The Missing Wife, All For You (winner of the Irish Independent Popular Fiction Book of the Year Award) and *Three Weddings and a Proposal*, as well as the bestselling short story collections *The Moment We Meet, The Season of Change,* and *Christmas With You*.

Sheila has always loved telling stories, and after working in banking and finance for a number of years, she decided it was time to fulfil a dream and give writing her own book a go. So she sat down, stuck 'Chapter One' at the top of a page, and got started. Sheila is now the author of over twenty bestselling titles. She lives in Dublin with her husband.

Praise for *Three Weddings and a Proposal*

'Reading a Sheila O'Flanagan novel always feels like sitting down for a cup of tea with a friend . . . She writes with such warmth and empathy' **Beth O'Leary**

'A glamorous, blockbusting, empowering read . . . Sheila knows just what it is to be a woman' **Veronica Henry**

'Great characters and many twists and turns . . . A great read!' **Katie Fforde**

'Sheila's books always make you feel as if you've spent time with a good friend' **Carole Matthews**

'Insightful, pacy and authentic . . . Terrific' **Patricia Scanlan**

'An involving, thought-provoking novel . . . I was drawn in from page 1' **Sue Moorcroft**

'[A] won... ...overy, I can'... ...or'

By Sheila O'Flanagan

SHEILA O'FLANAGAN

THE NO.1 BESTSELLING AUTHOR

three weddings and a proposal

REVIEW

First published in Great Britain in 2021
by HEADLINE REVIEW
an imprint of HEADLINE PUBLISHING GROUP

First published in paperback in Great Britain in 2022
by HEADLINE REVIEW
an imprint of HEADLINE PUBLISHING GROUP

1

Cataloguing in Publication Data is available from the British Library

ISBN 978 1 4722 7266 9

Typeset in Galliard by Palimpsest Book Production Ltd, Falkirk, Stirlingshire

Printed and bound in Great Britain by Clays Ltd, Elcograf S.p.A.

MIX
Paper from
responsible sources
FSC
www.fsc.org   FSC® C104740

Headline's policy is to use papers that are natural, renewable and recyclable
products and made from wood grown in well-managed forests and other
controlled sources. The logging and manufacturing processes are expected
to conform to the environmental regulations of the country of origin.

HEADLINE PUBLISHING GROUP
An Hachette UK Company
Carmelite House
50 Victoria Embankment
London EC4 0DZ

www.headline.co.uk
www.hachette.co.uk

three
weddings
and a
proposal

Chapter 1

I'm very close to spending a hundred thousand euro on a silver bracelet when my mobile rings and the theme from *Frozen* blasts around the office at a pitch that could break glass. I pull open the bottom drawer of my desk, shove the leather bag with the ringing phone into it and close the drawer sharply with my foot. Elsa is now muffled, but the mobile continues to vibrate as she informs me that the cold never bothered her anyway.

'What did you say?'

Denton, our expert, is in the auction room, and Elsa's advice to let it go has clearly knocked him off his stride.

'Nothing,' I tell him. I take a deep breath. 'Where are we now?'

'The last bid is at ninety thousand,' he says.

Will ninety-five finish it off, or will I have to go to the limit? In all honesty, I hadn't expected it would get this high. The bracelet is antique, but although it's sophisticated and stylish, it isn't *haute joaillerie*. However, it belonged to Lady Annabel Ansley, who was a well-known model back in the day, and as she was wearing it the night she was photographed snogging one of the Beatles in the back of a car while her husband was giving an important speech in Parliament, it has a bit of sixties notoriety. Also the three stones set into the silver bangle are emeralds, and emeralds, even small ones, are popular right now.

I increase my bid to ninety-five.

'OK,' says Denton.

I pace behind the desk as I wait for his feedback. Conrad really wants this bracelet for Bianca's thirtieth birthday, and Conrad usually gets what he wants, at the price he's prepared to pay. He seldom exceeds his self-imposed spending limits, even when it comes to his stunningly beautiful (and much younger) girlfriend. So if the bidding goes much higher, he'll be disappointed. And I don't want him to be disappointed. I never want him to be disappointed. He depends on me to deliver.

'Ninety-eight,' says Denton.

Oh, for God's sake! People who spend this sort of money on silver bracelets shouldn't be haggling over a couple of thousand. *I* shouldn't be haggling over a couple of thousand, even though it's not my money to spend and even though if I had a spare hundred thousand lying around I wouldn't blow it on jewellery, I'd use it to help pay down my mortgage. It would be nice to be a silver-bracelet-with-emeralds kind of person instead of a mortgage-paying-down kind of person, but I'm not the multimillionaire businessman Conrad Morgan, I just work for him. And he was as specific about the upper limit he was prepared to go to for the bracelet as he is about any of his business ventures.

Conrad started his investment company over fifteen years ago, and he didn't get to where he is by overpaying for anything. He can be flexible when it comes to personal things (although he's being ferocious about his potential divorce settlement with Martha), but he set a hundred thousand as the limit for today's auction, and as he's left the bidding to me, I'll stick to it and take the flak if the bracelet goes to someone else for a few grand more.

'A hundred thousand,' I tell Denton. 'And that's it.'

All of a sudden, it's quiet in the office. The triple-glazed windows have effectively shut out the sound of the Luas tram that's passing by, while Elsa has stopped singing in my desk drawer. It's as though she knows she's muddying the waters. The only sound is my breath as I wait for news from the auction room.

'Congratulations!' Denton's voice comes down the line. 'You're now the proud possessor of Lot 25. An antique silver bracelet with emerald stones, formerly the property of Lady Annabel Ansley.'

I heave a sigh of relief. I really wasn't looking forward to telling Conrad that Lady Annabel's bracelet had gone to someone else.

'Thank you.'

'My pleasure,' says Denton, and I know that he means it, because he lives for bidding at auctions and he especially loves buying jewellery. 'I'll get the paperwork organised and have it sent around as soon as possible. Great to do business with you as always, Delphine.'

'And with you.' I end the call and allow myself to relax.

In the desk drawer, the theme tune from *Frozen* recommences. I didn't choose it. My ten-year-old niece, Noemi, who's a *Frozen* fanatic, changed it a few weeks ago and I keep forgetting to change it back.

I take my bag from the drawer and the phone from the

bag, then look at the caller ID. My younger brother, André. This time I answer.

'Jeez, Delphie, this is the third time I've called. Is there no chance you'd listen to your voicemail and phone me back?'

'I'm sorry,' I say. 'I've been busy.'

'Yeah, well, we're all busy.' His voice mellows. 'Listen, I wanted to check with you about your plus-one for the wedding.'

I stifle a groan. He texted me yesterday about the plus-one and I told him I'd get back to him asap, but I was busy and forgot. I don't want to admit I forgot. My brother's wedding is the family event of the year and we're all supposed to be as excited about it as he is. But quite honestly, the incessant messages in the wedding WhatsApp group about the venue and the timetable and the menu and just about everything else are doing my head in.

'It isn't till the end of the month,' I say. 'What's the rush?'

'That's only a couple of weeks away,' he reminds me. 'Tory is doing the place cards today. She needs to know what name to put beside you.'

Until André got engaged to Victoria Palmer, formal occasions weren't on his radar. He was a frayed-jeans-and-bare-feet kind of person who thought suits and ties were the work of the devil. Now he owns a tuxedo and is badgering me about plus-ones and place cards.

'I haven't really had time to think about it properly,' I say.

'Oh, come *on*, Delphie.' He sounds exasperated. 'You've had months.'

Well, yes, I have. But when André got engaged, over a year ago, I was going out with Paul and I assumed he'd come along. However, Paul and I broke up long before the invitations were sent out, so I pencilled in Danny, my regular plus-one standby instead. Rather stupidly, I didn't get around to actually inviting him until a few weeks ago, when he told me he was going to Las Vegas that weekend and wouldn't be available. I was so annoyed with myself for not having asked sooner that I pushed it to the back of my mind. It's not like me to put things off – I'm usually the model of efficiency when it comes to organisation – but André's wedding wasn't high on my priorities.

And now, suddenly, it is.

I know it's really important to him and I know I should've dealt with it as soon as Danny told me he'd be away instead of filing it away under things to do when I get a minute. Because I didn't get a minute, and now I feel like a really bad sister. I *am* a really bad sister.

I silently curse Danny and his unavailability, though I can hardly begrudge him his trip. After all, he's turned up at two events for me in the last few months while I haven't had to help him out even once. Danny and I dated back in our college days, but although we got on really well together, the chemistry was never there to turn it into anything else. That's fine by me. I like having male friends who are simply friends. I enjoy their company. I like knowing it's not going to be anything more. But as I mentally begin to run through a list of alternatives, I realise that I've fewer available friends than before, and I feel a knot of anxiety in my stomach.

I should have realised sooner that they'd all begun to couple up. Bob and Stan, stalwarts in the past, both got married and have had to be scratched off my list. Giles moved to Australia to be with his girlfriend, and Steve, though a great companion for a social night out, has started dropping hints about wanting to settle down. Which is why I'm not keen to ask him to a wedding. I don't want him to think that settling down with him is on my mind. How have I not noticed the change in the status of so many people in my life? How has it passed me by?

I've had plenty of other things to think about, that's how. Work has taken up a big chunk of my time and I've socialised less than before. Nevertheless, I go to yoga classes (I'm trying to be a bit more mindful, though I haven't really succeeded because my thoughts wander when I'm supposed to be relaxed) and I played badminton all through the winter, which got me off the sofa when I could've been slouched in front of the TV. Now that summer's coming, I'm back jogging again, even if I usually do that on my own. And I regularly meet Erin and Sheedy, my two closest girlfriends, for drinks and a bite to eat. Like me, they're in no rush to hitch themselves permanently to a man. Erin is divorced and not inclined to give marriage another try, and although all three of us have gone through phases of intense dating, for now, at least, nothing has changed. But somehow things around us have, and now my pool of single male friends is shrinking rapidly.

Which is a bit of a problem when it comes to the wedding of the century.

I open my contacts list and start to scroll through it, but there's no forgotten name leaping out to meet me. In fact I see another one to scratch off. Jim Blake has got engaged for the third time.

Maybe I shouldn't bother with anyone. After all, I'm a grown woman and I don't actually need a plus-one to enjoy myself. In fact I'd probably have a better time without some casual acquaintance I'd feel responsible for at my side;

someone I'd be fretting over in case they were regretting having come with me. At André's wedding I'll be surrounded by family, so it's not as though I'll be sitting in a corner like an ageing, wilting wallflower. But the trouble is that weddings are all about being part of a couple, and despite my perfect contentment about my current single state, turning up by myself seems a little tragic. I know I'm letting how other people think affect how I feel, which I always try hard not to do, but I can't help it. As I finish scrolling and realise that my list of plus-one options is, in fact, currently zero, I feel the knot of anxiety tighten into a hard stone of panic.

I really don't want to face my family's reaction to turning up alone. Ridiculous as it sounds, the Mertens clan has the unerring ability to turn me from a success into a failure based on my dating profile. It doesn't matter that I have a good job. It doesn't matter that I bought my own house two years ago. It doesn't even matter that I'm the only one who hasn't had some kind of notable drama or crisis in her life (if you exclude the time my passport was stolen and I got stuck in Caracas for a week). If they see me by myself at the wedding, they'll decide that I'm putting a brave face on missing out on love and they'll be sorry for me and despairing of me in equal measure. And while they might nod sympathetically at my repeated assurances that I'm very happy with my status, they'll somehow find a way to inform me exactly why it is that I'm approaching my thirty-eighth birthday and am still single. Which, in the eyes of every last one of them, is definitely a life fail.

The last time we were together as a family (at Easter, when Mum invited everyone to dinner; seventeen opinionated people around the table), she remarked that I'm too picky when it comes to future life partners. As my siblings and their significant others chimed in, the general consensus was that being as demanding as I am means I'll die alone with only my cat for company. The fact that I'm mildly allergic to cats and therefore wouldn't dream of letting one over the threshold is irrelevant.

No matter what they think, I'm not demanding. I'll admit to cutting my losses early on if I don't feel things are working out with someone, but I continue to hold out a certain level of hope that the man of my dreams is out there somewhere. Nevertheless, I accept that as time goes by, this becomes an increasingly unlikely prospect. Meeting the right man would certainly be a bonus, but the quest to do this doesn't occupy my waking hours. Yet whenever I say this to my family, they make me feel like I'm protesting too much. Honestly, I'm not. My future husband doesn't have to be Mr Perfect, but he has to meet some minimum standards. Which involve more than being a random solvent single man!

In any event, as I've told everyone more than once, unmarried childless women are the happiest subgroup of the population, so I need a proper incentive to change my status. I'm not quoting made-up statistics here; it's a finding of a professor of behavioural science at the London School of Economics. And in this day and age there's no need for an unsuitable man to whisk a woman down off the shelf and confer married status on her before she gets so old she's pitied and invisible. I earn a decent salary, so I'm not in danger of succumbing to genteel poverty like a heroine in a Jane Austen novel – though obviously in a Jane Austen novel I would've been given up as a lost cause by now and would be a slightly pitied maiden aunt. On the other hand, I might have become one of those formidable spinsters who sits in judgement on everyone else and terrifies them with a gimlet look whenever they cross her path.

I'd quite like to be a formidable spinster if it didn't conjure up pictures of statuesque women with stately bosoms, booming voices and hairy chins. The male equivalent, bachelor, sounds fun-loving, carefree and attractive. Despite putting mortgage repayments over emerald bracelet purchases, I can be fun-loving and carefree, and I happily go to the local beauty salon, where Letizia deals with all of my hair removal needs.

Can I be a formidable spinster at André's wedding?

'Well, Delphie?' My brother sounds understandably irritated by my lengthy silence.

I think frantically but to no avail, and finally tell him I'll let him know for definite by the end of the week.

'Delphie! She's doing the cards right now.'

'I'm not one hundred per cent sure of who's coming yet,' I say.

'Your list of potential dates is that long?'

'Not really,' I admit. 'I'm sorry, André, honestly. I promise I'll get back to you as soon as I can.'

'Oh, OK,' says André, who in fairness is generally the most easy-going of my siblings. 'But if everyone was as blasé as you, poor Tory would never get those cards written. So when you've decided what unfortunate soul you're going to terrorise by bringing him to what we hope will be a wonderful weekend, please tell me straight away.'

I ignore the touch of sarcasm in his voice and assure him I'll get back to him as soon as possible.

'It's going to be great,' he says. 'You'll have a good time. So will your plus-one.'

'I know. I do, honestly. I'm truly sorry to have put it off. I'll get back to you as soon as I can.'

I end the call and put my phone back in the desk drawer.

I draw up a shortlist.

There isn't a single name on it.

I've been staring at the blank sheet of paper for over a minute when Lisa Hannigan walks into the office and asks if I've had time to read the research and analysis document she's done for our latest client briefing. I know she's anxious about it because she's asked me face-to-face instead of messaging me.

'I'm sorry, Lisa, I've been caught up in other stuff. I'll look at it right away.' I crumple up the blank sheet of paper and throw it in the recycling bin.

'It's just that we're reporting on the switches we've made in the Preferred Cornerstone funds and I want to make sure it sounds reasonable before I send it out,' she says.

'I thought it wasn't being sent until Friday?'

'Yeah, but Justin wanted a look at it too and he'll probably have some changes. I wanted your input first.'

Justin Delaney is head of company operations and is next in line to Conrad. His job is to know what's going on everywhere in the firm, but he has a tendency to get involved in things that don't concern him, and the client research stuff isn't really any of his business. I remind Lisa, who only joined Cosecha a couple of months ago, that she's the one whose opinion matters. She leaves looking a lot happier and I find the document she's sent me and go through it. I send her a reply saying that it's fine, even though there are a few slight changes I'd make myself. But they wouldn't have a major impact on the report, and I'm not going to ask Lisa to change something just for the sake of it.

Another dozen or so emails landed in my inbox while I was reading Lisa's report, so I deal with them and then contact Conrad's insurance company so that I can add the Lady Annabel bracelet to his policy. I've already emailed the details, and Carrie Bryant, the adviser I deal with, is up to speed and tells me how much extra it will cost.

'That's fine,' I say, although the amount Conrad pays in insuring jewellery is a breathtaking sum – far more than the value of any piece of jewellery I've ever owned.

'It's a beautiful bracelet, isn't it?' says Carrie. 'Lucky woman.'

'Sure is.' I'm agreeing to both.

'I wish I could afford gorgeous stuff like that,' she continues. 'The most expensive piece I own is my engagement ring. And I'm thinking of getting the diamond reset since my divorce.'

Carrie left her husband after he hit her for the second time. Although I know her well after years of dealing with Conrad's insurance needs, I'd no idea that her husband was abusing her until she told me why she'd moved out.

Women are good at hiding things. We're good at getting on with things too. I buy my own jewellery, although it's usually Swarovski crystals, not antique emeralds.

There's no need to wait for Prince Charming to have nice things for yourself.

I start a new shortlist and have added and crossed out two names when Conrad phones me from his business meeting in Geneva to congratulate me on acquiring the bracelet.

'I'm sorry I had to go to the limit,' I say.

'It was there for a reason,' he replies.

'I would've liked to have got it for a bit less,' I admit.

'I don't mind. Bianca will love it. It'll go perfectly with the dress she plans to wear.'

'Great,' I say.

'Has it arrived yet?'

'Hopefully later this afternoon,' I tell him. 'I'll keep it in the safe till you're back.'

'If you can get a flight before the weekend, would you mind bringing it to Palmyra instead? Otherwise you can courier it, but I'd like to go through a few office things with you face-to-face too.'

'Aren't you coming back here first?'

'No,' replies Conrad. 'I'm heading straight there. Bianca flew out last week.'

I know she flew out last week. I dealt with her travel arrangements.

Palmyra is Conrad's house in Mallorca. He moves his family there for six weeks at the beginning of summer; then, when it's getting too warm, they come back to their holiday home in the south of Cork until the end of August.

Well, he used to do that when he was married to Martha. Things are different now he's with Bianca. They haven't yet settled into a pattern, and maybe they won't. Despite the fabulous bracelet and the extravagant birthday party he's planned for her, it's not certain that she's going to be a permanent fixture in his life. And even if she is, his divorce will take some time. There wasn't a prenup, you see. When Conrad and Martha got married over twenty years ago, they didn't even think of it.

But now they've split up, there are a lot of assets to divide. The apartment in New York. The house on Lansdowne Road. The mews off Anglesea Road (which is where he lives with Bianca when they're in Dublin). The holiday home in Cork. And, of course, Palmyra, which is in Port d'Andratx on the south-west coast of Mallorca. Although he deals in financial assets, my boss has the very Irish desire to own tangible things. Specifically property. But he doesn't buy houses or apartments simply as investments. He's lived in every one of them. Well, strictly speaking, he only ever stays in the NY apartment (which is actually quite small) when he's in the States on business; in fact Martha used to stay there more often when she went on shopping weekends with her mum. And although the Cork home is spacious, he and Martha took it on as a total wreck when the price was dropped during the last recession. Palmyra – well, Palmyra is beautiful. He bought it the year I joined the company.

It sounds like I'm making excuses for him, or that I'm trying to play down his wealth. I'm not. By any standards, Conrad Morgan is a very rich man. But he doesn't act like it. He's easy-going and friendly, and a great boss. And until his marriage went belly-up, I always thought he was a good husband and father too. Well, I guess he's still a good father. And marriages do go wrong.

But I feel a little guilty about that, because it was me who introduced Bianca to him in the first place. It was when we were planning to do a presentational video of the Cosecha funds. I thought Conrad could do with a bit of sprucing-up and I suggested he chat to Bianca, who's an image consultant. She was recommended by Erin, who'd gone to her when she was up for promotion in the law firm where she works. Bianca

13

gave Erin some great tips on looking good, and they certainly helped her feel more confident at the series of interviews she had to go through.

'A what?' asked Conrad when I made the suggestion.

I looked at him critically. Financiers are usually portrayed as sharp-suited, well-groomed men with expensive taste in shirts and cufflinks. Conrad is not naturally that kind of man. He's tall and thin, with wayward ginger hair that flops into his eyes, and he looks uncomfortable in the dark suits that are almost obligatory in the industry. The video was going to be seen by some very important clients. I wanted him to look less like a tech geek and more like someone who manages billions of other people's money.

He met her. She gave him a complete makeover. We got the business we were hoping for.

And he got the image consultant too.

Chapter 2

Denton arrives with the bracelet later that afternoon. It's stunning in real life and I suddenly understand why the bidding went up to the level it did. The dark green emeralds gleam like cat's eyes under the ceiling lights.

I slip it onto my wrist.

'Suits you,' says Denton.

It suited Lady Annabel better. There was a picture of her in the catalogue with her arm around whichever Beatle she was kissing, the bracelet clearly visible on her slender wrist. The bracelet itself would have identified her, because it's quite distinctive, but so was Lady Annabel, with her golden hair in a sixties beehive secured by a diamond clip. There was another photograph of her in the brochure too, this time dressed for a formal ball, wearing a figure-hugging black dress and long white gloves, with the bracelet on her right arm. She was very beautiful back then and she's very beautiful now, even in her eighties. She appeared recently on a programme about ageing gracefully and told Emily Maitlis that ageing disgracefully was much more fun. Emily asked her about the Beatles episode, because it was headline news back then – the English always love a bit of posh snogging in their gossip stories. Lady Annabel laughed at the idea that it was anything other than an innocent flirtation and pointed out that she and her husband had remained married until his death a few years earlier. She didn't, however, comment on the understanding they were supposed to have had that meant that he did his thing and she did hers, an arrangement that had led to him being named in a paternity suit in the early nineties.

I unclasp the bangle from my wrist and break the connection I suddenly felt with Lady Annabel and her world. I'm sure Bianca won't care about the life story of the woman who owned it; she'll just be pleased that Conrad bought it.

Anyhow, none of that is my concern. All I have to do is deliver it.

Although it's not an everyday occurrence, delivering precious jewellery to his overseas home is one of the perks of being the executive assistant to the CEO. I'm lucky to work for a boss who has given me the encouragement and opportunity to expand my original role. These days, as well as everyday admin tasks, I arrange client events, liaise with our legal advisers and work alongside Conrad on a variety of investment projects. I also oversee our corporate responsibility programme, which means managing the relationships and funding for the charitable institutions we support. While this is undoubtedly the most satisfying part of my work, purchasing a gorgeous emerald bracelet is certainly the most glamorous thing I've ever been asked to do, even if it was a personal rather than professional request.

I go online and am pleased to find that I can get a direct flight to Palma early the next morning with a return to Dublin later that night. I text Erin and Sheedy to tell them that I have to cancel our plans to meet after work tomorrow. Erin sends a sad emoji face in return and Sheedy replies with *Jammy!* and a laughing face. Erin and I used to work together at Haughton's, the law firm where I started out after college. She's a couple of years older than me and one of the most competent women you could ever hope to meet. Sheedy took over my job when she joined, but she now has her own practice and employs three people. My best friends are strong, ambitious women. And so, I hope, am I.

It's after six when I leave the office, but I decide to call in on my parents on the way home to show Mum Lady Annabel's bracelet. I'm feeling guilty for not having dropped by in ages, but I've been really busy over the last few weeks and there simply hasn't been time. So instead of continuing home to Malahide on the train, I get off at Killester and walk the couple of hundred yards from the station to my parents' house.

It was one of the homes built for Irish veterans of the First World War and started out as a slightly bigger version of the cottage by the sea that I bought for myself a few years ago. But with five children, it was inevitable that Mum and Dad would eventually need more space. Fortunately, like most of the houses in the development, there was a long garden and plenty of room to add on. So now their cottage is a good-sized family home. It needs to be because my sister Viviane and her boyfriend Jason are living there, along with their baby Charley. Additionally, the rest of the next generation have regular sleepovers with their grandparents. They're a fixture almost every weekend and there isn't a day that goes by without one or other of the grandchildren having a supposedly impromptu visit. Mum loves it, though. In

17

fact it wouldn't surprise me to hear that she loves her grandchildren more than her actual children.

When I arrive, Noemi, Phoebe and Elodie, my brother Michael's daughters, are playing in the front garden. Elodie, the youngest at five years old, sees me first and runs over to hug me as I walk up the garden path. I swing her into my arms, kiss her, then put her down again, thinking that I won't do that again in a hurry because I've nearly put my back out.

'Hi, Auntie Delphie.' Noemi releases Phoebe from the stranglehold she has on her. 'We've already had tea. You're too late.'

'That's OK,' I tell her. 'I'm just here to see Granny and Grandad.'

'Grandad's out,' Phoebe informs me. 'He's gone to the pub to do his crossword in peace.'

I grin. It's Mum who loves having the family around all the time. Dad's more of a loner. He deals with the fact that his house is being perpetually invaded by distancing himself to do his crosswords. Clearly I get my solitary nature from him.

Mum, Vivi and my sister-in-law, Nichola, are deep in conversation when I walk into the kitchen, and I realise that I'm interrupting an intensive analysis of last week's pre-wedding dinner. Apparently it's become a thing for the bride to invite the female members of both sides of the family to a getting-to-know-you meal ahead of the main event, another piece of wedding lore I knew nothing about.

I wasn't able to go to the dinner. Conrad was making a presentation to a set of potential new clients that evening, and I had to be there. To be honest, I was happy enough to have the excuse, because it wouldn't really have been my thing, but I'm not sure Tory has forgiven me for not turning up. What with missing the dinner and being late with my plus-one, I'm probably deep, deep in her bad books by now.

'It was wonderful,' gushes Vivi as she takes out her phone to show me some photos. 'Superb food and a fantastic atmosphere. Tory's family are simply lovely. Really amazing people. We had a good old sing-song afterwards too.'

'Looks great,' I lie. Group singing after a few drinks is one of my least favourite things. I realise I sound like a killjoy, but I'm not. Honestly. It's just that I'm more of a soft-music-in-the-background-and-gentle-conversation person. (Unless I go to a gig with Erin and Sheedy, where I jump around with the best of them.)

'It was.' Mum cuts a slice from the carrot cake in the centre of the table and puts it and a cup of coffee in front of me. 'It's such a shame you missed it.'

'Oh, well, I'm sure the wedding will make up for it.' I eye the enormous chunk of cake dubiously.

'The frosting is sugar-free,' Mum says, reading my mind.

I try not to indulge in too many sweet things. That was difficult when I lived at home, because Mum worked in a bakery for fifteen years and she bakes the most amazing cakes. It was my downfall when I was younger and led to my overall sturdiness being more about being overweight than just tall, so I try to steer away from cakes and biscuits now.

Sturdy has always been Mum's favourite adjective to describe me, and I guess it's accurate. Back in my school days, despite my limited acting abilities, I was inevitably cast as the hero in our end-of-term plays opposite the talented leading lady, because I was (and still am) at least a head taller than every female I know. All I had to do was stride across the stage and look imposing while the heroine delivered her lines in a suitably feminine way. Even now, when I dress up in the most girlie way possible (not that I do that very often, because I'm not really a fan of pink or sparkles or looking like a Disney princess), I'm just too big to pull off a sweetly feminine look.

Mum used to bemoan the fact that, like my two brothers, I inherited the well-built genes from her own mum, my Granny Dunphy, a countrywoman who could probably shear a field of sheep even now. Well, maybe not. She's eighty-five. She hasn't lost the feistiness, though, and I hope I inherited that too. Anyhow, despite struggling with it a bit when I was younger, I like that my height gives me a certain advantage now. While I generally favour flatter heels in the office, I always wear stilettos when Conrad asks me to come to meetings with him. That way, I never feel passed over as the mere PA, which men in particular tend to do. When I want to appear extra tall and extra confident, I arrange my cocoa-brown hair in a high knot on the top of my head, thus adding another couple of inches at least. And although I don't spend my time trawling Instagram for beauty tips, I never go into work without applying a decent amount of make-up. Charlotte Tilbury is my one extravagance. Beauty armour is good in the financial world.

And every woman, no matter who she is, needs her armour of choice.

As I take a tiny forkful of cake, Vivi, who seems to maintain her neat size 10 figure without any discernible effort, digs into her own enormous slice. She's the elfin one of the family, a younger version of our other grandmother in almost every respect. It is, therefore, a little ironic that I'm the one named after Dad's mother. Granny Mertens is eighty-eight, slight and elegant, and despite having become a little more frail over the last year or so, she's as independent and opinionated as Granny Dunphy. With a bit of luck, they've both passed on the longevity genes.

Despite their very different backgrounds (Granny Dunphy worked on the family farm outside Dublin, while Granny Mertens' family settled in Ireland after Belgium was invaded in 1940), they're both strong, determined women and I love them fiercely. Granny Mertens is more into the finer things of life than Granny Dunphy, loving make-up, fashion and any excuse to dress up. She lives alone in the small family home in Marino that she moved into when she married my grandfather, while Granny Dunphy still lives on the farm with my uncle Sean and his wife. After Grandpa Mertens died, Mum asked Granny if she'd like to move in with her and Dad, but she wanted to stay put and so far is managing very well on her own.

'Good?' Mum looks at me enquiringly now as I take a larger forkful of cake than I intended.

'Delicious.'

'So what brings you here?' asks Nichola.

I hold out my arm and the silver and emerald bracelet, hidden by my jacket until now, slides to my wrist and sparkles in the evening sun.

'Oh my God, Delphie!' Mum's eyes widen. 'Are those real emeralds?'

I nod.

'Who gave it to you?' asks Vivi, whose eyes are equally wide. 'Are you seeing someone new? If he's giving you presents like that, he's a keeper for sure!'

21

'It's not mine.' I explain about Bianca's birthday and the auction. 'I'm wearing it for safe keeping,' I add. 'So that if my bag is nicked, at least I still have the bracelet.'

'Won't your boss mind?' Mum sounds slightly disapproving, but it's not me wearing the bracelet she's disapproving of. It's Conrad. She blames him for the fact that my perennial excuse for not going to things is that I'm working.

I tell her he'll be fine with it and then relate the history of Lady Annabel and the Beatle.

'Can I try it on?' asks Nichola.

I take it off my wrist and she slides it onto hers.

'Are you holding out for someone like Conrad?' Her glance flickers from the bracelet to me and back again. 'I can see why. I love Mike with all my heart, but I'd certainly be tempted by someone who could buy me emerald bracelets for my birthday.'

'Love isn't about material things,' says Mum.

'I know,' says Nichola. 'But isn't it beautiful, Josie?'

'Yes.' Mum sounds grudging. 'Though when I married Julien, we didn't have a spare penny to rub together, and we're still together after all these years, so I don't think it's money that makes a good marriage. Especially,' she adds, 'as Conrad Morgan isn't even married to the woman he's bought it for.'

I'm not going to agree with her, even though my sympathies in general lie with Martha, who has become a friend over the years, rather than Bianca, who I've only ever dealt with professionally. I was horrified when I discovered she and Conrad were seeing each other. I still feel uneasy when he mentions her name. But I didn't say no to buying the bracelet for her.

'Anyhow . . .' I finish the cake and my coffee. 'I should be heading off. I've an early flight tomorrow.'

Mum gives me a concerned look. She doesn't like me flying.

'Have you given Tory the name of your plus-one?' The look Vivi gives me is wicked, not concerned, and I wonder if everyone knows that Tory is waiting on me to come up with a name. The bush telegraph works very quickly in our family, but even so, why should the name matter to anyone other than my brother and his fiancée?

'André called me a dozen times today,' I say, not caring that I'm exaggerating. 'I told him I'd let her know by the end of the week.'

'It's not fair to—'

'D'you have someone in mind?'

Mum and Nichola speak at the same time.

'I have a couple of possibilities,' I lie. 'The date's a bit problematic, that's all. And not everyone wants to come to a three-day bash.'

'If it's one of your casual acquaintances, you're going to need to book an extra room,' says Mum. 'You'd want to get on that straight away. There mightn't even be one available.'

'I think we're all agreed it'll be a casual acquaintance,' I say. 'And I'll probably suggest that whoever it is only comes for the Saturday.'

'Oh, you can't do that,' protests Mum. 'Tory has stuff planned.'

'Not everyone's coming for the entire weekend,' I point out. 'Only family.'

'And plus-ones,' Nichola supplies. 'Don't worry, Delphie. You can bring a ninja plus-one who turns up for the church and afters and then disappears.'

I laugh and so does she.

She's not the worst, really.

That's Lindsey, Martin's wife.

It's after eight when I get home. I put Bianca's bracelet into the safe in my wardrobe, change into a T-shirt and leggings and go for a short jog along the seafront. I don't run quickly, but it clears my head. As I arrive back at my house, Lyra Casey, my next-door neighbour on the left, comes out of hers with her two basset hounds. We exchange hellos and then she heads off in the direction I've just come from, the dogs walking very properly on the leash ahead of her. Lyra's around the same age as Mum and recently retired from her job as a court reporter. We occasionally go out for a drink together, and she gives me details of past criminal trials that make my blood run cold.

The house on the other side of me is much bigger than mine, and is home to Peter, Katie and their two boys. The boys are six and eight, and from April until the end of the summer I spend every evening throwing their errant footballs back over the dividing wall between our properties. Whenever I see her, which isn't often because, being a working mum, she's always in a rush, Katie apologises profusely about the footballs and I tell her not to worry; as long as Liam and Cathal don't send one through my window, it's fine.

After a shower to freshen up, I pour myself a large glass of water, add a slice of lemon and throw back today's footballs before checking out the half-finished jigsaw on the trestle table near the window. Jigsaws became a thing for me during the virus lockdown months, and I've kept doing them because they're a disconnection from technology and the general amount of rushing around I seem to do. This one is of a Caribbean sunset, a palette of pinks and golds, blues and greens. I slot enough pieces into place to finish the top corner, then move to the window seat that looks over my back garden. I was very lucky to get this place, as it was totally renovated before I bought it, which means that although it's compact, the space has been cleverly used. Originally a single-storey home with tiny rooms, the previous owners knocked down the wall between the kitchen and dining room, which flooded the area with light. It's made even brighter by the folding glass doors stretching the entire width of the house at the back. They also used the attic space to add a mezzanine floor with an additional bedroom and bathroom.

I knew I wanted it the moment I stepped inside. Although everything is painted in neutral shades, there's a real warmth about it that's exactly what I need when I close the door behind me. In the summer I can open the back doors and take advantage of the south-facing garden. In the winter I close the plum-coloured drapes and feel cocooned from the outside word.

I wouldn't have managed to buy it without Conrad. House prices in Dublin are ridiculously high and the bank's criteria for mortgage lending were crucifyingly tight. Even though I'd saved up a deposit and could afford the repayments, as a single person buying on her own they still wouldn't lend me as much as I needed. Conrad stepped in with a company loan to make up the difference. It's part of the reason I'll never say a bad word about him.

I had a big house-warming when I moved in. It was a beautiful evening, and with the patio doors opened to their fullest extent, people moved from house to garden and back again, telling me that my new home was very 'single professional woman'.

'You won't want to have kids here,' Lindsey said as she looked around. 'It's too gorgeous, and besides, there isn't room.'

'I'm guessing that a hundred years ago entire families were raised in places like this,' I remarked. 'So I'm sure I could manage a child if I wanted.'

'And do you?' She looked at me intently. 'Is there someone in your life at last? Are you becoming broody now that you're a homeowner?'

'Are you mad?' I laughed. 'You're absolutely right, Lindsey. There isn't a hope in hell of me having a baby to mess up my fabulous new house.'

I could see her mentally noting how shallow I am, but I didn't care. It's not that I wouldn't love a child if I had one; it's simply that I don't want one. Not yet. Maybe not ever. Married or not.

No weddings. No pink sparkles. No children.

'You try so hard not to care about what's important in life,' Lindsey told me. 'But one day you'll realise there's more to it than clipping around an office with a briefcase.'

That's why I don't get on with her. I like clipping around the office, though I've never had a briefcase. I don't judge her for wanting something different. I just wish she didn't always judge me.

I check the weather for my day trip to Mallorca in the morning. The forecast is for clear skies and a balmy twenty-two degrees.

Despite what Lindsey might think, I'm living my best life.

Chapter 3

It doesn't feel quite so much like my best life when I have to get out of bed at 4.30. I'm not good at getting up in the dark, which means I'm bleary-eyed until I've had my shower followed by a shot of coffee. Then I get dressed in a lightweight pastel blue suit and a pair of low-heeled sandals. There's no need to be a total glamazon today.

The taxi turns up on time, and at that hour of the morning it takes less than twenty minutes to get me to the airport. I have another coffee along with a croissant in the Butlers café before heading to the gate and getting on the plane.

I'm inappropriately dressed, as most of my fellow passengers are off on their holidays, and despite the fact that it was only eight degrees in Dublin this morning, they're wearing shorts and sleeveless tops. I've somehow managed to end up sitting beside a young couple who are on either their honeymoon or their first ever holiday together, as they spend the entire flight wrapped around each other, only surfacing when there's a brief interlude of turbulence and the cabin crew tell them to fasten their seat belts.

I don't think I've ever been so consumed with passion that I literally couldn't keep my hands off the person I'm with.

27

At least not in public. Does that mean there's something wrong with me? Am I unable to give my heart and soul completely? Is it that my family are right and I'm far too picky? Or could it be that I simply haven't found the right man?

I run through my list of ex-boyfriends. Fran. Aaron. Ed. Jamie. Barney. Paul. Whenever I start a relationship with a man, I wonder if this is it. If he's the one who's going to turn me into the kind of woman who binge-watches rom coms and starts dreaming of the day she walks down the aisle. Or, more realistically, if he's the one that I realise I can't live without. It hasn't happened yet. There's no doubt that I was in love with all of my boyfriends when we were dating. But madly, crazily, stupidly in love? Devastated by the end of the relationship? That's different. The closest I came was with Ed. And he was the only one who dumped me. Every other time I ended it.

I cried after Ed.

But not for long.

I open my iPad and try to ignore the steaminess of what's going on beside me, but it's hard to concentrate on a cost–benefit analysis of Conrad's latest project when the couple should be getting a room, so it takes me a lot longer than I anticipated to read everything through.

They're still wrapped around each other when we touch down at Palma, nearly three hours after boarding the plane. I take my bag from under the seat in front of me, and while we're waiting to disembark, I remove Bianca's bracelet from my wrist, put it into the box it came in and place it in the zipped compartment of my handbag. Given that Conrad has sent a driver to collect me, I think it's safe to say I'm not going to lose it now.

I inhale the warmth of the island and feel the heat of the sun as I walk down the aircraft steps and into the terminal building. I've never actually holidayed in Mallorca, but I've overnighted at Palmyra a few times while Conrad and Martha were there.

The driver is waiting in the arrivals hall, holding up a card with my name written on it in black marker. I walk up to him and follow him to the car park, where I get into the comfortable BMW.

The traffic is heavy on the motorway that circles Palma, and the driver mutters beneath his breath as he adjusts the air conditioning. I lean back in my seat and don't let it bother me. I'm more of an occasional driver than someone who likes to be behind the wheel, and I definitely prefer being driven in heavy traffic, particularly when it's on the wrong side of the road.

The pace picks up a bit once we've left the city traffic behind, and suddenly we're on a clear stretch of road with stunning views to the aquamarine sea below. I take a short video to add to my Instagram story. My account, ForwardsInHighHeels, is followed by quite a few business-people, who always enjoy photos of my trips. I often post a photo of my shoes with the name of the city I'm in. It's the only social media I get involved in, apart from having a LinkedIn profile. I'm not great at sharing.

I post the video, then settle back for the final part of the journey. Conrad's house is set up in the hills behind Port d'Andratx to take advantage of the same views as I'm seeing now. It usually takes about forty-five minutes to get there, but today we do it in less than forty. The driver pulls up outside an iron gate set into the yellow brick wall that forms the boundary of the house, and presses the intercom. The gates slide open and he drives the short distance to the house itself. Realistically, I could've got out at the gates and walked, but the driver isn't having it.

Palmyra isn't a typical Spanish house. There's no whitewash or bougainvillea, no terracotta tiles or grilles on the windows. It's starkly modern, built in the early 2000s by a Spanish pop star, but sold when the same pop star was done for tax evasion and had to pay a massive fine. Conrad heard about it, came to see it, and bought it within a week.

I love modern architecture but can't help thinking there's a touch of an office building about the place. It's basically two large white cubes one on top of the other, all angles and no curves. Outside, where I'm waiting for someone to open the double doors and let me in, the front garden is granite tiles and stones. To my left, a futuristic fountain shoots water into the air, while on my right are modern urns filled with cactus plants. It's not restful. But it's definitely striking.

It's Conrad himself who opens the door.

'Delphie.' He smiles at me, his eyes almost navy blue in his angular face. 'Come in. Come in.'

I step over the threshold.

Most of the ground floor is open-plan and – like my own house – flooded with light, although this is the sharper, brighter light of the Mediterranean. The internal space is broken up by tall plants and verdigris screens, while green marble floor tiles have a cooling effect. When Martha lived here, they were covered by a variety of brightly coloured rugs, but those have gone, along with the portrait of her and the children that used to dominate one of the walls. Now it feels as much like an office inside as it looks outside.

'Let's go to the den,' says Conrad.

I follow him into a room with spectacular views over the sea. Whenever I come here, I wonder how on earth Conrad leaves this place for Dublin, where his office view is of glass and steel buildings. If I had a view like this, I'd never leave, which is why, I suppose, I'm the executive assistant while he's the CEO. For all my ambition, I'm never going to be in a position to own a place like Palmyra.

'The bracelet?' asks Conrad as he sits behind his big glass desk.

I take the slim red jewellery box out of my bag and hand it to him.

'Nice,' he says. 'A little slimmer than I expected.'

I nod. 'But it sits beautifully on your arm.'

'You tried it?' He looks amused.

'How could I not? Besides, it was safer to carry it that way until I got here.'

He turns it over in his hands. 'The emeralds are a bit smaller than I expected, too.'

Is he having second thoughts? Surely not. I imagine for a moment what it would be like to spend a hundred thousand pounds on a piece of jewellery and have second thoughts about it. I feel a hollow in the pit of my stomach.

'But it's beautiful,' he acknowledges. 'Bianca will love it. Well done at the auction.'

'I'm pleased it worked out,' I say. 'Denton did the bidding. But you know what auctions are like – anything can happen.'

'Somehow, though, nothing ever seems to happen when you're involved, Delphie. Everything goes exactly to plan.'

'Is that a good thing or a bad thing?' I ask.

He laughs. 'Good, obviously.'

'Glad to hear that.' I take out a folder and hand him some paperwork. 'Here's the amended Caldwell documentation. It's a final draft, so if you can go through it, I can have everything ready for signing when you're back.'

Caldwell is another project he's involved in. It's a bit sensitive, as it involves buying a portfolio of distressed mortgages – a legacy of the financial crash over a decade ago. But Conrad has plans that don't involve repossessing the properties. He's not a cold-hearted man. He is, however, fanatical about getting what he wants at the right price.

'It's tricky, but I think it'll work out,' he says as he skims through the documents. 'It'll probably be a few weeks before we sign off on it, and I'll have some additional numbers for you to run first. Also, I wanted to talk through a few other bits and pieces with you, but I'm waiting on a couple of calls, so if there isn't anything else, we could take a break before we finish up the business side of things.'

'Only this.' I take my iPad from my bag, open a file and push it towards him. 'I was working on it on the flight over. I thought it was ready to go, but you might want to check out the projections on page three. I'm not sure Justin's using the right benchmark, but I haven't had time to clarify it. Obviously a different benchmark would skew the end valuation.'

Conrad frowns as he looks at the file. 'Can you forward it to me?'

'Of course.'

'I wasn't expecting you to have even looked at it yet,' he says as he sends the forwarded file to his printer.

'I wanted to get as much off my plate as I could before my brother's wedding,' I admit.

'Surely that's not for ages?'

'They're doing the place cards as we speak.'

'You don't sound terribly enthusiastic.'

'I thought it was weeks away,' I confess. 'Now it's almost on top of me and I need to buy myself an appropriate dress and find myself a plus-one.'

'Which is the more important?' he asks.

'Hard to say.'

'I'm sure you'll manage.'

'I'll be taking a half-day on the Friday beforehand,' I say. 'I've got to get myself to some godforsaken castle in the country for an evening of family entertainment.'

He laughs. 'You sound so glum. But it'll be fun, I'm sure.'

'Oh, it'll be fine when I'm there. I'm not really a social person, that's all.'

'Rubbish,' says Conrad. 'You're brilliant at all the Cosecha events.'

'That's different,' I reply. 'When I'm corporate Delphie, I know exactly who I am. When I'm with my family . . . well, let's say I regress somewhat.'

'I can't honestly say I'm looking forward to Bianca's party myself,' he admits. 'Everyone who's even remotely related to her is coming, and I'm not sure I can hack it.'

'You hack all the Cosecha events.' I turn his words back on him and we laugh together. Although he's a financial genius who's built up an amazing business, and I'm more of a practical person than an innovator, we understand each other. That's why we work so well together.

When I saw her at Mum's the other day, Nichola asked if I was holding out for someone like Conrad, but there's never been a hint of anything more than a brilliant working relationship between us. It would be nice to meet a man who was as supportive of my career as he is, and as encouraging, but Conrad has his flaws too. Sometimes he believes his own publicity. Sometimes he thinks he can have it all. That's when I have to bring him back to earth. It's an empowering position to be in.

'Anyhow, I'm assuming you're here for the day and getting the evening flight,' he says. 'Did you bring your swimming things?'

I did, but I didn't like to presume I'd be able to lie out by the pool as I used to in the days when Martha lived here. Back then, I'd finish whatever business I had with Conrad and then hang out with his wife. Martha took a great interest in Cosecha's charitable funding and was the public face of the community grants initiative I set up as part of it. Sometimes we stayed by the pool, but we often headed off to the beach and had lunch together afterwards, leaving Conrad to keep an eye on the children. Killian and Connie are nineteen and fifteen now. I haven't seen them since their parents split up.

'Bianca's out by the pool,' says Conrad when I nod. 'You could join her for a while and we can do the rest of the business stuff after I've finished with my calls.'

It's a command rather than a suggestion, so I leave him to his own devices and walk through the house to the pool.

It's an amazing pool, overhanging the cliff on which the house is perched. It's partially shaded by tall palm trees as well as the pergola at one end, which is where Bianca is sitting reading a magazine.

'Hi,' I say. 'How are things?'

I've met Bianca fewer than a dozen times since Conrad left Martha for her, although I saw quite a bit of her when she was doing image consulting for him. The thing is, although I'm much closer in age to her, I feel emotionally closer to Martha, who's nine years older than me. I can't help feeling Martha hasn't been given the respect and the reward she deserves in the current situation. I know she'll be financially OK, despite the fact that Conrad has hired a solicitor who has a fierce reputation, but she was a real asset to the firm too. She accompanied him to events and entertained in their home, always being charming to clients and potential clients alike. And, of course, she raised their two children while he was travelling the world. Conrad was not (and never has been) a hands-on dad. Like I said, he has his faults.

And one of them was falling for his twenty-nine-year-old image consultant. Who, let's face it, is a total babe.

She puts down the magazine she's been reading and pushes her enormous sunglasses onto her head.

'Delphie,' she says. 'Conrad told me you were coming.'

'And now that I'm here, I hate that I have to go back later.'

She smiles at me. 'It's lovely, isn't it?'

'Amazing.' I perch on the sunbed beside her.

'Are you going to stay for a while?'

'My flight isn't till this evening,' I say. 'Conrad's making a few calls, so he suggested I chill out here for a while.'

Bianca picks up her phone and checks the time. 'I was thinking of having some lunch. As you're here, we could go to Tim's together.'

Tim's is a restaurant overlooking the bay. I used to go there a lot with Martha. Although I'm yearning for a swim, I say that lunch would be lovely, and Bianca asks me to wait for her while she changes into something more suitable. While

35

I wait, I think how her desire to have lunch with me is a command rather than a request too. The fact that the tables have been turned and the power between us has shifted isn't lost on me.

I gaze out past the pool to the vibrant blue of the sea and wonder what Martha is doing now. I haven't spoken to her much since she and Conrad split up – it's awkward because I know bits and pieces about the settlement they're negotiating and I don't want to be caught in the middle. But I miss her. She was smart and witty and fun to be with. Until Connie was born, she worked as an interior designer. It was during the boom times in Ireland, so she was always busy. She often said that Connie came along at the right time, because the crash happened around then and she was too caught up in her new baby to care that the bottom had fallen out of the housing market and, as a consequence, the interior design business. It was a stressful time for Conrad too, although obviously I wasn't working for him then. I'd just graduated with my law degree and was hawking my résumé around town.

Times change, I remind myself, as a cluster of floral seeds from the nearby palm tree lands on the surface of the pool. Nothing stays the same. And that's a good thing. Because otherwise there'd never be opportunities to do something new, even if there's currently nothing new I want to do.

Nevertheless, I can't help feeling sorry about bringing Bianca Benton into Conrad's life. I wasn't aware of any cracks in his relationship with Martha at the time, but there must have been. On one of the rare occasions I met her afterwards, my divided loyalties made our normally easy-going conversation difficult. She told me that Conrad had succumbed to the classic mid-life crisis of an older man wanting someone younger and more beautiful than his wife to make him feel good about himself. I couldn't really defend him yet didn't want to agree. Given that he already had so much to feel good about, it seemed sad to me that he'd become such a cliché. Nevertheless, Martha was probably right, although she never gave Bianca credit for being smart as well as beautiful and younger. After all, Bianca continues to run her own business, though I suppose the necessity to make a living out of it has diminished.

I turn around as I hear her walk up the steps that lead to the pool. She's changed into a loose white dress that shows off her tan. Her golden hair is tied back and she's wearing a floppy sunhat to protect her face. She looks young and hip and kind of boho. I feel a thousand years older than her in my blue suit and sandals.

'Let's go,' she says, and leads me through the house again.

It's a five-minute drive to the restaurant, and she takes us there in a brand-new BMW convertible.

'It's a hard life,' she says with a smile after we've bagged a table at the water's edge and a waiter has brought us a bottle of water.

'Sure is.'

'Thank you.' I think she's talking to the waiter, but I realise she's looking at me.

'For what?'

She grins. 'Introducing me to him.'

'It wasn't meant to be that kind of introduction.'

This time she laughs. 'I know.'

'I liked Martha,' I confess.

'Why wouldn't you?' she asks. 'I'm sure she's a very nice woman. She wasn't making Conrad happy, that's all.'

'She thought she was.'

Bianca shakes her head. 'Not for some time.'

Is that true? I wonder. Or is it something Conrad says to her? Either way, it's not for me to get involved.

'You're very discreet,' she says when I stay silent.

'Things change.' I echo my thoughts of earlier.

'Exactly.' She grins again and lifts her glass. 'To happy changes.'

'Happy changes,' I say, and begin to study the menu.

When we get back to the house, Conrad is doing lengths of the pool. I've never actually seen him in his swimming shorts before, and as he gets out of the water, I wonder if Bianca has had him working on his body too, because he looks very fit.

'Nice lunch?' he asks.

'Lovely,' replies Bianca. 'Delphie is such good company.'

Actually the lunch was more enjoyable than I'd expected. The food was great, and Bianca – well, she's amusing to be with. She doesn't take herself too seriously and she seems to be crazy about Conrad. She's also crazy about the money – she admitted to me that she can't entirely get her head around the fact that she can pretty much buy whatever the hell she likes whenever the hell she likes. When I said I couldn't quite imagine that myself, she said that it was amazingly easy to get used to.

'My grandma used to tell me that I should marry well,' she said. 'Naturally I'd tell her that she was old-fashioned and that women married for love, not money, but . . .' And when she saw the expression on my face, she winked and said that it *was* love, not money, but that perhaps she wouldn't have moved in with Conrad if he hadn't been so wonderfully wealthy. 'Though even then I didn't realise exactly how much money he had,' she admitted. 'It's obscene, Delphie.'

'You should ask him to give Martha a decent settlement,' I said. 'She helped him make the company what it is now with all her work behind the scenes. He doesn't need to bicker over money.'

'I didn't realise you were so deep in Martha's camp.' Bianca gave me a suddenly frosty look.

'I'm not in anyone's camp,' I told her. 'But Conrad couldn't have succeeded without her help, and the divorce is taking up a disproportionate amount of his time. He doesn't need to score points off Martha. He'd be better off looking towards the future.'

She shrugged at that, and thinking that perhaps I should've kept my mouth shut, I didn't say anything more. But I'm right about the divorce. Unfortunately it's the one thing I don't feel able to talk to my boss about. I'm happy to give him my opinion on business matters. I stay out of his personal life.

'Give me half an hour to organise myself,' he says to me now. 'And then we can go through the other business. I'd planned to be back at the office on Tuesday, but there's an unexpected meeting in Singapore that I have to physically attend, so I want to get as much done as I can before that.'

'Will you need me to go with you?' It's a few years since I was last in Singapore with him. I practically maxed out my credit cards on Orchard Road back then and I like the idea of giving them another workout.

He shakes his head. 'Not this trip. But there's some prep work to be done, as well as booking my tickets. I'll give you all the details.'

'OK.'

Bianca says she's going to change into her bikini and tells me I should do the same. I smile at the thought of sitting opposite Conrad wearing a bikini (which I don't have; I prefer the full cover of a swimsuit) but tell her I'll definitely have a swim afterwards.

The talk with Conrad takes nearly two hours. He's in full business mode now, and as well as the Singapore trip, he wants to discuss various investments, potential clients and, finally, office politics. Conrad both loves and hates office politics and always wants to know what's going on.

'Any problems?' he asks.

I shake my head. 'Justin's throwing his weight around, but otherwise all is well. Numbers were good for last week – I sent them to you, didn't I?'

'Yes, you did. And it's not as though Justin doesn't have quite a bit of weight to throw around.' Conrad focuses on the politics rather than the profits. 'He's a good man and a great deputy, but he can be a total arse sometimes.'

It's mainly me Justin throws his weight around at and is a total arse towards. He doesn't like me. He thinks I'm too close to Conrad. That I know stuff I shouldn't know. I probably know more about the company than him, but that's all. I don't say anything in reply to Conrad. He's right about Justin, who is actually a very good deputy despite being an arse.

I decide to throw a little more office politics into the mix. 'Kyle Dunne is trying to poach Ernest's clients,' I say. 'Chris Marshall and Didier Lamont are arguing about the Hoffman trust fund for no good reason that I can see. And Emily Hunt and Mark Gaskill have gone public with their relationship – though I realise that's not politics, just gossip.'

'Tell Didier I want a review of the fund,' says Conrad. 'Let's see if there's anything they should be arguing about.' He leans back in the chair. 'I like Emily. And Mark. She's way out of his league, though.'

Emily is one of our investment managers. She's sharp as a tack. Mark is in client relations. They got it together at the Christmas party last year, but they've been keeping it under wraps – a rather futile gesture, as everybody knows they left together and have been accidentally bumping into each other at the water cooler ever since.

'Oh, I dunno. They seem happy.'

'He'll hold her back,' says Conrad. 'Men do, you know.'

'Do what?'

'Hold women back when they're working together. You feel bad if you're getting more recognition. The men feel bad too. But you feel bad for them, whereas they feel bad for themselves.'

I think about this for a moment and conclude that Conrad is right. He's very woke for someone who's dumped his wife for a younger model.

'Anyway,' he continues, 'I had something else I wanted to put to you, Delphine.'

He hardly ever calls me Delphine. It's always Delphie. So now I'm anxious. My heart beats faster and my mouth is dry. I eye the bottle of water on the desk in front of me, but I don't make a move for it.

'It's about your place in the firm,' he says, and I feel the same lurch in my stomach as I did when the plane hit the turbulence earlier. I've done good work for Conrad over the years, but his words are making me anxious. I think suddenly of Bianca, and I wonder if this is anything to do with her. Perhaps she doesn't like me being so close to her boyfriend. But that can't be it, surely. She's younger and prettier than me and has no qualms about wearing bikinis.

'You look concerned,' Conrad says.

'I didn't think there was anything about my place in the firm we needed to talk about,' I tell him.

'But there is. And our conversations today have only confirmed it for me.' Conrad sits back in his chair and looks at me speculatively.

'What?' I ask.

He sits up straight again. 'I've made a decision, Delphie. I want you to join the board as a director.'

'What!' I look at him in astonishment. 'You do? Why?'

'Delphie, I'm only going to say this once, but in my entire career, no man has ever asked why he's being asked to join the board. He assumes it's because he's done great work and that his expertise will be invaluable.'

'Yes, but—'

'And so, Ms Delphine Mertens, I'm asking you to join our board because you've done great work and your expertise will be invaluable. Not forgetting the many ways in which you saved me from myself over the last year, and your timely observations on some of our investment opportunities. More people are applying for our community funding programme than ever before. The story in the *Irish Times* last March was excellent for the Cosecha brand. There's definitely room for expansion there, and you're the one to lead it.'

The grants for this programme, to voluntary groups within communities, range from a few hundred to a few thousand,

and I'm really proud of having come up with the idea, although I wasn't expecting any reward for it.

'Besides,' Conrad continues, 'we need more diversity, and I can't think of anyone more suitable than you.'

Am I the token woman? I don't want to be the token woman. I want to be there on merit.

'You're not the token woman,' he says, as though I've spoken aloud. 'You're a valuable member of the team. There's nobody else at Cosecha better qualified to be a board member.'

I'm starting to smile and I can't stop it turning into a huge beam of delight.

'Thank you,' I say. 'Thank you very much. Does this change my job?'

He shakes his head. 'Not essentially, although I think we should retitle it Senior Executive to the CEO. Executive Assistant doesn't really have the clout for what you do, and the thing is, Delphie, you do a tremendous amount and you always have the best interests of the company at heart.'

'Thank you.' I don't usually blush, but I feel my cheeks warm at his praise.

'Anyhow,' he adds, 'we're a director short since Tim Power retired a few months ago, and it's about time we filled the vacancy.'

'I'm . . . well, not speechless, but nearly speechless. And very grateful. Thank you.'

'Don't be grateful,' says Conrad. 'Be confident that you've earned it. And you have. Drawing my attention to the mistake Justin made with the benchmark only confirms it.'

He's right. Catching Justin's mistake has saved us money, but more than that, I've worked hard over the years. I absolutely deserve my promotion. I know my family think I put my job before everything else, and I do, but I'm not as pushy about it within the company as they might think. Yes, I've wanted to move upwards. But I couldn't imagine there was anything more for me than being Conrad's executive assistant. The fact that there is, and that he's recognised it, is tremendously exciting.

'You're right, of course.' I smile at him. 'Thank you. How do the other directors feel about it?'

'I'll be speaking with them when I get back. They'll be fine with it, Delphie, they all appreciate your loyalty to the firm and your commitment to its success. And they know you're smart and have legal experience, which is invaluable.'

My legal experience is limited. I haven't needed to use it in any meaningful way since leaving Haughton's and I was only a lowly associate when I was there. But I do try to keep up to date with what's going on. And I'm good at problem-solving. So yes, I have skills.

'Anyhow.' He leans back in the chair. 'That's all the business done with for the day, so if you want to celebrate by jumping into the pool, be my guest.'

Should about-to-be-appointed board members jump into the CEO's infinity pool? I ask myself.

Of course they should.

So I change into my swimsuit and I do.

Chapter 4

I'm tired but very, very happy as I take my seat on the flight for Dublin later that evening. I haven't said anything to anyone about my board appointment yet. It's not something I want to share until it's done and dusted, though I know Erin and Sheedy will be delighted with the news. It always amazes me when I read stuff in the papers about women being bitchy to each other at work. I've never met anyone who wasn't supportive, and I try to be supportive in return.

I wonder, suddenly, how Tory would feel if I asked one of my girlfriends along as my plus-one. What's the definition of a plus-one anyhow? There's no requirement that they have to be a date, is there? And certainly not someone you're in a long-term relationship with. So wouldn't it be more fun to bring along a girlfriend with whom I'd definitely have a good time than some random man? If it was an office situation, wouldn't Erin or Sheedy be the best person for the job? And wouldn't the man simply be a beneficiary of gender quotas?

I smile to myself as I think this through. And then I sigh, because leaving Tory out of it, me turning up with a girlfriend would unleash the hounds of hell in terms of family questioning and opinion.

'Sorry. Excuse me. I'm at the window.'

I feel a surge of disappointment. I was hoping the plane was fully boarded and the seats beside me were going to be unoccupied. But I stand up to make room for the late arrival.

'Thanks. Thanks. Sorry again.'

He takes his place and I hold back an exclamation. But he doesn't.

'Delphie? Delphie Mertens. You've got to be kidding me.' He's looking at me in absolute astonishment.

'Ed Miller. This is a surprise.'

'It's lovely to see you,' he says. 'You look great.'

'Um. You too.'

'Seriously. It's been – how long?'

'Oh, I don't know. Ten years?'

It's been eight. But I've decided to round it up.

'Surely not. We didn't . . . I haven't . . . Gosh, whatever, it's amazing meeting you like this.'

He runs his hands through his once jet-black hair, now sprinkled with grey. Not too much grey, but enough to make him look distinguished. His square, contoured face looks distinguished too – those eight years (plus three months and a few days; I'm not anal enough to know it that precisely off the top of my head) have been good to him.

'What have you been doing with yourself?' he asks. 'Were you on holiday?'

'No,' I say. 'A business trip.' I turn my attention to the crew's safety demonstration, not because I haven't seen it multiple times before, but because we're near the front of the plane and the cabin crew member is standing right beside our seats. It would be rude to keep talking while she's explaining how the life jacket and whistle will save our lives in the unlikely event of us plunging thirty thousand feet into the sea and surviving.

'You always watched the safety demo,' remarks Ed as the plane pushes back.

'Always? We only took one flight together,' I remind him.

'You watched, though.' He grins at me. 'You even read the safety card.'

'I like to know what to do in a crisis.' Suddenly I relax and smile at him in return. 'How are you, Ed? Were you in Mallorca for business or pleasure yourself?'

'A holiday, of course,' he says. 'Who goes to Mallorca on business? Seriously?'

'Like I said, me,' I reply. 'My boss has a house here. Were you on holiday on your own, or have your friends abandoned you?'

He makes a face at me. 'I came with a group of guys,' he says. 'But I had to leave a day earlier than everyone else because I've a meeting tomorrow that I can't get out of. Are you still working at that investment place?'

'Yes.'

He considers this for a moment. 'It's worked out well for you.'

'I've just been appointed to the board,' I say. Because I have to say this to Ed. I have to show him that he did me a favour eight years ago.

Although it didn't seem like it at the time.

*

Even if I've never been head over heels in love, eight years ago I was certainly more in love with Ed Miller than I've ever been with anyone else.

We first met in the coffee shop near Haughton's. I was a junior associate, the one who went out to get the coffees for the group of us working on a commercial law case. It was complex and we were putting in long hours, arriving at the office at seven in the morning and often not finishing until after seven that evening. Which was why our eleven o'clock coffee from the excellent café on the corner was essential.

The first time I met Ed, he was behind me in the queue and I could sense his irritation at having to wait for my order of assorted lattes, cappuccinos, flat whites and Americanos.

'Sorry,' I said. 'I'm trying to keep a bunch of lawyers awake.'

'I'm not sure if that makes things better or worse,' he said. 'But fire ahead.'

The next day we arrived at exactly the same time.

'You first,' I said. 'There's only one of you but I'm ordering for an army.'

He grinned and then proceeded to order three flat whites and a macchiato.

'Sorry,' he said, though he clearly wasn't sorry at all. 'My turn to be ordering for the entire crew.'

The third time, a couple of days later, I was ahead of him in the queue again.

'Do you want me to order yours as well and get it over and done with?' I asked, much to the horror of the woman in line between us.

He shook his head. 'I can wait. It's only for me today.'

I ordered his Americano anyway.

'You didn't have to,' he said as I handed it to him.

'Coffee kindness,' I told him.

'Ed Miller. I like my coffee strong.'

'Delphine Mertens. I like people to be kind.'

'But you work for a law firm?' He gave me a sceptical look.

'It's a dirty job but somebody's got to do it.'

'Would you like to have coffee with me sometime?' he asked.

I decided I would. He was, after all, a good-looking man with a certain sense of humour, always desirable in a potential boyfriend (not that I was considering him as a potential boyfriend at that point. Not seriously). He got bonus points for being taller than me, and for being handsome in a corporate kind of way. His hair was perfectly cut, he was clean-shaven and he had dark brown eyes that were looking at me with warmth and amusement.

We met for coffee after work the following Friday, and then we met for lunch on Saturday and brunch on Sunday. We were both too busy to meet for anything other than a few words in the coffee queue the next week, but our weekend was spent together again. Even though I was too busy to think about him at work, Ed occupied a lot of my leisure time thoughts. I liked being with him. I looked forward to seeing him. I missed him when he wasn't there.

He was good in bed too. The first time we slept together, he asked me what I liked and what I wanted him to do. And then he did it, telling me it mattered to him that I was enjoying it as much as he was. Which wasn't hard, because good sex is as much about who you're with as how it's done. And I was very happy to be with him.

It was Ed who encouraged me to apply for an associate role at Cosecha after I'd shown the advertisement to him and told him that I was feeling undervalued where I was.

'The problem is, I don't think I'm qualified enough,' I said. 'I haven't got the sort of experience they want.'

'You've plenty of experience,' he told me. 'You've worked on some high-profile cases, Delphie. Big them up at the interview.'

'If there *is* an interview.'

There was. And I took Ed's words to heart.

'Women never think they're qualified enough, whereas men always think they're better than they are,' he told me when I learned that I'd got the job. 'You were probably way ahead of any guy who applied.'

He was being supportive, but he was also right. So I took him away for the weekend to celebrate.

My parents loved him. Erin gave him the seal of approval. And I was beginning to think that maybe I could combine a hopefully high-powered career with falling in love. I was pretty sure I was falling in love with Ed. I liked the feeling.

Then he told me about the job in Dubai.

'It's a great opportunity for me,' he said. 'I'd make an absolute fortune and it would polish up my CV no end.'

'No doubt about it,' I agreed. 'You're going to take it?'

'I have to,' he said. 'I'm sorry.'

'Why are you sorry?'

'Because it's for a minimum of two years and it's probably going to be five and there's no point in us trying to stay together for another five years while we're in different countries.'

He was stating this as a fact, without discussing it with me first. Without looking at other options.

'Are you breaking up with me?' I asked.

'It's the best thing to do,' said Ed. 'I've really loved our time together, Delphie. But you're like me, you want to get on in your life. You've got this new job at Cosecha. I know you're happy there, and you deserve to do well. I can't ask you to come to Dubai with me. Besides,' he added, 'it'd be tricky as an unmarried couple. Living together is frowned upon . . . actually, I think it's illegal, though mostly people don't get prosecuted. I couldn't put you in that position.'

I noticed he hadn't asked me to marry him, which would have put us in an entirely different position. I was hurt that he hadn't considered it, but also a little relieved that it wasn't a choice I had to make.

'So it's better this way. You concentrate on your career and I'll concentrate on mine.'

'I can't argue with that,' I said.

'I knew you'd understand.'

I did. But I wasn't sure I wanted to.

'We can keep in touch, of course,' he said. 'It's just – well, I won't be back at all for the first six months, and maybe not even after that.'

Even though I hadn't wanted to get married to him, I couldn't quite believe that he was able to shrug me off so easily.

I'm not a crier, but I was struggling to hold back the tears.

Nobody had ever broken up with me before.

It was a crushing experience.

Of course, I recovered. I wasn't as crushed as all that. But I'd been knocked sideways all the same and I found it hard to trust men afterwards. To believe them when they said they cared, to allow myself the luxury of thinking it could be forever. Besides, despite dating Jamie, Barney and Paul over the following years, I never once felt the same spark as I'd done with Ed. And so, as with the boyfriends who'd preceded him, I was the one who did the breaking up, before there was a chance of things getting too serious.

I'm not a cold-hearted person. I felt bad about the break-ups. But it was the right thing to do for everyone concerned.

'So tell me all about your career,' says Ed, jerking me back to the present. 'Appointed to the board! That's brilliant, Delphie. Really brilliant. You must have leaped up through the ranks.'

'Not entirely.' I fill him in on my move from associate to Conrad's personal assistant, executive assistant to the CEO and now director and senior executive to the CEO.

'It helps to hitch your wagon to a bright star,' muses Ed. 'And Conrad Morgan is a very bright star. Didn't he meet the American president a few years back?'

'Not that he really wanted to,' I remark. 'But yes. We have a lot of US investment funds. What about you? Are you still in Dubai, or have you come home? What's new in your life?'

'Oh, it's been all go.' He leans back in his seat. 'The first year was great. Then I met Carleen – she was working at one of the Jumeirah Beach hotels.'

'And it wasn't great after that? Why?'

'Obviously it was initially,' says Ed. 'We hit it off straight away. She's an events organiser and there's so much going on there that she was always busy. There's a work-hard-play-hard ethos, so . . . we played hard together.'

I keep my face expressionless.

'Ah, Delphie.' He grins. 'It was grand, there isn't some terrible punchline to this story. Unless getting married is it.'

'You're married!' I'd leaned back in my seat too, but I jerk upright again.

'I was,' he says. 'Divorced now.'

'I'm sorry.'

'Don't be. Playing hard with someone isn't the same as being married to them. It all went pear-shaped.'

'I'm sorry,' I repeat. 'So you're in Dubai without her?'

'Not a bit of it,' he replies. 'That's why it went pear-shaped. She got pregnant and insisted on coming home. I don't blame her for that; Dubai's not a place I'd want to raise a child. I'm working for an engineering company in Sandyford now. I miss Dubai, but I don't want to be the sort of dad who disappears from his son's life.' He opens the app on his phone and shows me a photo of a blonde boy in blue shorts and a red T-shirt, who looks to be around three or four. 'He's a great kid and I'm mad about him,' says Ed as I zoom in on the photo and tell him his son is gorgeous. 'But he wasn't in my game plan.'

'Still, you came home and gave it a shot.'

'It got to me, though. I resented having my plans disrupted, even if I've kind of made my peace with it now. Because I wasn't really committed to being home, I wasn't a great husband, or even a good dad, for a long time. So I don't blame Carleen for divorcing me. But I can't help feeling she got everything she wanted – being at home, the house, Joe – while I got nothing.'

'How long ago was the divorce?'

'It's two and a half years since we broke up. Three months since the divorce was finalised.'

I give him a sympathetic look.

'OK, all this sounds very "poor me" and I don't mean it to,' says Ed. 'Carleen and I are on a better track now, and I see Joe whenever I want.'

'You're happy working in Sandyford? Do you live there?' It's a fairly affluent suburb on the south side of the city, although Ed, like me, is a northsider by birth.

'It's a good company. I've an apartment in Ballinteer, close enough to cycle when I'm not out on a project.'

'You! On a bike!' I laugh. The Ed I dated wasn't a fan of cycling.

'Carleen's influence,' he says. 'It's good for me.'

I laugh again and he does too, and the atmosphere lightens.

'So, did you have a good holiday in Mallorca?' I ask.

'It was a stag party.' Ed looks slightly abashed. 'I know it's usually the twenty-somethings that have week-long stags in the sun, but hey, forty is the new twenty.'

'You're not forty!' I exclaim. 'You're . . .' I do some rapid calculations. 'You're thirty-nine.'

'I'm flattered you remember.'

'I'm good with numbers,' I remind him. 'Whose stag?'

'A pal from my five-a-side football team,' he says. 'It was fun, to be honest. Mainly golf and lying around in the sun. No real damage done, except to our livers.'

'Glad to hear it.'

'And you?' He puts the question casually. 'Did you get married yourself?'

'When would I have the time to get married?' I ask in return. 'And me tied to my globe-trotting boss.'

'I was never sure about you and getting married,' he muses. 'You always seemed to feel that there were better things you could be doing.'

I laugh, but inside I'm wondering if he really did think that. If, during our time together, he reckoned there was no point in asking me to marry him because I would've said no. I thought about that a lot after our break-up. Would I have gone with him to Dubai if he'd popped the question? Had I loved him enough to give up everything that mattered to me? I'm still not sure of the answer.

'Anyhow, like I said, you obviously made good choices,' he says. 'Are you seeing anyone now?'

'Not currently.' The words are out of my mouth before I think that perhaps I should have replied differently. I don't want Ed to think of me as a loser.

'In that case, how would you feel about meeting up again? I don't mean a date,' he adds quickly, as though it matters. 'Just, you know, coffee and a catch-up. We were together for nearly two years, but outside of that I've always enjoyed your company. It'd be nice to have a woman I could meet up with from time to time. I've not been good at that since Carleen.'

I'm not entirely sure how to take this, and Ed obviously sees the indecision on my face because he apologises for putting me on the spot and says that he's sure my life is as perfect as I've always wanted it to be and he doesn't want to trample all over it.

'Not at all,' I say. 'Nobody's life is perfect.'

'I feel better hearing that.' He grins.

'Actually . . .' The thought has come to me, and although I want to brush it away, I can't.

'Actually?'

'Are you doing anything the weekend of the ninth?' I ask. He thinks for a moment. 'No.'

'I'm asking you this because I know you're the one man who won't take it the wrong way, but . . . would you like to be my plus-one at a wedding?'

Chapter 5

It's after midnight when we touch down at Dublin airport and Ed and I part ways.

'See you at the wedding,' I say as a taxi pulls up at the rank outside the terminal building. 'I'll text you beforehand and confirm the room for Saturday night.'

'Sure.' He gives me a friendly peck on the cheek. 'I'm looking forward to it. And if you really need me to come on the Friday, I will.'

'Thanks, but you're doing me the most enormous favour by coming at all,' I say.

'No problem. It'll be something to do. I don't get out much these days.' He winks.

I get into the taxi, close my eyes and allow my shoulders to relax as we head for Malahide. It's been a busy day, but a brilliant one. Obviously the promotion is the biggest and best thing that's ever happened to me, and I can't wait to tell people, although, being slightly superstitious about these things, it'll only be a select few until it's done and dusted. Telling Ed didn't count because . . . well, because I had good reasons to tell him. Asking him to the wedding was something I did almost without thinking. I wouldn't have minded if he'd said no. The fact that he's agreed is the icing on today's cake.

I don't realise I'm home until the driver turns around and tells me we've arrived. I might have nodded off – after all, I was up very early this morning. I give him the fare, get out of the car and open my front door.

I love how the moment I step inside I feel totally at home. I love that everything is exactly how I left it this morning. I love that nobody has moved a piece of my jigsaw, or put away the cup on the drainer.

I love living alone.

Despite the late night, I'm up and out at my usual time and sitting behind my desk by eight o'clock. Although we have a working-from-home policy that I sometimes take advantage of, Conrad likes me to be in the office when he isn't there himself. I messaged him while I was on the Dart to ask if there was anything urgent he wanted me to look after, but he didn't respond, and I imagined Bianca telling him to ignore the beep of the text alert as they sat on the terrace sharing her clean-living organic breakfast preferences. (I know about her breakfast because she Instagrammed it last week; laid out on an iron table covered by a pristine white tablecloth, with the blue sky as a backdrop, were bright yellow bowls filled with various chopped fruits, chia seeds and nuts, some Greek yoghurt, a small pot of honey, and a lemon that she said was from her own tree. I'm not sure how she consumed the lemon – straight up or in a glass of water – and made the entirely bitchy assumption that it was there to make the post more colourful. To be fair, the breakfast looked very appealing and significantly healthier than the croissant and takeaway coffee I usually grab from the Spar near the office.)

At nine o'clock, I text André and tell him that Ed Miller will be my plus-one. He sends back a thumbs-up emoji. At 9.30, as I'm hanging up on a call to Berlin, my mum phones.

'Ed Miller?' she says without any preamble. '*The* Ed Miller?'

'I'm not sure who you mean by *the* Ed Miller,' I say, emphasising it exactly as she did.

'Of course you do,' she says. 'The Ed Miller you went out with before. Lovely Ed. Are you seeing him again even though he fecked off without you?'

'How quickly the Mertens bush telegraph works,' I remark, ignoring the question.

'Don't be silly. Tory dropped in to me a few minutes ago on her way to the train station and mentioned you'd finally given her a name. She didn't realise he was a *former flame.*' Even more emphasis from Mum.

'It was a long time ago,' I say. 'He's a friend now.'

'I thought he'd moved to the Middle East,' she says.

'Dubai,' I remind her. 'He's back.'

'Obviously.' She sounds sarky.

'We're not back together,' I say. 'He's just . . . a friend.'

'You can't call someone "just a friend" when you've already slept with them.'

This is the problem with my family. There's no filter. That's why Danny is usually my best bet as a plus-one. He's used to them. Fortunately, Ed is too. Or was.

'We've moved on to being just friends,' I say.

'How long has he been back?' demands Mum.

'A while.'

'How long have you been seeing him without telling me?'

'I haven't.'

'So you've asked him out of the blue?'

'Not exactly.' I don't give her any further information. 'I met him, I asked him, he said yes.'

'Huh.' She clearly wants to grill me further but decides to hold back.

'I thought you'd all be happy that you can put a name and a face to my plus-one and Tory can write her place card,' I tell her.

'She says he's not coming to the Friday dinner.'

'It's a family meal,' I remind her. 'He doesn't need to be at that.'

'He knows us and we'd have made him welcome,' she says. 'Other guests are coming on Friday night.'

'But not to the meal. Anyway, it's fine. He's busy.' It's a white lie.

'I liked Ed,' she says. 'But not that he broke your heart.'

'He didn't.'

'Of course he did. When you weren't locked in your room sobbing, you were mooning around the place like a lovelorn waif.'

I was living at home back then. It wasn't a great place to get over a broken relationship. I spent a lot of time in my room to get away from the sympathetic looks and unasked-for advice.

'I wasn't sobbing and I did go out with other people afterwards,' I remind her. 'I was fine.'

'Your heart wasn't in it.'

There's no pleasing her. Really there isn't.

'I've got to go, Mum,' I say. 'I've a meeting in five minutes.'

'Fair enough. I'm heading off to Pilates.'

'Enjoy,' I say.

'It's better than feckin' meetings, that's for sure,' is her response as she ends the call.

Erin phones me in the afternoon because I texted her and Sheedy about the director's position. Sheedy sent a message saying she was in court but we'd celebrate soon. She added lots of champagne and streamer icons. It's nice to hear Erin's voice.

'You deserve it,' she says. 'You really do.'

'Apparently so.'

'Stop downplaying it, Delphie,' she commands. 'It's fantastic.'

'I know,' I say. 'I'm trying to be assertive and proud, but until the other directors vote on it, nobody knows anything, so I'm staying low-key about it.'

'When's Conrad due back?'

I tell her about his trip to Singapore and say that he's not a hundred per cent sure of his return date yet. But it doesn't matter, because he's told me and that's the most important thing.

'I'm delighted for you,' she says. 'My friend the director.'

'I know. It sounds very grown up and important.'

'Because it is. Listen, I know you and I were supposed to meet up this weekend, but Fintan has asked me to go to a fundraiser with him. I've said no the last couple of times and I really can't refuse again. Let's get together with Sheedy very soon and have a proper celebration. As soon as our diaries are free. OK?'

Fintan is her on-off boyfriend. They're obviously on at the moment.

I agree on meeting up for a celebration, then remind her that I have the wedding of the year in my schedule too.

'Oh God, yes. I forgot about that. Did you find anyone to go with you?'

'Ed Miller,' I say as casually as I can.

'Ed Miller? *The* Ed Miller?' she squeaks, sounding exactly like Mum.

I explain about meeting him on the flight and fill her in on his backstory.

'Wow,' she says. 'And you don't mind asking him?'

'Why not?' I shrug, even though she can't see it. 'He's arm candy, that's all.'

We both laugh.

'Is he still attractive arm candy?' she asks when the laughter stops.

'Actually, yes,' I reply. 'He's aged better than me.'

'Nonsense.'

'It's true. But I don't care. At least he knows everyone and he can spend time catching up. Much better than dragging along someone who hasn't felt the full force of the Mertens en masse before. I thought of asking you,' I add. 'But I'm not sure they would've got it exactly.'

'I hate weddings,' Erin says. 'All that lovey-dovey stuff does my head in.'

'I can put up with the lovey-dovey stuff,' I say, although I'm definitely not the world's most romantic person. 'It's the plus-one element that stresses me out. As well as everyone asking me when it's going to be my turn,' I add.

'I'd seriously rather go to a conference on legal precedent than a wedding,' Erin says.

'And I'd rather listen to an analysis of market trends,' I

61

tell her. 'But hey ho, I'll self-medicate with bubbly and I'm sure I'll get through unscathed.'

'I can't wait to hear all about it,' she says. 'We'll definitely meet up soon.'

'I'll probably need to for the therapy,' I tell her, before ending the call.

I use the weekend to go shopping for a suitable dress, but I struggle to find anything I like. The stores are full of early summer clothes, but spaghetti straps and clingy fabrics don't suit me, while the more formal outfits all seem very staid. I panic-buy a floral dress from Ted Baker, but it's not really what I'm looking for. Not that I know what I'm looking for – I'm good at business suits or jeans and T-shirts. Everything else is hard work. However, the fact that I have a dress and a plus-one means I'm a lot more relaxed about André and Tory's big day, and I'm even starting to look forward to it.

I know they're totally pushing the boat out, but it won't be anything like Bianca's thirtieth. On Sunday morning I see that she's updated her Instagram account, and I scroll through her carefully curated photos and videos with a touch of envy at how stunning Palmyra looks at night.

Multicoloured lights are strung across the pool area, while candles in glass tea-light holders have been placed around the pool itself and flaming torches light the way from there back to the house, where the internal LED lights change colour every few minutes. I can't help wondering what Martha would have made of it all. It's not that she didn't enjoy a bit of bling, but I don't remember her ever flaunting it quite as much as this. More importantly, what do Killian and Connie think? I'm sure they've seen the photos too.

Bianca herself is stunning in a green organza dress, Lady Annabel's bracelet very visible on her arm as, in one of the videos, she blows out the candles while the band plays 'Happy Birthday' and fireworks fill the skies. There are lots more photos, including one of Bianca with Conrad in which he's gazing adoringly at her.

I put away my phone and go for a jog along the waterfront.

Conrad calls me on Tuesday afternoon to say he won't be back in the office as he needs to go directly to New York after Singapore. He wants me to book his tickets and meet him there. This randomness is one of the things I love about my job, although, like many businesses, we've embraced Zoom and cut back significantly on overseas travel. Nevertheless, Conrad prefers face-to-face meetings to virtual ones if possible, so I book the flights and message him to say I'll meet him at the Four Seasons, which is where I stay whenever I'm in New York on business. Conrad, of course, has his Central Park apartment; it might be small, but the views from its floor-to-ceiling windows are breathtaking.

It's a weird thing being the assistant (executive or otherwise) to someone like Conrad Morgan. You dip your toe into the privileges of wealth without having it yourself. You stay in hotels that you could never afford if you were paying for them out of your own pocket and eat at restaurants where the prices would make your eyes bleed. It's not like Conrad doesn't work hard and deserve the rewards, but the money he earns is totally disproportionate to what he does. He knows that too, which is why he's committed a lot of resources to the charitable sector, yet there's something ludicrous about having more in your bank account than you'll ever be able to spend. I occasionally think that having it all can be a burden rather than a benefit. Conrad is always worrying about his money, about how to protect it, how to spend it, how to save it, how to make it grow even more. He's never satisfied and nor are any of the people he deals with. There's always someone richer, always someone with a bigger house, a bigger car, a bigger plane. Always someone to make you feel that you're not doing as well as them.

But as I book my business-class flight, the only thought I have is that it's nice to share the benefits from time to time.

I'm one of the few people in the world who are not blown away by New York City. I'm overawed by its size and energy, but I can't help feeling a sense of desperation about it too. Everyone's trying to scramble to the top of the heap, and it's exhausting. Nobody talks, they shout. Nobody walks, they hurry. Nobody sleeps. It's a New York thing.

However, the three days of meetings go well, and I even get time to nip into Bergdorf Goodman, where I pick up a discounted Elie Tahari cocktail dress that's way more suitable for André and Tory's wedding than the floral Ted Baker. It's nice to think that the trip has been a success for both of us.

Over coffee in the Four Seasons we talk business. Conrad tells me that I was right about the files I was working on on the way to Mallorca, and that he gave Justin a bollocking for using the wrong benchmark. Which probably explains why his deputy was snippy with me when I returned to the office. Justin hates being caught out in an error. I allow myself a moment of satisfaction for being right, then our conversation switches to the more personal, and Conrad tells me that Bianca's party was fantastic and that she loved the bracelet.

'Who wouldn't?' I don't say that I've already seen Bianca's Instagram posts of the spectacular party. Conrad isn't an Insta person.

'I'll have to come up with something even better for Christmas,' he remarks.

'Surely not,' I say without thinking. 'Surely it's all about giving someone something they like, not something better than the last thing you gave them.'

He shakes his head. 'She'll always like something better than the last thing I gave her.'

'Well, yes, but . . .' I don't want to appear to be judging my boss, but I'm not sure how to say what's going through my mind without making it seem like I am. 'I'm sure she'll love anything you give her' is what I eventually come up with, and Conrad laughs and tells me I'm easy to please.

'Not at all,' I return, more confidently. 'Not when it comes to my work, anyhow.'

'You mean you're not pleased at your directorship?'

'I'm ecstatic about that,' I admit. 'What I mean is, I always want to do better.'

'And you always do,' he confirms. 'Sorry I wasn't in Dublin to talk to the other directors this week. I have to go to Mallorca again too, but as soon as I'm back in Ireland, I'll get everything in place.'

'There's no rush. And I'm very grateful to you for doing this.'

'It's nothing more than you deserve.'

Maybe not. But it's the first time I've ever got anything without asking for it. And it makes me feel really good.

Chapter 6

The week leading up to André's wedding is manic and I don't get time to meet up with Erin and Sheedy, who are keen to celebrate my elevation to the Cosecha board even if I have to wait for Conrad's return for it to be made official. While he's back in Mallorca, he's left me to deal with a number of outstanding issues, all of which are complex and time-consuming. Justin is in a foul mood and is riling the staff, especially Lisa Hannigan, who he doesn't get on with. Lisa camps in my office for half an hour, venting about him, and I tell her that it's nothing personal – he's one of those guys who annoys all the female staff at some point. She gives me a quizzical look as I say that she shouldn't let him get to her, while assuring her that she's a great analyst and Conrad is very happy with her work. I think she's going to ask more about Justin, but then her phone rings and it's a call she has to take so I get back to what I was doing and forget about it. Lisa will have to fight her own corner. That's one of the things I've learned about office life. Women want to be liked, but being liked isn't necessarily the way to get on. Being respected is a lot more useful.

There are some further minor crises, mainly relating to

things that Conrad has apparently forgotten about, but I manage to put out all the fires. It's actually a relief when Friday comes along and I take my half-day. Letizia does my nails and eyebrows at my local salon in Malahide before passing me over to Mindy, my hairstylist, who adds some party curls.

'It'll hold for tomorrow,' she says as she eyes her handiwork critically. 'Just don't roll around in bed too much.'

'Not planning on that,' I tell her with a grin.

'It's a wedding,' she says. 'All that love in the air. Who knows what might happen.'

I've filled her in on the extravaganza, although she doesn't think a three-day event at a castle is extravagant at all.

'Everyone does it now,' she informs me. 'Sure why not make the most of it? Isn't it the happiest day of your life?'

It's certainly the most expensive, and not only for the bride and groom, I reflect as I tap my credit card while totting up the cost of glamorising myself, the Elie Tahari dress (as well as the Ted Baker panic-buy) and, of course, the wedding gift – André and Tory have asked for money, and who can blame them given the extent of the celebrations.

If I ever do get married myself, it'll be a trip to the registry office in the morning followed by lunch in one of the nearby restaurants, and that'll be an end to it. Quick, simple and no stress for anyone. It sounds absolutely perfect to me, but perhaps I'm out of touch. Perhaps in a world where it's almost impossible to do what were once considered basic things – like buy a house and start a family on a single salary – it comes down instead to having a massive day out to show how much in love you are.

Having my own place as a single person is an absolute

luxury, and I'm aware that André and Tory somewhat resent the fact that I live alone in my cottage by the sea while they're paying almost as much in rent for their one-bedroom apartment in the city. I know I've worked hard for everything I have, but I sometimes can't help feeling guilty about my good fortune.

I get my stuff for the weekend together and then put my packed case into the car I picked up earlier in the town centre. I don't own a car myself, but I use an app to hire one whenever I need it, which suits me fine. I get behind the wheel of the Toyota hybrid, turn on the satnav and head out of the city.

My brother and his fiancée have been lucky with the weather. Last weekend, in typical early summer conditions, it was cold and grey, but today the sun is blazing down from a clear blue sky and the forecast is good until Sunday evening.

Even with leaving the house before three, the traffic is heavy, and it's gone half past four when I arrive at the castle. Mum and Dad are already sitting in the enormous reception area like a king and queen welcoming their subjects.

'At last.' Mum gets up and gives me a hug. 'I was hoping you wouldn't be late.'

'Dinner isn't until seven,' I remind her. 'I'm early if anything.'

'We all want to get together beforehand,' she says. 'We're only waiting on Martin and Lindsey now.'

I say nothing, but Mum can see that I'm not enthused about meeting my sister-in-law, and in an obvious effort to forestall any problems over the weekend, she tells me that Lindsey has been really good to her lately, and that she never means to be as sharp as she sometimes is.

I disagree, but I don't say so out loud. Lindsey revels in making barbed comparisons between her perfect family and my solitary state. Her unsubtle digs only reinforce my view that she regards me as some kind of non-woman for my unnatural lack of maternal instinct, and her frequent requests for me to babysit seem like a way to reinforce how lonely and meaningless my single life is.

Because I don't want to be on bad terms with my brother, and because I love my niece and nephew, I babysit for them whenever I can, though when I do, Lindsey always leaves me a list of instructions more suited to a nurse in a high-dependency unit than an adult looking after a child. The first time, I checked the house for hidden cameras in case she was monitoring me. I didn't find anything, but it wouldn't surprise me if she'd sewn a spy cam into one of the teddy bears.

'Everyone else is already here?' I stop thinking about my irritating sister-in-law and look brightly at Mum. 'Michael and Nichola and the girls? Vivi, Jason and Charley?'

'Yes,' she says. 'They came for lunch. A group of Tory's girlfriends arrived earlier too and are having treatments in the spa.'

'And the grannies?'

'We brought Granny Mertens. She's in the sun room enjoying the heat. Sean and Barbara haven't arrived with Granny Dunphy yet.'

'Sounds like it's all under control,' I say.

'Of course it is.'

'I'll check in and see you later, then.'

'Your hair is nice,' she says as I begin to walk away. 'You should wear it like that more often.'

Is there ever a time when your mother doesn't make some

comment on how you look or what you do or what you eat? Not if she's my mum, that's for sure.

We have a large private room for dinner, which is a good thing as there are thirty adults and ten children. Everyone's in high spirits and I'm very happy sitting beside Granny Mertens at one end of the table. She's talking to me in French, as she always did when I was small. She thought it would be useful for me to know another language, and it has been. At first we're both a bit rusty – she's searching for words that once tripped off her tongue, while I'm getting my tenses mixed up. But after a while the conversation begins to flow.

'How are you getting along at work?' She leans close to me because she's taken out her hearing aids. Sometimes, in noisy, clattery situations like now, she finds them too much. 'Josie says you're very busy. That you're back travelling the world again.'

'Not quite,' I reply. 'But when my boss asks me to join him in New York, I don't say no.'

'You're very lucky,' she says. 'I'd have given anything to have a job like that.'

Granny Mertens worked in a jam factory as a girl. The work was hard, the hours long and the pay low.

I agree with her that I'm lucky.

'Your mother also says that an old boyfriend is coming tomorrow,' she says.

I wonder if they've charged her with extracting information from me. I've always got on with both my grandmothers and probably confide in them more than anyone else, but I'm not going to allow them to become some kind of conduit for information to the rest of the family.

'There's nothing between Ed and me any more,' I tell her. 'It was a coincidence that I bumped into him and he was able to come.'

'Isn't there anyone you *wanted* to ask?' Granny looks at me quizzically.

'Not really,' I admit.

'What about that boy that came to Charley's christening?'

Poor Danny. I lugged him along to that even though, like me, he doesn't have a religious bone in his body, and I didn't really need a plus-one. But it was definitely an occasion where my life choices would have come up for discussion, and having Danny with me prevented that.

'He's in Las Vegas,' I tell her.

'But are you and he . . .?' She gives me the quizzical look again.

'Granny, there's no me and anyone. And that's fine. Really it is.'

'Of course it is,' she says. 'Stick to your guns, Delphie. Don't feel you have to settle for second best.'

'I won't.' I smile at her.

'*Bon pour toi alors.*' She smiles in return. Good for you.

I love Granny Mertens. I love her strength of purpose, her unshakeable determination. She reminds me of the heroines in the novels my mum used to read when she was younger, and which still line her bookshelves. They were dismissed as 'sex and shopping' books at the time, but the leading ladies all managed to forge business empires from humble beginnings, and went on to be rich and powerful and strong (even if their personal lives were a complicated mess). And I know that not everyone can be strong all the time, but I don't want to believe that we're always hanging on by a thread,

71

barely managing to keep all the balls in the air, being sucked under by the stresses of our day-to-day existence, let alone our business lives. I don't want to be the woman who cracks open a bottle of wine every evening and worries that she's making a mess of her life. I want to be the one who pours herself a whiskey and soda and celebrates doing great business deals! Well, maybe not whiskey and soda, owing to the fact that I don't like whiskey, but I want to be the sort of woman who could.

Granny Mertens asks me a little more about my trip to New York. She loves hearing my travel stories and I always have great fun telling her about the places I've been. I mention that I bought my wedding outfit in Bergman's, and she says she bought hers in Brown Thomas, where the sales assistants made a big fuss of her and ensured she found something that made her look elegant and lovely.

She *is* elegant and lovely, with her silver-grey hair and her still-high cheekbones. Her cornflower-blue eyes might be a little dimmer than they were in her youth, but they sparkle with enthusiasm when she's animated, as she is now.

'Were you sure that Grandad was the man for you when you first met?' I ask as the plates are cleared away.

She considers the question for a moment. 'I knew he was a fine man,' she says eventually. 'I knew he would make a good husband. He was ambitious. He wanted to do well in his new country. And he did.'

He moved from Kells to Dublin to work for the Guinness brewery at a time when it was one of the biggest employers in the city and the employees were generously looked after. He started out in the brewery itself but ended up as an executive. It was probably easier to move through the ranks back then, because experience counted more than degrees. Although, I think, that's what's happened to me in a way. I started off as nobody very important at Cosecha, and I'll soon be a director. So perhaps I'm following in my grandfather's footsteps. The idea is a pleasing one.

After dinner, we break into various groups, and I decide to go for a walk around the castle grounds. It's a warm evening, although with dusk falling the midges are out and I'm soon scratching my arms and thinking that it won't be a good look being covered in bites tomorrow. As I make my way back indoors, Noemi comes running to meet me and demands that I redo her golden plait, which has come undone.

I do as she asks and give her a massive hug before she races back indoors. Seeing her reminds me that my ringtone is still the theme from *Frozen*, so I take out my phone and change it to the more generic 'Reflection'; not that the ringtone is particularly important, because my voice calls are increasingly rare these days. It's all instant messaging and WhatsApp, which I actually prefer. Looking at the phone, I realise I've missed two messages, both from Ed and both confirming that he'll see me tomorrow. I send a thumbs-up in response. Then I check my business phone. There's nothing. Which is a relief.

I join the rest of the family in the lounge and order a Sauvignon Blanc.

I'll leave the whiskey for another time.

Chapter 7

My hair has survived a night's sleep and is curly but thankfully not dishevelled when I get up early the next morning. Mindy would be disappointed that there was no unexpected wedding sex to disturb it, but then as we haven't had the wedding yet, there hasn't been an opportunity for post-ceremony passion. I've occasionally slept with my plus-ones in the past (I'm not entirely immune to romantic influences), but it's generally been a strictly friends-with-benefits scenario. All the same, I'm not planning on wedding sex with Ed Miller. It was good before, but I don't want him to think I asked him along because I want to start a relationship with him again. I've never gone back to an ex and I'm not sure it's a good idea.

I've opted to have a room service breakfast, as it's a luxury to have a lie-in and I'm not good at casual chit-chat in the mornings. After a shower, I put on a loose dress and go outside. There are no midges now and I walk through the expansive castle grounds thinking that André and Tory really have chosen a fairy-tale location for their wedding. As I look back at the crenellated towers and leaded glass windows, I feel a buzz of excitement for the day ahead. However, as I imagine Rapunzel letting down her long hair, I also remind myself that back then, women wouldn't have married for love. It would have been for money and strategic alliances. And on the command of their male relatives. If Tory had lived when the castle was a functioning castle, she wouldn't be marrying someone like André. Her dad would have been trying to find her the equivalent of Conrad Morgan.

Thinking of Conrad means I check my business phone again, but there are still no messages from him.

'Hey, Delphie!' Vivi, with Charley in her arms, waves from the formal garden near the building itself. 'How's the head this morning?'

'Fine,' I reply. 'I only had two glasses last night.'

'I long to have a glass of wine again,' she says. 'But until I stop feeding the monster . . .' She aims a broad smile at Charley, who gurgles back at her. Then she eases him to the ground and holds both his hands aloft while he takes tentative steps on the gravelled footpath.

'He's doing well on it,' I remark.

'I know.' She makes a face. 'Best for baby and all that, but I feel like Granny Dunphy's milking parlour.'

'Should he not be on solids by now?' I ask. 'He's what? Eight months? Nine?'

'Of course he's on solids.' She gives me an exasperated look. 'He simply loves his boob and I like feeding him that way. Not all the time,' she adds, 'but it's nice to be so close to him.'

Breastfeeding is not one of my areas of expertise, so I keep my mouth shut.

'Come on, precious.' She gathers him into her arms again. 'Momma has to go and pretty herself up for later. At least I don't have to worry about him having a role to play,' she adds. 'Poor Nichola is going mad with her three as flower girls. Noemi is insisting on some complicated style for her hair, and Elodie has suddenly decided that she doesn't want to wear the same dress as Phoebe. Meanwhile Melissa told Lindsey that she wants to be a flower girl too, and not a ring bearer with Kevin.'

'I'm glad I'm nothing more than a spectator,' I agree. 'I suppose I'd better get dolled up myself.'

'It's kind of cool that Ed's going to be here.' Vivi gives me a thoughtful look. 'I always liked him.'

'So did I,' I tell her cheerfully. 'Let's hope we're still friends after this.'

'You said last night that you hadn't seen him in years.'

'Not since he went to Dubai.'

'I'm truly surprised that you're back with someone who broke your heart. But I like it.'

'Why does everyone think he broke my heart?' I demand. 'I was upset for a while, that's all. I'm not back with him either.'

'Well, I like that you've forgiven him for dumping you,' says Vivi. 'It shows you're not as chill as everyone thinks.'

I'm not sure, when I'm back inside the hotel, if she was using 'chill' in a positive sense. But I'll give her the benefit of the doubt.

Nobody could accuse me of being anything other than soppy in the church later. When Tory walks up the aisle on her father's arm and smiles at André, she looks so beautiful in her embroidered white dress, and is so undoubtedly happy, that a tear slides down my cheek. I'm not the only one who's sniffing; every single woman in the church is. And a few of the men have wobbly faces too.

Not Ed, though, who's standing beside me tall and handsome, and who gives me a grin as I wipe away the tear.

'You OK?' he murmurs, and I nod as he squeezes my hand. I suddenly remember how he would catch hold of it as we walked down the street when we were going out together. Ed was always far more tactile than me. He still is. When I met him after he arrived at the hotel an hour earlier, his first act was to hug me and tell me how good it was to see me.

'It's good to see you too,' I murmured as we brushed cheeks. 'Thank you so much for doing this. I really appreciate it.'

'It's lovely to do something different on a Saturday,' he said. 'Not that I don't look forward to having Joe, but it's good to get out of the T-shirt and sweatpants. You look fabulous, by the way, Delphie. I'm loving the curls.'

'Thanks.' I'm relieved the curls have held up and delighted that the Elie Tahari, with its rather daring neckline, is such a perfect fit. I accessorised it with my favourite Swarovski earrings and necklace, as well as my highest heels, which means I'm eye to eye with Ed.

'So it's the usual gang then?' He looked around the reception area, although the only people gathered there were friends of Tory's, a group of perfectly made-up twenty-somethings taking multiple selfies of themselves.

'Pretty much. Along with a few extras now. A selection of nieces and nephews and some in-laws.'

'Funny how you think things stay the same when you're not around,' he said. 'But they don't. Everything changes.'

'Oh my God! Ed Miller. It's great to see you again!'

I turned at the voice and saw Mum walking down the wide staircase in her bare feet. I frowned.

'Hello, Mrs M,' said Ed. 'It's good to see you too.'

'You've aged well,' she informed him, shaking his hand and then pulling him into a hug.

'While you, Mrs M, are looking younger than ever.'

'Call me Josie.' She beamed at the compliment. 'You did before.'

'I'm trying to be extra polite.'

She grinned and then turned to me. 'I was wondering if you were going to wear those sandals from last night, Delphie. But I see you're not. Can I borrow them?'

'The L. K. Bennetts? Of course you can, but why?'

'Because the bloody shoes I bought six whole months ago are crippling me already,' she replied. 'They're rubbing against my toes and I won't be able to last the church ceremony in them let alone the rest of the day. Your sandals were stylish, they looked comfortable and they'll go with my outfit. We take the same size, so . . .'

I bought them in London the last time I was there, though I've only worn them a couple of times. They've a kitten heel and are super comfortable.

'Are you sure you want to wear cast-off sandals?' I asked.

'Definitely,' she said. 'I was wrong when I told myself I could suffer for my looks. All I want is to be able to stand up without crying.'

I laughed. 'Come on, so. Let's try them out.'

Ed said he'd wander around the gardens and see me either there or back at reception for the bus that was taking all the guests to the local church for the ceremony. Like me, André isn't the slightest bit religious, but he went along with Tory's

78

wish to have a Mass in the beautiful church rather than a civil ceremony in the hotel.

'There's no point in walking down an aisle if there isn't a proper aisle to walk down,' she said, and he agreed with her.

I led Mum to my room, where she pronounced the sandals a perfect fit.

'You're not just saying that, are you?' I asked.

'OK, they're a little big, but the gel insoles I got for the toe-pinchers will help,' she said. 'I don't know what I was thinking when I bought them. Well, I do. They were lovely. But just putting them on is uncomfortable, let alone taking a step in them.'

'You're mad, you know that.'

'And are you mad to be rekindling things with Ed Miller?'

'I told you already, I'm not rekindling anything.'

'Well maybe you should.'

'Make your mind up, Mum.'

'It's just . . .' She sighed. 'All I want is for my children to be happy. And I know you are, Delphie. I know you have a good life. But with André getting married, nearly everyone is settled. It'd be nice if you were too.'

'What on earth are you talking about?' I looked at her in bemusement. 'I have my own house, for heaven's sake. How could I be any more settled?'

'But you've nobody to share it with.'

'Mum, you've often said that no relationship is better than a bad relationship. I can't believe you're now throwing that excellent advice to the wind and telling me that unless I'm married, I'm not settled.'

'I don't mean it like that,' she said. 'But life is so much richer if you have someone you love in it.'

'Possibly,' I conceded. 'But I haven't found anyone I love enough to share it with yet. I might never. But I'm certainly not going to stress about it. And I'm not letting you make me feel as though there's something wrong with me because of it.'

'I don't feel there's something wrong with you. Of course I don't. But Ed is a nice man who's had his chance to sow his wild oats, and you two were always good together. It seems like fate has brought you back together.'

'Sow his wild oats? For heaven's sake, Mum, Ed has been married and divorced since I first went out with him. He has his own baggage. I'm not getting involved.'

She sighed. 'It's up to you.'

'Yes,' I said. 'It is.'

Then I told her that it was getting late and she should scoot along and finish getting ready. I fixed my make-up, shook my head so that my curls danced around my face, and went to meet my ex-boyfriend again.

Ed releases my hand as we sit down, and the priest welcomes us all to the church and tells us how the ceremony will proceed. My attention wanders towards the beautiful stained-glass window behind the altar, and I wonder about the people who designed and installed it nearly two hundred years ago. Obviously, like the church, it was built to last, but did they ever wonder back then about the people who would sit in the pews and look at it after they were gone? Did they wonder what our lives would be like? Did they pray for us?

Despite my lack of interest in formal religion, I like sitting in old churches; I appreciate the sense of peace and tranquillity they bring. And so I enjoy the wedding ceremony, even though the soprano's exquisite interpretation of 'O mio babbino caro' has to compete with the asthmatic spluttering of the tractor in the field behind us.

The tractor's gone by the time we leave, and we shower my brother and his new wife with grains of rice, an activity that the children, in particular, take to with great gusto. I always enjoy throwing rice too, although I'm hopeless and a lot of it ends up in my own cleavage. After a barrage of official photos and unofficial selfies, we get into the coach and are driven back to the castle, which looks magnificent under the cloudless blue sky, and where a long red carpet waits for them.

There's a champagne reception on the terrace while the newly-weds are off having more photos taken, so I sit on one of the iron chairs while Ed, never a man for champagne, heads to the bar to get a pint of Guinness. Nichola joins me, a bright splash of fuchsia pink in the summer sun.

'Lovely ceremony,' she says as she sits down on Ed's chair. 'So moving.'

'Yes.'

'We're all intrigued by the return of Ed.'

'He was the only available plus-one,' I confess.

'Ever think of marrying one of them and saving on the stress?' She grins at me.

'Don't hold your breath,' I reply, and both of us laugh.

Ed returns with his pint and another glass of champagne for me, and smiles at Nichola. 'How are you?'

'Good. And you? I couldn't believe it when I heard you and Delphie were back together.'

'Oh, well let's see how we last the day before making any wild assumptions.' Ed gives her an easy smile. 'Delphie tells me you've got three girls now.'

'Yes. They were the flower girls.'

'And very good they were too,' says Ed, ignoring the fact that Elodie refused to scatter any of her petals in front of Tory as she was supposed to and is still hanging on to her basket as though it contains a hidden treasure.

Nichola grins at him and suddenly they're chatting away like old friends. Which they aren't. I don't recall Ed being particularly friendly with any of my family, although now that I think about it, he did seem to get on better with Michael, and consequently Nichola, than anyone else. In fact, I suddenly remember, the two men occasionally went to rugby matches together – both of them were season ticket holders for Leinster matches.

How had I forgotten all that?

I half listen to Ed and Nichola as I look around me at the guests, the women like multicoloured butterflies in their party dresses, the men in formal monochrome. Most of them have taken off their jackets now, because the sun is properly beating down on us and I'm starting to think I should've brought some factor 50 with me. Thinking of sunburn makes me also think of Conrad in Mallorca, and I take a quick peek at my phone. There are still no messages, which, to be honest, is a little unusual, as Conrad tends to contact me at least once a day regardless of whether I'm supposed to be working or not. Clearly he's remembered the wedding, which is progress. Or maybe Bianca has reminded him – we did chat quite a bit about it over lunch at Tim's. She wondered what her own wedding would be like. I was uncomfortable with the direction the conversation was taking and didn't really engage too much. But Bianca was happy to talk without interruption.

There's a slight commotion at the end of the terrace and I see that André and Tory have returned from their formal photography session. The photographer follows them outside and tries to marshal us all together for some group shots with the castle as a background. There's a lot of good-natured jostling for position, and I find myself, as always, at the back of the group.

'You know you look amazing?' says Ed, who's standing beside me.

'Aw, thanks.' I give him a cheesy grin.

'Seriously,' says Ed. 'All the other women look as though they've made an immense effort. You look chic and sophisticated without even trying.'

I glance at him, but his expression is serious.

'Thanks,' I say again, and then, as the photographer asks us to shuffle closer together, I move in towards him and he puts his arm around me. It's nearly six months since a man has put his arm around me, and a lot longer since that man was Ed. I hadn't realised how much I've missed it. I slide my own arm around his waist and move even closer.

Eventually the photographer is happy with the shots and the group breaks up again. Tory spots me and comes over.

'So,' she says, looking at Ed. 'The elusive plus-one. Pleased to meet you.'

'Pleased to meet you too,' says Ed. 'Congratulations. The service was lovely.'

'It was, wasn't it?'

'Yes. And what a fantastic location.'

I'm thinking that Ed is laying it on a bit thick, but Tory is lapping it up. She's positively purring as he rains even more compliments down on her, saying he's never seen a prettier

83

bride and telling her that he wouldn't have put money on André Mertens managing to snare a woman like her as his wife; then he tells her about André's twenty-first, when my darling brother got pissed out of his brains and fell asleep in the bushes on the seafront at Clontarf.

'I brought him home,' says Ed, which is actually true though I'd forgotten that part of it.

'Nobody tells me anything about André's wicked youth,' says Tory. 'I need all the gossip from you.'

'That's the only gossip I have.' Ed winks at her. 'The rest of his early years were totally blameless.'

She laughs and flits off to mingle, while Ed and I reminisce about that night. I was still living at home then, and had gone back by myself when we were turfed out of the function room that André had hired. I have a feeling it was dawn before Ed poured him in the front door.

'Oh, he was absolutely catatonic by then,' says Ed cheerfully. 'I bet he didn't get up for a few days.'

'I can't remember,' I say. 'But you were very good to make sure he got home.'

'I like André,' he says. 'I like all your brothers.'

I suppose he must have done if he'd gone to the rugby with Michael and saved André from himself. But I didn't realise back then how close to my family he'd become.

'I think they want us to go inside.' Ed nudges me and points to a hotel employee who's telling people that dinner will be served shortly. We join the general move to the ballroom, a high-ceilinged room with long mullioned windows, decorated in shades of rose and dove grey and almost overflowing with matching floral arrangements.

'Nice,' says Ed as we find our table. 'Not too wedding-y.'

'No,' I agree. 'Tory has great taste. Well, of course she has. She married my brother.'

He laughs. 'The Mertens family really stick up for one another, don't you?'

'Not always,' I say. 'But on a day like today . . .'

I pull out a chair and sit down. We're at a table with Granny Dunphy, as well as an aunt and uncle on Tory's side, one of her cousins and his wife, and an old friend of my parents who we always called Uncle Jerry, even though he isn't related to us at all. Granny D, who's on my left, goes into a long story about her own wedding, but I'm only half listening because I've heard it before. She's generally sharp as a tack, but in the last couple of years she seems to prefer talking about the past than the present. Meanwhile Ed carries on a conversation with Tory's aunt. I'm dying to know what it's about, because he seems to be engrossed. He's very good with people, I remember. He has an easy way of engaging with them and making them feel important. He made me feel important too, until the day we split up.

The reception carries on as all receptions do: a haze of goodwill towards the happy couple from people who don't see each other very often and are using the opportunity to catch up.

Tory's dad, a local councillor, gives his speech after the starter. It's a traditional speech, long on compliments to Tory and how lucky André is to have married her. André's speech comes after the main course, and I feel a burst of pride at how well he looks and how confident he is at speaking. He thanks everyone for coming and Tory for looking past all his flaws and marrying him anyhow. She gives a speech too, after the dessert, which is equally confident and witty. I don't really know her that well, I realise, despite the fact that she's been going out with André for a year and a half. (They got engaged after six months, but they'd moved into the apartment together after three.)

Granny D tells me that I'll make a great speech at my own wedding. She was very impressed by a presentation I did for Cosecha last November that was uploaded onto YouTube – she texted me after seeing it and told me that she was very proud of me. I was proud of myself. The pressure had been on to present our company in its best light and I know I did a good job. It should really have been Shane, our client manager, who gave the presentation, but Conrad had realised that the entire panel of speakers was going to be male and he needed me to step up to the plate, which of course I did. Just like he's asking me to step up to the plate as a director now.

'I know he's an old flame,' Granny D murmurs with a nod towards Ed. 'The divil you know, is it?'

'Granny!' I give her a pointed look. 'Ed's just here as a friend.'

'Lolz.'

I laugh. 'Seriously. There's nothing going on between us.'

'I'm not so sure about that,' says Granny D. 'I sense bit of the aul' chemistry there.'

'Honestly not, Granny,' I assure her. 'We're grown-ups with different lives now.'

'It doesn't bother me one way or another,' she says. 'All I want is for you to be happy.'

Just like Mum. At least she didn't say settled.

'And don't . . .' She hesitates before continuing. 'Don't do something because you feel you should.'

'What something is that?' I ask.

'Relationship-wise,' she says.

'I'm not doing anything relationship-wise.'

'Exactly. Don't do nothing for the wrong reason and don't do something for the wrong reason either.'

She's losing me.

'I had to get married, you know,' she says.

'What?' I look at her in astonishment.

'Oh, not that sort of having to get married,' she says. 'I wasn't pregnant. But I was the youngest daughter and there was nothing for me. I didn't have the same choices you do.'

'What d'you mean, there was nothing for you?' I ask.

'Well,' she says, 'the farm went to the eldest. That was Seamus. He moved in with his wife Peig before my parents passed away. Peadar became a priest. Eithne got married. I was left.'

'So why did you have to get married? Wasn't there anything else you could do?'

'It was the early fifties, pet, and we were living in the midlands. Dublin was like another country. It didn't occur to me that I could leave home and go there, and even if I had, I would've been a single girl on her own in the city. But I couldn't stay on the farm with Seamus and Peig. I had to do something. So I married your grandfather.'

Mum still has a black-and-white photo of their wedding hanging on the wall at home. Granny is wearing a mid-length dress with buttons down the front, and a small hat. Grandad is wearing a suit. They both look uncomfortable in front of the lens.

'I was only eighteen, and he was a lot older than me,' she says. 'He'd been married before.'

That's something I didn't know, and I look at her in astonishment.

'His wife died in childbirth. His sister raised the baby.'

'Oh, Granny. Why did nobody ever mention that?'

'Why should they?' She shrugs. 'It was a long time ago. Anyhow, your grandad had a decent farm and he was a good enough catch. So I married him and I had your uncle Sean, your mam and your aunt Margaret, and that made him happy because he had someone to leave his farm to.'

We used to visit Granny D and Uncle Sean on the farm when we were younger. My favourite time was when they were cutting the hay and we'd be allowed to clamber on the bales. I remember jumping from them into the field and being chased around it by my cousins. I was never a country girl, but I enjoyed those visits until I reached my teens and jumping from bales of hay lost their allure. Later, Uncle Sean built a small one-bedroomed bungalow for Granny to live in while he and his wife Barbara worked the farm.

'Anyway,' says Granny D into my silence. 'What I'm trying to say is that I ended up doing something I didn't really want to do, more for economic reasons than anything else. You don't have to.'

We're back to Jane Austen again. Women marrying for security rather than love.

'Did you love Grandad?' I ask.

She gives the question a lot more consideration than I expect.

'In the end, yes,' she answers finally. 'At first, marrying him was a transaction. He gave me a home. I gave him an heir. But he was a good man and he treated me well. So I can't complain.'

'But if you'd had money of your own? If you hadn't felt

you had to get married? What would you have done then?'
I ask.

She gives this question even more consideration.

'I think I'd have been one of those ladies who supports
the arts and has a salon in her home where people can get
together and talk about books and music and painting,' she
says finally. 'A few years later, maybe I'd have gone to London
and been part of the whole swinging sixties thing. Mary
Quant and miniskirts didn't make it to Longford,' she adds.
'Don't forget, *The Country Girls* by Edna O'Brien was banned
back then. And there was hardly any sex in it. I reckon the
real reason was because it showed women doing their own
thing, and broken marriages and people living together. We
wanted to pretend that it never happened.'

'You're quite the feminist, aren't you, Granny?' I'm amused
by the sudden vehemence in her voice.

'Your generation thinks you're the first to even notice
inequality,' Granny tells me. 'But we lived through much worse.'

'I suppose so.'

Her words have triggered something in me – a feeling that
I'm too complacent about what I have now, and too worried
about the smaller things.

'All any of us has to be is better than a mediocre man,'
Sheedy said when she set up her own practice. 'And that's
setting the bar pretty low. So I'm hoping I'll be brilliant.'

Granny certainly is. And I'm looking at her in a new light.

There are more speeches – from André's best man and
from Tory's maid of honour – and then we leave the tables so
that the room can be prepared for dancing. The evening is still
warm, so most people head outside again. Tory's girlfriends

Sheila O'Flanagan

begin taking even more selfies on the terrace. Once again I check my phone. Conrad is being really good about leaving me alone. It makes me realise how accustomed I've become to him calling me whenever the mood takes him.

'That was fun, wasn't it?' Ed hands me a Mertens Marvel, the after-dinner cocktail André and Tory created for tonight. (It's actually a martini with passionfruit and raspberry, and it's very moreish.)

'I got involved in a deep conversation with my grandmother,' I say. 'She was reminiscing about her youth. It was very interesting. Instructive, even.'

'Oh, those old girls are a lot tougher than you'd think,' says Ed. 'My grandmother was in the Irish Countrywomen's Association and was part of a group that organised the Turn on the Tap exhibition in the Mansion House.'

'The what?'

'It was an initiative to get a water supply to their houses,' he says. 'Back then, a lot of towns only had parish pumps, and the women had to go and fill containers. The men weren't too keen on the idea of piped water. They were afraid it'd push up the rates on their houses.'

'You're kidding me.'

'No.' He shakes his head. 'It was a real thing. Not just the exhibition, of course, but fighting for water for rural communities.'

I'm gobsmacked.

'Granny's photo was in the paper,' says Ed. 'She was notorious.'

'Flipping heck. And all I worry about is being the token woman.'

'Why would you worry about that?'

90

I remind him about my upcoming promotion.

'I'm betting it's entirely on merit, but either way it doesn't matter. It's fantastic.'

And it is. Women have come a long way since having to fight for piped water. And contraception. And equal pay – even if we haven't quite achieved that yet.

The hotel staff have done an amazing job and the ballroom is ready for the evening's entertainment. The main lights have been dimmed and strands of fairy lights are twinkling through the floral arrangements on the tables. The garden doors have been opened to make space for friends of André and Tory who weren't at the wedding ceremony itself but have now joined us, and the scent of lilies and jasmine floats on the evening air. André, who was in a band in his much younger days, has enlisted the services of some old friends, and they begin to play the first dance. André and Tory have chosen 'All of Me', and there's enthusiastic applause as they take to the floor. The band segues into 'Marry You', and then the riff from 'Dancing Queen' breaks out and almost everyone gets up to dance, including Mum, who's kicked off the L. K. Bennetts and is giving Meryl Streep a run for her money in the *Mamma Mia* dizzy blonde mum stakes.

Ed pulls me onto the dance floor too, and I whirl around with the rest of them. I'm not a good dancer, but I love Abba, who were Mum's favourite band when she was a teen, and I know the words to every song they play. I'm breathless by the time the band slows it down again, this time the soulful 'At Last' by Etta James, which gets both my grandmothers up dancing together. I point them out to Ed, who gives them a thumbs-up and then puts his arm around me and holds me close.

The sentiment in the song is so beautiful that I can't help feeling a little bit emotional as I remember the good times Ed and I had together. And the way I thought that maybe we'd be together forever. And the gap in my heart when he left. I wonder what songs they played at his wedding. I wonder what it was like.

'Carleen and I got married in Dubai,' he says, as though I've spoken out loud. 'A massive bash in the Burj Al Arab. It was a monumental waste of money.'

'I'm sure it was lovely.' I lift my head and look at him.

'Our marriage lasted two years,' he says. 'Do you want to know how much per year that was?'

'No. And stop being so mercenary about it.' I realise I'm being a bit hypocritical here, as I know approximately how much André and Tory's bash is costing and I do actually think it's a massive waste of money when they're always complaining about being broke. All the same, everyone – including me – is having a great time, so maybe it's worth it.

'It was an amazing day,' Ed admits. 'But totally over the top. We were both earning a lot of money, of course, and we got caught up in the whole blinging lifestyle. She loved it even more than me – at least until she wanted to start a family and come home.'

'I'm sorry it didn't work out.'

'Romance fades,' says Ed.

'I know.'

'But old friends last forever.' He gives me a gentle kiss on the forehead.

I rest my head on his shoulder again.

Chapter 8

It's getting too warm inside, so when Ed goes to the bar for another drink, I head out into the gardens again. There's a finger of pale pink light on the horizon where the sun has set but darkness hasn't yet reached, and although it's a little later than my walk last night, the midges don't seem to be out in the same numbers.

Other guests are strolling around, but I make for one of the wrought-iron benches, where I sit down and take out my phone. It's force of habit – if Conrad didn't message me earlier, he's not going to have done it now – but I can't help myself.

When I look at the screen, I see five missed calls. They're all from Justin Delaney. Fuck.

I listen to the message from each one, which is simply 'Delphine, call me right away,' and I'm about to do exactly that when Lindsey sits down beside me.

'I'm sorry, Lin,' I say. 'This is urgent.' I dial Justin's number.

'Do you have to be so rude?' she asks. 'I don't think there's a single time when—'

I hold up my hand to silence her.

'Justin,' I say when he answers. 'What's up? I've only just seen your messages.'

'Where the hell are you?' he demands. 'I've been calling you for the last hour.'

I've been dancing with my plus-one for the last hour.

'I'm sorry,' I tell him. 'I'm at a wedding and—'

'It's Conrad,' he interrupts me. 'You need to get here right now.'

'What? Why? What's happened?'

'Conrad's dead,' says Justin.

I hear his words but I don't take in what he's saying, and my 'What?' in response is both shocked and feeble.

'Conrad is dead,' repeats Justin. 'And we need you here.'

'But . . . but how? How can he be . . .?' I can't bring myself to say the word. I can't bring myself to believe it.

'An accident,' Justin says. 'We have to contact the clients immediately. I need you to unlock Conrad's database and I need you to make some calls. We've got to be ahead of this and tell them before they hear it from someone else. I'll be speaking to most of them, but there are a few I want you to talk to. And they're the ones we need to call first.'

'What sort of accident?' I'm still in shock.

'That's not important. What matters is you get here right now. Bloody Conrad and his OTT security settings – I can't get into the full database by myself.'

He's right. Conrad set it up so that he was the only one who could access our top clients, most of whom keep their holdings in a number of trusts. Justin can't match the right holdings with the right client without more information. Everything he needs is on Conrad's office computer. I could talk him through it, but it's better if I'm there.

I'm thinking about this practically when it hits me. Conrad is dead. I'll never see him again. I feel as though I've been punched in the gut.

'What sort of accident?' I repeat.

'We'll talk later. You need to be here now.' Justin sounds impatient.

'I told you, I'm at a wedding. It's outside Dublin. I can't get there quickly.'

'I don't care what it takes, I want you here as soon as possible.'

'Give me an hour.' I'm shaving time off, but I need to sound on top of things.

'Sooner would be better,' says Justin, and ends the call.

I turn to speak to Lindsey, but she must have walked off when I started talking to Justin. I didn't notice her go.

I hurry back into the castle and towards the reception desk. I can't drive back to Dublin after champagne and cocktails, no matter how sobering Justin's news has been, so I'll have to order a taxi. And I don't know how long that's going to take out here in the back of beyond.

'It'll take ten minutes to get here,' says the receptionist when I explain that I need one urgently. 'If you'd like to wait in the bar, I'll let you know when it arrives.'

But I don't want to wait in the bar. I don't want to get involved with anyone or anything. All I want is to get to Dublin as fast as I can. And it's a good start when the taxi arrives ahead of schedule. I'm following the driver to the car when I hear my name and see Ed hurrying towards me.

'Where are you going?' he demands. 'I've been looking for you.'

'I'm sorry. I have to get back. I'll call you.' I keep walking.
'Delphie! Hang on! What's the matter?'
I don't turn around.
I don't answer him.
I get into the car and tell the driver to go.

The taxi driver, after a few initial attempts to chat, stays mercifully silent. I open my phone's browser and type in Conrad's name. But the only articles I see are about him as a businessman; some detailing successes, others asking questions about potential sweet deals he's done. There are a few puff pieces too about his lovely home on Lansdowne Road and his 'summer retreat' in Cork. I think of Martha, who is probably in the Lansdowne Road house now. And of Bianca at Palmyra, dealing with whatever has to be done. But I can't believe Conrad is dead. He has too much personality to be dead. He's vibrant and alive and brimming with ideas for the future. It's impossible to think that he has no future at all.

Ed has rung me three times, but I haven't answered. I can't talk about this yet. There's a call from Mum too, and then text messages from Ed, Mum, Vivi and Lindsey. I respond to them with *Office emergency*, which elicits a *WTF* from Vivi and a horrified all-caps message from Mum about leaving my brother's wedding for some office problem, as well as a string of furious emojis from Lindsey. I then text Ed and say that there's a crisis with Conrad and I'm needed urgently but I'll be back as soon as I can. I can't bring myself to say he's dead. Maybe because I truly don't believe it. I want to turn off my personal phone, but I don't in case someone sends me an important, relevant message. Not that anyone would. But I'm a just-in-case kind of person.

It takes an hour and twenty minutes to reach the Cosecha offices. I get out of the taxi and am about to swipe my way into the building when I realise that I don't have my entry tag with me. I call Justin and tell him I'm outside, and he says, 'About bloody time,' and that he'll be down to let me in.

'Where the hell were you?' he demands when he opens the glass door.

'I told you. At my brother's wedding. In Offaly.'

Justin should have known where I was. Everyone in the office knew about the wedding. I follow him into the lift, realising that my low-cut cocktail dress and diamanté high heels are completely out of place. Despite it being a Saturday, Justin is dressed in a business suit. His tie is black.

'Finally,' says Grigor Shapolov, our media adviser, when I walk in. 'Can you access Conrad's files right away? And we've a list of his US clients you have to call.'

'What do you want me to say?' I step into Conrad's office. It's exactly as he left it. And as I left it yesterday.

'Here.' Grigor thrusts a piece of paper at me. In it the firm expresses its sadness at the loss of its founder, its commitment to continuing with his principles of outstanding performance combined with exceptional customer care, and its desire to honour his memory by being the number one choice for investment professionals.

'Right.' I look around at everyone else who's crammed into Conrad's office. Justin and Kieran and Didier and Shane. Behind their shocked expressions is something else, and I realise it's anticipation. Because things have changed, and when things change, there are opportunities. I feel sick that men who Conrad would've considered as friends are thinking like this. And yet I know they are. Because finance is a dog-eat-dog world. And they're ready for it.

I access the files and begin printing out information on clients and portfolios. The guys grab the pages and look intently at what's in front of them.

'We need to make sure we don't lose anyone,' says Justin. 'We need to lock them down and make sure there isn't even a hint of them thinking they should move their funds. Delphine, when you've finished talking to everyone on your list I want you to pass them directly to me.'

I'm about to ask him why, but I already know the answer. These clients know me, but they'll want to be reassured by him.

'Let's get cracking,' says Justin as he sits behind Conrad's desk. 'No time to waste.'

We start to work the phones, talking to our American clients, leaving voicemail messages for the European clients, who don't answer calls this late on a Saturday night, and the Far East clients, most of whom aren't up yet. Everyone I speak to is shocked, but hardly anyone asks very much about the accident itself, which is just as well, because I don't know anything more than what Justin told me while I was still at the wedding.

By the time we've finished messaging or talking to everyone, it's past two a.m. I lean back in my chair and rub my eyes.

'Good work, everyone,' says Justin. 'It's vital that we have control of the narrative here.'

'What exactly is the narrative?' I don't know if my voice is trembling because I'm upset or because I'm tired. 'What happened to Conrad?'

'It's out there now,' Grigor tells us. 'News reports. I'm sending our press release.'

'What happened?' I repeat.

'Conrad drove his motorbike off a cliff,' says Justin.

'Deliberately?' I look at him in complete horror.

'Of course not,' he says impatiently. 'I only have sketchy information, but it looks like he took a turn too quickly, skidded and kept going.'

'But there are barriers on all the roads near his house!' I exclaim. 'He shouldn't have—'

'None of that is relevant,' says Justin. 'All that counts is the result. And the result is that he ended up on the rocks at the bottom of the cliff.'

'Was he killed instantly?'

'I don't bloody well know.' Justin is exasperated with me. 'I told you, the information is sketchy.'

'Who were you talking to about it?'

'The grieving girlfriend,' he says. 'Interesting situation Conrad has left behind. A girlfriend in Mallorca and a wife in Ireland.'

I hadn't thought about that particular dynamic. Martha and Conrad are still married. What does that mean for her and the children? And what does it mean for Bianca?

'You've all been great,' says Justin as he looks around the office. 'Now you need to get a bit of sleep. I'll want Grigor and Shane with his team in here tomorrow. We need to be ready with a strategy for any liquidation orders we might get. Everyone else, take time out and be here at six a.m. on Monday. I'll email the rest of the staff so that they're all here then too.'

'Do you need me tomorrow?' I ask.

'No,' he replies. 'But stay on call. Right now, I want you to unlock Conrad's files and give me any other passwords I might need. Then you can get back to your pole dancing or whatever.'

'Excuse me?'

He winks. 'That outfit. More men's club than office, don't you think?'

'I was at a wedding!'

Justin's comment isn't one he'd have made when Conrad was around. Not after the incident a few years ago. But now, in changed circumstances, he feels OK about it. A sudden shiver of foreboding runs along my spine.

'You look great, Delphie,' says Didier.

'How I look isn't the issue here, is it? Conrad is dead!' I raise my voice at the end, and once again I hear it tremble.

'Hey, we're all upset. No need to go overboard,' says Shane.

But my colleagues aren't upset.

They're eyeing up their opportunities, and they all know it.

At first I think it'll be easier to go back to Malahide rather than the wedding venue, but then I remember I've left the car at the castle and that I'd have to return there anyhow. So I order another taxi and wait for it in the glass foyer of our building. When I see it pull up, I walk outside and get in. The driver checks that I really want him to drive to Offaly at this hour of the morning, and I tell him I do, and we agree the fare in advance.

Then I sit back and scroll through my personal phone again. I haven't had any more messages, but despite the hour, I text Ed and tell him I'm on the way back. Given that he didn't reply to my previous text, he's probably in bed by now and pissed off with me for abandoning him. Not that Ed's feelings are high on my priority list at the moment. I'm thinking of Conrad and how he didn't know that today was the last day of his life. Of him getting onto his bike and roaring down the twisting road near Palmyra, full of confidence in himself and his machine. Conrad was a person who accepted all life's challenges, who believed he'd overcome them. Had he thought everything would be OK even as he sailed through the air? Had he even had time to think?

I feel sick.

How can everything change in a second?

How can life be so cruel?

I should send a message of condolence to Martha. Or Bianca. Or both of them. But right now, I don't know what to say, and even if I could find the words, I wouldn't do it in a text or an email.

It's such a mess.

The drive to the castle seems much shorter than the drive to the office, and we arrive back more quickly than I expected. It seems wrong to be returning to a place where, earlier, everyone was in such good spirits. And where they'll be in good spirits tomorrow when André and Tory continue the celebrations with their barbecue. And nobody will care that my boss is dead.

I really don't want to be here. But even though it's a few hours since alcohol passed my lips, I've definitely drunk too much to drive tonight. I have to stay until the morning at least. Then I'll be able to explain to my brother and his new wife why I ran out of their wedding. I hope they'll understand.

It's quiet when I walk into the huge reception hall of the castle, but in the distance I hear the clink of glass and

101

the sounds of laughter. It seems that the wedding party is still going strong, despite the lateness of the hour.

Going strong might be an overstatement, but there's a small group of wedding guests in the residents' lounge. I recognise them as friends of André and Tory, though the bride and groom themselves aren't there. Jason, Vivi's partner, is among them, and so is Ed, who spots me the moment I walk into the room.

'Delphie!' he exclaims. 'Where the hell have you been?'

'I told you.' I'm suddenly bone tired and I practically collapse into one of the winged armchairs. 'It was an office emergency.'

'What sort of office emergency would need you to rush to Dublin in the middle of the night?' he demands.

You'd be surprised, actually. Because our clients are global, there have been other occasions when Cosecha staff have been called in to work through the night. And, of course, Conrad doesn't – didn't – care what time of day it was if he needed something. He called me, and I answered. Always.

But this is different. And it's become too much for me. I bury my head in my hands.

'Hey. Hey.' Ed hunkers down beside me. 'What's the matter? What happened?'

I take a deep breath and tell him, not quite believing it even now.

'Oh my God,' he says. 'The poor man. And poor you. You need a drink.'

'I'm not in the humour for champagne, Ed.'

'I know you'd probably prefer Bacardi and Coke, but the bar staff left us a bottle of Jemmy. I'll pour you a glass. It'll do you good.'

I don't drink Bacardi any more. Nor have I become the

formidable woman who drinks whiskey. But I feel the need for something. Ed goes to the bar, where the bottle has been left, and returns with a generous measure of Jameson.

'Shouldn't there be ice in it at least?' I ask.

'Unfortunately we can't get at the ice, and what was in the ice buckets for the champagne has melted. You'll have to drink it neat. But it'll do you good.'

I'm not sure there's any circumstance in which a medical professional would tell you that knocking back a measure of whiskey will do you good, but I drink it in a single gulp anyway. Ed is looking at me in surprise.

'I thought you were only going to have a sip,' he says.

'It was medicinal,' I say. 'So better to down it in one.'

'You're a hardy woman, Delphie Mertens,' says Ed. 'I can't do that myself.'

I exhale slowly and sit up straight as I feel the heat of the alcohol warm my body. 'I'm really sorry I ran out on you without explaining,' I say. 'I hope you didn't feel too much like a spare part.'

'When I got your text, I knew it was urgent,' he says, 'though I never expected it would be anything like this. Anyhow, I was well occupied with the dancing and drinking and the usual wedding palaver, so you don't have to worry about me. Your family might be a little less . . . understanding,' he finishes. 'Your mum was particularly annoyed.'

'She'll forgive me when she hears what happened.'

'Tory will too,' says Ed.

'Did she notice I was gone?' I'm surprised.

'Someone told her. She asked me. I said you'd headed off for a while but you'd be back soon. I don't think it mattered after that. Don't worry about Tory.'

'You're a good friend, Ed Miller.'

'I know.' He grins at me.

'I'd better go to bed.' I try to stand up, but flop back in the chair. 'I swear that wasn't because of the whiskey,' I tell him. 'I'm exhausted, that's all.'

'Let me help.' He takes me by the arm and makes sure I'm standing steadily on my high heels. Then he escorts me from the lounge and towards the lift.

'What room are you in?' I ask.

'One-two-one.'

'I'm in two-one-two.' Even as I say the words, I'm wondering if he thinks I'm suggesting he should come to my room. The whiskey, along with the fugue of grief, has addled my mind.

'I'll see you to yours,' he says.

I'm still wondering if he's got the wrong end of the stick, but when we reach the room, he waits for me to open the door and then tells me that he'll see me in the morning.

'I'm glad you were here,' I say.

'Me too.' He puts his arms around me and I lean against him. 'Sleep well,' he adds before letting me go.

And then, for a moment, I'm tempted to ask him into my room. Being honest, it's not that I'm looking for wedding sex, or emotionally shaken sex, or even friends-with-benefits sex. I just don't want to be alone right now. And Ed would be a good person to have by my side. But he's already walking down the corridor and he doesn't look back. I'm not going to run after him.

I close the door and stretch out on my bed.

I don't sleep a wink.

Chapter 9

At least, I don't sleep a wink until sometime after six, when the sun has already risen and the magpies are chattering loudly from the trees. For some reason the light and the sounds relax me more than the darkness, and next thing I know, it's nearly ten o'clock and it's the noise of the door to the next room closing that's woken me.

For a brief moment I've forgotten about Conrad and I think that my headache and lethargy are down to my excesses of yesterday, but then I remember and I'm caught by grief again. He was a good man. A thoughtful boss. A decent person. And now he's gone. It's impossible to accept. I need more proof.

I check the news on my phone, and find it's a trending story.

Irish financier plunges to death in holiday tragedy! screams one headline. I flick through more variations on the same theme; some of the stories include a picture of the area where the accident is supposed to have happened. I recognise the coastline. As always, it's utterly peaceful and beautiful, the blue of the sky and sea meeting on a horizon framed by the green of the tree-lined bay. Nobody would believe anything bad could happen there.

I feel sick again.

I check my work phone too, but there are no messages from Justin or any of the other people who were in the office last night. Even though I wasn't asked to be there today, I begin thinking of some of the ways we should evolve our future strategy, despite finding it hard to imagine the company without Conrad. And then I realise that actually I should be there with them, sharing my views. I hesitate with my finger over Justin's number. I should call him and clarify the situation. I should tell him that I'll join them in the office later. Yet I'm reluctant to make that call, as though my own personal issues are greater than those of our company. Or greater than the loss of Conrad. It would be a bit . . . unseemly.

Besides, I need to show my face at the wedding celebrations again.

I put the phone to one side and head for the bathroom.

My head will be clearer after a shower.

I'm still overwhelmed by thoughts of Conrad as I make my way downstairs, dressed in jeans and a T-shirt and wearing an old pair of Skechers. I'm sure I'm too late for breakfast, but there are a few people in the dining area, so I sit down in a corner of the room away from everyone else and order coffee and pastries.

'Delphie!' Lindsey comes over to me. 'What the hell were you up to last night? André was really upset when he heard you'd left, and poor Ed was devastated.'

'My boss died.' I interrupt her before she says something that will annoy me. 'He was killed in an accident. I had to go back to town.'

'I saw the news story. And I'm sorry, I'm sure it was a

terrible shock, but you didn't have to go running off like that. At the very least you should've taken Ed with you.'

'Why? He didn't know Conrad, and he couldn't have come into the office with me,' I say.

'It wasn't fair to leave him here with all of us,' says Lindsey.

'He told me he was fine. I believe him.'

'You're impossible.' She gets up. 'You've no idea how things work. You really don't.'

She might be right.

But I know what I have to do today.

I finish my third cup of coffee, then leave the breakfast room, much to the relief of the staff, because I'm the last person there and probably in their way. Normally I'd be aware I might be holding them up, but this morning I can't find it in myself to worry about it. Instead, I'm thinking about my directorship, caught between concern over what Conrad might or might not have done, and feeling guilty for even caring when he's dead and his family is grieving. I'm thinking a lot about his family too, and wondering how things will pan out between Martha and her children and Bianca. I'll send them both a card expressing my condolences as soon as I get home, saying they should contact me if they need anything.

I leave my phone in my bag as I walk through the big rooms of the castle and out to the terrace at the back. Mum and Dad are there, having coffee at one of the bistro tables. I suppose that for anyone who gets up before eight, as they always do, it's time for a mid-morning beverage.

'Delphie!' she exclaims. 'You're back.'

'Of course I'm back. I wasn't gone for very long.'

'I'm sorry about your boss,' says Mum. 'When I heard the

news, I guessed that's why you left, but I really don't know why you were needed in the middle of the night. What happened exactly?'

I go through it all again.

'That poor man,' she says. 'How horrible.'

I nod in agreement.

'And you were only there in Mallorca with him recently.'

'Yes.'

'It's all very upsetting, but why did they ask you to come to the office in the middle of the night?' she asks.

'To help organise the narrative,' I tell her. 'To unlock certain files. To offer support.'

'What the hell does "organise the narrative" mean?' Dad gives me an impatient look over the black rims of his glasses.

'Oh, you know. The PR and everything. How to frame the accident. How the company reacts. How to deal with our clients. All that sort of thing.'

'It was definitely an accident?' Mum, who watches at least two hours of Alibi on TV every night, is used to looking at the dark side. 'He was a rich man, after all. He didn't have any enemies, did he? Anyone that would benefit from his death?'

'Get a grip, Mum,' I say. 'Apparently he was driving along the road and lost control of his motorbike and went over the cliff.'

Both my parents are silent as they, like me, see it in their heads.

'I'm glad you weren't out there when it happened,' says Mum.

On one level, so am I. On the other, if I'd been there, I could have helped. I am – or at least was – closer to Conrad

108

than anyone. If you leave out the sex, closer than Bianca, I'm sure. And in the last year, closer than Martha too.

'Have you seen Ed?' asks Dad.

I shake my head.

'He was worried about you yesterday evening.'

'Oh, I saw him last night. Not this morning, though.'

'What time did you get back?'

'Two.' I shave more than an hour off my return, because two sounds reasonable whereas any time after three sounds late. 'There were quite a few people around. We had a drink.' Which makes it sound even more like I got back in time to be part of the party. As though my absence was very temporary. And as though my drink was social rather than something that Ed had decided I needed for the shock.

There's a sudden round of applause and the three of us look towards the French doors, where André and Tory have just appeared. He's wearing an ancient T-shirt and denim shorts. She's looking as elegant and beautiful as ever in a light summer dress, a huge pair of sunglasses covering her eyes.

She sees me and walks over to the table.

'You left,' she says. 'André says it was because of your boss. We saw it on Twitter this morning.'

I can't see her expression behind the enormous sunglasses, so I'm not sure how she feels about my absence. I don't go into the whole framing-the-narrative thing, but I say that I was needed to access information for the people concerned. I add that it was very traumatic, but that now that I'm back, I'm looking forward to the barbecue. Although I'm not looking forward to the barbecue at all.

'I'm sorry about Mr Morgan. I'm sure you're very upset,' says Tory.

'Of course I am, but I don't want to be a wet blanket,' I tell her.

'You won't be,' Tory assures me. 'We've lots of organised activities, like archery, clay pigeon shooting and boating on the lake, so there's plenty to take your mind off it. The barbecue will be ready at around one thirty. You're too late for the golf,' she adds. 'They teed off before breakfast.'

I took up golf a couple of years ago so that I could go on the company golf outings, but it's safe to say that I'll never be any good at it. Nevertheless, it's true that business chatter happens on the golf course and it's better to be there than not. I can hit the ball very hard, although unfortunately not always in the right direction.

But there's nothing that can possibly take my mind off what's happened. I tell Tory that I'll probably laze around as it's such a lovely day. André, who's stayed quiet, gives my shoulder a squeeze and tells me to take care. Feeling like I've done my duty by talking to the bride and groom, I say something about going to freshen up and find somewhere to loll with my book.

I don't really want to loll with a book at all. I want to go back to Dublin and be close in case anything happens. But I've committed myself to staying for the barbecue, so I will.

I go back to my room and text Ed. He doesn't reply until I'm on my way downstairs again.

Went out with the golfers earlier. See you at the barbecue.

He's doing all right, I think. He always did. He's a lot more sociable than I'll ever be.

I walk outside again and find a secluded spot near the lake. I put in my earbuds. When I said I was going to loll with

110

a book, I meant with my audiobook, which is the way I read these days. But I'm not interested or engaged with the psychological thriller I downloaded earlier in the week. The only thing I can think about is Conrad, and that he must have known as he sailed through the air that he was going to die. And I feel faint at the very idea of it.

I do, however, ultimately fall asleep, and it's the aroma of charring beef that wakes me. The narrator of the audiobook is still reading, and I'm shocked to realise that the lead character has turned out to be some kind of murderous psychopath. I've missed out on an entire chunk of the action and I'm not going to listen to it now because the twist has been revealed. I take out the earbuds and make my way back to the castle, where people are beginning to mill around two big barbecue grills. The chefs are turning the meat while the guests help themselves to rolls and salads.

I thought I wouldn't be able to eat, but I'm suddenly hungry, no matter how disrespectful that makes me feel.

I get in line behind some people I don't know, and when I make it to the top, I select a piece of grilled tuna and a glazed chicken thigh. I'm looking for space at a table when Ed appears at my side. He's carrying a plate with a double burger in a toasted bun.

'Where did you spring from?' I ask. 'And how was the golf?'

'I'm crap at golf,' he replies. 'But good at finding seating. Follow me.' He leads me around the side of the castle, where there's a tile-topped concrete table with three semicircular benches around it. 'Not the most comfortable,' he adds. 'But not bad either.'

There's a large jug of mint water on the table and he pours me a glass.

'So,' he says. 'How are you doing?'

'OK-ish.'

I take out my phone and check the updates on the story. There really isn't anything new, but there are photos of Martha and the children (much younger than they are now), as well as Bianca, along with those of Conrad. The ones of Bianca are very recent – one is definitely from her thirtieth birthday party, because she's wearing the green dress and Lady Annabel's bracelet. I think of Conrad's desire for her to have the bracelet and the joy of getting it for him, and I feel the grief well up inside me.

'I'm sorry you've had a bad weekend,' says Ed. 'I'm sure you were expecting a lovely time.'

'I'm the one who should be sorry for having dragged you along and then abandoned you. You've been amazing, Ed. Thank you so much.'

'I was fine,' he says. 'You don't have to worry about me.'

I didn't, when I went haring back to Dublin in the middle of the night. But I feel bad that I abandoned him without a word. When I say this, he reaches for my hand, gives it a sympathetic squeeze and tells me that he knew it must have been important.

'Besides,' he adds, 'I was living it up in a luxury castle, so there's nothing for you to feel bad about.'

'Life's become a bit . . . well, it gets harder, not easier, doesn't it?' I leave my hand in the comfort of his. 'You have to deal with stuff. Adult stuff. And sometimes you wish a proper grown-up would step in and look after it instead.'

Ed nods. 'My divorce is what made me grow up,' he says.

'You'd think it would've been becoming a dad, but that didn't make much difference to me. It made me feel more responsible, for sure, but being responsible actually meant feeling that I had to work harder, make more money. The divorce, though, that was a different kind of responsibility. It was for myself, but for them too. And . . .' he gives me a wry look, 'responsibility for how I felt. About Carleen and Joe. About what they meant to me and I meant to them.'

'Wow,' I say. 'That's very emotionally mature.'

'Yes, you wouldn't have known me in this phase.' He grins as he lets go of my hand and pours himself another glass of water. 'You went out with Ed Mark I. Now I'm Ed Mark II, the responsible adult.'

'It's hard work being a responsible adult,' I say.

'You've always been responsible,' he tells me. 'You're focused and assured and you don't let yourself get distracted. You're not the cute romantic heroine who falls over her own feet and is funny and charming. You're strong and forceful and don't have any self-doubts. It's refreshing.'

On the one hand, I'm flattered. On the other, he's made me sound like a bit of a hatchet job. I tell him that I have as many self-doubts as the next person but that I don't spend hours trying to analyse them, and he laughs.

Once we finish eating, I say that I should get going because Justin asked me to be on call in case I was needed.

'OK,' he says. 'Let's say our goodbyes.'

He takes me by the hand again and we walk back to the terrace, where the barbecue is in full swing. I find Tory, who's sitting at a table, a single chicken thigh on a bed of green salad in front of her.

'I have to go,' I say. 'It's been a wonderful wedding.'

'I hope you had a good time despite everything?' She pushes her sunglasses onto her head and looks at me.

'It was fabulous,' I tell her. 'And I'm sorry again that I had to cut it short last night.'

'Don't worry about it.' There's genuine sympathy in her voice. 'André told me how well you got on with your boss. All those trips you took together. It must be very difficult for you.'

I don't think she's being suggestive about my trips with Conrad, but I can't be sure.

'Anyhow,' I conclude, 'I really have to leave now.'

'Of course.' She gets up and flings her arms around me. 'I'm so happy to be your third sister-in-law. And hopefully your favourite.'

I smile as I disentangle myself from her embrace and say that she's certainly right up there, and tell her that I hope she and André have a brilliant time in Fiji and that they'll be really happy together.

'We will,' she says, and hugs me again.

I've a few other hugs to navigate on my way out – my two grandmothers, who are chatting animatedly together and who say nothing about my disappearance last night (they probably didn't even notice), and Mum and Nichola, who are keeping an eye on Phoebe and Noemi while Elodie has gone for a nap with her dad. This means even bigger hugs for my two nieces, who ask if I'm not being allowed to stay another night like them (I murmur something about having to go to work, and they give me sympathetic looks). Then I say goodbye to André himself, who I meet as I'm striding through reception. He also sympathises about Conrad and doesn't say anything about my leaving the reception. I assure him that despite everything, I've enjoyed the wedding immensely. The barbecue was a great idea, I add.

'Being married is wonderful,' he tells me. 'You should try it, sis.'

'Maybe one day.'

'Don't leave it too late,' he says.

I smile and say nothing as I walk to the castle car park, accompanied by Ed.

'Is there anyone you've ever come close to marrying?' he asks when we reach my car.

'No.'

'Did you ever think that we—'

'You went to Dubai and I forgot about you,' I say before he can finish his sentence.

'Your honesty is devastating.'

I give him what I hope is my most withering look, and he laughs.

'Listen, if you want to meet up again sometime, that'd be nice,' he says. 'Now that we're aware of each other's existence again.'

Ed was the perfect plus-one for the weekend. Nobody could have been more understanding about my abandonment of him. Or kinder when I returned. And my family seem to have forgiven him for dumping me. I've forgiven him too. I say that I'd love to meet up when I have a bit more time.

'I'll call you,' he says.

'Do.' I unlock the door. 'Thanks for everything.'

'You're very welcome.'

Neither of us moves. Then he leans in towards me and wraps his arms around me, pulling me tightly to him.

I could stay in the warmth of his embrace for longer, but

I really have to get going, so I break free and kiss him. It was meant to be a quick peck on the lips, but it turns into something longer when he kisses me back, and isn't quite the platonic goodbye I had in mind.

'Drive safely,' he says, when I free myself for the second time.

I get into the car and reverse out of the space. He waves at me and I wave in return.

My lips are still tingling as I drive out through the castle gates.

Chapter 10

The moment I step into my house, both Ed and the wedding are nothing more than distant memories. I open my iPad and check Cosecha's website, where the home page has been replaced by a black-edged photo of Conrad. That, more than anything up to now, underlines the reality of it for me. And the finality. Last night should have done it, with the calling of clients and discussion of strategies, but it's seeing the recent photograph of him – taken after his image makeover with Bianca – that hits me right in the solar plexus.

Conrad's gone.

He's never coming back.

I phone Justin and am diverted to voicemail. I leave a message asking if there's any further news.

He doesn't return my call.

I arrive at the Cosecha building at exactly six o'clock the next morning. Justin is already at his desk. I tap at the glass door of his office and, before he has time to say anything, step inside.

'How did it go yesterday?' I ask.

He shrugs. 'I was mostly with our legal advisers to make

sure we're on the right path going forward. Additionally . . .' he gives me a considered look, 'I was talking to Bianca. The government is providing consular assistance. Hopefully his body will be repatriated before the weekend.'

'It's all so awful,' I say. 'I can't get my head around it. But Conrad would have wanted us to follow his ambition for the company.'

'Will you go through his diary appointments this morning?' asks Justin. 'Tell everyone that I'll meet them in his place. We'll work out later if I actually can.'

I'd rather be talking about our future strategy. I could contribute to the conversations with our legal people too. But even as I open my mouth to speak, his phone rings and he waves me away and answers it.

I leave him and go to my own office, which is attached to Conrad's. Anyone who wants – wanted – to see him had to get past me first. That was always the power I had within Cosecha. The power of access to the boss. I'm diminished without it.

I sit behind my desk and open my laptop. Conrad's accident is no longer the top story in the online media, but it's still headline news. Not surprisingly, there are speculative pieces about how it might have happened, more biography, and – from the tabloids – stories about his split with Martha and his relationship with Bianca.

The Beautiful Blonde in the Life of one of Ireland's Wealthiest Men screams one headline, along with a (very sultry) photograph of Bianca that I haven't seen before. There's talk about how they became close when she was advising him on his new image, and the piece also credits her with his recent higher profile on the Irish social scene.

I stare at the photo for a moment, then call the florist and order flowers and a card for both her and Martha on behalf of the company. I also order flowers and a card from me personally, adding that either woman should contact me if there's anything I can do to help.

Unsurprisingly, neither of them responds.

Later in the morning, Justin calls the staff together in the reception area and says a few words about Conrad's accident and death.

'I know he would want us to carry on in his tradition of fearless ambition,' he concludes. 'More than anything, Conrad wanted Cosecha to be the most successful financial services company in the country. We owe it to him to redouble our efforts to ensure that's the case.'

There's a muted round of applause followed by an awkward silence. Then, although I'm not sure it's really appropriate, I move forward and stand beside Justin. I look at the faces in front of me and clear my throat.

'I worked as Conrad's executive assistant for many years,' I say. 'He was one of the most supportive men I ever knew. Yes, he wanted every person here to achieve their full potential. He encouraged me in so many ways, as I know he encouraged all of you too. I'll miss him as the founder of Cosecha and I'll miss him as my boss, but more than that, I'll miss him as a person who made mistakes but who never believed that they defined him. Who was always ready to admit when he'd messed up. Who looked forwards, not backwards. Justin is right when he says Conrad would want us to redouble our efforts for Cosecha. But in doing that, let's not forget that he was also someone who wanted us to

119

encourage each other and bring out the best in each other. I think he'd like that to be his legacy.'

'Hear, hear!' It's Lisa Hannigan who leads the applause after my impromptu speech, then Justin tells everyone to get back to their desks and keep the show on the road.

'Very touching, Delphine,' he murmurs as he walks past me into Conrad's office and closes the door behind him.

I sit at my own desk and begin rescheduling Conrad's meetings. On checking my emails, I see that a flurry of new applications have come in ahead of the deadline for this year's community grants scheme. But I don't have the opportunity to study them, as people drift in and out all morning, still in shock, telling me that they appreciated my words and asking me if I've any more information than what's in the media. The admin staff are more upset than the investment managers and directors, maybe because they're not framing their futures based on Conrad's death. I missed my opportunity to frame my own future earlier when I didn't manage to speak to Justin, but there's nothing I can do now, because the door remains closed and nobody's getting in.

The atmosphere in the office is depressing, and I'm glad when Erin messages me and asks if I'm free for lunch. She'll understand how I'm feeling. We agree to meet for pasta at 12.30.

She's at the table ahead of me, trim and chic in a navy suit with a zipped jacket, her signature satchel-style shoulder bag hanging from the chair. Erin is my friend, but she's also my greatest role model, because she's calm and practical and thinks things through before acting.

'Delphie!' She gets up and hugs me. 'This is awful. How're you doing?'

I give her a résumé of events and she fixes me with her clear blue eyes. 'You need to consolidate your position,' she says as she flicks her copper curls out of her eyes in her getting-down-to-business gesture. 'You want to make sure that you're OK. Thank goodness Conrad made you a director.'

'He promised to,' I say, and I can hear the doubt in my voice. 'I don't think he'd spoken to the others about it yet.'

'Have you?'

I shake my head.

'D'you have it in writing?'

I shake my head again.

'Get in there and tell them straight away,' she says.

'I was going to mention it to Justin, but he's very busy and . . .'

'And what?'

'It seems . . . disrespectful to be talking about something like this when a man has died.'

'Cop on, Delphie,' says Erin. 'It's your career. You think Justin or any of the others would give a fig about appearing disrespectful?'

'I know. But . . . Conrad was a good person, and I . . . Well, it's hard.'

She gives my hand a squeeze and says that she understands, but that it's important for me to stay strong, especially with Justin.

'I'll deal with everything,' I assure her. 'I'll be fine anyhow. I know more about that company and the people in it than anyone else.'

'You don't want to be fine,' says Erin, who's a partner in her law firm. 'You want to be unassailable.'

I nod and agree that I'll confront Justin when I get back.

121

Then she asks me about the wedding. The question disorients me for a moment, because it seems like a lifetime ago, but I give her the low-down.

'And Ed?' she asks. 'How did you get on with Ed?'

'He was great. Very understanding about everything. I'm glad he was there.'

She raises an eyebrow. 'Did you guys rekindle something?'

'He'll be a handy new plus-one.' I smile. 'He said he'd call.'

'Ooh,' she says. And then her tone changes completely and she tells me that Fintan wants her to move in with him. 'What d'you think?' she asks.

'It's what *you* think that's more important.' I'm happy to talk about her issues instead of mine for a while.

'I don't know what I think. That's why I'm asking you.'

Fintan is a sound engineer. Erin met him at an industry conference a couple of years ago. He was managing the acoustics.

'I love that he knows nothing about the law,' she told me after they'd spent the night together. 'I love that he couldn't care less about any of the cases I'm working on. Not that I'd tell him,' she added, 'but it's refreshing that he doesn't give a toss.'

I like Fintan, who I've met a handful of times. He's a bit rock-and-roll with his black T-shirts and black jeans, even though he mostly does the sound for voice-over recordings and works at corporate events rather than concerts. But he's a laid-back person and he treats Erin well, despite the fact that they break up more often than a Taylor Swift relationship.

I say this to her.

'All very true,' she says. 'But the break-ups are never serious and the making-up is great. Would it be a disaster if I did move in with him?'

'Is that all it is?' I ask. 'Moving in? Does he want to . . . to marry you?' It sounds weird even asking the question. Erin and I talk about work. And boyfriends. But rarely marriage. It's not usually on our radars.

'Been there, done that, worn the T-shirt,' she says. 'And so has he.'

'So what are you thinking?'

'Part of me would like to go on as I am forever. And yet . . .' She sighs. 'I'm forty years old, Delphie. Perhaps I should be re-evaluating relationships. Rethinking how I want to live my life.'

'What would moving in with him give you that you don't already have?' I ask.

She considers this for a moment. 'Someone who's there for me,' she answers eventually. 'When I come home late at night and I'm tired and fed up and hungry, it would be nice to think there was someone waiting for me with a glass of wine and some food.'

'I know Fintan is handy with a corkscrew, but is he good in the kitchen too?'

'I've no feckin' idea.' She laughs. 'He's never cooked anything for me. I've never cooked for him either. It's always either eating out or ordering in.'

'Well, that's something you need to check out before you make any major life decisions,' I tell her.

'It's a nice thought, you know,' she says. 'The idea that someone has your back. That someone will look out for you and look after you. That's what I expected when I married Lar. Not what I got, obviously.'

'Maybe Fintan's thinking the same,' I observe. 'Maybe he's imagining you waiting for him with a bottle of wine in your hand and a roast chicken in the oven.'

'He'd be so lucky.' She laughs.

'You've got to look at it from every angle. But,' I add, 'what's actually important is whether you love him enough to want to share your space with him. What would the living arrangements be like? Your place or his?'

'It'd have to be mine,' she replies. 'His apartment is too small.'

Fintan, like Erin, is divorced. He has a ten-year-old daughter who stays with him every second weekend and part of the school holidays. Erin's cleverly designed town house in Milltown, an upmarket suburb on the south side of the city, would definitely suit them better than an apartment.

'Dervla,' she reminds me when I can't remember his daughter's name. 'Apple of his eye. That's a good thing, isn't it?'

'Do you get on with her?' I ask.

'Most of the time,' replies Erin. 'I suppose there'll be adjustments to make when – if – Fintan and I move in together. Young girls are very possessive about their dads, aren't they? I told Trish,' she adds. 'She was squealing with excitement.'

Erin's sister is a couple of years younger than her. She's married and has embraced motherhood with a kind of demented fervour that has seen her post all sorts of earth-mother-type photos to her Instagram account and build up a fairly decent following of other mothers who go for that wholesome children-running-through-fields-with-daisies-in-their-hair thing. She's told Erin more than once that she's leaving it late for a second shot at marriage and a family. Every time she does, Erin rings me to vent about it.

'If this is right for you then go for it,' I say.

'If,' says Erin, and stabs at her pasta.

Buoyed up by lunch with Erin (after we'd dealt with her love life, the conversation returned to work matters and she urged me again to be strong and forceful), I'm determined to talk to Justin about the director's position as soon as I get back. But when I return to the office, he's not there and nobody is entirely sure where he's gone.

I walk to Kieran Dunlop's office on the other side of the building. There's no sign of him, nor of Didier or Mark. Where are they all? My heart starts to beat more rapidly. Are they together? Deciding things? Things that will matter to me?

The majority of Cosecha's shares are divided between Conrad and the current directors, Kieran, Didier, Mark and Justin. These four will drive the company forward, but I'm the one who knew best how Conrad's thought process was evolving. He'd scheduled a board meeting for the coming week where he'd planned to propose me as the newest director, but I don't know if he spoke to them about it. I should be with them. I should know what's going on.

I ask Emmy McBride, one of the admin staff, if she's seen any of them, and she shakes her head and says not in the last while.

'Did they go out together?' I ask.

'I think Didier and Mark left at the same time,' she says. 'But I can't be sure. Sorry, Delphie.' And then her face crumples. 'Isn't it awful about Conrad?' She reaches into her bag and grabs a tissue. 'I can't believe it. He was such a good person. He gave me time off when my mum was ill. He . . .' She dissolves into a fit of sobbing, and I'm so caught up in comforting her that I forget about office politics and concentrate on morale instead.

Justin arrives back at around 3.30. I'm watching to see if anyone is with him, but there's no sign of the other directors, so maybe I'm simply being paranoid. I get up and go to his office.

'I need to talk to you about something,' I say.

'A client?' he asks.

'No. It's—'

He holds up his hand. 'Right now I'm only giving my attention to clients,' he says. 'It's important that we retain their funds. Despite our best efforts we've lost the Barrington family trust and Halliwell's.'

Both are big income generators for Cosecha. Both used to deal directly with Conrad.

'Why would they pull their money?' I ask. 'It's not as though our investment management team has changed.'

'People are irrational,' Justin says. 'It doesn't matter that Conrad himself wasn't making all the investment decisions for them. That's what our investment managers are for.'

'That's exactly what I said to Marcus on Saturday night. I told him the company would carry on with Conrad's ethos and vision.'

'Well you obviously weren't persuasive enough,' says Justin.

'Will I call him again?'

'No.' His tone is firm. 'I'm going to get Didier to talk to him. They're both members of Portmarnock.'

Portmarnock is a prestigious golf club on the north side of Dublin. I'm not surprised Marcus Barrington is a member, and it makes sense to have Didier talk to him man to man. Annoying though that is.

'If that's all, Delphie . . .' Justin taps the keypad in front of him.

'Not exactly,' I say, but he interrupts me again to remind me that unless it's client-related, he doesn't have time, and so although I really want to talk about my directorship, I tell him it'll wait and go back to my office.

A few minutes later, I see Didier and Justin get into the lift together.

Shit.

What happened to me being strong and forceful? I should've insisted on talking to Justin first.

Chapter 11

I don't get the opportunity to talk to Justin the next day either, because he leaves for New York early in the morning. An email saying he'd be away until the weekend arrived in my inbox at ten p.m., and I read it with some surprise, because I'd have thought he'd have mentioned the trip when he was talking to me earlier. Or at least asked me to organise his travel, as I'd done for Conrad.

I drum my fingers on my desk. If I was dealing with anyone other than Justin, I wouldn't be quite so concerned. But he doesn't like me. He thinks I'm too much of a feminist. Too woke. Too . . . well, too much of everything he doesn't like in a woman. We've clashed a number of times, but most memorably at a staff event a few years ago, when he complained that the whole Me Too thing had gone too far and that it was impossible for men to know how to behave in an office any more.

Normally I don't take the bait, but there were lots of younger women listening to him and I could see the mixed emotions on their faces. It seemed to me that someone had to make the point that all men had to do was behave like civilised human beings in an office and there'd never be a problem. So I did. He countered that women liked compliments and attention no matter what, and I said that in the office we wanted compliments and attention for our work and not anything else. It all got a bit heated, culminating in him practically shouting at me that he was entitled to a certain amount of respect from junior staff members like myself. I retorted that respect had to be earned.

'Oh, get off your PC hobbyhorse,' he snorted. 'You're not unassailable here, Delphine Mertens. Don't think you are.'

'Neither are you.' I spoke as calmly as possible, which seemed to infuriate him even more.

'Tread carefully,' he warned, while the rest of the group watched us with varying expressions of anxiety, approval and apprehension. 'Don't think I can't see right through you.'

At that point, Conrad, who'd clearly been distracted by how loud the conversation was getting, came over to find out what was going on. Justin made a jokey comment about being lectured on white male privilege and how oppressed men needed respect too, and Conrad, looking at both of us, announced that Cosecha was, and always would be, a company of equal opportunity and respect for everyone. He then reminded Justin that as he was in a position of power, it was important that he always showed respect to every member of staff, and he added that the directors shouldn't be above reproach. Turning to me, he said that he trusted I would always respect those who deserved it. There was a round of applause from the female staff after that, but Justin's face was like thunder.

He's never forgotten and never forgiven me. Any available opportunity he has to make life difficult for me, he does. He likes coming into my office when Conrad is away and asking me to dig out unnecessary information or statistics simply to waste my time. He stands closer to me than is strictly necessary in an effort to intimidate me. It might intimidate some women – in fact, I know it does – but it's hard to intimidate someone who's looking down at you. Because I always stand up when Justin arrives, and I always slip on my heels before I do.

So his childish antics have never bothered me. Until now.

I take a bottle of water from the fridge and bring it into the garden with me. The boys next door are playing football, and I wonder how many times I'll have to throw the ball back before I go inside again. But even halfway through the water, it hasn't come over the wall. It's nice to see that their skills are improving.

My phone buzzes. I look at the message and see it's from Ed.

Hi Delphie. How are things going? Hope you're doing OK. I know it must still be tough. Do you fancy meeting up for a drink at the weekend?

I'm flattered that he's got in touch so soon, but Justin left a note on my desk asking me to stay available in case I'm needed to help out with Conrad's clients, for whom the weekend is an irrelevance. So I text back saying I'm not currently in control of my timetable but I'd love to meet him as soon as I am. He replies saying that whenever suits me is fine with him and to let me know. It's good to have something non-work-related to look forward to. And good that it's with Ed.

He's definitely more than your average plus-one.

*

I don't meet Ed, because it's all-hands-on-deck in the office and I end up being incredibly busy. Justin is on a whirlwind tour of client meetings and I'm dealing with his absence as well as company policy around Conrad's funeral, which eventually takes place the following week.

Obviously all the Cosecha staff are there (we've closed our offices for the day), as well as representatives from the business world, a number of politicians, friends, and – awkwardly – Bianca and her family as well as Martha, Killian and Connie. Martha and the children are sitting in the front row, while Bianca is directly behind them. The tension is palpable, but the humanist service is calm and dignified, and as we finally file out to the sound of Pavarotti singing 'Nessun dorma', I think that Conrad would have been pleased at how smoothly everything went, as well as moved by the kind words everyone had to say.

'Delphie!' Martha taps me on the shoulder. 'You'll be coming back to the house?'

'I . . . Yes, if that's OK.' She phoned the previous week to thank me for the card and flowers, and said that she planned to have drinks and canapés at the family home after the funeral. She asked me to help with the arrangements, and I organised the catering for her as I'd always organised it when she was having an event in her home. I wonder if Bianca has planned a rival reception back at the house she and Conrad shared. If so, she hasn't said anything to me about it. Unlike Martha, she didn't get in touch.

'I'm so sorry for your loss,' I add.

'Thank you.' Martha sounds tired as she squeezes my arm. 'It's been difficult.'

'You're doing great,' I say.

'I'm not so sure about that.'

'You are. And Killian was amazing.'

Conrad's son gave a short eulogy at the service. It's over a year since I've seen him, and he's grown and matured since then. He was eloquent today.

'Wasn't he?' She smiles slightly. 'His dad would've been proud.' Her attention is caught by someone coming towards us. 'I'm sorry, Delphie, I have to talk to some people. I'll see you later.'

She moves away and I begin to walk down the pathway from the cemetery to the main road, where I plan to get a taxi.

'Delphie!' This time it's Bianca who calls my name.

I turn around.

She's wearing a black dress with a light wool charcoal coat over it. Her blonde hair is pinned up and her make-up is expertly barely there.

'I'm sorry for your loss.' It's odd to say the same words to Bianca as I said to Martha earlier. 'How are you?'

'How d'you think?' She glances in the other woman's direction. 'I'm devastated and she's trying to take over with having everyone back to the house. Which should've been my house. But I won't let her muscle in. She can schmooze around all she likes this afternoon, but then it's over.'

'She knows everyone here,' I say as gently as I can. 'She feels obligated.'

'Obligated my arse,' says Bianca. 'She wants to make it seem as though she's the grieving widow. But she's not.'

Technically she is. But I don't say that. Instead I say that the entire experience must have been awful.

'Horrific,' she agrees. 'I never thought in my whole life I'd have to go through something like that.'

'What happened exactly?' I've imagined so many scenarios in my head, but I want to know the reality.

'Nobody's a hundred per cent sure.' Bianca's voice trembles. 'He was on his way to see his friend Johannes, who lives in that huge granite house set into the cliff. You probably know the road to it – it's really twisty and narrow. They think a small animal might have run out in front of him and that he swerved, lost control and went over the side.'

'Oh, Bianca.'

'It was the worst day of my life,' she says.

I don't have the words to respond.

'Are you going to Martha's?' she asks.

'Um . . . she invited me, yes.'

'Fine.' Bianca no longer sounds distressed. Her tone is firmer, more controlled. 'I'm in the dark about Conrad's estate. If you hear anything, please let me know.'

'I don't know if—'

'We're friends,' says Bianca. 'You were in our home shortly before the accident. We had a lovely lunch together at the beach. Conrad has been good to you. I want you to be good to me.'

'I—'

'She thinks she's entitled to it all.' Bianca's tone hardens. 'I've got to look after myself. If you hear anything worthwhile, I want you to tell me.'

'Well, I'm not sure that anyone will tell me anything, but . . .'

'I'm counting on you,' says Bianca, and she gets into the black car that has been waiting for her.

Lansdowne Road is an upmarket part of Dublin, better known to non-Irish people for the international rugby stadium at one end of it. Years ago, the majority of the stately Victorian red-bricks were used as offices, but they're gradually being bought up and restored as private homes again. In one of those weird coincidences that sometimes happen, the law firm where I started out once had its offices in the house that Conrad eventually bought. They'd moved into their current modern building before I joined, but there's still a picture of the ivy-clad three-storey-over-basement property in Haughton's reception area.

I've been to the house many times before, although not in recent months. The restoration was beautifully done, very much in keeping with the original features of the house. There's a real family feel about it, though Conrad also kitted out the basement as an office space, complete with a den and games room – he had a bar, full-sized snooker table and home cinema down there along with a variety of monitors keeping him up to date on the various financial markets.

When things blew up between Martha and Conrad over his relationship with Bianca, she, not surprisingly, told him to get out of the house. He refused, saying that he needed to use the office space, which led to a bit of a stand-off because Martha insisted that she wasn't leaving – it was the family home and that was where the children should stay. Then Conrad suggested the children could live with him and Bianca (something Bianca probably would've freaked out over if it had actually happened. I'm pretty sure that living with teenagers isn't part of her current life plan!). Naturally Martha was having none of that either. In the end, they agreed that she and the children could live in the house until the divorce had been hammered out, but Conrad would continue to use the basement level as a home office whenever he liked. Obviously him not actually living there made this a little inconvenient, but the Anglesea Road mews he shared with Bianca is only five minutes away by car. Neither Conrad nor Martha was particularly happy with the arrangement, especially when she saw him going into the basement with Bianca one evening. She phoned him from the kitchen and told him never to bring that woman to her home again.

I know all this because I had to contact Conrad's solicitor about it. In fact, over the last year, dealing with issues arising from Conrad's relationships with his wife and his partner has been the most demanding and stressful part of my job. But now Martha is in command of the house and she's welcoming people as though today is merely another of the many functions that she has helped host, while Bianca is nowhere in sight. Never underestimate the power of a legal arrangement. My years in the law firm taught me that, if nothing else.

I'm standing in a corner on my own, a little surprised that none of the Cosecha directors are here, and wondering if they're having yet another meeting – or even if they're at Bianca's instead – when Martha walks over to me with a glass of wine.

'Thanks for coming,' she says as she hands it to me. 'And for all your help with this. It was important to me to have people back here. It's what he would've wanted.'

'You know I'm available to help however I can,' I say.

Her smile doesn't reach her eyes, but when she tells me that she's always been able to depend on me, her words are heartfelt.

'I can't take it in that he's gone, to be honest,' I say.

'Me neither.' She breathes out slowly. 'He was such a . . . a live-wire of a man.'

'A good man,' I say.

'Not always.' Her face is expressionless.

'I didn't mean . . .'

'He made a fool of himself over that girl. A fool of me and the children too.'

I stay silent.

'Still, at least he didn't get around to making an even bigger mistake and divorcing me.'

It seems bizarre that after everything, Martha and Conrad were still married when he died.

'He wasn't going to divorce me at all,' adds Martha.

And yet there's a locked folder buried deep in his files and colour-coded in red that contains all the divorce information.

'He would've changed his mind sooner or later,' she continues. 'Partly because of how much it was going to cost him, and partly because there's no way on God's earth he could've put up with that girl for very long.'

Martha met Bianca early on in the image consultancy phase, then followed her on Instagram. She told me later that, based on Bianca's relentlessly upbeat posts and stories, she thought the younger woman was a bit of an airhead. I reminded her that Bianca ran a successful company so she wasn't stupid, but I couldn't help feeling that Martha was more comfortable with the idea of Conrad leaving her for a fortune-hunter than someone who had a business of her own. After all, although Martha herself supported Conrad in every possible way, it's a long time since she had a paying job.

She may be right about Conrad and Bianca. But we'll never know.

'Anyhow,' she says, in a steadier voice, 'I wanted to ask if you were aware of any plans he might have made that included her. I haven't heard of anything, but have you? Is there any legal stuff you know about?'

'Gosh, Martha, I've no idea. It's all been between Henry and Oscar.'

Henry is – was – Conrad's personal lawyer. Oscar is Martha's.

'Is she a director of any of his companies?'

Conrad and Martha were joint directors of a number of shell companies he set up for future use. As far as I know he didn't set up any new ones with Bianca as a director, although she's an authorised signatory to one or two of his more recent ventures. When I say this to Martha, she shrugs.

'There's so much to consider,' she says. 'The firm, the properties, the investments . . . it's overwhelming.'

'I can imagine.'

'My priority will always be Killian and Connie,' she continues. 'This last year has been hard on them and I don't want them to think that their dad might have . . . oh, I don't know, behaved in a way that makes them feel ignored.'

'I very much doubt he did that, Martha. He adored them.'

'I know. But men do very stupid things sometimes. He already did something stupid by moving in with that woman. So you'll let me know if you hear anything, won't you? If there's any sort of arrangement I wouldn't know about? Oscar's great, but he might not see things as quickly as you.'

Bianca wants me to let her know if I hear anything. So does Martha. It's uncomfortable being caught between them.

'How are things going for you?' Martha asks when all I do is nod.

'Oh, fine.'

'Conrad thought very highly of you, you know.'

I feel a lump in my throat and I can't respond.

'He said you had brains to burn. He wanted you to take on more responsibility at the firm.'

'I know.' My voice comes out as a croak. 'He spoke to me about it.'

'I'd be glad if you did too,' says Martha. 'You understood his vision, Delphie, and you can make sure they carry it on. I'll do my best too, of course, in whatever way I can.'

She's talking as though they never even split up. As though his relationship with Bianca never existed. And as though the last time I saw them together she wasn't screaming at him that he was like every other pathetic man going through a mid-life crisis by banging a blonde.

'I'd better go,' I say as I put my barely tasted wine on the table.

'It was lovely to see you.' She pulls me into a hug. 'Maybe we could have a coffee together soon?'

I tell her I'd be delighted to, and check that she has my mobile number.

'Of course,' she says. 'I never delete contacts.'

Me neither. That's why I had Ed Miller's number in my phone after nearly ten years.

I look back as I leave and see a room full of men in dark suits. The only women there are Martha, Connie and the people serving the food and drinks.

I walk down the steps, hail a cab and go home.

Chapter 12

I'm barely in the door when I get a message from Mum telling me that she's seen me on TV. It takes a moment for me to remember that the news media were at the crematorium and that people were filmed arriving at the service. I didn't think I'd be in the shots, but when I look back at it on catch-up (because who can resist seeing themselves on screen), I'm easily identifiable as I walk along the gravel pathway to the chapel in my black Louboutins, my dark hair ruffled by the breeze. The camera pans across the crowd, and I see Bianca standing beside Tiernan O'Dowd, Cosecha's IT guru. I wonder if Tiernan even knows who she is. Then, out of nowhere, Grigor swoops in and diverts his attention in what looks like a choreographed move. Bianca is left on her own and I'm suddenly in shot again, along with one of the politicians.

I text Mum back and tell her I've seen the TV, and she rings me immediately to ask what the funeral was like.

'Not exactly a cheerful day out,' I reply.

'No, but it was very high-profile,' she says. 'All those famous people.'

'Conrad was fairly famous himself.'

139

'I didn't realise he was quite so rich.'

They did a run-down on him during the coverage, talking about how he'd built up the business from nothing, competed globally and brought valuable business to Dublin. It was all illustrated by stills of him meeting with various well-known personalities. There was talk too of the intricate restoration work he'd done on the Lansdowne Road house, along with aerial shots of his Cork home. The report concluded with the information that he left behind his wife of over twenty years and his two children. There was no mention of Bianca.

'He used to say that there was always someone richer than you.'

'Feck's sake,' says Mum. 'It's far from that sort of thinking the man was reared. It says he was from Cork himself originally. I'm surprised they didn't bury him there.'

'He came to Dublin as a child,' I tell her.

'I didn't see any mother and father,' she says.

'No. They were both killed in the tsunami of 2004,' I tell her.

'Oh, the poor man!' Her voice, which was mildly critical, softens. 'What an awful thing.'

'After that, he poured everything into the business,' I say.

'And now he's gone too. So sad.'

'Yes, it is.'

'How are you?' asks Mum. 'I'm sure it's been difficult.'

She never thinks that any of my normal days at work might be difficult, or that heading to New York, Singapore or even Mallorca at the drop of a hat isn't always fun. But she totally understands how difficult the emotional stuff can be.

'It has been,' I admit.

'I wish you had someone to look after you,' she says.

'Oh, I can look after myself. I'm good at office politics.'

'Not in the office, you eejit. Now. At home. When you're sad. It's not a good time to be alone. Did you ever think about internet dating?'

It takes me a moment to fully process her words. I reply by saying that I've spent the day at a funeral, so it's hardly the appropriate time to talk about internet dating.

'How about Ed, then?' She's completely unperturbed by my reaction. 'OK, so it didn't work out the first time, but he was lovely at André's wedding.'

'I've no plans to get back with Ed,' I tell her, although I'm definitely going to see him again. But I don't want to say this to Mum. Not yet.

'I'm not suggesting you rush into something with the wrong man. But you need to give yourself an opportunity to find the right one.'

'I know. Don't worry about me. I'm fine.'

'But today's been tough,' she says. 'Would you like me to come out to you?'

I'm more touched than I would've imagined by the fact that she's offered, but I tell her that I'm exhausted and I'll probably chill for a while before heading off to bed.

'Do,' she says. 'Look after yourself. Take it easy. Come for dinner on Sunday.'

'That'd be nice. Really it would.'

'I'll see you then, so. Take care in the meantime.'

'I will.'

Leaving the phone on the kitchen counter, I go to the fridge, contemplate having a glass of lemon water, then open a bottle of rosé instead. I pour myself a generous glass and take it outside, where I sit on the wooden bench that catches the evening sun. Next door the boys are playing football again, using the dividing wall as a goal. It's hard to believe that life is going on as usual for them while I'm feeling so dislodged by the events of the last couple of weeks. But a wayward ball over the wall confirms that it is.

As I throw it back, my phone buzzes with a text from Ed.

How did it go today? he asks. *I saw you on TV. Is it wrong to say you looked amazing?*

Everyone must have been watching the news. But I smile at the text all the same.

Yes, it's wrong to say that, I reply. *It was an emotional day. Home now.*

I'm in Howth myself, so not that far from you. Just finishing up a work thing. Would you like some company or would you prefer to be alone?

I told Mum not to bother coming to see me. Do I want someone else around me instead? Do I want it to be Ed? I hesitate for a while before finally sending him a yes.

I'll be there in half an hour.

I change from my black clothes into a white T-shirt and jeans and refresh my make-up, adding a little blusher and my favourite nude lipstick. Then I fold the patio doors open so that the sunlight sweeps from the garden into the house. I retrieve my wine glass from the garden and refill it. I'm a third of the way through it when the doorbell sounds.

Ed follows me into the house and asks how I'm doing.

'A bit ragged, to be honest,' I reply.

'It's been a tough time for you. If I can help at all . . .'

He's saying the same things to me as I've said to Martha and Bianca, and for the first time, I feel the impact of Conrad's death in a deeply personal way. He was my boss, but he was also my friend. And I really, really miss him. I look out over the garden as I try not to cry.

'You OK, Delphie?' asks Ed. He puts his hand on my shoulder and I turn to him but don't speak. He holds me close, and once again I'm comforted by his arms around me.

I give myself a moment, then move away and take the bottle of rosé from the fridge.

'No wine for me, thanks, I'm driving,' he says. 'Water or non-A beer would be fine.'

He studies my half-finished jigsaw while I add more wine to my glass. As I hand him a beer, he picks up a piece and slots it into place. It's near the bottom edge, a part I haven't been concentrating on. He adds another piece, and then another. Before he tries to finish it for me, I suggest we go into the garden, where we sit on the bench.

I feel suddenly awkward in his company, but then the ball flies over the wall again and nearly knocks the beer from his hand. Clearly the boys haven't improved as much as I thought.

'Liam, Cathal – I have a visitor in the garden. Can you keep the kicks low!' I cry as I throw it back.

'Sorry, Delphie!' yells Cathal. 'We'll play a different game.'

'Thank you!'

'I never thought of you as someone who gets down with the kids,' remarks Ed.

'When we were small, our next-door neighbour used to go nuts every time we lobbed a ball into her garden,' I say as I sit beside him. 'It was never deliberate, but she made us feel as though it was. Years later, I was talking to her and she said how much it annoyed her at the time. But that now, when she was so much older, she missed having young people around. So I try to embrace it.'

He laughs. 'Seriously?'

'Seriously. And if today tells me anything, it's that life is fleeting and we should embrace as much as possible.'

'That's very true.'

We sit in silence while the sound of Cathal and Liam's laughter floats on the air. I'm transported back to the times when my brothers played football or all of us played rounders and the balls soared into Mrs McGinty's garden. She seemed ancient to us back then, although she was only in her fifties. But she was in her late seventies when she talked about missing younger people and I understood what she meant. I might not want children myself, but there's definitely something about their zest for life that's inspirational. We may be driven to want to achieve more as adults, but children find a joy in simply being alive that somehow fades the older we get.

I'm being maudlin. I'm not usually maudlin.

'Have André and Tory been in touch from their idyllic Pacific island?' asks Ed.

'They posted pictures on their social media. It looks amazing.'

'I've never been to Fiji,' says Ed.

'Me neither.'

'What's the most exotic location you've visited?'

'Probably Singapore, although it ended up being more about the shopping than culture for me,' I reply. 'I was supposed to go to Malaysia when the pandemic hit, so that got knocked on the head.'

'A lot of things have been knocked on the head then and since,' says Ed. 'You must have been lonely by yourself.'

I give him a non-committal smile. I feel guilty for knowing the multiple lockdowns were a lot worse for other people than for me. At the start, I was in the office helping to organise remote working for the staff, which was extremely stressful, but once it was sorted, I soon got used to working from home myself, and not having to commute was a blessing. Because he was away so often, a lot of my management of Conrad had always been done remotely, so it made no real difference where I was. And although I'd never have admitted it out loud, not having the pressure to turn up to a Sunday lunch at Mum's every week was a bit of a relief. Of course I worried about her and dad, and both my grandmothers, but we phoned and FaceTimed regularly and they all seemed to have coped remarkably well. From my point of view, although the restrictions were frustrating, the deli was still open for takeaway food, and I got together with Erin and Sheedy on Zoom most weekends, so despite some hard and exhausting days, my situation was reasonably good.

I don't say any of this to Ed.

'I'm sorry, I'm not exactly great company today,' I tell him after we've sat in silence again for a few minutes. 'You're not having much luck with me. I invite you to a wedding and run out on you, and now you've very kindly come to cheer me up but my head's not in the right place for it.'

'That's OK,' he says. 'I wouldn't expect it to be. I only came to . . . well, offer a bit of support if you needed it.' He drapes his arm across the back of the bench so that it's resting gently against my shoulders. I lean towards him and feel myself relax.

Meeting him on the plane was a stroke of luck. I couldn't have invited anyone better to the wedding, and having him at my side now is reassuring. He knows me and I know him. We have a shared past. A shared understanding of each other. Even if he left me, he also loved me, at least for a while. And today, with the realisation that we never know what's around the corner brought so sharply into focus, I want someone to love me again.

I'm hyper conscious of him as he makes casual conversation about his life in Dubai and the difficulty of his return to Dublin, but I'm also drifting off into memories of Conrad and of today's funeral. And my thoughts turn to Martha and Bianca too, both wanting me to keep tabs on the other person as though I was their personal spy.

'Delphie?' Ed gives me an enquiring look and I realise he asked me a question but I haven't a clue what. I sit up straight again.

'Are you OK? You've gone into a world of your own.'

I tell him that I've been thinking about the meaning of life. He nods and says it's not surprising. 'I did a lot of that after my divorce,' he adds. 'Well, strictly speaking, before the divorce. When I realised that I'd made a mistake marrying Carleen.'

'Were you in love with her?'

'You're in a kind of bubble when you're living the expat life,' he replies. 'Emotions are heightened. Lots of our friends were getting married, throwing massive parties. She wanted that and . . .' he sighs, 'I wanted it too. It was a statement about what we'd achieved together. I kind of forgot there was more to it than showing off.'

'I'm sorry it didn't work out,' I say. And I am.

'Going to Dubai was good for my career,' he says. 'So that part worked out. But I didn't treat you very well when I left. I should've talked it over with you. I'm sorry about that.'

You broke my heart, I say. But not out loud.

146

'It was a decision you had to make for yourself. And I was fine,' I assure him. 'Anyhow, you wouldn't have changed your mind, and the only other option was me going with you. Which, in all honesty, was unlikely.' And that's why my heart didn't stay broken very long. I had my own dreams and plans.

'That's what I thought at the time. You'd made the move to Cosecha and I told myself . . .' He shrugs. 'The most important thing in my life at that point was my career. With everything that's happened over the past few years, I realise that relationships matter more.'

'We were good together back then,' I say. 'And I was hurt at the way you left me. But I moved on and so did you, so no regrets. Anyhow,' I add brightly, 'you have your lovely son, so it's not all bad.'

'He's been the making of me,' he says as he takes out his phone and shows me a video of Joe kicking a football around the garden. 'It took me some time, but I finally stepped up to the plate as a good dad.'

He scrolls through photos of Joe, and others of Dubai, the Burj Khalifa, the Burj Al Arab and an aerial shot of the Palm Jumeirah. There are photos of the beaches too, and he stops at one of a group of women wearing brightly coloured kaftans and wide-brimmed straw hats as they pose in the waters of the Persian Gulf.

'He's the image of his mum.' He points to the curly-haired woman in the centre of the photo. 'That's Carleen with her Jumeirah Jane pals.'

I raise an enquiring eyebrow.

'The rich expat women whose life's work is to spend their hubbies' tax-free dollars,' he explains.

'Are there Jumeirah Johns?' I ask.

'Not that I know of.' He grins. 'You'd never have been a Jane, would you?'

'Neither was Carleen. You said she was an events organiser.'

'And a home bird, in the end.' He notices the time on his phone. 'It's getting late and I haven't eaten properly today. Would you like to go for a bite?'

'Thanks, but I can't face food at the moment.'

'Or perhaps a drink?'

I glance at my almost empty glass.

'Quite honestly, I've probably had enough.'

'OK then,' says Ed as he gets up from the bench. 'Time to go.'

I apologise again for not being better company, and he tells me not to be silly.

This time when he puts his arms around me, he holds me more tightly and I'm expecting him to kiss me. But instead he releases me again and the kiss, when it comes, is the merest graze of his lips against mine. I'm both relieved and disappointed that it isn't anything more.

I stand at the door until his car has disappeared around the corner. I'm glad he came, though it's a pity he was driving, because otherwise he could have shared the rest of the wine with me. As it is, I've drunk most of the bottle myself. I can hold my drink, but I haven't eaten much today and I'm feeling woozy. I'm about to go back inside and lie on the sofa for a while when Lyra Casey steps out into her front garden.

'Delphie,' she says. 'I saw the funeral on the news. How are you?'

People keep asking me how I am, but it's not about me. It's about Bianca and Martha and Killian and Connie. Everyone else is irrelevant. Nevertheless, I tell her I'm fine and agree that it was a terrible tragedy for everyone concerned, and then she asks about Conrad's wife and I don't know if she means Martha or Bianca, but she adds, 'The mother of his children,' and I tell her that Martha was very dignified.

'Poor woman,' she says. 'And poor you too, Delphie. I know you were very close to your boss.'

I nod.

'You look exhausted,' says Lyra. 'And I bet you haven't eaten. I've got a lasagne in the oven. Why don't you come in and share it with me?'

I wasn't hungry, but suddenly lasagne sounds delicious.

'I couldn't,' I say.

'Of course you can,' says Lyra.

And so I do.

Chapter 13

My eyes are gummed together and my mouth is as dry as a sack when I wake up the next morning. I groan and roll over to look at my clock. It takes me a few seconds to focus, and then I see that it's ten past eight. I shoot upright in the bed and my brain seems to ricochet off the inside of my skull.

I shouldn't have shared another bottle of wine with Lyra. And red, too, which is far more likely to give me a hangover than white or rosé. But she opened it to go with the lasagne and I couldn't say no. I was sitting in her house talking to her (God, what did I say? I can't even remember) until after midnight. And now I'm going to be late for work for the first time in my life.

I take a quick shower before getting dressed in my dark purple suit with its fitted jacket and mid-length skirt. I wear my Skechers to get to the train station, carrying my high heels in a tote bag. I change into them in the reception area of our building before taking the lift to the third floor.

The atmosphere is less subdued today. There's more noise, more conversation, more chatter. I don't say anything as I walk to my desk. I leave my bag on top of it and then stop where I am. Because there's someone in Conrad's office and for a nanosecond I think it's him. But it's not. And it's not that I could even have mistaken Justin Delaney for Conrad Morgan; it was simply the shape of someone there that made my heart skip a beat.

'Justin.' I step into the office.

'Ah, Delphine, you're here.'

'I'm sorry I'm late,' I say.

'I assumed you were working from home.'

'I need to talk to you,' I tell him, even as I rage at myself for being hung-over when I'm about to have one of the most important conversations of my life.

He glances at his watch. 'An hour.'

'OK.'

I'm relieved to know we're finally going to have a discussion. I get some water from the cooler and swallow a couple of paracetamol, then sit at my desk and open my laptop. There are still hundreds of emails in my inbox. The most recent is from the organisers of an investment conference in Stockholm that Conrad was due to speak at next week. I was to have gone with him. The organisers offer their sympathies and say that they've arranged an alternative speaker. Of course they have. Life goes on.

As I forward the last of the emails to the relevant investment manager, Justin emerges from his office.

'Let's go,' he says.

I pick up my mobile and follow him to the wood-panelled boardroom. It's one of the only spaces that can't be viewed from the office floor. Conrad was big into openness and transparency, but he said that privacy was important too.

Justin closes the door behind us.

The windows of the boardroom overlook the Liffey, which is sludge green beneath today's grey skies. Justin waves me to a seat with my back to the windows and sits facing me.

'So, Delphine,' he says.

'Did Conrad tell you about the director's position?' I get straight to the point.

'Excuse me?'

I've caught him off guard, which is a good thing.

'The director's position,' I repeat. 'He was going to recommend appointing me to the board.'

Justin stares at me for a moment, then starts to laugh.

'Good one,' he says. 'You had me there for a moment.'

'I don't know why you're laughing. It's a fact.'

'Really?'

'Yes.'

'And when did he tell you this?'

'When I was at Palmyra. He was going to get all the paperwork together and call a meeting when he got back.'

'He never said a word to me about it,' says Justin.

'Maybe not,' I concede. 'But he told me.'

'In writing?'

I shake my head. 'But he'd made the decision. We talked about it in Mallorca and again in New York.'

'I'm sorry, Delphine, but he had plenty of time to tell me, and he didn't. To believe anything so ridiculous I'd need to see it written down.'

'Why is it ridiculous?' I demand.

'Oh come on, Delphie. What qualifications do you have for being a director?'

'Leaving aside my law degree,' I say, 'you know perfectly well that I've advised Conrad on multiple projects, and I've

152

been managing the corporate responsibility programme for years. I'm entirely qualified.'

'I don't think so,' says Justin.

'And yet Conrad did.'

'Oh, well. We all know what Conrad was thinking as far as you're concerned.'

'Excuse me?'

'Let's not go there.' Justin is dismissive of his words and their implication, but I feel a wave of anger surge through me. I don't get time to say anything else, though, because he opens the slim folder he's brought into the boardroom with him and then looks up at me.

'We've done a review,' he says.

'Who's we?' I ask.

'The current directors.'

'A review of what?'

'Of the company. Of our strategy. Of how we operate in a post-Conrad world.'

'You didn't ask for my input.'

'There will have to be changes,' he continues, as though I haven't spoken. 'Of course there are technical issues to do with his shareholding and other corporate matters that will need to be dealt with over time, but we have to move on.'

'Of course.'

'And we need to do that in a dynamic way.'

I nod again.

'I'll be taking over as CEO,' says Justin, and I can hear the satisfaction in his voice. 'Didier will be my second in command.'

Didier. That's a surprise; I thought it would be Kieran. But Justin's elevation isn't. Not for the first time, I wish

153

Conrad had listened to me about splitting the chairman and CEO roles, which is best practice though not a legal requirement. It didn't matter when he was the one in charge, but Justin needs someone to keep him in check. A strong chairman would do that. Didier most certainly won't.

At that moment the door opens and Kieran walks in. He nods at me but says nothing as he sits beside Justin.

'I was about to inform Delphine of our new structure,' Justin tells him.

Kieran nods again. I feel my heart beat faster.

'We've got to be leaner going forward,' Justin tells me. 'More focused.' There's an edge to his voice that's a little disconcerting. 'And we really don't see your current role fitting in that structure,' he continues, with a quick glance at Kieran. 'I don't need an executive assistant.'

It takes a few moments before his words sink in, and I stare speechlessly at him as he continues.

'It's a role that Conrad liked because having someone dedicated to him made him feel important. But it's not necessary,' he says. 'It's not a good use of our resources. So we need to make a change.'

I'm finding it hard to breathe. But when I eventually manage to suck in enough air to speak, I tell him that I've already reminded him of my responsibilities, which are absolutely necessary to the smooth running of the company. 'Besides which,' I add, 'I organise—'

'I'm a perfectly competent organiser,' Justin interrupts me. 'Why would I need someone to look after my schedule or remind me of things when the watch on my wrist does all that? Why would I need someone to make calls for me when I can use voice commands on my phone? Why would I need

154

someone to plan my travel when I have the internet in front of me?'

'That's only a fraction of what I do,' I protest. 'And you know it. This year's community grants—'

'We spend far too much time on that responsibility stuff,' says Justin. 'The grant scheme is ridiculously time-consuming. In future we'll contribute to a couple of charities and that'll take care of it. As for everything else, Conrad would've been able to deal with it all himself if he hadn't spent his time banging image consultants and swanning off to his pad in Mallorca.' He looks at me. 'You were more of his enabler than anything else, which, given the way you've spoken about gender-related issues in the past, is a bit of a joke, don't you think? Anyway, we've done an assessment of our more critical needs and we think you'd be best placed working in compliance. Kieran agrees.' He glances again at his fellow director, who nods.

I'm horrified that they might be thinking about stepping back from the community grants scheme. Conrad was proud of it and its impact. And as for sending me to compliance – they're having a laugh, they have to be. It's a hotbed of red tape and box-ticking. It would be an absolute nightmare. Unless Justin is offering me head of compliance, which wouldn't be my favourite job but would at least recognise that I'm a senior member of the firm.

'So that's that,' he says. 'You'll be reporting to Frank Maher. Your salary going forward will have to reflect the type of work you'll be doing.'

So it's not head of compliance. It was never going to be. And what does he mean about my salary? What sort of work will I be doing?

'The vacancy is for an administrator,' he continues, 'so there'll have to be a reduction in your pay. Realistically, Delphine, you were massively overpaid for what was basically a secretarial role. One in which you simply ran around after Conrad and his family. You even helped Martha with the funeral arrangements, something that had absolutely nothing to do with Cosecha. Conrad's funeral was a private affair. You knew that but you were still on the phone to Martha every day. But that's you, Delphine. Wanting to put yourself about in places you shouldn't be. Having ideas well above your abilities. At least this way you'll be concentrating on the firm and earning your salary.'

I stare at him wordlessly before managing to say that helping Martha was the right thing to do both personally and because she's the widow of the company's founder. I say that anyone would've done the same, especially as, for all we know, she could be a significant shareholder in the future, and then remind him yet again that I was Conrad's executive assistant, not his secretary, and that I have a wide range of experience that the company can ill afford to lose.

'I was on call twenty-four/seven,' I say. 'My salary reflected that, and the complex nature of my work.' I take a deep breath before I speak again, this time with a sideways look at Kieran. 'If you remember, I pointed out an error in the Dellalio proposal a few weeks ago that could've been very costly for us as a firm. Worth my current salary to prevent that, don't you think?'

The Dellalio proposal is the one where Justin used the wrong benchmark. I see his jaw tighten at the reminder.

'What error?' Kieran speaks for the first time.

'It would have been spotted when the proposition was

being looked over again,' says Justin before I can speak. 'You didn't single-handedly save the firm, Delphine, no matter what you might choose to believe. And regardless of what you think about your situation under Conrad, the truth is that we'd been taking a look at staffing arrangements long before his accident. He knew that.'

'He wanted me to be a director!' I can't keep the frustration out of my voice.

'Even if that were true, it was an emotional rather than a practical thought,' says Kieran. 'The board wouldn't have passed it.'

They would. If Conrad had proposed it, they would.

'But the board has taken this decision.' Justin glances at the paper in front of him and then looks me straight in the eye. 'Conrad's death has simply speeded up the restructuring we were discussing before. There's nothing more to say. You should go to the first floor immediately and settle in.'

I'm not going to break him down. So I say that sending me to compliance is ridiculous and that if he feels the need to move me, I'd be more valuable in operations.

'It isn't up for discussion.'

'I should have been consulted,' I object. 'And there should be a discussion about my role as a director too.'

'We're doing you a favour by redeploying you within the company at all,' says Justin.

'You're demoting me!' I cry.

'No we're not,' says Kieran. 'We've taken a look at our future needs and we're assigning you to a job that's suited to your talent and experience.'

They're stabbing me in the back.

'You can't reduce my salary,' I say.

'We're offering you the best possible alternative given that your job no longer exists,' Kieran tells me. 'It's up to you to decide if you want to accept it.'

'How much?' I ask.

'If you know everything about the company as you say, then you'll know how much the compliance admin staff are paid,' says Justin.

I do. It's about half what I currently earn. I can't afford a fifty per cent pay cut. How will I pay my mortgage on that? If I can't repay my mortgage, I could lose my home. My stomach lurches at the thought and I'm suddenly afraid that I might throw up onto the polished boardroom table.

'Anything else?' Justin's tone is challenging.

It's becoming even harder to breathe, and it takes me a moment to say that he's not really talking about restructuring the company. That what he's actually trying to do is force me out.

'You can't use some kind of fake restructuring to get rid of me,' I say.

'We don't want to get rid of you.' Justin keeps his tone pleasant, but I can detect a triumphant undertone. 'We all agree there's a place for you here because you're an experienced employee. But that place is not in an unnecessary job at a ridiculously high salary.'

'You needed me the night Conrad died,' I remind him. 'You needed me to unlock files and call clients and—'

'And that was an admin task you did for us,' says Justin. 'So you can use that experience in Frank's department. You don't have any special skills, Delphine. There's nothing that sets you apart.'

'I have a law degree!'

'And we have legal advisers we pay good money to.'

They should've got legal advice on this. Because I'm not going to let him destroy my career. But right now there's a pain in my chest, and I wonder what he'd do if I had a heart attack in the boardroom. And then I think that me having a heart attack would solve all his problems, so I get my breathing under control again and say that I'm not going anywhere until I get some professional advice.

'We're perfectly within our rights to move you,' Justin says. 'And if you don't take up this position by tomorrow, then you're in breach of your contract with us.'

All the Cosecha contracts state that staff can be moved within the company. Nevertheless, it's not as clear-cut as he's making it out to be.

'It's up to you,' he says. 'Why don't you take the rest of the day off to think about it, and you can start your new role tomorrow. But one thing . . .'

I look at him.

'If you leave, you'll have to repay your company loan.'

My stomach lurches again.

I've been assiduously repaying the loan that Conrad arranged for me when I bought my house, but there's still a sizeable sum outstanding and I don't have the spare cash to repay it.

'I checked,' says Justin. 'It's repayable on demand if you leave Cosecha for any reason.'

I don't know what to say.

'So there you are.' He stands up. 'I'll tell Frank to expect you tomorrow morning. They start at eight in compliance, Delphine, and they don't like people working from home. Be on time.'

He walks out of the boardroom, followed by Kieran, who doesn't even look at me. I stay where I am, unable to move.

I don't know how long it is before I regain the use of my limbs. But when I do, I pick up my phone and head straight to the ladies', where I lock myself in a cubicle. I'm no longer the strong, capable woman I've always prided myself on being. I'm the woman whose life is crashing around her and who is choking back the tears.

Chapter 14

Kieran once told me that women aren't good leaders because they cry too much. I laughed at him and said he was a sexist fool. But here I am, about to prove him right.

As I lean against the cubicle wall, the door to the ladies' opens and I take a deep breath. I will not be heard sobbing in the loo. I squeeze my eyes shut and swallow hard while I wait until whoever it is leaves. I've managed to hold back the tears. And even though I'd classify them as tears of rage, I'm proud of myself.

Nevertheless, when I emerge from the cubicle and see myself in the mirror, I look terrible. My skin is blotchy, and because I've rubbed my eyes, I've smudged my allegedly smudge-proof mascara. I pinch my cheeks to bring up their colour and then stand in front of the mirror taking slow, steady breaths until I feel a little more together. I remind myself yet again that I'm a strong, confident woman, then I text Lisa Hannigan and ask her to meet me in the building lobby with my handbag and iPad.

'What's up, Delphie?' she asks as she hands me both. I realise that I've forgotten about my Skechers, which I left

161

under my desk when I came in. I wish I'd remembered to ask her to get them too.

Obviously I'm not going to tell her what happened. It'd be all around the office in seconds and I'm damned if I'm going to have people find out about a move I don't want to make before I have time to do something about it. I take my bag and tell her that I have a bit of an emergency to deal with.

'To do with Conrad?'

I give a non-committal shrug.

'It's so hard believe he's gone,' says Lisa. 'I loved what you said about him to the staff. It was so true. Now I keep looking up and expecting to see him pacing the floor like he did whenever he was thinking things through.'

'Me too,' I say.

'It feels so different,' she says.

'I know.'

'It'll be OK, won't it?' There's anxiety in her grey eyes. 'The firm will be fine?'

'Of course it will.' I speak with an assurance that I don't feel. 'Conrad was the captain of the ship, but he had an excellent crew.'

She smiles. 'Thanks, Delphie. You always know what to say to people. At least you're still here.'

I give her an encouraging smile. 'You'd better get back. That analysis won't happen by itself.'

'I've a mountain of stuff to do,' she tells me. 'See you later. Do you want me to call you if anyone's looking for you?'

'Nobody will be looking for me,' I say. 'See you soon.'

Or maybe never again, I think, as I leave the building. If

I don't accept Justin's proposal, this could be my last day in Cosecha. But it can't be. If I was ever going to leave, it surely wouldn't be like this. Besides, I can't afford to leave. Justin has trapped me. Unless I can find a way to fix it.

Everything can be fixed.

Conrad said that to me once when a deal looked like going sour and costing the company millions. You just have to have the right strategy, he told me as we pored over the files together. I have to find the right strategy to deal with Justin and the other directors.

I go into the café around the corner and take out my phone. I scroll to Erin's name.

Need to talk asap. Want your advice.

Sure. After work?

Was wondering if you could meet for coffee now.

There's a pause.

Need time to finish something up. Can you make it to the café near me?

See you there.

Heidi, the barista, is used to me coming in and then suddenly leaving without getting anything. She's used to a lot of her clients doing that. So it doesn't bother her that I give her an apologetic smile and say, 'Can't stay.'

I turn towards the Liffey and head across the Samuel Beckett Bridge, then walk up Macken Street and towards the tiny café where Erin and I always meet when I'm on her side of town. It's only a kilometre, but I'm not used to walking that kind of distance in my heels any more, and my feet are aching by the time I get there.

It's another ten minutes before she arrives, full of apologies.

'What's the problem?' she asks when she's got a cappuccino in front of her.

I tell her, outlining the situation about my company loan too.

'You're joking!' She puts the cup she'd raised to her lips back on the saucer without tasting the coffee.

I shake my head.

'This is outrageous. Did he give you anything in writing?'

I shake my head again. 'Sorry. I should've asked. But I wasn't thinking straight.'

'No. Well, who would be.'

'I should have been,' I say. 'I'm supposed to be a good crisis manager.'

She leans across the table and gives my hand a squeeze.

'Are you OK?' she asks.

I feel the tears brim in my eyes but blink them away.

'I'm . . .' I pause. 'I will be,' I amend. 'It's so . . . so out of the blue, Erin. I mean, I knew there'd be changes, but . . . I told Justin about the directorship. He thinks I'm either making it up or that Conrad was doing it because . . .'

'Because why?'

'He thinks we were sleeping together.'

'Delphie! Did he say so?'

'Not in so many words. But he didn't have to. His meaning was quite clear.'

'Even more outrageous.'

'He's been out to get me for years. An opportunity presented itself and he took it. And Kieran let him. I liked Kieran. I thought he was one of the good guys, but he sat there like a nodding dog, reinforcing everything Justin said.'

'Do you have anything at all from Conrad to back you up?' asks Erin. 'A text? A WhatsApp message? A voicemail?'

'No.'

'Shit.'

'I'm an idiot. I should've known Justin would pull some kind of stunt. And I don't believe for a minute that they would've voted it down if Conrad had put it to them. But without him, with Justin in charge . . . well, they're going to support him, not me. They already have, haven't they?'

'I'm so sorry,' says Erin.

'I let him blindside me. I should've been watching my back, because this was too good an opportunity for him to miss. I'm such a fool.'

'You're not,' she says. 'This sort of thing happens all the time in business.'

'Not usually to me.'

'Do you have a plan?'

'No. Not yet. I probably shouldn't have rushed out. I should've talked to people who might support me. But I was too . . . too humiliated.' I look at her in despair. 'I suppose I've got supporters in the company, but Justin has the directors. I'm not sure what I can do to change things.'

And yet I have to do something. I can't let him ruin my career.

'Can you recommend an employment lawyer?' I ask. 'I need some expert advice.'

'Luke Granahan,' says Erin immediately. 'He's our guy and he's brilliant. Maybe have a word with Sheedy too. I know she doesn't specialise in this, but she might have some suggestions.'

It's a plan. I feel better with a plan. I'm good with plans.

'Don't worry,' she says. 'We'll sort it.'

But I *am* worried. Because the truth is that Conrad was wrong. Not everything can be fixed. We ended up losing money on that deal, even if it wasn't as much as it could have been. And nothing I can do will ever bring him back. He's gone forever.

I have to be strong. And determined.

But I'm not sure it's enough.

When Erin goes back to her office, I walk to Grand Canal Dock and get the train home. The first thing I do when I get in the door is kick off my high heels and stick an assortment of plasters over my blisters. Then I change into a pair of cotton trousers and a long-sleeved T-shirt before retrieving my personal laptop from the small bedroom that doubles as a study.

I'd forgotten that my home screen is a photo of Conrad and me together at an industry awards event that was won by Cosecha. In his speech, Conrad said he couldn't have done it without me. I suddenly don't feel like looking for my contract. I bury my face in my hands and stay there, not moving, for at least five minutes before I get up, walk into the kitchen and open a bottle of wine. I don't care that it's mid afternoon and that I've barely recovered from my hangover. I pour a generous amount of white Zinfandel into a glass and sit down in the small armchair near the patio window.

I'm remembering that awards night – the excitement of being nominated and the delight at winning. Conrad bought champagne for the table and the next day he asked me to get gift vouchers for one of Dublin's top restaurants so that he could give one to every single member of staff. 'It's a team effort,' he said. 'Everyone deserves to share in it.'

He was such a good man to work for. That's why I stayed with Cosecha even when in my early years I was occasionally offered jobs at other firms. Each time the head-hunter suggested to me that I was being under-utilised where I was. That I could challenge myself a little more. That I could be more ambitious for myself. But with Conrad's encouragement, I carved out a greater role for myself in Cosecha. I took on more responsibility although I didn't make a song-and-dance about it within the company. Perhaps I should have. That way Justin and Kieran and Didier would have seen me as someone who mattered.

I stayed because of Conrad.

I would never have left him.

But now he's gone.

And as I gulp my wine, I wonder if staying at the company for so long was a monumental mistake. I was smack in the middle of my comfort zone. I haven't been rung by a head-hunter in years. I'm a woman who's nearer forty than thirty, potentially looking for a new job in a competitive market. It's all very well to tell myself I've got good qualifications, but so have plenty of other job-seekers, and they're younger, keener and – crucially – cheaper than me.

I tell myself that I'm catastrophising. I have a tendency to do that. To see the pitfalls in every given situation. It can be useful in my professional life. It's destructive now. I need to believe that Luke Granahan will advise me on how to get my career back on track. I need to believe that I can sort this out. But as I refill my glass, I think of the culture at Cosecha. It's never been one to accept failure, and although I haven't failed, I've been knocked off my perch. If I accept Justin's proposal, I'll never go back to being who I was before. Powerful. A part of the inner circle. I'll be Delphie in compliance, nothing more.

There are no second chances at Cosecha. Especially for the women.

I take another glug of wine and open a job search site to scan for executive assistant roles. There are quite a few, but all of them pay considerably less than I earned at Cosecha.

Maybe Justin's right.

I was cosseted and looked after by Conrad.

Now I have to look after myself.

Erin calls as I'm filling my glass with the last of the wine. I realise that by now I'm more than halfway to being a woman who drinks wine and despairs about everything in her life. A woman who's afraid that everyone else is doing better than she is. One beset by doubts. I'm Ed's Manic Pixie Dream girl without the charming cuteness.

'Are you OK?' asks Erin.

'Of course.' I try to pull myself together.

'Can you meet Luke this evening?'

I'm in no fit state to meet anyone.

'What time?'

'Seven?'

'At your office?'

'Yes.'

'OK.'

It's just gone five. I make myself the strongest cup of coffee imaginable and then stand under a tepid shower. Afterwards I put on my winter make-up to hide the pallor of my cheeks and the dark shadows under my bloodshot eyes. I get dressed in a pair of navy trousers that I can wear with flat shoes, and a plain white blouse. I need to look businesslike and competent. The sort of person who could easily be a director of a financial company. The sort of woman who doesn't cry in the loo. Though the truth is, I'm exhausted, my head hurts, and all I want to do is curl up on the sofa and sleep. But I keep some of my wits about me, and before I leave, I find my contract on the laptop and email it to myself. I also locate a copy of the loan agreement and email that too.

I nod off on the train, and when I jolt awake, I think for a moment that I've missed my stop. But we're only at Tara Street and there's one more station to go. Most of the passengers are commuters looking at their phones, oblivious to what's going on around them. I'm usually that commuter staring at her phone too.

Erin meets me in the lobby of Haughton's. If I'd stayed here, I could've worked my way up and used my degree instead of letting it become irrelevant. I could've been like Erin. A partner with a great future ahead of her instead of someone who only has a past.

But I wouldn't have had the opportunities I had at Cosecha, I remind myself as we take the lift to the fourth floor. The travel. Staying at great places. The feeling that I was interacting every day with important people. And the immense satisfaction I got from seeing the difference our annual funding to the charities we supported made. I thought I had it all. I shouldn't regret my choices. And yet I can't help a nagging feeling that I've allowed something to slip by me without even noticing.

'Here we are,' says Erin as she taps on a glass door and

shows me into a corner office. 'Luke, this is Delphie. Look after her. She's great.'

Luke Granahan is around the same age as me, his hair cropped so short it's almost shaven. He's wearing a well-cut suit and black-rimmed glasses, and as he steps out from behind his desk to greet me, I realise that in my flat shoes he's significantly taller than I am. Ridiculously, that gives me confidence in him.

'I'll leave you two to it,' says Erin. 'Drop in to me when you're done, Delphie.'

I nod, and then wish I hadn't, because it makes me feel dizzy.

'Well,' says Luke, going back behind the desk and sitting down. 'Let's see what we can do here.'

I take the seat in front of him and tell him that I have a copy of my contract and the loan agreement. After I've emailed them to him, he studies them carefully, then asks me to recall the meeting with Justin. As he listens and asks me more and more questions, I can't help feeling that I'm not half as clever or important as I've always thought.

'Your supposed redeployment isn't part of a general reorganisation,' he says. 'And obviously you weren't consulted beforehand, which, given that you advised Conrad on staff matters, you could have been. Is there anything else?'

I tell him about the run-in with Justin at the party. And about the more recent episode when I highlighted his mistake to Conrad.

'I don't know if it's relevant,' I add. 'But the next time I saw Conrad . . . the last time . . .' My voice breaks, and it takes me a moment to compose myself again. 'Well, he said he'd had words with Justin about it. I'm sure Justin wasn't happy. Nobody likes having their mistakes pointed out to them by the boss. Maybe I should've spoken to him about it first, but I only realised when I was working on the plane, so . . .' I look pensively at Luke. 'I mentioned it when he was presenting me with the so-called restructuring and he jumped in very quickly to prevent further discussion, presumably in case it weakened his position as incoming CEO.'

'*Would* it weaken his position?'

'I don't see how. There have been other mistakes in his past but they haven't held him back. He's the kind of guy who fails upwards, and now he's the top man. All the same, I'd be happy if this changed it.'

'Delphie, I specialise in employment law.' He removes his glasses, polishes them, then replaces them. 'When something goes wrong for someone in a company, I try to get the best possible resolution for them. Bottom line, though, the best resolution usually isn't trying to turn the board of directors against the CEO. Even if he is a prat.'

I was feeling suddenly hopeful, but now, even though Luke's description of Justin is accurate, I'm deflated again.

'They've handled this abysmally,' he says. 'The role he's offered you is a demotion. He wants you to leave and he's trying to find a way to make it happen. Realistically, fudging a restructuring plan isn't going to cut it, and I'm sure they already know that.'

'So why are they doing it this way?' I rub my temples to ease my headache. 'Luke, I'm in financial trouble if I take their offer, but it'd be a lot worse if I leave. I have a hefty mortgage as well as the company loan, and he's well aware of that. If he really wants me to go, you'd think he'd at least allow me enough time to pay off the loan. But even if he does, I might still lose my house.' My house – my home – is a symbol of everything I've achieved. The fear of losing it is paralysing.

'I'll do my very best to make sure there's no chance of that,' says Luke. 'Is there any other job in the company that would be appropriate for you?'

'Not at this level.' I give him a despairing look. 'They're gutting corporate responsibility, and although I could be up to speed in compliance very quickly, they're not talking of moving Frank, who heads it up. I suppose they could – should – beef up human resources, especially if getting rid of some of the staff who were loyal to Conrad becomes a thing, but although I'm good on the admin side of HR, I don't have enough detailed knowledge or experience of the finer details. Although I could learn, if they gave me the time.'

'I'll discuss it with him,' says Luke. 'Alternatives should have been part of the procedure, obviously.'

The thing is, we weren't much for procedures in Cosecha. Conrad ran it as an innovative, nimble company. His belief that the staff were better paid and looked after than anywhere else meant total loyalty from us all. People did leave, of course, and sometimes people were fired for poor performance. But it was always handled discreetly in house by Conrad; in all my time there, nobody ever consulted a legal firm about employment issues.

There's always a first time. I just never thought the first time would be me.

'Is there anything else I should know about?' Luke asks. 'Any complaints about your work?'

'I worked directly for Conrad. Nobody ever needed to complain about me.' It feels like a second hangover has lodged in my head. 'It really is all because of Justin.'

'I'm sorry about that,' says Luke. 'Constructive dismissal is probably our best route.'

He's right. It's increasingly obvious that I don't have a future at Cosecha any more. Not as a director. Not as human resources manager. Not even as Delphie in compliance. Not at all, as long as Justin is in charge. And perhaps I don't want to be there any more if Justin is in charge.

I feel a pain in my chest again.

'Don't worry,' says Luke. 'We'll look after you.'

'Thanks.'

'I'll get a letter to him by eight o'clock in the morning.'

I'm negotiating my exit. I never thought this would happen to me. I hold my breath to steady my nerves, but I know I'm shaking, and I swallow hard a few times.

Luke opens a drawer in his desk, takes out a box of tissues and pushes them towards me.

'I'm fine,' I say.

'Delphine, you're being forced out of your job. It's OK to be upset.' His voice is warm and comforting.

Although the lump in my throat feels like a rock, I manage to keep control of myself. I ignore the box of tissues and stand up. So does Luke.

'I'll take care of everything,' he says. 'Don't worry.'

I would've preferred to sort it myself. But I can't. I need him on my side.

'Thank you,' I say.

'It was good to talk to you,' he says as he shows me out of his office.

What's good is knowing I have a professional in my corner.

*

I close the door gently behind me and walk along the thickly carpeted corridor to Erin's office. She sees me through the plate-glass wall and waves me in.

'How did it go?' she asks.

'Pretty much as I expected. Luke is going to get into negotiation with Justin on constructive dismissal.'

'That's what I thought,' says Erin. 'Poor Delphie, you look shattered.'

'Downing a mid-afternoon bottle of wine will do that to you.'

'I'm impressed you made it here, in that case,' says Erin. 'Shows your fighting qualities.'

I give her a weak smile.

'I texted Sheedy. She's in Slattery's.'

Slattery's is an old-style Dublin pub that has managed to move with the times yet retain a traditional feel. It's one of our favourite places to socialise.

'I've already drunk more than enough today,' I say.

'You can rehydrate with some water.'

I don't want to go home yet. I don't want to be on my own. I want the support of my friends. So I agree.

Sheedy is holding seats for us at an outside table. When we arrive, she gives me a hug.

'How's it going?' she asks.

'You didn't have to come haring in to meet me.' I hug her back.

'Don't be ridiculous. We're the Three Musketeers. We stick together. And it's horrible what they're doing to you.'

It's certainly a challenge. But maybe I deserve it. Was I so caught up in being Conrad's assistant that I forgot to cultivate relationships with everyone else? Was I too remote? Too arrogant about my position? Too damn complacent? And yet I always thought Kieran and Didier respected me at least. I was wrong.

'Sure you won't have anything stronger?' asks Erin as she orders gin and tonics for herself and Sheedy and a sparkling water for me.

'Water's fine,' I say.

'So,' says Sheedy when the drinks are in front of us. 'What's the plan?'

I give her a run-down of my meeting with Luke.

'It's surreal,' I finish. 'A short time ago I was excited at the thought of being a director. Now Justin Delaney wants me out the door.'

'That man was always a prick.'

'A pompous prick.' It makes me feel better to say it.

'A particularly pompous prick who'll get his comeuppance,' says Sheedy.

'He won't,' I say. 'No matter what happens, he'll have the job he always wanted and I'll be out of his hair.'

'Not necessarily,' Erin says. 'Who knows what plans the other directors have? And if you get a good settlement out of it, they may question Justin's judgement. Either way, you've got to get something better from the situation. You did so much there, Delphie, but Conrad was the only one who really saw it.'

Erin has put her finger on the issue. Regardless of my role at Cosecha, many people, like Justin, would have assumed that my main task was to look after Conrad. So despite my fancy title, despite what I know I contributed, they thought of me as an extravagantly titled secretary too. I always considered myself to be as successful as Erin and Sheedy, but maybe

I was fooling myself. And yet Conrad had told me I deserved my promotion. That I wasn't the token woman.

Was it true? Or was he simply pandering to my sense of self-importance?

'Of course it was true,' says Sheedy, when I wonder this aloud. 'You were a senior person in the company, Delphie. Luke will leverage that.'

But he won't get me my job back.

'I'm sorry,' I say, when she starts offering more advice. 'I'm not at my best right now. I'll have forgotten everything by tomorrow.'

'You don't look great,' she agrees. 'Would a brandy help?'

I wanted to be a whiskey-drinking woman. Perhaps I'll become a brandy-drinking woman instead. Although I dislike that almost as much as whiskey. I say no to the brandy, but then decide I'll join the girls in a gin and tonic.

'Let's stop talking about me for a while and talk about you,' I say when I've taken a sip and felt myself relax a little. 'How are things going?'

'Oh, you know yourself. Busy enough. Some good cases, some not. Enough to make you lose your faith in humanity, that's for sure.'

Sheedy often says that the stuff that passes over her desk makes TV dramas look tame. I was never interested in family law myself. It's full of hurt feelings and bruised egos. Plus there are the violent cases, the ones that make you truly despair. That's why I went for corporate law, where it's pretty much only about egos.

Mine has taken a battering today, that's for sure.

I wonder if there'd be an opening for me with Sheedy's firm. She employs three people at the moment. Would she have space for a fourth? But what could I bring to the party? What use would any of my current skills be in a bitter divorce case?

I take a larger gulp of the gin than I intended. It's comforting in a way wine isn't, but it's blurring my vision. I tell my friends I'm going to the loo and walk as steadily as I can to the ladies'. There, I lean against the wall and try to tell myself that what I'm going through is a crisis but not a total disaster. I'm in a much better position than many people facing similar circumstances. I only have to worry about myself. Things could be a lot worse.

But right now it doesn't feel like that.

When I return to the bar, Sheedy and Erin have switched topic and are talking about Erin's situation with Fintan.

'Have you made a decision about moving in with him?' I ask.

She takes a sip from her glass, then puts it back on the table. 'On the one hand, the idea of having someone around all the time is sort of enticing,' she says in the way she always does when she's talking through a legal issue. 'And it would get my damn sister off my back. You know Trish, she's as bad as your sister-in-law. Never lets an opportunity to criticise my ageing single state pass her by. On the other hand, more importantly, Fintan comes with baggage. But who doesn't have baggage when they're forty? On yet another hand, how long would it be enticing for? Would I get fed up with him after a few weeks? Am I being selfish for thinking that a man with a ten-year-old daughter is too much trouble? But is he my last hope of a stable relationship? Or of having a child of my own?'

177

'A child of your own?' I focus on her last point and blink a couple of times to sharpen my focus as I look quizzically at her. Given that she broke up with her first husband over the issue of having children, this would be a major U-turn for her.

'When I went for my last smear test, the doctor asked me about it,' she says. 'He mentioned that I was leaving it a bit late.'

'The cheek of him!' exclaims Sheedy.

'He was simply stating a fact,' says Erin. 'It is late. But it doesn't have to be irretrievably late. I do know that if I want to do it, the window of opportunity is very narrow. And maybe now . . . maybe now's the time.'

I find it hard to believe she's saying this. Erin is the woman who drew up an actual plan for her career after her divorce. She showed it to me: a proper flowchart with options and potential decisions already marked on it. There was a box for 'remarry' linked to a box with 'have a family' inside. She'd put a big red X through both of them.

'Would you move in with Fintan just to get pregnant?' I'm trying not to sound judgemental, but evidently I don't succeed, because Erin tells me not to be judgemental.

'I'm not,' I retort. 'I'm . . . well . . . it's not something you wanted before.'

'I don't honestly know if I want it now,' she admits. 'But that damn doctor has put doubts in my mind. What if some part of me does want a child and I leave it too late? What if I could become that Instagram mum with her perfect son and daughter? What if I let the chance pass me by and regret it forever?'

'I'm not sure that thinking you might want a baby is a

good enough reason for moving in with anyone,' remarks Sheedy. 'If you do live together, it should be because you think it's your best life. Would it be better than what you have now?'

'I don't know,' says Erin. 'But it would be nice to have someone there all the time. To unblock drains and unscrew the lids on jars and stuff like that.'

I smile properly for the first time that day. 'You said before that you wanted him to uncork bottles of wine and cook for you. Now you want him to move in to open your marmalade in the mornings? I have a little gadget for that, you know.'

'OK, that sounds particularly shallow,' she admits. 'I'd want him for more than cooking, cleaning, jar-opening and potential parenthood duties.'

We all laugh, but we don't press her any more on her decision. After all, she was married before. She knows what she wants from a relationship. In all honesty, there may be only one thing that everybody really wants, and that's someone to love who loves them in return. But as for everything else – surely that's up to each individual person. I think of Lindsey, who's utterly adamant that a woman isn't a real woman unless she has a baby. And Trish, who thinks Erin should want the same things as her. We're all very different people. We do want different things. And nobody should be telling us that our choices are the wrong ones.

I know what I want. I want to turn back time. I want to make everything the way it was a couple of weeks ago. I want Conrad to still be alive, still be my boss. I want to feel secure about myself and my place in the world. But I'm racked with self-doubt. I've never been in this situation before.

I've no road map to deal with it.

Chapter 15

I'm awake at 6.30 the next morning and asking myself whether I should go into the office or not. What would happen if I tried to sit at my old desk? Would Justin manhandle me kicking and screaming, to the compliance department? Or would he fire me on the spot for not being where he wants me to be? Do I even want to go back knowing what a shit-show Cosecha will be under him? But I can't simply roll over and let him do what he likes.

I play with various scenarios in my head, but none of them work out well. I don't want to be humiliated in front of everyone. Being marched unwillingly to compliance would be humiliating. But so would walking there of my own accord. Delphine Mertens, once the boss's right-hand woman, now checking procedures. I can't bear it.

I'm being ridiculous in thinking all these things, because I shouldn't do anything until I hear from Luke. I send an email to the generic office address saying that I'm working from home. Not that I'll be doing much of anything, because my head hurts, my eyes are gritty and my mouth is like the bottom of a hamster's cage. When I look in the mirror, I'm horrified at how pale my face is and how lank my hair appears.

My eyes are still bloodshot. It's going to take industrial quantities of Optrex to whiten them again. But right now, I can't be bothered. I flop onto the bed and allow the room to spin around.

My stomach lurches and I jackknife off the bed, making it to the bathroom just in time to throw up into the sink.

Which is not a pleasant experience.

This is when I could do with a man in my life I think, as I pull the duvet around me afterwards. It would've been nice to have someone hold my hair out of my face while I barfed. It would've been nice to have someone help me back to bed and tell me that I was going to be OK. To bring me paracetamol for my pounding head. To be alongside me and tell me not to worry about a thing. But it's only me, looking after myself, the way I've always done, and it's suddenly a lonely place to be.

I think of Ed, who's promised to be in touch, but I can't call him and tell him to come and mind me because I've poisoned myself with alcohol, no matter how comforting it would be right now.

My phone beeps. It's Lisa, with a query about a webinar she's hosting. I give her the information she needs, then ask if Justin is in the office.

Not yet, she responds. *Do you want him to call you when he arrives?*

I tell her no, it's fine, that if he needs me he'll get in touch.

At that moment an email arrives. It's from Luke and it includes the letter he's sent to Justin asking to meet to discuss the company's proposed restructuring and the initial proposal he's made me. I like the way he's worded it. It makes it sound

181

like the opening salvo in a negotiation rather than Justin's take-it-or-leave it approach.

Luke knows what he's doing.

And that means I have someone alongside me after all.

After Luke's message I fall asleep and don't wake up until two p.m. I've never slept so late before – even as a grumpy teenager, I was always out of bed by 9.30 at the latest. It's not that I'm a morning person particularly; it's that I like being up and out and doing things. But today, although there are plenty of things I could choose to do, there's nothing I absolutely *have* to do.

I decide a walk along the seafront will clear my head. At least walking seems like something constructive. When I get back in, I check my emails again, but there's nothing from either Luke or Justin. I thought Justin might have sent me something a bit ranty when I didn't show up, but I suppose he's not going to commit anything to writing when he has a solicitor's letter on his desk.

I put Cosecha out of my mind to think about my future employment prospects. It wouldn't do any harm to update my CV and my LinkedIn profile. I've never been a big user of the business social media site, but as I always checked out the profiles of potential new hires for Cosecha, I have to assume that any new employer will do the same for me.

It doesn't take me long to get lost in a rabbit warren of potential jobs and other people's profiles, which distract me from the overall updating of my own. By the time hunger drives me to the kitchen, I've got a whole load of new buzzwords for my CV as well as a list of companies to send it to, should it become necessary.

I'm feeling significantly more positive about my future as a professional woman by now, but one look at the contents of my fridge reminds me that I've yet to crack my inner domestic goddess. The shelves contain nothing more than milk, butter and a selection of yoghurts close to their sell-by dates. I think of Mum and her insistence that you can make nutritious meals from leftovers. But I have no leftovers. I have no food in the house at all. Well, that's not strictly true. There are two M&S ready meals that would definitely be past their sell-by dates if I hadn't shoved them into the freezer when I first bought them. They've been there since last Christmas.

I'm not actually hopeless when it comes to eating, although I don't cook very much from scratch. I usually pick up something from the deli on the way home from work. Their freshly prepared meals probably work out cheaper than buying individual ingredients that would moulder away in my kitchen. At least that's what I've always told myself. But I haven't been to the deli today.

I close the freezer door and open the cupboard instead. At least I have cream crackers. They'll go with the butter. And some salted caramel slices that were an impulse buy last week. So I haven't become the useless singleton who can't cope. I can cope. I just haven't needed to.

I butter the crackers and make myself a cup of tea. It's a long way from lunch in Port d'Andratx with Bianca. Or dinner in New York with Conrad. Or even Italian in the docklands with friends or colleagues. I think of the jobs I've been looking at online and can't help feeling that I'm setting my sights too low. Perhaps the recruitment agencies will come up with something better.

I need them to come up with something better.

I'm not hungry any more.

I throw the crackers into the bin.

I'd forgotten about lunch at my parents' house until Mum texts me on Sunday morning telling me to be there by one. My first instinct is to say I can't make it, but if I do that, there'll be a flurry of texts asking what I've found that's better. Besides, ducking out will leave me on the judged step again, although this time being judged for the wrong thing. Mum will assume that even though it's Sunday, it's a work-related reason. It's happened often enough before.

I dither for ages before deciding that I'll go. So for the first time since Thursday, I wash my hair, do my make-up and decide what to wear, rather than just pulling on a T-shirt and leggings. The make-up hides the dark circles under my eyes, and I notice that my skirt is looser around the waist than it used to be. It's not really a silver lining, though, is it?

When I get to Mum's, Vivi opens the door. She and Jason have been living with my parents ever since she got pregnant with Charley. The pregnancy was unplanned, although the two of them had been talking about moving in together before she announced it. But they'd been struggling to find anywhere, and when Mum suggested they use one of her spare bedrooms, Jason moved in like a shot. In all honesty, I think she likes having them. And it gives them an opportunity to save up for a home of their own.

Mum greets me with a smile as I walk into the kitchen, then tells me I'm looking a bit ragged. Clearly the make-up hasn't been as effective as I thought.

'Bad night's sleep,' I say.

'Are you still upset about Conrad?' asks Vivi.

'Of course,' I reply. 'It's only been a couple of weeks.'

'I understand,' says Vivi. 'But you need to get over it, Delphie.'

I'm over the shock of Conrad's death, even though there's a gaping hole in my heart at his loss. But obviously I'm very much not over the shock of losing my job, although my family doesn't know about that yet. In a late development yesterday evening, Luke sent me an email saying that Justin was considering the situation and that in the meantime I should regard myself as on gardening leave. Gardening leave is usually the period when you've given your notice at a company and they don't want you working in case you acquire sensitive information to take to a competitor. You're on the payroll, but not part of it any more. When it happens at Cosecha you're given a cardboard box to put your belongings in, and you leave with a security guard at your side, never to return. My situation is somewhat different. I'm out of the office, but my stuff is still there, because I haven't been completely thrown to the wolves yet. And who knows, perhaps there's an unlikely chink of light at the end of the tunnel.

I'm not going to say anything to Mum and Dad. They'd only ask questions I can't answer. I plan to avoid the topic of work if I can. It shouldn't be too hard. My family never talk about my job if they can help it.

'Tarragon chicken for lunch,' says Mum. 'I hope you're hungry.'

'Anyone else coming?' I don't say that I'm not hungry. She'd be horrified at that.

'Lindsey and Martin might drop by later. But it's only you for lunch. Well, along with Vivi and Jay, of course.'

Usually at least one of my brothers and his family are there too. I'm beginning to wonder if she had an ulterior motive in asking me.

Dad, who's been reading the Sunday papers in the living room, joins us in the kitchen. It's part of the original house; the long, narrow dining area was added shortly after André was born.

'If I had the time and the money, I'd knock it down and do a much better job,' says Mum as we're sitting at the table. 'Back then, it was builders not architects who added bits to houses. There wasn't a lot of joined-up thinking.'

'Yours is a good example,' Vivi says to me. 'It's really clever how they opened it up. Jason and I would love something like that.'

Jason, sitting opposite me, winks. I like Jason. He works in a tech call centre, telling people to switch their computers off and on again. (I'm not being sarky. He told me that half the problems people ring up about really are solved by switching their computers on and off again. When I asked him if it wasn't the first thing everyone did, he gave me a dark look and told me never to underestimate the stupidity of the general public. I laughed at that.)

The conversation around the table continues to focus on houses, extensions, new-builds and the cost of it all.

'At least you're sorted,' Vivi tells me. 'You've always had it easy, Delphie, you lucky sod.'

I swallow the piece of chicken I'm chewing and it gets stuck in my throat. It takes a lot of eye-watering coughing to dislodge it.

'Are you all right?' asks Dad, when I've drunk a full glass of water.

I nod, and wipe my eyes with my napkin.

'Sure?' asks Mum, as my eyes continue to water.

'Delphie?' Dad looks at me. 'Is everything OK?'

And so, despite my intention not to say anything, I tell them that there are lots of changes happening at Cosecha and that my current position is under scrutiny and that there may be some restructuring and that it's a difficult time. I say that I'm out of the office for a few days and Dad comes straight out and asks if they've fired me.

'Of course not,' I reply.

'Are they making you redundant?'

'No,' I say. 'But until they resolve things, I'm out on full pay. It's fine. I have a great employment solicitor looking at the situation for me.'

'A solicitor?' He stares at me. 'What about the union? Can't they help?'

Naturally there isn't a union in Cosecha. Conrad never would've allowed it. Besides, the staff wouldn't have wanted it either. Dad has never understood that. He was the union rep in the state agency he worked for before his retirement, and he fought ferociously for better pay and conditions for his colleagues. Having someone like Dad on my side against Justin would make a big difference, I think, as I explain that Luke has everything under control.

'You'd be better with a union rep,' says Dad.

'So is this lawyer getting you a better job in the company?' asks Mum.

'Or a better settlement if I decide to leave.' I want to present it as my decision, not something forced upon me. I don't want them to know that there's a knot of fear in my stomach and that Mum's cooking tastes like ashes in my mouth.

187

'I know you liked working for that Conrad chap, but in all honesty, a good state job with a decent pension is hard to beat,' says Dad.

He has a point, as he has an amazingly great pension that allows him to live a life very similar to the one he had when he was working. Except now with the free time. To be fair, both he and Mum concede that they were lucky starting out at a time when there were jobs for life and pensions to go with them. But they always point out that they had nothing much other than the four walls of their house in the first ten years. The furniture was all second-hand and they kept to a very strict budget. There were no designer accessories or unnecessary gadgets. No eating out or holidays abroad. No Netflix or Prime or Sky. They didn't even have a landline for the first two years – they had to use a public phone box two streets away for calls. It was a different time. A different life. Yet they could afford for Mum to give up work to raise her family, even though she went back to the bakery eventually.

'No such luck for us,' Vivi says. 'It doesn't matter how hard we work, we're always going to be chasing the dream.'

'I'm sure everything will be fine for you, Delphie,' says Jason. 'You have an impressive CV.'

'Jason's right,' agrees Vivi. 'You're on the pig's back, aren't you? Out on full pay with the chance of a sweet pay-off at the end of it. And you can take your own good time about finding something else.'

I'd like to think that was true.

'And no matter what, you have your lovely house,' she adds.

'I hope I can still afford it.' I need to inject some realism into the conversation. Somehow my situation with Cosecha seems to have morphed from a potential disaster into something I should be grateful for. Yet every time I think of my mortgage, my stomach ties itself into knots of fear.

'Rent it out for a while if you're stuck,' suggests Vivi. 'That's what everyone does.'

'And where would I live myself?'

'There's always a bed for you here,' says Mum. 'I'd be happy to have you.'

'How much are your monthly repayments?' asks Vivi while I digest the notion that both my mother and my sister think I could simply live at home again. 'I'm sure it's cheaper than renting.' She gives me a speculative look. 'Jay and I could always move in.'

I feel like I'm in a parallel universe. Is Vivi seriously suggesting that she'd move into my house while I live with our parents?

'I'll be fine. There won't be any need to move out of my house,' I tell her as firmly as I can.

'Have you heard anything from Ed?' Mum shifts the conversation, and I'm not sure if it's because she's realised this is difficult for me or because she really does want to know if I've seen him. I tell her that he dropped around after the funeral and she looks pleased.

'He's matured well,' she says. 'Naturally I was angry with him when he left you, but everyone makes mistakes.'

'He was great at the wedding,' adds Vivi. 'Even when you disappeared, he still partied.'

'No reason for him not to,' I say.

'Someone else might have gone to their room and sulked,' she points out.

'Will you see more of him, d'you think?' Mum gets to the question she really wants to ask.

'Maybe.'

'Ooh, Delphie. He could be your knight in shining armour and rescue you,' says Vivi.

'Rescue me? From what?'

'Your situation.'

'I don't think Ed will be offering me a job,' I tell her.

'No, but you can reboot your youthful romance.'

'I hardly think that's rescuing me.'

'He'll be rescuing you from being alone,' says Vivi.

'I like being alone.'

'You've always done fine by yourself,' Mum agrees. And then she adds the twist. 'But your life would be easier if you had someone in it. Especially now.'

I don't say anything as I remember how I thought the same thing when I was being sick.

But I don't plan on being sick again.

Nevertheless, I mull over our lunchtime conversation when I get home. There's absolutely no chance of me moving out and letting Vivi and Jay move in. As for being rescued by Ed, or any other man for that matter, that's not what I need right now.

Mum didn't serve wine at lunch, but I pour myself a glass now, having got over my aversion to it. If you can't poison your liver after the death of your boss and being told your job doesn't exist, when can you? My sensible side says never. My emotional side adds another drop to the glass.

My phone rings. It's Ed. I tell him I'm just back from Sunday lunch at Mum and Dad's.

'I loved Josie's lunches,' he says. 'Especially when she produced an enormous cake afterwards.'

She made pavlova today, but I couldn't face it.

'I'm just leaving IKEA,' he says. 'I was there to buy a new desk, but I stocked up on meatballs and Daim bars. Joe's mad about them and I remembered that you love them too. The Daim bars, not the meatballs, I mean. So I bought extra. I thought you might like me to drop them over to you.'

'Oh, Ed. That's lovely of you. Though obviously right now I couldn't possibly eat another thing.'

'No worries, I can hang on to them for later,' he says.

I haven't had a Daim bar in ages, but just thinking about them makes me want one. I tell him that I'd love him to drop by and he says he'll see me soon.

I'm still holding my phone when it vibrates with a message. It's Sheedy, saying she's nearby and asking if I fancy a visit from her. I text back, *Of course*, and five minutes later she arrives carrying a box with four iced doughnuts inside.

Do people think I need a sugar rush?

'Would you like one with your coffee?' I ask, after I thank her.

'Not a bit. They're for you, so you can comfort-eat.'

I laugh and tell her I comfort-ate at Mum's earlier but that I'll have one this evening. I put the box in the fridge and pour the glass of sparkling water she's asked for. I stick with rosé for myself.

Not surprisingly, the talk turns to my situation at Cosecha. Sheedy is trying to make me look at it in the same positive way I spun it to my parents.

'Onwards and upwards, Delphie,' she says when I've filled her in. 'Have you registered with a head-hunter?'

I tell her about my LinkedIn surfing and CV updating and say that I'll be contacting an agency in the coming week. I add that I've had some more conversations with Luke Granahan and that I'm leaving it all in his hands now.

'You've got the best in him,' Sheedy assures me.

'I didn't think about my future enough while I was in Cosecha,' I say. 'I didn't look outside my circle. A man would've.'

'Not necessarily.'

'A man would always have been thinking ahead,' I say. 'Justin was. Kieran was. Didier was. All the guys in the firm had plans for what would happen if Conrad left. Not this particular scenario, of course, but . . . That night, they swung into action and they didn't let emotion get in the way. I felt loyalty to Conrad and his memory. Their only loyalty was to themselves. And I'm not saying it was necessarily wrong,' I add, before Sheedy has a chance to speak. 'Just that they played a different game and won, and I'm an absolute idiot.'

'Let's see what Luke comes up with before you write yourself off as a complete loser.'

The doorbell rings and startles both of us. I'd forgotten about Ed.

I go and answer it and lead him into the living room. He's carrying the three bags of mini Daim bars he's brought for me, as well as three bags of meatballs he asks me to put in the freezer so that they don't start to defrost.

Sheedy looks at him in astonishment. 'Ed Miller,' she says. 'What a surprise.'

'Sheedy Collins! I certainly didn't expect to see you here.'

I glance from one to the other. As far as I recall, Sheedy never met Ed. We split up around the same time as she joined Haughton's.

'Ed was my client,' says Sheedy. 'I handled his divorce.'

'Oh.'

'What's your connection?' Ed looks at me.

'We're friends,' I say. 'Through Erin.'

'You never mentioned you used to be at Haughton's,' Ed says to Sheedy. 'If you had, I would've asked you about Delphie.'

'As far as I remember, we were too busy concentrating on the job in hand to talk about anything else,' says Sheedy. There's an edge to her voice that surprises me.

'It's really good to see you,' says Ed.

'How do you and Delphie know each other?' Sheedy asks him.

'We dated. Briefly,' says Ed.

'Not that briefly,' I remind him. 'It was nearly two years.'

Sheedy looks at me in surprise. 'I don't remember an Ed,' she says.

'It was before your time,' I reply. 'There've been others since.'

'Anybody got anything for a bruised ego?' Ed sounds plaintive, and we laugh.

The atmosphere suddenly lightens. I ask Ed if he'd like a drink and he opts for coffee. While I busy myself at the machine, he and Sheedy chat, mainly about how things are between Ed and Carleen since the divorce.

When I join them with coffees, and a bowl filled with the mini Daims (Sheedy takes three; she's a bit of an addict too), we move on to talking about Conrad, Cosecha and the situation I find myself in.

'What a complete shower of tossers!' Ed is furious on my behalf. 'You're not going to let them get away with it, are you?'

'My employment solicitor is on the case,' I tell him.

'I hope you've a good one.'

'One of Erin's colleagues,' Sheedy says. 'Very competent.'

'It's a disgrace you have to take this route, Delphie,' says Ed. 'You'd think Cosecha would treat someone as loyal and as hard-working as you better.'

I'm comforted by Ed's reaction and his unconditional support.

'Still, you're a smart woman and I'm sure it'll work out in the end,' he adds. 'And you never know – this could be a great opportunity.'

Maybe everyone is right and the current catastrophe will turn out to be a good thing. But I had a good thing. I didn't realise how good until it was taken from me.

'I'd better be heading off,' says Sheedy, when she's finished her coffee. 'I've a busy day tomorrow and I need to do a bit of additional prep.'

'OK.' I follow her to the door. 'Thanks for dropping by. I hope Ed being here hasn't chased you away early. I can't believe you two know each other.'

'He was a good client.' She shrugs. 'Keep me in touch with what's going on. If I can do anything to help, I will, though I think you're in good hands with Luke.'

'Sure.'

We give each other a hug, then she gets into her car and drives off.

'That's mad, you two knowing each other,' I say as I sit beside Ed again.

'Dublin's a village. Everyone knows everyone. She was a great solicitor.'

'Still is.'

194

'Gave me some excellent advice. Didn't let me feel hard done by.' He grins. 'I moaned incessantly at her and it was water off a duck's back.'

That's Sheedy all right. Nothing fazes her.

We sit in silence for a couple of minutes, then Ed asks if I'd like to come to dinner with him.

'Ed! You know I've eaten at Mum's. I couldn't possibly—'

'Not today. I completely understand that Josie's lunches could keep you going till tomorrow. Sometime during the week. Or the weekend.'

'That'd be lovely,' I say.

'Great.' He smiles. 'I'll be in touch.' Then he looks at his watch and says he'd better be off because he's picking up Joe from Carleen's mum, who lives in Drogheda, a forty-minute drive away.

'And you're on the opposite side of town.' I frown. 'Where does Carleen live?'

'Skerries,' says Ed.

'Crikey. That's a lot of driving for you.'

'It's OK when the motorway isn't too busy.'

I remind him not to forget his meatballs and he follows me into the kitchen.

'Oh, and why don't you take a couple of these for yourself and Joe?' I open the fridge and take out the box of dough-nuts Sheedy brought. I'll never get through four of them on my own. I open the lid and take out two.

'Delphie, I don't want to be critical, but is that all you have in your fridge?' Ed sounds horrified as he peers into it and sees wine, milk, butter and yoghurt and not much else.

'I have a just-in-time policy towards shopping,' I tell him.

'Maybe you should keep one of these.' He indicates the

meatballs. There's one bag of each type – meat, fish and vegetarian.

I laugh. 'I'm fine. Really I am.'

He doesn't look convinced.

'Don't worry about me. I've Daim bars and doughnuts.'

'I'm not sure that's a balanced diet.'

'You sound like my mother.'

This makes him laugh.

I walk him to the front door and open it. Before he steps outside, he leans towards me and kisses me. This time it's more than a gentle graze against my lips. This time we kiss the way we did after André and Tory's wedding.

We've definitely moved on from the plus-one scenario.

'I'll be in touch about dinner,' he says. 'Given the state of your fridge, you need it!'

I watch him walk to the road, where he gets into a Volkswagen Golf. He's right about the state of my fridge. Not that it was something he'd have noticed before he got married and had a child.

Ed Mark II is very different to Ed Mark I.

Ten minutes after Ed leaves, my phone rings again. Clearly I've become the go-to person for phone calls on Sundays. I'm surprised, though, to see that this call is from Martha.

'Delphie,' she says when I answer. 'How are you?'

I reply that I'm fine and ask how she is.

'Coping,' says Martha. 'It's difficult.'

I'm sure it is.

'I'm trying to sort things out and I need you to do something for me, if you don't mind.' She's speaking in the brisk tone she used when she was asking me about Cosecha's community projects. She loved being involved with them, and her support was invaluable. 'Can you check if there's a set of keys to the Bandon basement in the Cosecha office? And a set for Palmyra too.'

Bandon is the name Conrad gave to the Lansdowne Road house. It's named after the town in Cork where he lived as a child. Maybe it's because he travelled so much that he had such a strong sense of home.

I know there are keys to the basement in the Cosecha office, and I say this to Martha. 'But don't you have a set yourself?' I ask.

'He changed the locks when he moved out.' Martha's voice is brittle. 'I could get a locksmith, but I don't want to if there's a set of keys I can use. I'm not planning on going to Palmyra soon, but I'd like those keys too if possible.'

I tell her that it's not keys she needs for Palmyra but a passcode. Conrad had new locks installed a few months ago that can be opened with an app.

'An app!' She sounds horrified. 'Does that woman have it?'

I explain that even if Bianca has the app, Martha can change the passcode if she logs in with Conrad's PIN. Although I suggest it might be worth checking with Bianca herself first.

'D'you know the PIN?' She ignores my suggestion.

'No. But it'll be saved on his laptop.'

'Well, if you could get me the laptop and the keys, that'd be great. The laptop was his personal one, so I'd like to have it.'

'I think it's still at Palmyra,' I tell her. 'It's not in the office.'

'I really hope *she* doesn't have it.' Martha groans. 'I don't want to have to . . . Oh, Delphie, there's so bloody much to think about! Oscar expects me to know about everything. Laptops, keys, codes, insurance policies . . . my head is melted.'

I'm not surprised she's feeling overwhelmed. I sympathise, and she apologises for dumping on me, suddenly sounding less like the wife of the boss and more like the warm-hearted woman she really is. 'I know I'm being a pain, but I'd really appreciate if you could check where the laptop is, and get the keys too.'

'It might be better to be more formal about things and ask Oscar about them,' I say.

'Oscar will want to send a damn letter to Cosecha,' Martha snorts. 'You know what solicitors are like. You were Conrad's trusted assistant, Delphie. I'd rather you did it for me.'

I tell her why I can't.

'What!' She sounds both astonished and angry, and I'm comforted by that. 'They want to get rid of you? Is Justin Delaney out of his mind? You keep that place together.'

'I might have thought I did, but I didn't,' I say. 'I kept Conrad together.'

'It's so unfair.' She's still angry on my behalf. 'You're a million times better than Justin. Than any of the others on that board.'

'Not at investments and not at stabbing people in the back,' I tell her.

She digests this for a moment and then reminds me that there are procedures for letting people go and that it doesn't sound like Justin followed them.

'I've consulted an employment solicitor,' I say.

'Oh, Delphie. Conrad would have . . .' Her voice trails off. 'This is awful.'

'It was a shock,' I agree. 'But these things happen in business.'

'All the same. You're an essential part of Cosecha. I can't imagine it without you. Conrad would be furious. *I'm* furious!'

Her anger is reigniting my own, but I say what I've been telling myself ever since going on gardening leave: that they managed before I came and they'll manage after I've gone.

'Conrad worked better after you arrived.'

'Perhaps,' I tell her. 'But Justin isn't Conrad.'

'That's for damn sure.'

'We'll see how things work out,' I say.

We're both silent for a moment, and then she asks me if there's any chance I could still go into the office and get the stuff she wants. 'Because although I could go in myself, I can't face it. Not yet. And I'd really like them as soon as possible.'

'I'm not sure I can face it either,' I admit.

'You're right. I shouldn't have asked.'

But now that she's taken the pressure off, I suddenly want to do this for her. And I have a reason for going in anyway, because I need to collect my personal possessions. At first I thought that leaving them there was a sign I might come back, but that's not at all likely now.

'I might be able to go in if you really want me to,' I say.

'Not if it puts you in a difficult position.'

'It doesn't.' I'm suddenly feeling stronger. More determined. 'I'll go in tomorrow.'

'Thanks,' she says. 'You're a star, Delphie.'

'Let's see if I can get your keys before you start complimenting me.'

'I wish I knew where the laptop was for sure,' she says.

'You don't need it for his passwords,' I point out.

'But you said they were on it.'

'Yes, but it was automatically backed up to an off-site server. You can connect to that online.'

'Seriously? Could I do it now?'

'Yes, but you have to use the desktop computer at Bandon.'

Which is in Conrad's locked basement office.

'I presume there's a password for the desktop too,' says Martha.

'Of course, but I know it,' I tell her. 'And you can check the location of the laptop from that computer as well.'

'Oh, Delphie, I knew I could depend on you.'

Exactly as Conrad used to.

She ends the call.

And just like that, I feel energised again.

Chapter 16

I arrive in the office at eight the following morning. I'm wearing a maroon Louise Kennedy suit, paired with a cream silk top. I've put my hair up and am wearing my highest heels, as well as industrial quantities of Charlotte Tilbury. I'm also carrying my oversized Tommy Hilfiger bag and channelling my inner Billy Ikehorn, the heroine of my mum's favourite sex-and-shopping novel, *Scruples*. I'm glad that I decided to do this for Martha. It's good for me too. I swipe my entry card and am a little surprised when the door opens immediately. Honestly, this place is falling apart without me. One of the key things to do as soon as someone leaves is disable their card.

'Is it true?' Lisa Hannigan is the first to see me as I come in. 'Have you been fired, Delphie?'

'Is that what people are saying?'

'Oh, well, you know. The rumour mill has gone into overdrive.'

'I haven't been fired,' I say. 'But I may not be back.'

'I can't believe they'd let you go,' she says.

I shrug, and she gives me a smile that's a mixture of sympathy and fear. Her fear is for her own job. Because if I can be let go, so can anyone. I pat her on the shoulder and walk to my office, where Norah Black, one of the admin staff, is sitting in my chair. She's in her twenties, and although good at her job, not overly ambitious. Her eyes open wide in surprise when she sees me.

'Good morning,' I say. 'Can I help you with anything?'

'I . . . I'm . . . Justin asked me . . .'

'Is he in?' I glance towards Conrad's office, which is empty.

'No,' replies Norah. 'He's away. He asked me to be here in case he needed anything.'

'Here, at my desk?'

'Yes.'

I take out my phone and press record. 'Can you say that again, Norah?'

'Why?'

'I want to record you saying it, that's all.'

'I'm not sure—'

'For heaven's sake! Just say what you said to me.'

She hesitates, but then repeats that Justin asked her to sit at my desk in case he needed anything.

'There you go. That wasn't difficult. Now you can scoot back to your own desk, because I have things to do.'

'But you're on gardening leave,' she protests. 'You're not supposed to be here.'

'I have some personal matters to deal with,' I tell her. 'It's fine, I won't be doing anything I shouldn't.'

She looks at me for a moment, then gathers up her things and disappears. I presume she's going to let somebody know I'm here, but it doesn't really matter. I send the recording to Luke before opening my desk drawer and taking out my set of keys to Bandon, which also include the keys to the basement. Then, feeling like a spy, I walk into Conrad's office and slide open the door to his low-rise filing cabinet. I hunker down and check the folders, select the slimmest and remove it.

'What are you doing?'

I stand up at the sound of Kieran's voice.

'Martha asked me to look for something for her,' I say. I'm looking him directly in the eye. In my heels, that's easy.

'You shouldn't even be here,' says Kieran. 'How did you get past security?'

I hold up my ID card.

'How come you still have that?' he demands.

'Justin could have disabled it, but he didn't. He's not a details man, Kieran, as you know. He made a cock-up of the Dellalio deal, but luckily for him, I was here to save his bacon. Not for much longer, though. He'll have to plough ahead unchecked. Because you didn't notice the mistake either.'

'For God's sake, Delphie . . .'

'Anyhow, this gives me a chance to thank you so much for your support during his little chat in the boardroom.'

'It was a business decision.'

'My arse.' I use my most pleasant voice, even though I want to spit at him. 'Justin has always wanted to get rid of me, and you guys have obviously decided that I faff around doing nothing all day, despite all the support I've given you over the years. Meanwhile, Norah was sitting at my desk when I came in.'

'You know how things work,' says Kieran. 'New leader, new broom. Besides, Justin needs someone he can trust.'

'So you decided I should be canned because he doesn't trust me?'

'I didn't say that.'

203

'Sounds to me like you did.'

'Stop twisting things, Delphie.'

'You're a crowd of back-stabbing shits,' I tell him. 'I wish I'd remembered that when I came haring in from my brother's wedding to unlock files and call clients. I would've stayed with the people who matter instead.'

'Delphie—'

'Shove it.' I walk over to my desk and this time open the bottom drawer.

'You can't take anything from the building,' says Kieran.

At that moment, Didier comes striding across the floor.

'Get away from that desk,' he says.

'*Et tu*, Didier.' I make a face at him.

'You shouldn't be here.'

'As of now, I'm still on the payroll. I haven't left.'

'That doesn't give you the right to turn up at the office.'

I ignore him and remove three pairs of emergency tights as well as a packet of Tampax and the hairdryer that I kept in the drawer.

'I'm entitled to remove my stuff,' I say, as I put them into my bag along with my Skechers. 'I can't imagine you want my sanitary products, Didier. But the main reason I came is for these.' I dangle the keys to Conrad's home office. 'Martha asked me to collect them for her.'

'Why couldn't she do it herself?' asks Didier.

'Possibly because she couldn't bear to see what you guys are doing to a great company.' I drop the keys into the inner pocket of the bag. I also pick up the folder. 'Anyway, I'm off now. Have a nice day.'

'Hey! What's that you're taking with you?' Kieran holds out his hand for the folder.

'It's a photo album.'

'A what?'

I can understand his surprise. People don't have photo albums any more. I certainly don't. All my photos are digital.

'A photo album.' I hand it to him and he flicks it open. Inside are photos of Conrad, Martha and their children, four to a page, protected by transparent sheets and all neatly noted with the date and place they were taken. There are five pages in the album. 'It's personal to Martha. I knew she'd want it.'

'Right.' He gives it back to me. 'You've got what you came for, now go.'

I feel the eyes of everyone in the office on me as I sweep out without another word and stab the button to call the lift. When I reach the ground floor, I realise they haven't taken my ID card away. I bet they'll forget to disable it again too.

They really are hopeless.

I call Martha when I'm outside the Cosecha building and tell her I've got the keys to the basement.

'Can you meet me at the house?' she asks.

'It'll take me about half an hour to get to you.'

'Text me when you're at Grand Canal Dock.'

'OK.'

I take the Luas as far as Connolly and transfer to a Dart. When it leaves Grand Canal Dock, the station before Lansdowne Road, I text Martha. By the time I reach Bandon, she's standing at the top of the steps that lead up to the red-brick house, waiting for me. She's wearing a bright blue jacket over jeans and a T-shirt, and her glossy brown hair is tied back in a short ponytail. She looks at least ten years younger than when I saw her at the funeral.

'Delphie.' Her smile is bright. 'It's good to see you.'

'You too.'

And it is. My friendship with Martha was always complicated because of my status as an employee of her husband, and yet most of the time we were just two women who enjoyed each other's company and who wanted nothing but success for the same man.

I walk into the house and we go downstairs to the door that leads to the basement. I hand her the keys. She unlocks the door and we walk inside. There are monitors everywhere, and I know that when they're switched on, they show statistics from financial markets around the world. Of course Conrad could have replicated his office anywhere, but the equipment needs space and that's what he had here.

'All that time spent holed up down here and for what?' asks Martha as she opens the plantation-style shutters to allow light into the room.

'For making money,' I reply. 'He was great at making money.'

She nods. 'I liked that he did, of course. No matter what people say about the best things in life being free – if that's even true – it's nice to be able to afford the second-best things.'

I laugh and she smiles. Then she laughs too and suddenly our laughter is uncontrollable. When we finally stop, she wipes her eyes.

'I never stopped loving him.' She's halfway between laughter and tears. 'Even when he went off with that girl. It wouldn't have lasted, Delphie. You know that.'

Conrad and Bianca seemed happy together when I last saw them at Palmyra. But Martha could still be right about them.

'She was a gold-digger.'

It's funny how women who have relationships with wealthy men are called gold-diggers. Even by other women. It's as though they're a dangerous breed, always ready to pounce on an unsuspecting male target. As though the man in question doesn't have any choice in the matter.

'You liked her, didn't you?' asks Martha.

'I didn't dislike her,' I respond cautiously. 'I regret introducing her to him.'

'Oh, he was in mid-life-crisis mode,' says Martha. 'He was ripe for the picking. And when she started changing his clothes and making him get his hair cut and wear different glasses . . . well, he thought he was that person. Young, dynamic . . . Thing is, I always thought of him as young and dynamic. Fifty isn't old. It's just not thirty any more.'

'I understand.' And I do. Because it's the same in the office. The younger investment managers are all keen and ambitious. All wanting to make their mark. But Justin and Didier and Kieran were equally ambitious, snapping at Conrad's heels, jostling for position. Everyone wanted to be him. Everyone wanted what he had. It's Justin who's succeeded.

'I knew he'd leave her eventually,' says Martha.

'But you were getting divorced.' I have to bring some realism into her interpretation of events. 'You had Oscar working on it.'

She shakes her head. 'He knew and I knew it would come to nothing.'

I think of the hidden folder on Conrad's laptop and wonder if she's right.

'But,' she says as she switches on his desktop computer, 'we don't know what sort of financial juggling Conrad might have been up to in order to keep his mistress in the style to which she wanted to become accustomed.'

It's unfair to call Bianca his mistress. She was his partner. Even if only temporarily.

'It's hard for you, isn't it?' Martha gives me a shrewd look. 'Your loyalty is to Conrad, not me.'

'Martha, we've been friends for years. But he was my boss and . . .'

'And you have to cover for him. Did you know of anyone else? Before this Bianca person?' This time the look she gives me is penetrating.

'No!' I exclaim. 'Absolutely not.'

'I'm sorry,' she says. 'The whole thing has left me . . . unmoored. I loved him but he hurt me. And we didn't get the chance to fix it.' Her voice wobbles. I put my arms around her and allow her to rest her head on my shoulder. After a moment or two, she straightens up and sniffs. 'It's not easy,' she says. 'And maybe people are right. The best things in life really are free and the worst things are free too. Because I thought nothing could hurt me more than when he told me about Bianca. But hearing about the accident was even more devastating. It was like losing him twice. I was always there when he needed me,' she adds. 'But I wasn't there when he needed me the most.'

'I'm so sorry, Martha. I really am. And if there's anything I can do . . .'

'You're doing it.' She wipes her eyes. 'You're going to get me into his computer.'

I sit down in front of the monitor and power it up. When the log-in window appears, I type in the password to unlock it. Then I take the slim folder out of my bag and open it.

'Oh my goodness!' exclaims Martha as she sees the photos. 'Where did you get these?'

'Conrad kept it in the office,' I reply.

'I didn't know . . . That was sweet of him.' She goes to flick through it, but I tell her to wait. She looks at me in surprise as I put it down beside me again. I double-click on an icon and another log-in screen opens. As I begin typing the password, Martha realises that it's the date the first photo of her and the two children was taken, fifteen years earlier.

'Just the date?' she asks. 'That seems very simple.'

'And the place.' I type 'Brittas' with a capital B. I add a percentage sign afterwards. Conrad always used a percentage sign at the end of his passwords.

A 'please wait' message appears on the monitor, and I wonder for a moment if Justin has managed to get into Conrad's computer and change things after all. But I tell myself that a man who was too idiotic to think of disabling my ID card certainly wouldn't have managed this. Besides, he didn't need to, because I transferred the lists of clients that had been exclusively Conrad's to the office server the day after the accident.

'Is this the up-to-date record of everything?' asks Martha when the home screen appears again.

I shake my head. 'Conrad was using his laptop at Palmyra. I need to sync the two and then you'll have everything.'

My fingers fly over the keyboard and the desktop begins the sync. The monitor bar suggests it'll take ten minutes.

'It probably won't take as long as that,' I say when Martha offers to make us both a coffee while we wait.

'Oh, let's have the coffee anyhow,' she says. 'It's gloomy down here.'

209

Even with the shutters open, the basement doesn't get a whole heap of light. So I agree, and we walk up the stairs and into the main house together.

The kitchen is bright and cheery after the office. It's big enough for my entire house to fit in, with an enormous centre island, Carrara marble tiles and New England-style cupboards in a pale Farrow & Ball blue. I remember when Martha had it done. Conrad was going mad about the disruption.

She makes coffee in a cafetière and hands me a cup, along with a piece of biscotti.

'I talked to him the day of the accident,' she says as she sits on one of the high stools at the countertop.

I look at her in surprise.

'Killian wanted to go to Palmyra with a few friends during the summer,' she explains. 'I was trying to work out a time. I didn't want him to be there when that woman was there. Conrad said he'd get back to me. It was the last conversation we had.'

'I'm so sorry, Martha.'

'I asked the children if they'd like to go to Palmyra after the funeral, in case they wanted to see where it happened. But they preferred to stay here and go to Cork.'

'Are you sure you don't want to go yourself?'

She shakes her head. 'I can't make myself do it yet. Besides, I know I must sound like a privileged cow, but there's so much to think about when it comes to Conrad's estate, it's all I have time for. Oscar's on to me every single day.'

'Is the will complicated?' I ask the question cautiously.

'According to Oscar, Conrad didn't make any significant changes to the one he drew up a few years ago,' she says, and I can hear the relief in her voice. 'That would mean he left everything to me and the children. I know he set up trust funds for them.'

'Nothing at all to Bianca?'

'Not that I know of. Thankfully.'

'Ouch.'

'Tough,' says Martha. 'She didn't build a life with him. He didn't change anything because deep down he knew it was a fling.'

'What about the mews house they were living in?' I ask.

She gives me a self-satisfied smile. 'His,' she says. 'And therefore mine.'

'Is she still there?'

'I know you think I'm being hard-hearted, but I'm not as cold as all that. I've asked Oscar to send her a notice to quit. I'm giving her three months from the end of this, which should be plenty of time for her to find somewhere new.'

'That's generous,' I concede, although I'm pretty sure Bianca won't see it that way. She'll be furious. And hurt.

'Anyway, I'm really grateful for all your help,' says Martha. 'And I really am sorry about the whole situation at Cosecha. It's very wrong. I own some shares myself,' she adds. 'I could talk to Justin for you.'

It's kind of her, but it would probably do more harm than good. I say this, and she nods.

'Like you with Oscar, I'm leaving it in the hands of my solicitor,' I add.

I finish my coffee, then suggest that the sync has probably finished and we should check the computer. So we go back downstairs, where I log in to the desktop again. I'm pleased to see that all the files have been updated. I go into the app where Conrad keeps his passwords securely protected. The code to unlock the front door of Palmyra is a simple set of numbers, and it's as well he saved it, because as far as both of us can see, they're random.

'Might be her birthday, I suppose,' says Martha gloomily as I type in the last two digits.

'She's thirty, not twenty-five,' I tell her.

'As if that really matters.' But Martha looks more cheerful as she makes a note of the code.

'As soon as you download the app to your phone and log in as Conrad, you'll be able to change the codes to lock and unlock the doors,' I tell her as I do some more scrolling. 'His ID is simply his name and a four-digit number.'

'The year we bought Palmyra,' observes Martha.

'You've got everything you need,' I say. 'You don't need the laptop to access anything now. You'll find most of the passwords in that app. Anything that isn't there is work-related.'

'Even so, I'd like to get hold of the laptop,' says Martha. 'I don't want anyone else appropriating it.' She looks thoughtful. 'There's other stuff at Palmyra I want too.'

'Oh?'

'Some jewellery. Things I left behind the last time I was there when I didn't realise I wouldn't be back. They're more sentimental than anything, but I'd like them now. And I want his watches.'

Conrad collected watches. Some of them were new, some vintage. Not all were valuable, but many were.

'I'm sure you'll get there sooner rather than later,' I say. 'Don't you have a legal representative in Mallorca too? Now that you have the app to unlock the door, you could let him in.'

212

'Would you go, Delphie?' she asks. 'I'd really appreciate it.'

I look at her in surprise. 'Why on earth would you want me to go?'

'It's my home!' she cries. 'Just as much as here or Cork. I don't want people I don't know tramping around it.'

'The solicitor in Mallorca is hardly people you don't know,' I say as mildly as I can.

'I've only met him once,' she says. 'Besides, he's not you.'

I'm flattered that Martha has asked, but going back to the island knowing what happened to Conrad would be hard. And the very idea of walking into his house makes me shiver. Yet she's looking at me with a beseeching expression and I can't say no.

'Go for a few days and bring someone with you,' she says. 'Turn it into a bit of a holiday. You've got time on your hands while you sort out what you're going to do yourself. A different location might help you make up your mind about your next steps.'

'Well, I—'

'Obviously I'll pay for your flight and your stay. And for your time. I realise you could be looking for work instead.'

'You don't have to pay for anything,' I tell her.

'If you've lost your job, you'll need the money,' she says.

'I'm not destitute.' Although as I say the words, I know that Luke is making a very different point to Justin.

'Let me pay for the flight at least. You can go and come back in a day if you prefer.'

'I'll think about that part,' I say. 'But if you want me to go, I'll go.'

'I really, really appreciate it,' she says.

'You'll need to let me know the code for the house when you change it.'

She nods.

'I'll organise it in the next couple of days,' I tell her. 'I'll text you when it's sorted.'

'Perfect,' she says.

We hug, and then I leave.

Despite being unceremoniously dumped from the company, it appears that I'm still involved in Conrad's personal life.

I'm not sure how I feel about that.

When I get on the train back to Malahide, I take out my phone and see that I've missed two texts. One is from Bianca. The other from Ed.

I look at Bianca's first.

Have you any information on Conrad's estate? she asks. *His lawyer hasn't told me anything and I'm completely in the dark about what's going on. I'm entitled to know, Delphie. I was his fiancée. Why don't they read the will?*

People have a mistaken idea, gleaned from movies, that wills are supposed to be read out in a solicitor's office so that everyone knows what they might have inherited. The truth is that the executor doesn't have to let anyone know anything until they're ready to finalise it. Besides, Bianca wasn't Conrad's fiancée. He hadn't asked her to marry him.

I realise I'm still stuck between the two women in his life. I've been able to help Martha, but what can I possibly say to Bianca? I don't want to be the one to break the news that she probably hasn't been left anything, or that Oscar will be ordering her out of her house. I'm certainly not going to tell her that Martha wants the jewellery from Palmyra and has

214

asked me to get it. In any event, the jewellery has nothing to do with Conrad's estate. It was hers, not his.

In the end, I send a reply saying that I've no useful information to share, but that I'm sure Oscar will be in contact with her soon. I add that I'm in the process of leaving Cosecha.

My phone rings.

'You're leaving!' Bianca sounds as shocked as Martha.

I explain the circumstances.

'They're sharks,' she says. 'Conrad used to say there'd be a feeding frenzy if anything ever happened to him. Seems like he was right.'

Conrad never said that to me. Maybe he assumed I knew.

'I guess I have to look after my own interests,' says Bianca. 'I can't rely on you for help.'

'Sorry.'

'Oh, well, I'm sure you'll be fine. Conrad was always generous with you.'

Why does she think that? My salary? My loan – would he have told her about that? My directorship?

'Did he say anything to you about making me a director?' I ask.

'No.' She sounds surprised.

'It doesn't matter now, I suppose.'

'I'm sorry if things haven't worked out for you, Delphie,' she says. 'But at least you haven't lost the love of your life.' Her voice breaks.

Martha and Bianca were the women Conrad loved, but I was part of his life too. It's no wonder I've been all over the place this last while.

I tell Bianca that I'm sorry I can't help.

'Don't worry,' she says before she ends the call. 'I'll take care of myself. I'm good at that.'

I'm still thinking about Bianca and Martha when I look at the message from Ed.

I've ended up in town today. I was wondering if you'd like to meet up? Maybe have that dinner?

I wasn't expecting him to get in touch until later in the week. But I haven't eaten today and I'm feeling properly hungry for the first time in weeks. So I say yes, and suddenly I feel cheerful again.

As I walk into my own house, my mobile buzzes.

I drop my bag on the kitchen table and answer it.

'Hi,' says Luke Granahan. 'I've sent you an email from Justin at Cosecha. He's made an offer.'

'Already?' I grab my iPad and open it.

'Yes,' says Luke. 'You have a case, Delphie, and perhaps those incidents you spoke about have influenced him even without the audio you sent earlier, because . . . well, let's see what you think.'

I access the email. Justin is prepared to write off the outstanding balance of my company loan as well as make a reasonable severance payment to me if I leave the company immediately. It's an unbelievable turnaround. Instead of threatening me, he's practically bribing me to leave. If he'd made me this offer himself instead of suggesting I work in compliance, I might even have taken it there and then. So why didn't he? Was it simply to humiliate me? Hurt me? Dent my confidence? If so, I guess he succeeded. I've never felt less sure of myself than in the last couple of weeks. But did he also think I'd roll over at his 'restructuring' excuse? Didn't he realise I'd get advice? Get someone to work on my behalf? Did he think I was that much of a fool?

Knowing Justin, he probably did.

I read the offer again.

'Well?' asks Luke.

'It sounds . . . good.'

'I agree. It's more than I expected, if I'm honest. Are you going to accept?'

'What do you think?'

'It leaves you debt-free, with a lump sum and able to get on with your life,' says Luke. 'So it's definitely worth your serious consideration.'

'I'm not entirely debt-free, Luke.'

'Debt-free from Cosecha,' he amends. 'Your skills are in demand and I'm certain you'll get a new job, Delphie, so don't worry about your mortgage. I can go back and see what else I can squeeze out of him, but I'm not sure it's worth it.'

There's a part of me that feels I should try to negotiate some more, but Luke is right. This is an astonishingly good deal. Messing around won't make it substantially better. No matter how awful I feel about everything, it gives me time and space to think about my future and what I need to do next.

'OK,' I say.

'We'll accept?'

'Yes.' As I speak the word, I'm overcome with regret and sorrow. But I also feel a sense of relief at making a decision.

'I'll let him know,' says Luke. 'I'm sure I'll have the paper-work by later today.'

'Justin's away at the moment,' I say.

'We'll do it online,' Luke tells me. 'Don't worry.'

Conrad used to use a digital signature sometimes. But he always preferred doing it properly. On paper. With a Montblanc fountain pen.

I end the call with Luke and go to the fridge.

But I don't open the wine. I stick with a celebratory glass of water.

The time for drowning my sorrows is over.

I hope.

Chapter 17

I call Erin and tell her I've got an agreement.

'Great,' she says. 'You're better off out of it, Delphie.'

'I'm coming around to that way of thinking,' I admit. 'But it's hard.'

'If you fell down yesterday, stand up today.'

It's a quote from H. G. Wells and she has it on a little plaque on her desk. Erin likes the motivational stuff.

I call Sheedy too, but she's in court, so I send her a text, which she responds to with a thumbs-up emoji. Then I take out my laptop and open the same Cosecha portal that was on Conrad's desktop. I log in with the password Conrad used whenever he wanted to be incognito on the system. It still works, and I find the folder I'm looking for, insert a flash drive into the laptop, copy the folder and delete the original from the computer.

It's the one that contains information on Conrad's divorce and I've been anxious about it ever since I gave Martha access to his files. It's unlikely she'd find it, and of course it's password-protected, but after our session at Bandon, she might work it out. I really don't want her to access it. The multiple emails that went back and forward between Conrad and his solicitor would only hurt her. I suppose it's my own legal background that made me save it to a flash drive. But as soon as everything is cleared up, I'll trash that too.

I look at the folders again and open the one marked 'Caldwell', which contains all the documentation about the distressed mortgage deal Conrad was working on. I know I'm crossing a line here, but I have a proprietorial interest in this deal because it was a discussion with me that encouraged him not to allow people to lose their homes. I talked about how hard it was to buy a home and how important it was that anyone who did should be able to stay in it, and asked him to think about people as well as profit. And he did. If I'd stayed at Cosecha, I would've been involved, at least peripherally, in making sure the deal closed on good terms for the mortgage holders as well as the company. I'm a bit afraid that with Justin in charge, it won't. But so far, nothing seems to have changed, and I'm relieved.

I remind myself that this is nothing to do with me any more, and that the only reason I logged on was to delete the divorce folder. I shouldn't be looking at company files, but I check Conrad's emails anyway. They're all marked as read, so someone from Cosecha must have gone through them.

I close the computer. The clients aren't my worry. The emails aren't my worry. Nothing to do with Cosecha is my worry. None of it is part of my life any more.

I recall another quote that Erin uses a lot. This time it's from Eleanor Roosevelt. 'With the new day comes new strength and new thoughts.'

That's going to be me from now on.

*

I'm in the mood to celebrate when I meet Ed at Davy Byrne's pub in Duke Street. He's already waiting at an outside table, a pint in front of him. I order a Prosecco and fill him in on my severance package.

'That's definitely worth celebrating.' He beams at me. 'How're you feeling?'

'A lot better than this time yesterday,' I acknowledge. 'Now I need to start looking for a new job.'

'There's no rush,' he says as my Prosecco arrives. 'It's the summer. Take a break, have fun and enjoy your freedom. Cheers!' He raises his glass, and I laugh as we clink them together. I say that I'm not very good at breaks but agree he has a point, and he says I should go somewhere warm and tropical. I tell him about Martha's request that I go to Palmyra for her.

'And will you?'

'I feel obliged to,' I say. 'And anyway, it might be good for me to visit one last time. If for nothing else than some kind of closure.'

'It's not a holiday, though, is it?' he says. 'You're looking after her because she's your boss's ex. You should go somewhere decadent and exciting. What about Malaysia, given that you missed out before? Or Dubai? Carleen used to rave about the Spa at the Burj Al Arab.'

'Martha's not just my boss's ex,' I say. 'We're friends too. Not close friends, but friends all the same.' I take another sip of Prosecco as I think about his suggestion, then say that a decadent holiday sounds a bit pre-pandemic and I'm not quite ready for it yet. 'Anyhow,' I add, 'isn't the Burj horrifically expensive?'

'They might be doing deals now,' he says. 'I'm surprised you never went before.'

'It's odd,' I agree, 'because Conrad did some business there.'

'Did you enjoy your trips with him?'

'What wasn't to enjoy?'

'You were working.'

'I liked my job.'

'And him?'

'He was a good boss.'

'And as a person?' Ed's tone is casual, but I can hear the intent behind it.

'I never had that sort of relationship with Conrad,' I say.

'I didn't mean—'

'Yes you bloody did. Why are all men the same? Why can't you believe that a woman can spend time in your company without wanting to fall into bed with you? I had no interest in sleeping with Conrad. None whatsoever.'

'Look, Delphie—'

'It wasn't a quid pro quo,' I interrupt him. 'And I'm offended you'd think it might have been. I travelled and stayed in great places because I was his assistant, not his lover.' I drain my Prosecco and slam the glass onto the table. 'Thanks for this, but I think I'll head home.'

'I'm sorry,' says Ed. 'I really am. I'm an idiot.'

'No,' I say. 'You're like every man who thinks that all women should be bowled over by whatever the hell it is you can give us. You can't seem to believe that we can manage on our own. That we're happy on our own.'

'I can. Honestly. Don't go, Delphie. It's not my fault I'm a Neanderthal.' He looks at me with a pleading expression.

'Of course it's your fault.'

He hangs his head and then peeps up at me from behind his hair.

'Oh, stop it.' I can feel myself giving in.

'Seriously, Delphie, I said the wrong thing entirely. I know you're a hard worker and you deserve everything good in life. And I know you've done it on your own terms.'

'Huh.'

'Stay. Let me buy you dinner. Not because you can't afford to do it for yourself, but because I'd like to treat you.'

I look at him without speaking. He gives me another pleading look and I concede to myself that I might have overreacted.

'Oh, all right,' I say, and then smile. 'Only because I'm a poor out-of-work woman who doesn't know where her next meal is coming from and I need to take advantage of helpless men whenever I can.'

He laughs. So do I.

And when we've finished dinner, I let him pay the bill without making a fuss.

Afterwards, we go back to his apartment in Ballinteer with its panoramic views of the Dublin mountains. He lived with his parents when we were first dating, and I remember their large suburban house being stylish yet homely, but Ed's apartment, with its grey walls and lack of decoration, is a little impersonal. However, his presence is evident in the sweatshirts and jackets draped over chairs and the assortment of work-related gadgets on the same IKEA desk as I have in my own study. Beneath the desk is a plastic storage box filled with colourful Lego, along with a bright blue child's chair.

The balcony, where he leads me, is more restful, and welcoming in the warmth of the evening. I settle into a comfortable chair, enchanted by the strands of multicoloured solar lights on the side walls.

'Joe likes them,' he says as he hands me a glass of wine.

'So do I.'

The wine, in a large glass that he's filled almost to the brim, is probably one too many, but I'm not drunk, just slightly fuzzy. We don't talk as we listen to one of his playlists, and I feel my eyes close. The music is soft and soothing. And then so is the touch of Ed's hand on my cheek.

I open my eyes and give him a languid, lazy look.

'I'm too comfortable here,' I say.

'It's nice to have company. I don't often. Well, except for Joe. And he's into "The Wheels on the Bus" rather than Hozier and Billy Joel.'

I smile. And I know it's an encouraging smile, because I see the flicker in his eyes as he moves towards me. Then his lips are on mine. It's distantly familiar, but it doesn't evoke strong memories of the past. He was a good kisser back then, and he's better now. He said he's changed, and he has. He's gentler, more thoughtful, less rushed. I like the confidence of his touch as his hands slide gently along my sides then slowly ease my voile blouse over my head. I murmur about us being overlooked by the adjoining block of apartments, and he pulls me upright. For a second I think he's going to try and lift me, and I worry about him putting his back out, and what it will do to our moment of romance, but then he leads me indoors and into the bedroom. It's very male, with its plain walls and dark bed linen and lack of soft touches. But I don't need any other soft touches, because his fingers are soft enough and so are his lips and so is his bed.

224

Nothing else matters except the here and now and the pleasure of it all.

Ed said I should treat myself.

And I am.

I'm awake before him the next morning, and I slide out of the bed and make my way to the bathroom. It's as stark as the bedroom, with grey stone tiles on the walls and floor and harsh lighting over the mirror. I squirt some toothpaste onto my finger and rub my teeth before deciding that I won't use his shower. There's only one bath towel on the rack and it's already been used. I've had sex with my ex, but using his towel is, weirdly, a step too far for me. I splash water onto my face and pat it dry with the hand towel, which smells strongly of his Boss aftershave. Then I walk as quietly as possible into the bedroom and get dressed in the darkness provided by the heavy blackout curtains.

I'm almost ready to leave when Ed rolls over, then sits upright. I'd forgotten this about him, that he wakes instantly and needs no time to know where he is.

'Delphie?' he says. 'Where are you going?'

'I've got to get home,' I say.

'Why?'

'Things to do.'

'What sort of things?'

'I've a meeting with my solicitor.'

'Oh.'

He gets out of bed and opens the curtains. He's naked. He never sleeps in pyjamas or shorts and T-shirts. His body, in the early morning light, is slacker than it once was, but fit enough, that's for sure. He stands a bit taller as he notices me looking at him.

225

'Sure you wouldn't like to come back to bed first?' he asks.

'Nope. I need to get across town and change.'

'Why?' He winks at me. 'It's not like you're going into the office.'

'I'm going into my solicitor's office. I have to dress appropriately.'

'You look fine,' he says.

'Perhaps. But I'd feel better in a less flimsy top and skirt.'

'Spoilsport.'

'That's me.'

'Let me make you coffee.' He pulls on a T-shirt and a pair of joggers and follows me into the kitchen, where he puts a pod in the machine.

'Last night was fantastic,' he says as he's handing me the coffee.

'Yes.'

'We should do it again.'

I hadn't planned this when I first asked Ed to come to the wedding with me. I thought he'd just be a useful addition to my dwindling group of single male friends. But we've definitely moved on from that.

I tell him I'd love to do it again.

He puts his arms around me and kisses me.

I feel a lot more relaxed than this time yesterday.

Perhaps, instead taking another step forward, it's time to take one back.

Chapter 18

One of the advantages of spending the night with Ed (despite having to wear clothes that clearly identify me as a dirty stop-out among the morning commuters) is that when I meet Luke Granahan later that morning, my head's in an entirely different place to what I expected. I have, of course, had time to shower and change into a far more suitable skirt and jacket, although it does occur to me that my current lifestyle doesn't actually need skirts and jackets. But I feel properly dressed and properly professional as I sit in front of him and add my signature to the agreement that Justin has already signed from Luxembourg. I do it quickly and without thinking too much about it, although when I put the pen down on the desk afterwards, I'm conscious of feeling bereft. As though part of my life has been forcibly wrenched away.

'So,' Luke says. 'That's that. The termination money will be in your account by the weekend. I'm sure you'll get another job soon, Delphie. In the end, this will work to your advantage.'

'I hope so.'

'Shitty things happen to everyone at some point.' He's more relaxed now with the business out of the way. 'The trick is managing to turn them into opportunities. After all, great things never come from comfort zones.'

I don't mind Luke saying that my redundancy is an opportunity. From him, it sounds like it could possibly be true. And if I do get a job fairly soon, then I'm actually in a far better position financially than before, given the write-down of my company loan and the lump sum that will soon be sitting in my bank. As for my comfort zone, I often thought there was too much emphasis put on challenging yourself with something new. What's wrong with being confident where you are, being happy in your role? I was happy at Cosecha, but it definitely was a comfort zone and I allowed myself to become complacent. That will never happen again.

'Thanks for everything you've done,' I say. 'I really appreciate it.'

And then, to my complete mortification, tears well up in my eyes. Once again I'm in the position of being in his office and wanting to cry. But this time he doesn't reach for the box of tissues. He waits while I compose myself.

'I'm sure it's a great relief to you,' he says.

I nod.

'They treated you badly, Delphie. I can see that you're a capable woman. I think Justin is scared of you.'

'He's hardly any reason to be scared of me.' I clear my throat. 'He got rid of me, after all.'

'But at least he didn't do it on the cheap.' He grins. 'Looks like he didn't want to go head to head against you. I don't blame him.'

'I'm going to take that as a compliment.' I make a face at him.

'Sometimes throwing money at a problem is a good idea,'

says Luke. 'Let's be grateful he decided to do that. Or that his colleagues persuaded him to. And you, Delphie, take care of yourself. I'm sure you'll find something worthy of your talents.'

'Thank you for everything again.' I'm feeling better now I know I'm not going to cry.

'You're more than welcome. I hope everything goes smoothly for you from here on, but if you need any further help, don't hesitate to call me.'

He stands up, and although I'd like to wrap my arms around him and thank him for everything he's done for me, I don't. I behave like the professional woman I am, thank him politely, remind him to send me his bill, and say goodbye. Then I make my way to Erin's office.

'All done?' she asks when I tap at her door.

I nod, and this time there are hugs.

'Will we go out later and celebrate?' she asks.

I agree enthusiastically and text Sheedy, who's up for it too.

Celebrating being shoved out of my job.

Not something I ever thought I'd do.

City centre two nights in a row, I think, as I wait for the girls at a table outside the pub in Duke Street. Losing my job has turned me into a social butterfly! I'm rehydrating with water, but as soon as Erin arrives, she insists on champagne, and so we share a bottle before switching to gin and tonics. Still, at least now I'm drinking with friends to celebrate, not alone and miserable.

Like Ed, Sheedy thinks I should take some time out to get over everything. She reminds me that the death of someone close and changing jobs are two things that rate highly on the stress-o-meter, and that I need some time to look after myself. I ask her when she ever looks after herself, and she says she's not the one who's gone through a trauma. She adds that she tells all her divorce clients to be kind to themselves.

'I'm not a divorce client,' I remind her.

'Divorce is high on the stress-o-meter too, so it's basically the same. You need a break.' She takes out her phone and starts googling sun holidays. That's when I tell her and Erin about Martha's request for me to go to Mallorca.

'But that's great!' exclaims Sheedy. 'You can combine it with a few days at the beach.'

'My plan was to go over and back in a day if I can,' I say. 'That's what I usually do.'

'For crying out loud, Delphie.' Sheedy looks at me in disgust. 'You have free time. Why don't you use it?'

'Because . . .' There isn't a because. There isn't a reason. I wait a moment before continuing. 'Holidays are still . . . well . . . a bit . . . you know. Besides, I shouldn't splash my money on days away,' is what I eventually come up with.

'Delphie Mertens!' This time it's Erin who looks at me and shakes her head. 'A few days in Mallorca would be lovely, and it won't break the bank. Don't be ridiculous.'

'Tell you what.' Sheedy looks expectantly at both of us. 'Why don't we all go? We've never gone on holiday together before.'

We've always had other people in our lives to holiday with. We still do. The most we've ever done together is an overnight spa break.

'Port d'Andratx isn't very big,' I tell them.

'That's a good thing,' says Erin. 'Anyhow, there must be a few hotels nearby.'

'Well, yes, lots. But they're quite touristy.'

'We *are* tourists,' says Erin. 'Besides, it's a sun holiday. We'll be on the beach most of the time.'

'This looks nice.' Sheedy shoves her phone in front of my face. 'What d'you think?'

She's found a small hotel between Port d'Andratx and Santa Ponsa. It describes itself as 'boutique', but I've driven past it, and 'quirky' seems a better word.

Sheedy starts looking at dates and says there's some midweek availability. 'We'd have to share a family room,' she announces. 'But I'm sure we can manage.'

I can't remember the last time I shared a room with anyone who wasn't a boyfriend.

'It'd be a laugh,' she says. 'And we could stop you from being maudlin, Delphie.'

'I wouldn't be . . .' My voice trails off. Maybe, given the circumstances, I would.

'Will I book it?'

This is an alcohol-infused idea. But we all agree. And so, when I wake up the next morning, I realise that I'm going to Mallorca with the girls. I've completely jettisoned my comfort zone.

When I tell Ed about it, he says it's a great plan, and that he wishes he could come too. I point out that it's a girlie trip, and he nods and says that perhaps we could have a short break ourselves sometime. Then he reminds me to go all out and enjoy myself. It's a little irritating that everyone seems to think I don't know how to enjoy myself. I do. And I will.

Mum gets in on the act too, when I call around a few days later. I drop by in the middle of the day, something I've never done before. She's in the kitchen, baking.

'It's so lovely to see you, Delphie,' she says as she plants a floury kiss on my cheek. 'How are you doing?'

I phoned her to tell her that I'd sorted out my situation, and that although I'd decided to leave Cosecha, I'd got a great package so she didn't need to worry about me. She said that she never doubted for a second that I'd come out on top. She said I always do. Then, like everyone else, she told me that taking a bit of time out would be a good thing. Now I tell her that's exactly what I'm doing, as I explain about the trip to Mallorca.

'So . . . it's a holiday with your friends but you're also picking up stuff for Martha?'

'Yes.'

'Are you planning to take the rest of the summer off?' she asks.

'Not really,' I reply. 'A few days is enough for me. Then I'll be job hunting.'

I don't mention that I was up until two in the morning looking at LinkedIn, trying to find something to match my skills and experience. As yet, I haven't seen anything that's right for me, and despite my jazzed-up profile, nobody has approached me either. It's a little bit worrying.

'Josie, d'you know where my glasses are?' Dad walks into the room. 'Oh, hi, Delphie. How're things? Your mum tells me you've sorted the whole job situation.'

'My employment solicitor was great,' I tell him.

'It probably wouldn't have come to that if you'd had a union rep,' he says.

232

'Times have changed, Dad. I'm happy with how things have worked out.'

'Hopefully it's for the best,' he says, still looking around for his glasses.

'They're on the bookshelf,' Mum tells him as she fills pastry with apples she stewed earlier. As she points him to the right bookshelf, it strikes me that her skills are my skills. Multitasking. Looking out for someone. Making sure they're on the right track.

That's what I did for Conrad every single day.

It's a shock to suddenly realise that the skill set I possess is the same as my mum's.

It's more of a shock to think it might be most suited to being a wife.

Chapter 19

Ed offers to drive me to the airport for the Mallorca trip. When I tell him it makes no sense for him to come across town when a taxi will have me there in fifteen minutes, he explains that he has an early appointment at an industrial complex nearby, and that he's happy to pick me up at the crack of dawn. It's thoughtful of him, but I'd've preferred to be in control of my own timetable, and I'm anxiously checking my watch when he pulls up outside the house. I don't say anything about him being nearly ten minutes late. It really doesn't matter. But it does mean that Erin and Sheedy are waiting for me in the departures hall when I arrive.

'This is a brilliant idea,' Sheedy declares as we tuck into a full Irish breakfast before heading to the gate. (The only time I ever have a full Irish is when I'm on holiday.)

'Which? The food or going away?' asks Erin.

'Both,' says Sheedy. 'I can't believe how much I need this break.'

'Me too,' says Erin. 'Mind you, Fintan was a bit put out I didn't ask him about it.'

They haven't moved in together yet. Erin is still thinking it through.

'I was late because Ed wanted to drop me off and I was waiting for him,' I confess. 'It was mental really, but he insisted.'

'That's very sweet,' says Sheedy.

I glance at my friend. She looks strained. Maybe she's the one who needs a holiday the most. She works the hardest of all of us.

We finish our breakfast and head to the gate, where boarding has already started. As we take our seats, I remember my last trip to Mallorca: the loved-up couple on the way out, meeting Ed on the way back. I never imagined, on that return trip, that I wouldn't see Conrad again. And now I'm going back on a quest for his widow. I'll walk into his house, a house he left not realising he wasn't going to come home. I'll see the things he left behind. I'll remember him sitting behind his desk, telling me he wanted me to be a director, not knowing what the future had in store.

A knot of sorrow and anxiety tightens in my stomach.

But the girls, on either side of me, either don't notice my sudden mood swing or else have decided to ignore it, because they start talking about all the things they want to do while we're away.

'It's only a short break,' I remind them. 'It's not a big deal.'

'Yes it is,' Erin protests. 'I haven't been out of Ireland in eighteen months. I'm really looking forward to this.'

'Girls on tour.' I grin. 'Let's be having us.'

Because I'm familiar with Palma airport, I'm the one who's hired the car. Even though I've never actually driven on Mallorca before, I know the roads and I'm confident about where we're going. But as we travel along the coastal route, I can't help thinking again of the last time I was here and how hopeful I was about my future when I left. Once again I'm trying to hold back the tears. Once again I succeed.

I'm going to be fine.

The quirky hotel is called La Perla, and is painted a deep pink with vivid green shutters over the windows. The reception area is tiled with white marble and dotted with indoor palms.

As soon as we're checked in, we head to our room, which is on the third floor. It's spacious, with an additional lounge area that has a couple of armchairs and a sofa bed. This leads to a large outdoor terrace that overlooks the backs of the nearby buildings. There's also a small bathroom with a large shower. It's not the five-star luxury I've grown accustomed to, but it's clean and bright, and when Erin opens the shutters at the windows, we're treated to a breathtaking view towards the sea.

'I feel like I've stepped back in time,' she says as she turns to us. 'I went to Cuba during my gap year and stayed in a place exactly like this.'

'It's very gap year all right.' Sheedy grins. 'But I love it.'

'Me too.' I lug my bag to the lounge area. 'I'll take the sofa bed.'

'Not at all,' says Sheedy. 'I will.'

'No, I will,' says Erin.

We exchange knowing looks. None of us really wants the sofa bed.

'There's no point in you taking it,' Sheedy says to me. 'Your feet will hang over the end.'

'I always sleep kind of sideways in a bed,' I tell her. 'So it's nothing new for me.'

Erin has a closer look. 'It's more of a kid's bed, Delphie.'

'And none of us are kids,' I say.

'I'm the shortest,' says Sheedy. 'I'll take it. No arguing.'

We concede that Sheedy is probably best suited to the sofa bed, then hang our clothes in the single wardrobe before trooping downstairs and ordering drinks in the hotel bar. We can either take them to the tables at the front of the hotel, or to a small paved garden to the back. We elect to sit at the front to watch the world go by. Not that there's a lot going on – the hotel is sandwiched between a shop selling a variety of beach paraphernalia and a small hairdresser's. Further along the road is another bar, then a bank, then a restaurant that calls itself an *arrocería*, which I know means it specialises in paella – as evidenced by the big paella dish hanging outside.

We're all drinking water, it being meltingly hot right now, and Erin suggests that perhaps we should go to the beach.

'I thought there was a pool.' Sheedy frowns. 'I'm sure I saw a picture of one when we were booking.'

'The beach will be more fun,' says Erin.

Sheedy confesses that she's not really a beach person, and we express our horror that she's agreed to come on what is essentially a beach holiday when she doesn't like the sea and the sand.

'I do,' she protests. 'I don't like crowds, that's all.'

'I'm sure it's properly spaced out,' says Erin.

'It's not that,' says Sheedy. 'My image of me on a beach is always something romantic and dreamy. It's not lying in a row waiting to be toasted or dodging kids with their buckets and spades.'

'Sheedy has a point,' I say. 'We don't have to go to a big beach. There are some gorgeous little coves where you could pretend you were alone in the world.'

'I didn't say alone in the world,' protests Sheedy. 'I said dreamy and romantic.'

'And alone until Prince Charming strides topless across the beach wearing . . . what? Shorts? Jeans? Nothing at all?' Erin winks at her.

'I'm sort of seeing the long hair, white trousers and barefoot look,' says Sheedy.

Erin nods. 'Fintan would be like that. Only black trousers probably. You know what he's like.'

We do. Fintan is more rock-and-roll than dreamy and romantic.

We finish our drinks, then decide to see if La Perla has a pool. The young girl behind reception assures us that it does. It's on the roof. We take the rickety lift to the top floor, and there it is, although it's more of a plunge pool than a swimming pool, with half a dozen loungers shaded by navy umbrellas ranged along one side.

There's nobody else around.

'This works for me,' says Sheedy. 'Given that we were up so early this morning, I think an hour or so here would suit me very well.'

We all agree that some lying out by the pool is an essential part of our girlie holiday. So we get changed into our swimsuits, lash on the sunscreen and fall asleep.

We've decided to leave my trip to Palmyra until the end of our stay – mainly because I don't want to have the responsibility of Conrad's watches and Martha's jewellery for longer than necessary. And so, even though I feel a constant low-level anxiety about what I have to do, I push it to the back of my mind and try to take advantage of our days in the sun.

And I absolutely do take advantage of them. In fact I'm enjoying myself so much I don't know why we've never gone away together before. Despite minor differences about the beach versus the pool during the day, and paella versus pasta at night, we get on really well. We take a trip to Palma to wander around the streets of the old town and see the cathedral (though afterwards we all admit that when you've seen one cathedral, you've pretty much seen them all). We find a glitzy marina bar where we sip cocktails and watch the sun set in a palette of rose gold light. We make a day trip to the inland town of Sóller, and take the vintage tram through the lemon and orange groves to the picturesque coastal village with its mountainous backdrop overlooking an aquamarine bay. We decide that if we ever return to Mallorca, we'll actually stay here, because it's so pretty and tranquil. Then we change tack completely and go to an outdoor club, where the music is loud and all-enveloping and where we dance until we're ready to drop.

The club isn't my usual thing at all – at least not for years – but it brings me back to my student days and it doesn't bother me that most of the people there are a lot younger than me. The men don't seem to care that Erin, Sheedy and I are older than the rest of the clubbers, or that we're not up for heading off into the night with them. It takes a while to realise that they don't want us to head off for the entire night; that they're happy for some quick action without even exchanging names. Casual sex has always been out of my personal comfort zone and not something I'm sure is safe to do anyhow; yet an hour after arriving, I find myself in the arms of an absolute body-builder of a man whose name (I think) is Thor, and all I can think about is what it might be like with him. He's on holiday from Finland. Or Iceland.

I haven't had that much to drink, so it's not the alcohol fuelling me, but when he leads me into one of the side streets, where it's dark and hot and the sounds of the club are nothing more than a background beat, I'm ready for whatever might happen. Thor has clearly done this before and hustles me into an almost hidden laneway between two houses, where he assures me he's fit, healthy and has full protection, which, though it could be a passion killer, is actually reassuring. His hands are all over me and mine are all over him, and as I feel him pushing up my floaty skirt, I don't care that the stones of the wall I'm leaning against are digging into my back, because I'm hot and sweaty and I want this more than anything.

When we've finished, I'm still hot and sweaty. And exhilarated.

'We wait a minute and we do it again?' asks Thor.

'Yes,' I reply.

And we do.

Erin and Sheedy are dancing together when I get back to the club, and Erin pulls me by the arm and asks if I'm OK. I nod enthusiastically and she raises an eyebrow, and I shrug and give her a self-satisfied smile, and I realise that I've blasted right through my comfort zone tonight.

Not that I'll be boasting about it.

'So what was everybody's highlight?' asks Sheedy on the second-to-last night when we're at dinner together. 'The cathedral? Sóller? The antiques market?'

240

Erin laughs. 'The clubbing,' she says. 'At least as far as Delphie's concerned.'

'I never thought you had it in you,' says Sheedy.

'Well, I did,' I say primly. 'Twice.'

They guffaw.

'OK, not something I'd normally do, but God, ladies, it was . . . amazing.'

'I'm envious,' says Sheedy. 'It should've been me. You two are at least getting it on a regular basis.'

'I'm not . . .' I falter. I suppose I might be getting it on a regular basis with Ed in the future. Though maybe not any more if he hears about Thor.

'What happens on tour stays on tour,' Erin insists as I voice my concern. 'And you needed to do something mad, Delphie. You're always so . . . so proper.'

Am I? I thought that with my succession of boyfriends, I was actually a bit out there.

'You have proper relationships,' Sheedy tells me when I say this. 'They all end, but they're real at the time.'

'One of the great things about this holiday has been that it's just us,' muses Erin when I acknowledge that relationships are all very well but sometimes you have to do something for yourself. 'That's the difference between coming away with the girls and coming away with a boyfriend. We don't have to second-guess each other.'

She's right. Whenever I've gone on holiday with a man, I've always tried to figure out what it was he wanted to do and fall in with that. Not because I'm a doormat, but because if I choose something he's not happy about, I don't enjoy it myself. Which *is* a bit doormatty now that I come to think about it. I've never stopped to think that my needs could be equally important as his. So am I a doormat after all? Or is it simply because all women are conditioned to think that if the man is happy, they should be happy too?

'It's certainly been fun,' I agree. 'Not just the sex, ladies. The fact that even with Martha's thing at the back of my mind, I've managed to relax more than on any other holiday.'

'Maybe it's because on your other holidays you were thinking about work,' observes Erin.

'You might be right,' I concede. 'But you and Sheedy are thinking about work and you've had a good time too, haven't you?'

'I deliberately muted all my notifications,' says Erin. 'It's the best thing I ever did.'

'Me too,' Sheedy agrees. 'During the day, anyhow. I've got to be honest and admit I check them all before I go to bed.'

We've all spent time on our phones checking things before going to bed. In my case it's mostly been Twitter for the news rather than anything else. I've had messages from Ed too, one every morning and one at night, the first telling me to have a good day, the second hoping I have. I've usually responded by sending him a photo. Not of me, but of the beautiful scenery, to which he's invariably responded with a cheery emoji. I like getting his texts. It's nice to think that he's looking out for me.

I was afraid I might feel guilty about the meaningless sex with Thor, but I don't. It was a necessary moment of madness and I've put it behind me. Besides, Ed and I aren't an actual couple. OK, we might be moving in that direction, but we're not there yet. Sleeping together could simply have been a pleasant way to end an evening, just as having sex with Thor was a crazy interlude in a mad night out. So there's no residual guilt, just a sense of satisfaction whenever I think about it.

'I'm thinking that I definitely will move in with Fintan,' Erin announces when we take our after-dinner drinks to the garden at the back of the hotel.

Sheedy grins. 'Has this girls' holiday persuaded you?'

'I do love him,' Erin says. 'He's good for me. He makes me not take myself too seriously.'

'Did you talk to him about children?' I ask.

'Only peripherally. I haven't made up my mind about that yet. I'm not sure if my potential desire to have a baby is some kind of panic reaction because time is running out. I don't know if I really want a child or if it's that I hate the option being taken away from me.' She grimaces. 'Bloody biological clock. I don't feel a hundred per cent ready for a baby, yet my body is telling me that I was ready twenty years ago!'

'Having it all,' says Sheedy. 'The impossible dream.'

'I'm afraid that if I had a baby I'd turn into my sister and be an all-consuming mother,' confesses Erin. 'You know me, no half measures.'

Sheedy nods. 'You'd be the kind of mother who has targets and charts stuck to the fridge. Every day would be accounted for.'

'That's my worry,' admits Erin. 'I'd look at the poor kid as a kind of project management task.'

'You wouldn't,' I assure her. 'You'd be a great mother.'

'People always say that to women,' says Erin. 'As though we're genetically cut out for looking after babies and children even when we're not. Not all mothers are good mothers. And the problem,' she adds, cutting off Sheedy, who's about to speak, 'is that you don't know if you'll be any good or if you'll like it until it's too late. You can bail out of a job. You can't bail out of being a mum. It's the ultimate job for life.'

I think of how my mum constantly worries about all of us and I nod in agreement. Sheedy nods too, and Erin asks us if we ever want to settle down.

Settle down. Mum's favourite phrase. It's odd coming from Erin's mouth.

'I don't have time,' Sheedy tells her.

'Do you ever feel you're missing out?' asks Erin.

'I would if I wanted to be married with kids,' agrees Sheedy. 'But I don't.'

I mention how all my male friends have coupled up in the last few years. How difficult it was for me to find a plus-one for André's wedding. How lucky it was that I bumped into Ed.

'The lovely Ed,' says Erin. 'Divorced, of course. Not that I can talk – at least I got it over and done with before I hit thirty! But the most likely scenario for all the men we're going to meet now is that they're divorced with previous families and God only knows what baggage lurking in the background.'

'Sheedy handled Ed's divorce,' I tell her.

'Really?' Erin looks surprised. 'I suppose there's a limited number of hot-shot divorce lawyers out there. Ed, as I recall, was a man who always wanted the best.'

'True,' I say. 'And he got that with Sheedy. He praised her to the skies.'

'Rightly so,' says Erin. 'And now that she's made him footloose and fancy-free, he's come back to you.'

'Making me second-best?'

'Oh, God, no!' exclaims Erin. 'I didn't mean . . .'

244

'It's fine.' I grin. 'He wasn't the best for me back then. I've no idea if he's the best for me now.'

'I have to say something.' Sheedy, who's been silent during our exchange, sounds a little uncomfortable.

We look at her expectantly.

'I should've told you sooner, Delphie, but I didn't quite know how to put it.'

'What?' And when she hesitates, I repeat it a little more forcefully.

'I slept with Ed.'

My third 'What?' is a controlled shriek.

'I slept with him. After his divorce. We went out a few times and I . . .'

I stare at her.

So does Erin.

Sheedy stares back.

'Bloody hell, Sheedy,' I say. 'You could've mentioned it sooner.' Before I slept with him again myself, I think, but I don't say that out loud.

'It wasn't until I met him at your house that I realised who he was,' she says.

'You should've said so then.'

'I didn't know how,' she says. 'He was sitting there in your living room, after all. It was awkward.'

'He didn't tell me either.' I drum my fingers on the tabletop. 'Was it a conspiracy of silence between you?'

'No,' says Sheedy. 'I thought he might say something. But then I realised he hadn't. And I didn't want to . . . I'm sorry, Delphie.'

I rub the bridge of my nose. My annoyance with Sheedy (though it's more than annoyance, if not quite as strong as anger) has dissipated a little. It's not like she slept with him when I was going out with him. It's just that she kept quiet about it.

'It was a shock,' says Sheedy when I say this to her. 'I was so surprised to see him that I couldn't say a word.'

'Oh, well.' I can't blame my friend for sleeping with a man I've slept with myself when she didn't know he was an ex, or that I might sleep with him in the future. Ed should've said something before he got into bed with me. But he didn't.

He's the one to blame for that.

Chapter 20

The following day I text Martha and tell her that I plan to go to Palmyra to get her stuff. She responds by asking me to let her know when I arrive at the house so that she can open the door for me. I hope the app works. I've never seen it in use, and I'll feel a bit daft if I end up standing on the step unable to get inside.

Erin, Sheedy and I talk about the visit at breakfast, which is served in a bright room that overlooks the garden.

'Do you want us to come with you?' asks Erin as she loads a dollop of Seville marmalade onto a slice of toast.

'I assumed you would.' I look at her in surprise.

'We thought you might prefer to do it alone,' she says.

I shake my head. 'I'd rather have company,' I say. 'I'm not sure how I'll feel.'

'Whatever you want,' Sheedy says.

'Thank you.' I give them both a grateful smile. 'Thanks for everything, girls. For supporting me. For coming with me. For being around.'

'All for one, remember?' says Sheedy.

I smile at her.

'Will we head over after breakfast?' asks Erin.

'Sure.' I hesitate slightly.

'What?' Sheedy looks at me.

'Before we go to the house, I'd like to go to the scene of the accident,' I say.

'Oh, Delphie! Are you sure? Isn't that a bit morbid?' asks Erin.

'Maybe,' I concede. 'But there's something in me that needs to see where it happened. I'd like to be able to tell Martha I went too.'

'Martha isn't really your concern,' says Sheedy.

'She kind of is,' I counter. 'I'm already getting her stuff. I'd like to be able to say that I . . . well, that I paid my respects at the scene.'

'If you must.' Erin looks concerned.

'It's a closure thing,' I tell her. 'There's a part of me that thinks he's not really gone. That it's some sort of cosmic joke. That he'll turn up and fix everything. Give me my job back. Make me a director. Be there for me again. Until I see where it happened, I can't stop myself thinking that way.' I rub the back of my neck, where tension I haven't felt all week is suddenly building up. 'I used to think it was really weird of people to want to go to the place where a loved one died, but now I understand it.'

'A loved one?' Erin gives me a quizzical look.

'I didn't love him,' I assure her. 'Of course not. But he was an important person in my life and I . . . I cared about him.'

'OK.' She folds her napkin and drops it on the table. 'Let's go.'

'You haven't finished your coffee yet.'

She drains the cup and grins at me.

'Now I have.'

We get up from the table and leave.

I'm wearing a long-sleeved tunic top over my shorts because even though it's not yet 10.30, the sun is high in the cloudless blue sky and I want to protect the arms that I managed to burn by falling asleep at the pool the other evening. The heat of the morning is tempered by the breeze coming from the sea, but the car's air con is having to work hard. The atmosphere is tense as I negotiate the narrow, twisting road. I take the fork towards Johannes's house, and after a hundred metres, I see where the low barrier has been damaged. This must be where it happened. I stop the car and turn off the engine.

It's quiet up here in the hills and the view to the dark blue sea is spectacular. I get out of the car and walk to the edge of the road. Erin and Sheedy follow me.

'Be careful.' Erin's voice is shaky. 'This is definitely dangerous.'

I walk a little closer to the edge. I can see the fall from the road to the water below. It's not sheer. There are outcrops of rocks from the cliff face. It's very likely that Conrad hit one of them on his way down. I can hear it now, the thud of his body as he impacted off the cliff. Horrible though it is to think it, I hope the first hit killed him. I hope he didn't really know what happened. I hope he didn't suffer.

I feel myself sway before Sheedy and Erin grab me by the arms.

'Sit down,' commands Sheedy.

But I don't. I stagger to the other side of the road and, in the shelter of the cliff, throw up this morning's breakfast.

Erin goes to the car and brings me a bottle of water. I take a sip.

'Sorry,' I say.

'Don't be. You must be devastated.'

'I never thought it would be so . . . so . . . brutal.'

They don't say anything. After a few minutes, we get back into the car. I take a deep breath and rest my hands on the steering wheel.

'Are you sure you're OK to drive?' asks Sheedy.

'Yes.' I'm feeling better, though certainly not a hundred per cent. I'm worrying about how I'm going to turn the car on this road. Before the accident I probably would've done a three-point turn without a thought. But now the only thing I can think about is taking us all over the edge. I decide to go the long way round, not caring that it'll add twenty minutes to what should be a five-minute journey. I say this to Erin and Sheedy and they're both fine with it. So we climb higher to even more breathtaking views before turning onto a narrower road that brings us downhill again, this time inland, which is better for all our nerves.

I've stopped shaking by the time we pull up at Palmyra.

'Is this it?' asks Erin when I park outside.

'Yes. I don't have a fob for the electric gate,' I tell her. 'But there's a pedestrian entrance.'

It's deserted in the hills. That's why Conrad loved it. The only people who come are people who need to be here. We get out of the car and I enter the code to the pedestrian gate. It's an old-fashioned keypad, not linked to the codes for the house, so Martha won't have changed it.

The gate swings open and we walk inside.

As soon as I pass through, I'm overcome by memories so

strong that my entire body starts to tremble. I can almost see Conrad at the front door beckoning me into the house. I can see Martha – no, now it's Bianca – lying by the pool. I am in the past and the present and it's overwhelming.

'OK?' asks Sheedy, even as Erin exclaims over the contemporary garden design and the starkly modern architecture of the house.

I nod.

'This is like something out of *Grand Designs*,' says Erin.

My body has stopped trembling. I feel strangely calm again. As though everything is as it should be. As though Conrad is here. I take out my phone and text Martha.

A minute or so later, I hear the front door unlock. I turn the handle and push it open. The house alarm is silent. Martha has already switched it off from the app.

'Wow,' says Sheedy as we step inside. 'It's stunning.'

I can't help feeling a little proprietorial as I lead them across the marble tiles of the open-plan salon and slide open the huge patio doors. This time it's Erin who exclaims as we step outside. Obviously someone is looking after both the garden and the pool, because there are no stray oleander blossoms blowing around, and the water is crystal clear. The stylish sunloungers are still in place beneath the canvas pergola, although the thick cushions have been put away.

'I could live like this,' murmurs Erin as she steps into the shade. 'I really could. Gosh, Delphie, it's no wonder you stayed working for him when he got you to drop over to places like this on a regular basis.'

I can see them again – Conrad and Bianca, Conrad and Martha. Conrad and the children. Laughing and joking. Living

251

the good life, without a care in the world. I visualise Conrad as I last saw him, climbing out of the pool, his body fitter than it had any right to be thanks to Bianca's almost carb-free regime. I wonder how he felt about that. Had looking good become as important to him as it was to her?

'Do you feel better for coming?' asks Sheedy.

It takes me a few moments to nod.

'I should've brought what's left of the water in from the car.' Erin wipes beads of perspiration from her brow. 'It's really hot today.'

'There's an outside fridge,' I say. 'If it's plugged in, there'll be water in it.' I walk past the pool to what Martha called the summer kitchen. It was part of the original house that had been here before the pop star had demolished it to build his own, but he'd kept the kitchen, and Martha loved it. It's a small covered area containing a cooker, sink, granite worktop and fridge. The fridge is plugged in and switched on. And it contains bottles of water, as well as half a dozen beers and a bottle of Freixenet cava.

We glug back water and the girls continue to exclaim about the gorgeousness of Palmyra while I bask in the reflected glory of having relaxed by the pool with Martha in the shade of the gazebo.

Thinking of Martha reminds me of why I'm here, so I leave Erin and Sheedy leaning over the glass balustrade admiring the view while I go in search of Conrad's laptop and the other things she wanted.

I look into the office first and see the laptop on the desk. Once again the memories flood back. Of sitting opposite him. Of feeling excited and valued, like someone who mattered. I can see him smiling at me, happy for me as he told me about the directorship. I clench my jaw and turn away. I'll take the laptop after I find Martha's jewellery.

She thought she'd left it in a safe that's set into the floor of her walk-in wardrobe, but as I walk up the marble stairs, I wonder if Bianca or Conrad might have moved her stuff somewhere else so that they could use the safe themselves. It's beyond weird walking into the master bedroom, a striking room decorated in shades of white and silver. I'm betting Bianca gave it a makeover when she moved in. Martha preferred things more vibrant.

The door to the wardrobe is opaque glass. I push it open and am met by rails of summer dresses and skirts, colour-coordinated exactly as I'd do if I had a massive wardrobe myself. Clearly Bianca and I are more alike than I imagined. One wall is taken up by shelves of shoes and sandals, and drawers that, on investigation, contain T-shirts and tops. I wonder if she has any plans to have them collected, or to collect them herself, though she'd have to arrange that with one of the solicitors.

When I turn around, I see more rails, this time containing men's trousers and shirts. It's heart-stopping to know that these belonged to Conrad. I notice the pale blue shirt he was wearing the day I was here. I can't help touching it.

I lean against the shelves and try not to imagine his body at the bottom of the rocky cliff.

It takes me a moment to steady myself again, but then I look for the safe, which Martha said was beneath the shelves in the back corner of the wardrobe. When I see it, I kneel down and key in the code she gave me. The lock clicks open and I lift the door.

The safe is empty apart from a single item I immediately

recognise. It's Lady Annabel's bracelet. The one Conrad bought for Bianca. The one I brought here. I take it out and hold it up to the ceiling lights. The gleam of the emeralds beneath the lights is seductive. I slide it onto my wrist, remembering again the day I bid for it, remembering that Conrad was a little miffed that it wasn't bigger. It's the nicest gift he ever bought for anyone. Even Martha.

Why did Bianca leave it behind?

I peer into the safe again, as though I can miraculously magic up the watches and jewellery that Martha wanted me to get for her. I even check it with the torch on my iPhone in case I'm missing something. But I'm not. Then the phone rings, and it's Martha, asking me if I've found everything yet, and I have to say that I'm still looking but that there was nothing in the bedroom safe.

'Maybe she moved it all,' says Martha.

'Or perhaps Conrad did,' I suggest. 'Don't worry, Martha. I'll find it for you.'

I close the safe and walk out of the wardrobe. I check the drawers in the dresser, but there's nothing. Nor is there anything in the two bedside units.

If Conrad moved his watches, he must have moved the jewellery too. And in that case, they must be somewhere in his office. I leave the bedroom and make my way downstairs again.

Sheedy and Erin are deep in conversation as they lean over the balustrade looking towards the sea. They don't even notice me.

When I re-enter Conrad's office, I put the laptop (along with the very expensive Montblanc pen that's lying beside it) in the large canvas bag I brought with me, I add the framed photograph of Killian and Connie that's also on the desk, then turn around to look at the walls. There's a painting of Bantry Bay opposite his desk. The bruised purples and moss greens of the Irish winter scene have always looked slightly out of place in the bright Mediterranean light, and when I once remarked on it, Conrad told me that there was a safe hidden behind the painting.

'Not very original,' he laughed. 'But it reminds me of home. And it's kind of cool to have something you see in the movies in your house, isn't it?'

I grinned at him and called him a big child. He agreed that he was, then told me to join Martha by the pool.

I walk over to the painting, and as I lift my arm to swing it to one side, I realise I'm still wearing Bianca's bracelet. I'll replace it when I've finished here. But in the meantime, there's something comforting about the feel of it against my skin, reminding me of better times.

Behind the painting, I study the office safe. It's bigger than the one in the bedroom, but, like that one, it's electronic and needs a code. I don't know what it is. Martha didn't give it to me. I don't know if she's even aware of the safe's existence. I text her to ask and she rings me back.

'I forgot about that one,' she says. 'I don't know the code to it either. Besides, he probably changed it after we split. You know what he was like about security.'

'He was strict about digital security, but I doubt he'd have changed this, particularly if you didn't even know it existed. Could you take pictures of the photos in the album and send them to me?'

'What album?' And then she remembers the folder I took from Conrad's office. 'Oh, yes. Of course. One of them might be the clue. Give me a few minutes, Delphie.'

A short time later my phone buzzes with the photographs.

I scroll through them and stop at one that was taken at Bantry Bay four years ago. It's the only one with nobody in it at all. I glance from it to the painting that covers the safe and back again. Even though the photo is summery and bright and the painting darker and more atmospheric, they're definitely of the same place. It's worth a try.

I enter the date below it onto the keypad, add Bantry and a percentage sign, then press unlock. There's a smooth whirring sound and the door glides open. I applaud myself for my powers of deduction, then exhale sharply as I see the contents of the safe.

There are three of the vintage watches Martha wanted – a Rolex, a Tag Heuer and a Patek Philippe. There's also a Tiffany box containing a gold tie pin, and a red box with a wedding ring inside. Conrad's wedding ring, engraved with the date of his marriage to Martha. Finally I remove a velvet pouch that contains a silver locket, a rose gold friendship bracelet, a Swarovski lady's watch and a slim silver ring set with three red stones.

I recognise all of them. Martha used to wear them a lot in Mallorca. She always said that if she lost any of the jewellery on the beach, it wouldn't be the end of the world because it was cheap and cheerful, although Martha's idea of cheap isn't generally the same as mine. But these are the pieces she wanted me to bring back to her.

I put the watches and the jewellery in my bag and then allow myself to look at the other item in the safe.

It's an enormous bundle of cash in fifty- and one-hundred-euro notes. At a quick glance I estimate about twenty or thirty thousand euro, but it could be even more.

I've never seen so much cash in one place before. It doesn't seem real.

Conrad always liked to have access to cash as well as his many cards. But this much? I suppose, though, that to someone like him, twenty thousand would be loose change.

I pick up one of the wads and flick through it. A thousand euro. I was off in my original estimate. There's about fifty grand here and I doubt very much that anyone else knows about it. Martha would surely have mentioned before I came if she'd been aware of it. And Bianca – well, I can't see Bianca leaving fifty grand behind. Although she left the bracelet, didn't she?

I stare at the money and my mind goes into overdrive.

Conrad's death changed everything for everybody. For Bianca. For Martha. For his children. For me.

Bianca lost the man she loved and the lifestyle she thought she deserved.

Martha lost her husband of over twenty years – the husband she thought would come back to her.

Killian and Connie lost their beloved dad.

And I lost my boss and my job. I lost my chance to be a director of the company too.

Money and things can't replace a person, but Bianca will still have everything Conrad bought her. Martha and her children have their homes and their inheritance. I have nothing.

Fifty grand would compensate me for all that I lost. For the grief that Justin put me through. I deserve it.

Don't I?

I look at the wad in my hand. It would be tricky to get all the money into my bag. But I could try. Who would know, after all? Who would even care?

Bon pour toi alors. I hear my grandmother's words again. Good for you. Take your chances.

I imagine what I could do with fifty grand.

Quite a lot.

But I'm not a thief.

I'm not a woman who has casual sex in the street either, am I?

Yet I did.

I turn the money over and over in my hand. Then I think of the deal Luke Granahan got for me. The one where Cosecha wrote off my loan. The deal I was so happy with. I've already been compensated for all I lost. And this money isn't mine.

I shove it back into the safe and lock it.

Then I replace the picture and rejoin my friends.

'We thought you'd got lost,' says Erin. 'I guess you could, in that house.'

'It's really not that big.' I push my hair out of my eyes.

'Delphie!' exclaims Erin.

'What?'

'Did Martha ask you to get that too?' She points to Bianca's bracelet on my wrist.

'Oh, crap!' I exclaim. 'Bianca left it in the upstairs safe. I couldn't help trying it on, then I got distracted. I'll put it back now.'

'Can I try it on before you do?' asks Sheedy. 'It's absolutely stunning.'

I nod, and she fastens it around her own wrist and admires it before passing it to Erin.

'Did you find Martha's stuff?' Erin asks as she hands the bracelet back to me and I put it on my arm again.

'Most of it,' I reply. 'Though three of the watches are missing. Maybe Conrad brought them back to Dublin. I'm surprised he didn't return Martha's things to her, though. None of them comes even close to the value of the bracelet. He hardly kept them as some kind of negotiating tactic. That'd be silly.'

'It never ceases to amaze me how bloody silly men are,' says Sheedy. 'They always get hung up over the stupidest things. And they're always surprised that their wives want a divorce. They can't believe they'd want to leave them. Can't accept it.'

'Even if they've been having affairs with women half their age?' I ask.

'Especially if they've been having affairs.' Sheedy grins. 'They say what Martha thought. That it was a fling. That it didn't mean anything. That they love their wives.'

'Was Martha prepared to take him back?' asks Erin in surprise.

'Isn't that what you said, Delphie?' Sheedy looks at me and I nod.

'I wouldn't,' says Erin. 'Cheat on me and it's over. I can't understand how any woman could forgive and forget.'

'Money talks,' says Sheedy. 'And there's a lot of money at stake here.'

I think again of the fifty thousand in the safe. I don't mention it, or my moment of weakness, to my friends.

'Does Bianca know her bracelet is here?' asks Erin.

'She must, surely,' I reply.

'I'm surprised she hasn't been back herself before now in that case,' says Sheedy. 'How does she feel about her situation now, d'you think?'

'A bit vengeful, I reckon,' I say. 'She believes she's entitled to something, but the trouble is, Conrad didn't change his will, so everything goes to Martha and the kids.'

Sheedy nods. 'It's always messy where there's money involved.'

'And even when there isn't,' remarks Erin.

Both of them are speaking from experience. Death and money always create work for the legal profession.

'I'll put the bracelet back in the safe and then we'll go,' I say.

'Let's take a selfie of ourselves first,' says Erin. 'It's such a stunning place.'

'I used to take a photo every time I came,' I confess. There's a selection on my phone from over the years. It's an unchanging vista, a stark reminder that people come and go but the earth still turns and the sun rises every morning no matter what.

The thought comforts me rather than making me despair.

Things change, but they stay the same too.

And then I hear the voice.

I don't believe it.

'Shit.' My phone slides out of my hand and cracks onto the ground.

'What the hell are you doing here?' asks Bianca as she steps out of the house.

Chapter 21

She's wearing cut-off jeans and a white T-shirt, her blonde hair tied back and her sunglasses pushed onto her head. Following behind her is a younger man who looks vaguely familiar. He's also blonde, his Ray-Bans hiding his eyes. My look flickers between the two of them.

'What are you doing here?' she repeats as the three of us stare at her.

'What are *you* doing here?' As I bend down to retrieve the phone, I remember I'm wearing her bracelet. My heart skips multiple beats as I pick it up with my other hand. The screen is now a network of spiderweb cracks.

'Is *she* here too?' Bianca almost spits out the words.

'No,' I say. I glance at the man and then back to Bianca, an unspoken question in my eyes.

'My brother,' Bianca says before he can speak. 'Josh.'

I remember him now, from the funeral. He was in a suit then.

'Hi,' says Josh.

We murmur hellos.

'Is anyone going to tell me what you're doing in my home?' demands Bianca.

'Martha asked me to collect a few things of hers that were here.'

'She had no right,' says Bianca. 'Everything here belongs to me.'

'I'm really sorry,' I tell her. 'You know I am. But the thing is, it's Martha's house. Everything is Martha's. She's his widow and he left it all to her.'

'Bitch.'

I don't know if Bianca is talking about me or Martha.

'How did you get in?' I ask suddenly. 'She changed the door code.'

'I have a key,' says Bianca.

'Oh.' I want to laugh. It doesn't matter how clever the security is, or how many codes you have, when an old-fashioned key overrides everything.

'And why are you here?' I put my earlier question to her again.

'I left things behind,' says Bianca. 'I wanted to collect them.'

Oh God. She's here for the bracelet. Perspiration that has nothing to do with the heat breaks out on my brow.

'I'm sure it's fine to take anything that belongs to you, but I think you should've asked permission first,' I tell her, as I make sure the bracelet is well hidden by my sleeve and wonder frantically how I'm going to put it back in the safe without her knowing.

'Who should I have asked?'

'Well, like I said before, this is Martha's property.'

'But they're *my* things,' says Bianca. 'And there's no way I'll ask that cow's permission to get them.'

I groan internally. I'm stuck between a rock and a hard place. Bianca looks at me defiantly.

'I guess you can collect whatever you're here to collect,'

I say. 'But then I have to lock up. Martha will want to know that the alarm is set.'

'It's not up to you to tell me what I can and can't do,' says Bianca.

She's sort of right. I'm the hired help when it comes down to it.

'Anyhow, I'm not leaving,' she adds.

'What d'you mean?'

'I came to get my stuff, but I'm staying for a week. Here. At Palmyra.'

I stare at her. I totally understand where she's coming from, but I can't let her stay. At least not without saying something to Martha. Who won't let her stay, although I hope she doesn't think I'm going to be able to stop her. I'm certainly not going to get into some kind of tussle over it. I have a sudden mental image of trying to wrestle Bianca out of the garden, which almost inevitably concludes with us both ending up in the pool.

'Martha's expecting me to leave the house and set the alarm,' I tell her. 'I can't not do that.'

'Yes you can.'

'I really can't.' I shake my head. 'She'll know. I'll have to call her.'

'Go ahead.' Bianca gives me a defiant glare.

I look at my phone. 'It's not working. I'll call from the landline.'

'I'll go with you.'

'It's probably better if you stay here.'

'No.'

'Let Delphie make the call.' Erin steps forward. 'Wait with us.'

263

'And who the hell are you?' demands Bianca. 'What makes you think you're entitled to order me around?'

Erin introduces herself, adding that she's a partner at Haughton's. When Sheedy does the same and says she's the owner of Collins and Associates, Bianca opens her eyes wide and looks at all of us in bemusement.

'What's this? A legal convention?'

'No,' says Erin. 'Just a trio of friends.'

'All friends of Martha?' Her tone is scathing.

'We're friends of Delphie,' says Sheedy.

'Are you staying *here*? In the house?'

'Absolutely not,' says Erin. 'We're at La Perla.'

Hearing the name of the hotel seems to placate Bianca a little. Perhaps because it's not the kind of luxury hotel she likes to stay in herself.

'Oh, all right.' She sits on one of the chairs beside the pool.

'How about I get you a drink of water or something?' suggests Erin.

'There's cava in the fridge.' Bianca gets up again and walks towards it.

My mobile starts to ring and everyone looks at me in surprise.

'It must have managed to fix itself,' I say feebly.

The call is from Martha. 'How's it going?' she asks. 'Any luck with the safe combination?'

'Yes,' I reply. 'But there's been a slight . . . complication.'

I hear her sharp intake of breath as I fill her in on Bianca's arrival and her plans to stay at Palmyra.

'That woman is *not* staying in my home,' she says, her voice taut with fury. 'You have to get rid of her.'

I don't remind her that Bianca was staying in the house when Conrad died. That it hasn't been Martha's home for quite some time. That it was only a summer house anyhow. I don't say anything at all.

'I'm going to talk to Oscar. I'll get back to you.' Martha ends the call and I'm left holding my cracked phone and looking between Josh and Bianca.

'It might be a good idea to call your own solicitor,' I suggest.

'Why should I? It's an unfortunate accident of timing that's she's the widow, not me,' says Bianca.

I've no reply to that. Arguing about who should be mourning a dead man is an uncomfortable thing to do.

'What stuff did she want you to get, anyhow?' asks Bianca. 'Nothing of hers is here.'

'She thought she left a few personal items behind, trinkets mainly.' I don't say anything about Conrad's laptop or his watch collection. Nor do I mention the hoard of cash in the office safe.

'I asked you to tell me if she was up to anything,' she says. 'But you didn't. You came here without saying a thing. You're a two-faced wagon, Delphine Mertens.'

A two-faced wagon with her emerald bracelet on my wrist. How the hell am I going to put it back without her knowing? Without her accusing me of theft and maybe even calling the police? Ending up in a cell wasn't in the girls-on-tour plan.

My phone rings again. Martha tells me that she's taking out an injunction to stop Bianca accessing the house and that her Spanish solicitor will be there shortly.

'I understand that,' I say to her. 'But Bianca has left some personal items here and she wants to get them.'

'What sort of personal items?' demands Martha.

'Her b—' I almost say 'bracelet', but realise that if I do, Bianca will know I've seen it. 'Her bits and bobs,' I amend as a river of sweat runs down my back.

'Slightly more than bits and bobs,' says Bianca. And then, loudly enough for Martha to hear, she adds that she doesn't care what injunctions Martha takes out, she's staying where she is because she has nowhere else to go.

'She's not staying in my home for a second more than she needs to get her stuff and leave!' cries Martha. 'It was bad enough knowing she was swanning around in it when Conrad was alive. She's certainly not doing it when he's dead.'

'It's as much my home as yours!' Bianca shouts in the direction of my phone. 'I lived here with him.'

'Tell her to pack up and go,' says Martha.

'I'm not going anywhere,' retorts Bianca.

She turns on her heel and walks back into the house, followed by her brother, who hasn't said a word. Martha tells me to wait until the solicitor arrives with the injunction. 'It's a trespass order,' she says. 'The house is mine and she's trespassing.'

'OK.' I end the call, thinking that this is a complete mess. Yet bizarrely, there's a part of me that likes being flung into being the centre of Conrad's world again. Even if the centre of it means standing between his wife and his lover wearing the latter's emerald bracelet.

I follow Bianca inside, accompanied by Erin and Sheedy. Erin whispers an unnecessary reminder about the bracelet that's practically burning my arm at this stage, and I murmur that I'm trying to figure out a way to get it back into the safe before Bianca sees it.

266

'Give it to me,' says Erin. 'I'll do it. You stay with her.'

'Thanks.' I slip it to her.

When I follow Bianca into Conrad's office, she's opening and closing the drawers in his beechwood desk.

'Find anything?' I ask, knowing that she won't.

'He used to leave surprise gifts for me,' she says. 'In all sorts of places. So I'm checking. I'm not walking out of here until I have everything.'

There are more drawers in the shelving units, and to give Erin time to replace the bracelet, I suggest Bianca tries them all.

When she doesn't find anything, she says she'll get the stuff she knows is upstairs. As I turn to follow her, I see Erin waiting for me with a worried expression on her face.

'I couldn't put it back in the safe,' she mutters. 'It's locked.'

It must have locked automatically after I closed it. My gut spasms.

'I put it in one of the bedside drawers.'

'Best you could do.'

'Hopefully she'll think she left it there.'

'Fingers crossed.'

When I go upstairs, Bianca is opening the door to the walk-in wardrobe.

'You don't have to supervise me,' she says. 'I'm not taking anything that's not mine.'

'You're right. I'll wait for you outside.'

But even as I begin to go down the stairs, I hear Bianca's shriek and hurry back into the bedroom.

'It's gone!' She looks at me ashen-faced. 'My bracelet is gone.'

'The emerald one?' I keep my voice as neutral as I can.

'Are you sure it was there?' I should get an Oscar for my acting skills.

'Of course I'm sure,' she snaps. 'I'm not an idiot.'

'But it was such a traumatic time,' I say. 'Maybe—'

'Maybe nothing,' says Bianca.

'Were you wearing it the day of Conrad's accident?' I ask.

'I . . . don't remember.' There's sudden doubt in her voice and she sits on the floor of the wardrobe.

'Perhaps you were and you left it someplace else without thinking,' I suggest.

'Perhaps.' She gets up slowly and begins opening drawers.

I keep quiet and walk to the full-length window that looks out towards the sea. It's a spectacular view and I'm going to stay here looking at it until Bianca finds the bracelet herself.

'Oh!' It seems like an eternity before she does. 'It's here.'

'Where?' I turn around.

'Here. In the bedside drawer. I must have . . . but I wouldn't have.' She shakes her head. 'It's on his side of the bed. That makes no sense.'

She puts on the bracelet and I heave a sigh of relief.

'It was a difficult day,' I tell her. 'I'm sure you were traumatised.'

'Even so,' she says. 'He taught me to be very careful with expensive things. That bitch must have been here. Nobody else would move it.'

I simply remark that at least nobody took it and everything's OK. I also tell her that Conrad wanted her to have that bracelet very much.

'You were the one who bought it, weren't you? You bid for it at the auction?'

'Yes.'

268

'And you brought it here the last time you came.'

I nod.

'You did everything for him.'

'Not everything.'

Her eyes flicker. 'Did you love him?'

'I cared for him,' I say shortly.

'Did you ever sleep with him?'

My voice is cool when I tell her I never even thought of sleeping with Conrad and that I'm insulted by her question. I feel better for having regained some of the high ground I lost after raiding the safe.

'I . . . Oh, don't mind me.' Bianca sighs. 'My head is all over the place.'

She walks back into the wardrobe and starts taking mountains of clothes from the racks.

'I hadn't the time to pack everything,' she says as she throws an assortment of dresses, skirts, shorts and tops onto the bed. 'Besides, I couldn't even think about it. Not when . . .' Her voice suddenly breaks and she stumbles to the dark green velvet chair in the corner of the room, where she sits down and buries her face in her hands.

'I'm sorry, Bianca. I really am.' I kneel in front of her and she raises her tear-stained face to me.

'I saw him lying there. He was broken, his body at all sorts of angles. It was horrific. I still see him in my dreams.'

'Oh, Bianca.'

'I had to go to the hospital and wait,' she continues. 'There was nobody with me. It was awful.'

'I'm sorry,' I repeat.

'And she . . .' Bianca swallows hard and wipes away more tears, 'she has the nerve to parade around as the grieving widow when he couldn't have cared less about her nor she about him.'

'I don't know—'

'All she wanted was the money,' she continues. 'She was on to her solicitor every single day, badgering him, badgering Conrad. It was driving him crazy.'

There's nothing I can say. Bianca is truly distressed. But then so is Martha.

So am I.

And I can't pretend any more.

'It was me,' I confess.

'You what?'

'Who moved the bracelet.'

'What?'

'Martha gave me the code to the safe. When I saw the bracelet there it brought back memories and . . . Well, I tried it on. I'm sorry. I shouldn't have. One of my friends went to put it back, but the safe had locked itself and she couldn't.'

'Why didn't you say so sooner?'

'Because I was afraid you'd think I'd taken it for Martha. Or for myself.'

Her eyes narrow. 'And would you have? If I hadn't turned up?'

'Of course not.'

She stares at me. 'Are you sure about that?'

'Certain.'

She stands up and gives me a look of disgust.

'Get out,' she says, so I do.

It's a relief when José Roig, the Spanish solicitor, arrives and takes control. While Sheedy, Erin and I sit in the shaded pool area, he stays with Bianca as she packs up her things. She arrived in a hired Mercedes SUV, the exact same model as the car that Conrad kept on the island and which I presume is still in the garage attached to the house. She brought three large suitcases with her, and by the time she's ready to leave, she's filled them all.

'You can tell the bitch I'm going back to Palma,' she says when she's ready to leave. 'I've managed to get a suite in the Glòria de Sant Jaume.'

It's an exclusive boutique hotel in the centre of the city. I've stayed there myself a couple of times.

'I'm really sorry, Bianca,' I say.

'Like I believe a word out of your mouth,' she responds. 'But you can show how sorry you are by telling me everything that's happening though with Conrad's estate in the future. Because you might have left Cosecha but you're still hand in glove with Martha, and I bet you know more than you're letting on.'

She's right. All the same, there's nothing I can do to change things, no matter how much I might sympathise. I murmur something non-committal. She gives me another look of disgust, then gets into the car with her brother and drives away.

I'm relieved at that thought that we'll probably never see each other again.

Erin, Sheedy and I have the last evening meal of our stay at a stylish restaurant overlooking the bay. It's late by the time we get to eat, and the sun is sliding into the sea in a kaleidoscope of rose and orange. The anchored boats bob up and down on the gentle swell of the water as the lights from the surrounding buildings begin to twinkle in the dusk. It's picture perfect, and despite the anxieties of the day, I feel myself relax. Even if the events of this afternoon were stressful, it was good to feel needed again.

Not that there was much for me to do after José Roig arrived. He made it very clear to Bianca that she had no right to be at Palmyra, and though she argued vociferously with him, she eventually gave up. He called Martha when Bianca had gone, and then Martha called me again to get the fuller picture.

'Thanks for being there,' she said. 'And thanks for looking after things for me. You're a true friend, Delphie.'

I'm glad she thinks so, because I'm not sure what I am right now.

Erin and Sheedy are still talking about today's events. In the past, I never discussed my boss's private life, but now I fill them in on the details of his and Martha's separation and his affair with Bianca.

'Although it's not simply an affair if he moved in with her, is it?' I say.

Sheedy looks thoughtful. 'Who owns the house they were living in?'

'Conrad. Martha's given her three months to leave.'

'Does she have her own house too?'

'I don't know,' I say.

'I'm thinking Fintan and I should sign a prenup if we get married,' says Erin. 'I know I'm not a multimillionaire like Conrad, but it might be a good idea.'

'So you're not thinking it's forever?' I ask.

'I'm a lawyer,' says Erin. 'I like to have all the bases covered.'

No matter how much you love someone, or you think you love someone, you still have to look after yourself.

Our flight back to Dublin arrives ahead of schedule, just before midnight. As we walk into the arrivals hall, I tell the girls that despite the drama at Conrad's house, I really did enjoy myself.

I've hardly finished the sentence when I see someone waving at me.

'Ed.' I look at him in surprise. 'What are you doing here? Is everything all right?'

'Of course. I texted to say I'd pick you up.'

I didn't bother switching my phone from flight mode when we landed, but I do it now and the text comes through.

'It's really good of you to come, but you honestly shouldn't have bothered. It's such a trek for you.'

'I've missed you,' he says.

'He's very keen.' Erin, beside me, murmurs into my ear while Sheedy steps forward and says hello to him.

'Hi, Sheedy,' he says. 'Did you all have a good time? Lots of girlie chit-chat?'

There's the faintest hint of tension in his voice.

'It was lovely,' she tells him. 'We all got on fabulously. As you'd expect.'

'You really came to meet me?' I smile at him.

'Of course. Why wouldn't I?'

'We'll leave you to it,' says Erin. 'We were going to share a taxi into town anyhow.'

We group-hug.

'He's besotted,' whispers Erin. 'Make the most of it.'

'And I had hot sex with someone else,' I remind her.

273

'What happens on tour . . .'

'Are you OK about . . . well, you know?' Sheedy glances towards him.

'At the time, he was getting divorced from someone else. And, you know, Ed and I aren't exactly . . . well, I don't know if we're going to be a long-term thing. So we're good, Sheedy, don't worry.'

She looks relieved, though I still have to completely process how I feel about my friend and my ex-maybe-now-current-boyfriend having slept together.

We agree to meet up again soon, then the girls head towards the taxi rank and I follow Ed to the car park.

'You honestly didn't have to pick me up,' I say as I fasten my seat belt.

'It's late,' he says. 'I thought it would be a nice thing to do.'

'It is. Thank you.'

Being picked up from the airport is something that seldom happens to me. I'm used to heading for the taxi rank. I try to decide if I feel guilty that I cheated on him, although it's hardly cheating, because having sex with someone doesn't necessarily mean you're an actual couple. Even though we're definitely more than friends.

'Thanks again for the lift home,' I repeat as he pulls up outside my house and cuts the engine. I get out of the car, only now realising that the Dublin night, while cooler than Mallorca, is nonetheless quite balmy. The moon is high in the sky, its silver light reflecting in the water of the estuary.

'Did you want to come in for a coffee?' I ask, even as I realise that asking someone in for a coffee after midnight can't possibly be construed as offering them a hot drink. So

I add that coffee at this hour might keep him awake all night and that he probably wants to go home and sleep.

'Surprisingly, coffee doesn't really have much of an effect on me,' he says. 'As soon as my head touches the pillow, I'm out for the count.'

'Lucky you.' I open the door and he follows me inside.

I leave my wheelie bag in the hallway and walk into the kitchen, where I switch on the internal lights and the LED lights in the garden.

'Oh, that's pretty,' says Ed.

'It was a bonus,' I tell him. 'I didn't see the house at night before I bought it. It's lovely to look out on. Or to sit out in.'

I switch on the coffee machine and tell him that I have decaf if he prefers. He tells me he's fine with the caffeinated version, but I go for decaf myself because otherwise there isn't a hope in hell I'll be asleep before dawn.

'Would you like it outside?' I ask when it's ready.

'Why not?'

We take our coffees into the garden and sit on the wooden bench.

'Thanks for the lift home,' I say.

'Happy to do it. I always feel sad for people who walk out with nobody there to say hello.'

I laugh. 'It's no different to getting a bus or a train. You wouldn't expect to be picked up from the bus stop, would you?'

'Ah, Delphie!' He laughs too. 'I might be a sap, but I think air travel is different.'

I agree that it's certainly become more complicated.

He puts his arm around me and draws me close. Then he

275

kisses me and leads me back inside, where we go up to my mezzanine bedroom and make love. And it is making love rather than the mindless sex of Mallorca, because there's a connection between Ed and me and it's been there for a long time. I was afraid that getting back together with him would be a weak thing to do. But I'm moving forwards, and having him in my life is a reminder that not every step has to be into the unknown. That familiar things and familiar people are important too.

And if this is my comfort zone, it's good to be back.

It's only when (true to his word about coffee not keeping him awake) he's sound asleep beside me that I remember I've left the back doors wide open and the suitcase with Martha's stuff in the hall. I slide out of bed and tiptoe downstairs to close the doors again.

Then, as always, I set the house alarm.

Which, let's face it, is more secure than having someone sleeping in my bed.

Chapter 22

It's Ed getting up the following morning that wakes me. I wonder at first if he was trying to sneak out of my house like I did from his, but he leans over and kisses the top of my head.

'I was going to make us some breakfast,' he says.

'That'd be a miracle,' I observe. 'Because there's nothing breakfasty in the house at all. I used milk sachets from the aeroplane in your coffee last night.'

'Eggs? Butter? Orange juice?' He looks hopeful.

'Not a chance. But,' I add as I swing my legs over the side of the bed, 'there's a lovely café five minutes from here that does excellent pancakes.'

'Pancakes it is,' he says.

'D'you mind if I nip into the shower first?' I ask.

'Can I join you?'

'Well . . .'

He does. And a lot of soap and lather precedes some very pleasurable activities that carry on until the water runs cold.

'Why did I ever break up with you?' he asks after we've walked to the café and ordered pancakes and coffee. 'Long showers and breakfast by the sea is so much fun.'

'Because you wanted to go to Dubai,' I remind him.

'I'm back now.' He grins. 'We could make this a regular thing.'

I already go to the café most weekends. Though I usually have my iPad with me and spend the time scrolling through Twitter. I say this to him and he makes a face at me.

'Much better to have a conversation with a real person,' he says. 'Especially if that person is me.' He hesitates for a moment and then says that sometimes it might be him and Joe, and how would I feel about that?

'More importantly, how would Joe feel about it?' I ask.

'People are of secondary importance to him when there's food involved,' replies Ed. And then he adds that Joe is a very happy-go-lucky boy and he'd love me to meet him.

'I'd love to meet him too,' I say.

'I have to pick him up in Skerries a little later,' he says. 'Would you like to come?'

I don't answer straight away, partly because I'm eating the last of my pancake, but mostly because although I've said I'd love to meet Joe, I'm not sure I'm ready to take that step right now. I'm trying to think of the best way of saying this when I'm saved by the beep of my phone. It's hard to read the message on the cracked screen, but it's Martha asking if I can call to her today with the laptop and jewellery. I hesitate for a moment before I send a reply saying I can get to her in a couple of hours.

She responds with a thumbs-up and thanks in return.

'I'm really sorry,' I say to Ed when I tell him my plan.

'You'd rather go to Martha's than meet Joe?' He sounds hurt.

'Not at all,' I assure him, although he's not entirely wrong.

'But I'd really like to get her stuff out of the house. The jewellery isn't much, but the watches are quite valuable and I'm not keen on having them, or Conrad's laptop, at home. My insurance wouldn't cover them if something happened, so it's a bit of a worry having them there. I'd love to meet Joe another time, honestly.'

He finishes his coffee in a single gulp and then looks at me. 'I can't help feeling that whenever anyone connected to Cosecha tells you to jump, you ask how high. It's not healthy.'

'Cosecha is in the past and Martha won't be asking me for any favours after this,' I point out. 'So it's no big deal.'

'I guess not,' he concedes. 'It would've been a nice opportunity for you to see Joe today, that's all. But like you said, maybe next time.' He looks at his watch and grimaces. 'Actually, I'd better get going.'

We walk back to the house together and he gives me a quick kiss before getting into his car and driving away. I know he's disappointed with me for prioritising Martha over Joe, but I really do want to hand over her stuff as soon as possible. And in the meantime, I can get my head around the prospect of meeting Ed's son.

I bring my case upstairs and unpack, taking the watches and Martha's jewellery from the zipped compartment inside. I shiver a little as I recall how I left it downstairs with the back doors open last night. It's not anything I'd ever do if I was on my own. It just goes to show, I think, how having someone around makes you let your guard down. How you come to depend on them. Assume they'll look out for you. But you can't make those assumptions. The best person to take care of you is yourself.

*

It's almost as warm as it was in Mallorca, and the passengers on the Dart are wearing shorts and T-shirts. There's a lingering scent of coconut in the air, which I'm guessing is due to suntan lotion. Everyone is cheerful and chatty, and I wonder whether it would always be like this if the sun shone in Dublin every day. Because most times we sit or stand in silence, avoiding eye contact and focusing instead on our mobile devices. But this morning is different, and I'm buoyed up by the cheeriness of the people around me.

Martha's wearing shorts and a T-shirt too. I didn't go for shorts myself; I'm fine with them on the beach but always feel they make my sturdiness look even sturdier in town. So I chose a pair of wide cotton trousers in faded green and a white V-neck top instead.

'Come in,' she says as she opens the door. 'I'm in the garden. It's too hot to be inside.'

A couple of comfortable outdoor chairs are set beneath one of the cherry blossom trees. There's a jug of iced water on a small table nearby.

'Would you like anything stronger?' she asks as we sit down. 'I have wine.'

'No thanks.' I shake my head. 'I'm giving my liver a rest.'

'I wanted to apologise to you,' she says as she pours water into a patterned picnic glass.

'To me? For what?'

'You were doing something for me and you got stuck in the middle of a situation and I bossed you around. I kind of forgot it wasn't up to me to do that.'

'It's fine.'

'Seriously, though. It's not. I've been very self-centred over the past few weeks and I need to rein myself in a bit.'

'Martha, your husband died!' I exclaim. 'It's not self-centred, it's self-care.'

'But you lost your job,' she reminds me. 'I should've been a bit more . . . well . . . whatever.'

'You were angry on my behalf. You offered to talk to Justin. I appreciated that.'

'I asked you to go into the office and get the keys for me and you did. You helped me with the laptop and Palmyra and everything. I presumed on our friendship, but also on your relationship with Conrad, and I shouldn't have.'

'It's fine, Martha, really. And I'm over losing my job now.'

'You can't be.'

'Well, not entirely,' I concede. 'All the same, I have to move on.'

'I keep telling myself I'm moving on too,' says Martha. 'Maybe when all this is done with, I really will.' She waves her hand in the general direction of the house.

'Done? Are you thinking of selling it?' I look at her in surprise.

'I don't know what I'm thinking yet,' she confesses. 'This is my home and I've always loved it, but there're only three of us living here and we're rattling around in it. So who knows. There's so much stuff to work through,' she adds. 'Home stuff. Business stuff. It's hard.'

There were only four of them until Conrad left. So it's not much of a difference in terms of the number of people rattling around. But I don't say this out loud.

'Have the solicitors got everything in hand?' I ask.

'I hope so,' she replies. 'Henry is looking after the business side of it, Oscar is looking after me and José is keeping an eye on Palmyra.' Her jaw tightens. 'I know it was awful for you, but I'm glad you were there when she showed up. Goodness knows what would've happened otherwise.'

'She was there to collect her own things,' I say as mildly as I can. 'She'd left a lot behind.' My stomach lurches as I remember the bracelet. I know Bianca is convinced I was going to take it, and although I know I wasn't, I can't help remembering how I felt when I saw the money in the safe. I thought I knew myself and my own character very well, but I suppose there's always a part of us that can surprise us. And then I think of my moment of casual sex and wonder if my capacity to surprise myself has even more hidden depths.

I reach into my bag and take out the watches and jewellery and put them on the table in front of us. I take out the laptop and Montblanc pen too. Martha picks up Conrad's wedding ring and looks at the inscription inside before closing her hand tightly around it.

'I couldn't find any more than three watches,' I tell her after a moment's silence. 'I looked everywhere.'

'Maybe he gave the others to *her*,' says Martha. She puts the wedding ring back on the table between us.

'Maybe.' I clear my throat. 'Martha, the watches were in the safe in Conrad's office, along with something else.'

'Oh?'

'Money,' I say. 'Cash.'

'How much?'

'I didn't count it, but quite a lot,' I reply. 'Anywhere between twenty and fifty thousand, I reckon.'

'Oh,' she says again.

'I was surprised,' I admit.

'Did you take it?'

I don't say that I was tempted to stuff a few wads of cash

into my tote bag along with everything else, but her assumption that I might have done shocks me.

'I didn't mean to imply that you might have taken it for yourself,' she says quickly. 'I meant do you have it with you?'

'No,' I say. 'I wouldn't risk walking around with that kind of cash.'

She nods. 'Forty thousand,' she says. 'That's how much.'

'Really?'

'I once said to him that he should keep some cash. Just in case. I was always a bit paranoid that one day there'd be some kind of electronic meltdown and everything we had would somehow disappear. So I suggested ten thousand for each of us. It was a joke, really. But he took me seriously. He always took me seriously.'

'Oh, Martha.'

It's as well I didn't turn into a thief, given that she knows exactly how much was there.

'He took me seriously during the divorce too,' she says. 'He was terrified of it.'

'Is that why you think he wasn't going to divorce you after all?'

'He wasn't going to divorce me because he wasn't a fool,' says Martha. 'This girl turned up when we were going through a bit of a bad patch. Bad patches had happened before and we always got through them. We'd have got through this one too.'

I'm not going to argue with her, no matter how wrong she might be. She might not be wrong at all. Conrad did get sudden wild enthusiasms. Mostly about business opportunities. Occasionally about investments in art and culture. Sometimes about one of the charities we sponsored. There's no reason why he couldn't have had a wild enthusiasm for his image consultant too.

'Relationships are all about give and take,' says Martha. 'They're hard work. Sometimes you think you're doing all the giving and none of the taking. But you have to know exactly how much it's worth giving before you pull back.'

'And you thought it was worth letting him move in with Bianca?'

'I thought it was worth giving him a dose of reality,' she says. 'Middle-aged men are so predictable. Especially rich middle-aged men. When they become aware of their own mortality, they want to assure themselves that they can still attract young women. They surround themselves with youth because that way they see youthful faces reflected back at them and can fool themselves into thinking that's how they look too. Conrad's makeover didn't turn him into a thirty-year-old again, the same way moving in with a thirty-year-old didn't knock twenty years off him, no matter what he might have thought.'

'You seem very sure of that.'

'I knew my husband,' says Martha.

We fall silent as we both think of him.

I accept what Martha's saying about middle-aged men in general. You see it all the time, especially in business. And even more with older men, who somehow believe that pretty young women are attracted by their personality rather than their bank balance. Bianca was no fool. She admitted to me that she probably wouldn't have looked twice at Conrad if he hadn't had money. But then she also said that she loved him. Maybe she just wanted to believe that she loved him. Maybe he wanted to believe that too.

'I worried about you for a while,' says Martha suddenly. 'You and Conrad.'

For crying out loud! Not her too.

'His previous PA was besotted with him. That's why he got rid of her. I would've preferred him to hire an older woman. Someone whose head wouldn't be turned by the lifestyle. But he told me he'd picked someone from the staff. A smart girl, he said. Head screwed on the right way. Sharp as a tack. Committed to doing well.'

I feel myself blush.

'When I got to know you, I was fine with it,' Martha says. 'I know you two had a rapport, but I never thought you'd sleep with him.'

'We understood each other,' I agree. 'We wanted the best for each other. Nothing more.'

'I'm meeting Henry tomorrow.' She refills our glasses with water. 'To talk about the business. The structure. I have to decide what to do about Conrad's shareholding. I finally went through the will in its entirety with Oscar, and although Conrad added a codicil a few years ago detailing some additional charitable bequests, nothing else has changed. The bulk of the estate comes to me and the children. He also left this to you.' She picks up the Montblanc pen and hands it to me. 'You might as well take it now.'

'Are you sure?' I hold the pen in the palm of my hand. I remember him buying it when we were in Geneva for a meeting. 'Strictly speaking, shouldn't I wait for Henry to give it to me?'

She shakes her head. 'Just take it.'

'Thank you. I'll treasure it.'

I will. Although I won't carry it around with me. It's worth over three grand and I'm forever losing pens. I put it into the zipped compartment of my bag. The same one in which I put Bianca's bracelet when I took it out to Mallorca before her party.

'Are you going to sell your shares, or do you want to be involved in the business?' I ask Martha after I've taken a sip of water.

'There's a lot of work to be done before I decide what steps to take,' she says. 'I have to sit down and talk to Henry. But it sure would piss Justin Delaney off if I got involved. And I wouldn't mind doing that.'

I laugh.

'Cosecha has been so much a part of my life,' she says. 'But I can't keep looking back. I have to move on, like you.'

'I've only made baby steps in moving on so far.' If I exclude getting back with Ed, having sex with a complete stranger, contemplating raiding Conrad's safe and being accused of stealing Bianca's bracelet. I finish my water and tell Martha I should go.

'Oh, please stay for a bit longer,' she says. 'I'm all alone today. Killian is in Cork with some friends. Connie is with friends too. It's good that they're getting out and about again, but it feels weird to be on my own.'

I hesitate for a moment, then relax back into the chair.

I wonder what it was like to be married to Conrad. To have to put up with his lengthy absences and his obsession with the company. To know that the business came first. It would have been hard. The people who love you don't want to take second place to your hopes and dreams.

Perhaps that's why my relationships don't last. Because although I'll never succeed on the massive scale of Conrad

Morgan, my professional hopes and dreams have always come ahead of personal life. None of my boyfriends have put up with it. But Ed knows me. And that's why this time could be different.

I stay with Martha for another hour or so before I tell her that I really should leave. It's been pleasant sitting in her garden reminiscing, and sharing good memories of Conrad has been therapeutic for both of us.

As I walk down the steps, I wonder if I'll ever see her again. Our friendship centred around Conrad and Cosecha. Without him, and without the company, I'm not sure what will keep us in touch.

I feel I owe it to Bianca to tell her what I now know for sure about Conrad's will. I compose a short email on the train, edit it a few times, then send it to her. I say that I'm sorry he didn't look after her.

She doesn't reply.

When I get home, Mum calls and invites me to another Sunday lunch. André and Tory are back from their honeymoon and will be there. They're going to show us their wedding and honeymoon videos. I explain to Ed, who calls just after I've committed to going to Mum's, that it's impossible to say no to her.

'She's a proper Irish mammy,' I tell him. 'She totally rules the roost.'

'I know.'

'Why don't you come too?' The words are out of my mouth before I can stop them.

'I'd love to,' says Ed. 'Will I pick you up?'

When I text Mum to check that it's OK, she's enthusiastic. *OF COURSE*, she replies in all caps. *ED IS ALWAYS WELCOME.*

So we rock up together, and in the end I'm glad, because it means that I'm not the only one who hasn't got someone with them. And rather like being alone at a wedding itself, watching wedding videos when you're single feels wrong. As though you're having to pretend too hard to be delighted for the happy couple. Even when you are.

Anyhow, Ed is great and oohs and aahs in all the right places at both the photos (most of which Tory has shared on Instagram already) and the videos (which she hasn't). I'm glad I don't appear much in either, although there's a moment when the camera lingers on Ed and me dancing to 'At Last'. I'm resting my head on his shoulder and we look as if we've been together for years. Then, somewhat out of the blue, he asks me about being his plus-one at his niece's wedding in a few weeks' time, and I say I'd be delighted.

'Wedding fever,' says Nichola, and for a moment I'm convinced she's going to ask Ed if he's popped the question, but thankfully she doesn't and I release the breath I didn't even realise I'd been holding.

Then Vivi asks Tory and André if they've heard my news, and Tory looks at me (and then my engagement finger) with great anticipation only for her expression to turn to surprise when I tell her that I've left Cosecha.

'For something better, I hope?'

I give her a potted history of the situation.

'Oh, but that's terrible!' she exclaims. 'Poor you, Delphie.'

'I'm sure I'll find something,' I say.

'I hope you've signed on now that you're out of work.'

Being a councillor's daughter, she's very up to speed on people's rights.

It's not like I haven't thought about it. Luke mentioned it too. But I don't know anyone in Cosecha who ever left the company and went on the dole – even people who were terminated. (Which sounds like something that happens in an episode of *Doctor Who*, rather than the reality of simply being fired. We never used the word 'fired' at Cosecha. It was always terminated. Or, in more casual conversations, canned.)

'If you need advice, you should talk to my dad,' she says.

'That's very good of you, Tory. I'm sure Delphie would be delighted to get Councillor Palmer's views,' says Dad. 'Of course I can advise her too, but I'm a few years out of the workforce now, so it'd be better to have someone who's completely up to date on her side.'

'It's fine, honestly,' I say. 'My solicitor took care of everything.'

'I'm sure she's not getting you a new job,' says Dad.

'Well, no. But everything else. And it's a he, not a she, Dad.'

'Good grief.' He looks at me in astonishment. 'I thought you and your squad of single women had the legal profession sewn up.'

I give him a withering look, and he winks at me, which makes me laugh.

'I bet you'll have something in no time,' he says. 'I have faith in my clever daughter.'

'Thank you,' I say.

'Why aren't you taking the summer off, Delphie?' asks André. 'I would, in your position. You haven't had much free time over the last few years. It's been all work, work, work. This could be the jolt you need to get you off the treadmill.'

'That's what I told her too,' says Ed, and there's a certain amount of satisfaction in his voice.

'I like being on the treadmill,' I tell them. 'Besides, I have bills to pay and a house to keep up. And work is fun for me.'

'Oh, come on.' André looks at me in disbelief. 'You were lucky with your job, but I can assure you that in general, work isn't fun. As far as your responsibilities go, you only have to look after yourself. And you could rent out your house. You'd probably end up making money that way.'

'I told her that ages ago.' Vivi chimes in with more things that people have told me already.

'Or Airbnb,' suggests Ed. 'After all, it's a cottage by the sea.'

'Oh, yes. Ideal.' André nods.

'I'm not renting out my home.' I interrupt their unnecessary attempts to sort out my life. 'I want to work. It's my thing.'

'We're just trying to help you see the advantages of your situation,' says Vivi. 'What if you headed off somewhere really remote to find yourself or whatever? Jason and I could be your tenants while you did yoga and other mindful stuff.'

'I already do yoga!' I don't mention the lack of mindfulness. I'm not a total hypocrite.

'Or me and Tory could rent it,' says André. 'Your place is much nicer than our flat.'

'Would you all stop!' I cry. 'It's my home. I live there. I want to keep living there.'

'But *if* you took a year off—' persists Vivi.

'I'm not taking a year off!'

290

'Delphie will take time off when she's ready,' says Mum.

'I'm sure I'll find a job soon.' I get up from the table and go to the bathroom. I need to get away from all this *Eat Pray Love* garbage.

My family don't understand me.

Even Ed Mark II doesn't understand me.

And quite honestly, I'm not sure that I understand them either.

Chapter 23

I've no immediate plans to sign on for the dole – or Jobseeker's Benefit as it's currently called – because it's not something I've ever imagined myself doing. But Mum and Dad continue to nag at me, and Councillor Palmer gives me a call to ask if I need help, so I go to the local job centre and discover that I'm not entitled to the allowance yet anyway.

'We'll be in touch with you about coming in for a discussion in the next week or so to talk about interviews and how to make the most of them,' says the woman behind the desk when I assure her I've already sent my CV to lots of companies.

I've interviewed people myself. I know how it works.

I'd better get a job before then.

It would be humiliating to be told how to do an interview.

I left my phone in to be repaired while I was at the job centre, and when I pick it up, I see that I've missed a call from Mum and she's left a message to call her back urgently.

She picks up straight away.

'It's Granny Mertens.' Her voice is shaky. 'She's in hospital.'

'What happened?'

'She fell,' says Mum.

An elderly person having a fall isn't good news.

'Did she trip, or was it something else?' I ask.

'She tripped,' replies Mum. 'Oh, Delphie, I asked her to live with us so many times, but she wouldn't. And now this happens.'

'She could just as easily have tripped in your house,' I point out.

'But I would have been there,' says Mum. 'As it is, she was on the floor for an hour. An hour!'

'What about her personal alarm?'

Last time Granny Mertens refused to move in with Mum and Dad, Mum begged her to get a rapid response alarm. She wears it around her neck and it can be used to alert the emergency services.

'She'd just had her shower. She wasn't wearing it.'

'Are you at the hospital now? Do you want me to come?'

'Would you?' Mum sounds relieved at my offer. 'Your dad's here too, but it's hard for him.'

'I'll be there as soon as I can,' I promise.

For the first time ever, I'm glad I don't have a job to go to. My grandmother is far more important.

Granny Mertens hasn't actually been admitted to a ward yet. She's on a trolley in A&E, but at least she has a cubicle to herself. When I arrive, she's hooked up to the monitoring equipment, her face almost as pale as the pillow behind her head.

'What are you doing here?' she asks when I lean over to kiss her. 'Such fuss.'

'Granny! You're in A&E. Of course we're fussing.'

'Well, I don't want fuss,' she says, and closes her eyes.

I exchange a glance with Mum and both of us step to the other side of the faded yellow curtain surrounding the cubicle.

'I think she's fractured her hip,' says Mum.

'Oh, no.'

'She'll have to move in with us now.'

I nod.

Dad puts his head outside the curtain. 'She's asleep at last.'

'You two go and get a coffee or something,' I say. 'I'll stay with her.'

They're reluctant at first, but eventually head off to the hospital café. There are no chairs, so I stand beside Granny's bed.

'Everyone thinks I've broken my hip.' Her eyes open and she looks directly at me. 'I think they're right.'

'Oh, well.' I try to sound cheerful. 'It's not the end of the world.'

'I'm eighty-eight,' she says. 'It might as well be.'

'You're not to think like that.'

'How am I supposed to think? That I'll be on my feet and hopping around in a couple of weeks? Not a chance.'

'You're a healthy woman, Granny,' I say. 'There's no reason for you not to recover.'

'My best friend died after she broke her hip. And she was only eighty-two.'

'You're not going to die!' I exclaim.

'We're all going to die,' she points out. 'It's simply a question of when.'

'Well, you're not going to die yet,' I amend.

'We'll see,' says Granny.

I don't want to have this conversation. I don't want to talk about her dying. She's too much of a live-wire.

She closes her eyes again.

'Are you in much pain?' I ask.

'Not if I lie still,' she replies. Then she opens her eyes again. 'What's all this I hear about your job?'

I suppose someone was bound to tell her. So I go through it all with her, and I can't help feeling that talking about something other than her possible fracture is cheering her up.

'You'll be fine,' she says when I'm finished.

'So will you.'

She laughs. It's a weak laugh, but full of mirth.

'Fingers crossed,' she says.

It's nearly five hours later when a junior doctor comes around and tells us that Granny has indeed fractured her hip, and that the best recommendation is surgery the next day.

'It's not without risks, of course, Mrs Mertens,' he tells her. 'But to be honest, there's no other option.'

She signs the forms and is eventually moved to a ward.

'Don't worry about me,' she tells us as we leave her for the night. 'I'll be fine.'

But of course we worry, and we worry all through the next day too, until we hear that she's out of surgery and recovering.

'First hurdle over,' says Dad in relief when he calls me with the news.

'When can we go in to see her?'

'This evening,' he says.

I say I'll be there, and he tells me that I'm a great help.

I feel a warm glow at his words.

*

295

Ed texts me a little later. I was in touch with him from the hospital, as he messaged to ask how my visit to the social welfare office had gone and I told him about Granny. He was very reassuring, reminding me that she's a fighter, and wishing her a speedy recovery. He asked if I'd like to meet, but I told him I was totally caught up with her situation at the moment. He replied telling me not to worry, and to call him when I had a chance. I immediately forgot about him. But now that he's texted again, I call him back.

'Sorry,' I say. 'It's been a bit mental here.'

'I understand.'

'I always thought Granny Mertens was indestructible, you know. She never seemed old to me. But yesterday, seeing her on that trolley . . .'

'She's a strong woman,' says Ed.

'Even strong women fade away eventually.' I can't help the wobble in my voice.

'Ah, Delphie. Don't upset yourself. I'm sure she'll make a good recovery.'

'I hope you're right. It's been . . . traumatic.'

'Can I help at all?'

'Thanks, but there's nothing you can do right now,' I say. 'I'll visit her this evening, see how she is.'

'If there's anything you need, let me know.'

'I'll call you when I'm leaving the hospital.'

'OK,' he says. 'Take care, Delphie.'

'You too.'

Granny is still a bit woozy when I arrive at her ward. She's hooked up to painkillers, but she tells me that everything seems to have gone well and she now has a nail and a screw in her hip.

'Held together like one of your grandad's DIY projects,' she quips.

I grin at her, but her eyes have already fluttered closed again. I take her hand and hold it. She gives my fingers a squeeze.

The doctor who meets with us a little later tells us that the operation has indeed gone well and that Granny has good bones for a woman her age.

'But of course recovery is more tricky with an elderly patient,' he reminds us. 'We'll get her into rehab as soon as possible, but we'd also recommend a nursing home for recuperation.'

We look at each other anxiously.

'I'm not keen on her going to a nursing home,' says Mum. 'I know there are great ones, but the risk of infection . . .'

'We'd rather have her at home,' says Dad.

'She needs rehab and physio,' says the doctor. 'And most nursing homes have great infection protocols now.'

We exchange more anxious looks.

'Can you tell us which ones are best?' I ask.

That provokes a whole new discussion, as the hospital can't be seen to recommend any home in particular, but they provide us with a list of potential places.

'Bringing her home would be a lot better,' says Dad.

We all agree, but we also agree that getting the right rehab is important too.

'Don't worry about it.' I keep my voice calm. 'I'll make some calls and see what we can sort out.'

'She's an old woman,' says Mum. 'They should keep her in hospital until they're sure she's OK to come home.'

But that's not how the health service works any more, we realise. Hospital stays are kept to the absolute minimum. If they could have her out tonight, they would.

After we've made sure that Granny is reasonably comfortable, we leave for the evening.

'Thanks for offering to look into the nursing homes,' says Dad. 'I don't think I could.'

'No problem.'

It is, after all, the kind of administrative thing I'm good at. And I'm glad that I've finally come into my own with my family.

I want to read through the brochures and check the websites when I get home, but my eyes are tired, so I leave everything on the table while I make myself a coffee. Then I suddenly remember I was supposed to phone Ed.

'Sorry it's so late,' I tell him. 'We were being given all sorts of info and time flew by.'

'Are you still at the hospital?' He sounds incredulous.

I tell him that I'm at home and apologise again for not calling when I said I would.

'I was getting a little worried,' he says. 'I know you have to concentrate on your gran, but don't forget to look after yourself too.'

'I won't.'

'Are you sure you don't need me to drop by?'

'I'm fine, Ed. Honestly. But thanks.'

He really is good to me. But tonight I want to be alone.

*

The rest of my week is entirely taken up with hospital visits and trying to find the right nursing home for Granny Mertens. It's harder than booking a hotel, because I'm trying to juggle all sorts of permutations. But eventually I find one that checks out well and will take Granny next week. Everyone, Granny included, is delighted. Mum and Dad are unnecessarily complimentary about the work I've put in, and I'm a bit embarrassed at how thankful they are for my efforts. Meantime, I've been so busy that I haven't followed up on any of the CVs I've sent out to recruitment agencies, which I apparently need to be doing to show that I'm a real jobseeker and not a benefits cheat. It's worrying that nobody has yet been in contact with me. But honestly, my head isn't in the right place for it at the moment anyhow.

On Friday evening, though, I go through the emails I haven't yet had a chance to look at and see that I've missed one from Martha. The subject is 'Thank you'.

Thanks again for all your help and for bringing back my things from Spain. Also for telling me about the cash. You're a brick, Delphie. You always have been. You wouldn't let me pay for your time, but I'm attaching a little something for you to express my appreciation. Martha x

The attachment is a voucher for an overnight stay at the Ardallen Lodge, a very upmarket hotel and wellness centre in the Wicklow Mountains. It opened a couple of years ago to rave reviews about its location, its style, the quality of its food and its superb spa. As I click on the link and look at the website's glossy photos of rolling hills and sumptuous rooms, I feel a wave of familiarity wash over me. This is the sort of life I understand. Booking rooms in amazing hotels rather than nursing homes. Elegant restaurants as opposed to hospital cafés. Quality time on my own, not dropping into Mum and Dad's every single day. Ardallen Lodge is right back in my comfort zone again, and the thought of being there is enticing.

For the moment, though, I'm the go-to person for Granny's care. And that's absolutely fine by me. It takes the pressure off everyone else. Taking the pressure off other people is another of my skill sets, though if I was still working at Cosecha, I'd have been running after Conrad rather than helping out with my family. Someone else would've had to research the nursing homes, keep Mum and Dad informed, make the afternoon hospital visits and keep Granny's spirits up.

I feel guilty as I realise how many times I've opted out in the past.

But I'm here now, helping. And I'll help when Granny comes out of hospital too. In the meantime, with everything in place for her, I browse the Ardallen gallery and imagine myself in the thermal suite, or getting a signature massage, or simply chilling out in one of the enormous bedrooms. I release a breath of sheer pleasure as I check availability. Except for a couple of midweek days next month, the lodge is booked up until the end of September. Making a quick decision, I reserve the first available night. If I get a job before then, I'll have to negotiate time off. I'm sure I can manage that.

I send a reply to Martha thanking her for the voucher and saying that if there's anything else I can do for her, to give me a call.

Then my phone rings and I'm back into my own family again.

*

It's Mum and she's calling from the hospital.

'Can you get here as soon as possible?' Her voice is tearful. 'Granny's taken a turn for the worse.'

'What?'

She was fine when I left earlier in the day, and looking forward to being discharged to the nursing home soon. She was a little anxious about her rehab and how that would go, but the physical therapists had already got her out of bed and taking steps around the ward. They had an entire schedule of therapy mapped out for her, and she remarked that it was surely something more suitable for a high-performance athlete than a woman of eighty-eight. We laughed about it, the two of us, and I kissed her goodbye and told her that I'd see her in the morning.

So how can she be worse now? How much worse?

'She blacked out and fell again,' says Mum.

'Oh no.'

'They're concerned,' she says.

'I'll be right there.'

I order a cab, because that's quicker than hiring a car with the app, but it takes over half an hour to get to the hospital. Mum is waiting for me in the corridor, and I can tell from her expression that things aren't good.

But I'm not ready to hear that Granny Mertens passed away ten minutes earlier.

I didn't think it was that serious.

I didn't think I'd be too late.

I stare wordlessly at Mum and she catches me by the arm to support me.

'Are you OK?' she asks.

I nod, but the truth is that I feel faint. It's all too quick, too sudden. Just like Conrad. It's as though death is stalking me, taking everyone I care about. I feel like I'm carrying some kind of contagion. That I'm not safe to know.

'She's in a room,' says Mum, leading me down the corridor.

I don't want to see her. I'm not ready. But the room isn't far and we're there before I have time to say anything. Mum ushers me inside, where Dad is sitting beside the bed. Granny is lying there and looks as though she's asleep.

Dad stands up to make room for me, but the first thing I do is hug him. He holds me very tightly before letting me go.

I'm not sure what I'm supposed to do. I don't know if I should touch her. In the end, I take her hand. It's not as cold as I anticipated, and I half expect her to squeeze my own hand in return. But of course there's no reaction from her at all.

'Can you talk to the hospital staff?' asks Dad, who suddenly looks every day of his sixty-eight years. 'I want to stay with her.'

I gather myself, then find a nurse, who directs me to the right person to talk to. And then I ring a funeral home and speak with a very kind man who explains what needs to be done. I agree with Mum and Dad that the funeral will be held on Monday, and then get back to the funeral director to make the necessary arrangements. I also ring the nursing home to say that Granny won't be coming to them after all.

I can't quite believe I'm doing all this. And I think of Martha, and Bianca, and the trauma they went through in dealing with Conrad's sudden death. Because while Granny's was sudden too, and certainly unexpected despite her fall, at least we can take some comfort from the fact that she'd lived a long, full life. Conrad was taken before his time. Nevertheless, it doesn't matter how long you've lived. For those closest to you, it's always too soon for you to go, and even as I deal with everything as efficiently as I can, my heart is breaking with the loss of my wonderful grandmother.

I used to love the randomness of life. But right now, I hate it. I hate how everything seems to be held together by the thinnest of threads, how all your hopes and dreams and plans can be brushed away in an instant. I hate how fragile it is.

Although maybe that's why it's so precious.

To my surprise, Granny Mertens' funeral is a joyful occasion and manages to truly be a celebration of her life. Obviously we're not joyful that she's gone, but the priest does his best to make us feel thankful for having her for so long, and equally thankful that her stay in hospital was so short. He's a young man himself, and I find myself wondering how he decided that religious life, rather than a career or a family, was right for him.

'I wanted to make a difference,' he tells me in the private room of the pub where we go for something to eat after Granny's burial. 'I didn't think I'd be able to do that in any other way.'

'But . . . God?' I look at him. 'How can you possibly believe in God?'

He smiles in return. 'When you see the goodness in the world, how can you not?'

Pretty easily, in my view, when you look at the rest of the world, but he's so earnest and kind that I don't argue with him. Instead, I look for Ed, who came to the funeral and who's been fantastic as always, saying exactly the right thing to Dad and fitting into the family dynamic in his easy-going way. When I find him, I ask if he'd like a drink and he says he'd murder a Guinness, so I go to the bar to order it.

'You insisted he was only your plus-one at the wedding,' says Lindsey, who's also ordering drinks. 'Is he your plus-one at funerals too?'

'We're . . . seeing each other,' I say.

'You don't get a second go at life,' she says, echoing my own thoughts. 'It's time for you to step up in a relationship. Ed's available and he obviously cares about you. You should be moving it to the next level.'

We're having regular sex, I think. Surely that's the next level.

'You can't have perfect,' she continues. 'And that's what you want, Delphie, but you'll never find it. It's all about making things work. You refuse to see that.'

'No I don't.'

'Getting married isn't an admission of weakness,' she adds.

'Jeez, Lindsey, give me a break. We've only just got back together. I'm not planning on marrying him.'

'In that case, what's the point?' she asks.

'The endgame of every relationship doesn't have to be marriage,' I remark.

'At some stage in your life you have to stop faffing around and make a decision. Especially when you've got a good man by your side.'

Lindsey has never been so forceful with me before. Maybe she feels empowered by the fact that I'm not working. Maybe she thinks that now I'll feel the need to have someone to look after me. But she doesn't have to make it sound quite so transactional.

'I'd better bring him this,' I say, nodding at the pint in my hand before she can say something else.

'Tory's been telling me more about the honeymoon,' Ed says when I sit beside him at the table where she's joined him. 'Fiji sounds amazing.'

'It was,' says Tory. 'You should visit.'

She's speaking to both of us, and maybe it's because of Lindsey's words that I'm conscious that Tory sees Ed and me as a couple with a future.

She and Lindsey seem to be singing off the same hymn sheet.

Do they know me better than I know myself?

Chapter 24

I spend a lot of time over the next couple of weeks going to Granny Mertens' house with Mum and sorting out her things. Dad doesn't want be involved. He can't bring himself to go through her possessions. Afterwards, he tells me he's glad I'm the one helping Mum, because he knows that Granny Mertens would have wanted it that way.

'She was very fond of you, Delphie,' he says. 'You were her favourite.'

I usually take this sort of comment with a grain of salt, but I'm unaccountably pleased at his words. I'm not sure Granny did have favourites – she certainly never treated any of her grandchildren differently – but I was named after her and I got on well with her, so it seems only right that I should do this.

'You've changed, Delphie,' Vivi observes as the two of us sit in the kitchen one evening after I've stayed for an evening meal. 'You're softer.'

'No I'm not.' I bounce Charley up and down on my knee and he gurgles his appreciation.

'You are,' she insists. 'You're here a lot more, and rushing around a lot less. And look at you there, playing with

Charley, happy as anything. Normally you don't have time to bother.'

'I've time for him because I'm not working,' I point out. 'But I will be soon, I hope.'

'And then you'll revert back to Delphie-Don't-Know-If-I-Can,' Vivi says.

Is that what they call me? I'm taken aback, and can't help a pinprick of hurt, but I ignore it and instead simply point out that I was very busy before and I expect to be busy again. But that I'm always around to help out.

'You're being unfair,' I add. 'Didn't I give André advice when his landlord was pressurising him over the rent? And what about the time Lindsey's holiday insurance wouldn't pay out and I contacted them for her? And babysitting? I'm always bloody babysitting Nichola's girls, Lindsey's kids too. But nobody ever thanks me for it.'

'Keep your hair on,' says Vivi. 'All I'm saying is that it's good you can give more time to family stuff. That's all.'

It's not all. But I'm not going to pursue it. All the same, I didn't realise everyone was keeping score. I didn't realise I was either.

'Ah, look, sorry if I sounded a bit harsh,' says Vivi as I pick up my phone and busy myself with looking at non-existent new messages. 'It's just that this version of you is a much easier one to get on with. Being back with Ed helps. He softens your edges, makes you laugh at yourself more.'

Mum walks into the kitchen at that point and agrees with Vivi that it's great I'm back with Ed, although she doesn't comment on my apparently softer edges.

'I'm happy for you,' she adds, 'especially now, when you've

gone through a bit of a bad patch. It's been hard for you and you're being so good to us.'

After Vivi's words, I'm comforted by what Mum has to say. I tell her that I was happy to help, and she smiles warmly at me.

I concede that having Ed around has been a massive bonus. It's not that Erin and Sheedy haven't been totally supportive, but they both lead busy lives, and although they're always at the end of a WhatsApp message, it's not quite the same as having someone ready to meet me whenever I want. Or to help with bringing some of Granny Mertens' stuff to the charity shops she specified in her will. Or to take my mind off things by insisting I abandon the search for an estate agent to value her house and instead have a decent meal and a glass of wine in a relaxed restaurant. We went back to his apartment that night. I didn't try to sneak away the next morning.

It was Dad who asked me to look after Granny's affairs. He's the executor of her will and, being an only child, the main beneficiary, but he's not keen on being involved in the admin work that her death entails. He was great with the union because he was passionate about it, but he prefers practical, hands-on things, like unblocking drains or painting walls or extreme gardening. When it comes to anything else, he tends to ignore it and hope things will sort themselves out. Faced with the details of Granny's estate, he prefers to take a step back. And I'm the one who's stepped up in his place.

But that's fine too, because it's legal and administrative stuff and right up my street. I've already been to Granny's solicitor and have begun the process of accumulating her assets. Not that there's much. But she had some savings and investments that have to be realised, and she owned the house where she was living.

It's a small mid-terrace in Marino. Single-storey with a dormer bedroom, it has a surprisingly large back garden, which means that it could be extended like so many of the houses in that neighbourhood. And because it's close to the city, it's an area where prices are higher than you'd expect for a house that size.

It seems that Dad never really thought about the fact that he'd inherit her house, because when I talk to him about valuations and selling it, he looks at me and shakes his head and says he doesn't want to think about it.

Sooner or later he will. But in the meantime, I don't mind doing the thinking for him.

I finally get called to some interviews, and the first one really gets my hopes up. It's with a small financial services firm which is looking for a senior administrator, and although the job description is more limited than I'd like, the company has a good reputation. I meet the CEO, who's a man around my own age and who met Conrad on a couple of occasions.

'A tragic loss,' he says about my former boss, and I agree with him.

The interview goes well, but I'm surprised to feel a slight sense of dissatisfaction at the idea that if I get the job I'll be back in the same environment as I was before. A part of me wonders if I shouldn't be doing something different. Something better. More fulfilling.

As I leave after forty minutes, I tell myself not to be stupid. My job with Cosecha was very fulfilling. This could be too. A job is what you make it, after all. My mood improves as I walk towards the train station, and is improved even more by Erin texting me to ask if I'd like to go for a run with her that evening. There was a time when we ran quite a lot together, but we haven't coordinated well this year. I ask if she wants to run along Sandymount, on her side of town, or if she'd prefer to come to Malahide.

'I haven't been to Malahide in ages,' she says. 'How about we meet up around six?'

That's perfect for me, as it gives me time to talk with the valuer about Granny Mertens' house. She's a smart and sassy woman who tells me that there's strong demand in the area and there'll be no problem at all selling it. She gives a ballpark figure that's sure to surprise Dad. But I don't call him or drop by my parents' house, as I feel I've done enough already today.

When I arrive home, I realise that it's only 4.30. When I was with Cosecha, I wouldn't even be thinking of finishing the day yet. Somehow time has changed for me. I don't feel it necessary to do a million things before lunch, or cram in another million afterwards. I've slowed down.

Have I changed that much, or is my slower pace of life a temporary thing?

When Erin arrives, we head out along the coast road, which is busy with people walking and running. We don't talk until we've covered a few kilometres, which is about all I can manage. I used to be a lot fitter, and so, says Erin as we sit on the low wall near the Martello tower, did she.

'And we have to get back,' I remind her.

'I'll be OK after a rest,' she assures me, and I reply that I'm not sure I will.

'We can always walk,' she says. 'Delphie, there's something I wanted to say to you.'

Her tone has changed; it's both serious and slightly hesitant, and I give her a sharp look.

'Nothing awful,' she says. 'It's just that your old company, Cosecha, wants to change its legal advisers. And they've asked us to pitch for the business. I'll be the one pitching.'

'Oh.' I don't know what to say.

'I realise it's a bit awkward,' she says. 'But obviously—'

'It's not awkward at all,' I tell her. 'You're entitled to take them on.'

'Well, yes, but—'

'Honestly, I'm fine with it.'

'I'm meeting Justin Delaney tomorrow,' says Erin.

'Fucker.' I can't help myself.

'Yeah, I know. But I won't be thinking of him like that. I'll be thinking of him as a prospective client. All the same, I'd hate to think you'd feel bad about it.'

'I truly don't,' I say, although my feelings are mixed, to put it mildly. Mainly because I think how great it would have been if I'd been there and was doing business with my friend. Power women together. But not now. She's a power woman and I'm in the unfamiliar territory of being an interviewee rather than an interviewer. 'Anyhow,' I add as brightly as I can, 'my connection with them has been entirely severed, so it's fine. Why are they changing?'

'Haughton's have the expertise they need in terms of dealing with Conrad's shareholding,' says Erin. 'Obviously there are issues with what should happen and the directors' buyout, and they want us to lead on that.'

'Don't worry,' I say. 'I won't badger you.'

'Thanks. I wanted to tell you myself so that you wouldn't suddenly hear it anywhere else and think I was trying to keep things from you.'

'You're a good friend, Erin Kiely,' I say. 'You always have been.'

'There's something else,' she says. 'Fintan and I are moving in together.'

'I'm glad you finally made a decision,' I tell her. 'Is he OK about living in your house?'

'He didn't think Dervla would want to stay there. So I'm going to rent it out and we're getting a new place together.'

'Right. Good idea.' I say this positively, even though I'm not sure it is.

'The new place is still in Milltown, so I'm happy. It's slightly bigger than my own, and we're moving in this weekend.'

'Sounds great.'

'Maybe we'll have a moving-in dinner party.' She grins. 'I'll be a gracious hostess.'

We both laugh. Fintan definitely isn't a dinner party person, so that's never going to happen.

'Well, drinks with you and Sheedy,' she amends. 'We've been remiss about catching up.'

'Look forward to it,' I say.

She switches the topic to my job prospects, and I bring her up to speed on today's interview.

'Sycamore Investments.' She nods. 'I know it. Was it Tom Greene who interviewed you?'

'Yes.'

'He's a good guy.'

'I thought so too.'

'I bet he'll hire you.'

'Fingers crossed.'

She glances at her watch. We've been sitting in the evening

sun for nearly thirty minutes, and she says she'll seize up if we don't get back. So we start on the return journey, at a significantly slower pace than on the way out.

I feel good, though. More like the Delphie I was before. Everything is falling into place again. As I open the front door, I'm thinking about today's interview and telling myself not to depend on a good outcome but to keep looking and widen my search. This is my opportunity to shake things up, after all. I shouldn't tie myself down.

As soon as we've rehydrated, Erin heads home and I have a shower. Then I make myself an omelette. I bought the eggs a few days ago because Ed mentioned that omelette and chips is Joe's favourite food and I wanted to practise making one. Feeling very Nigella, I add some chopped herbs I picked up in the deli, then open the patio doors, set the table properly and take a bottle of wine from the fridge. I've cut back significantly on my alcohol consumption, but a home-cooked omelette deserves a glass of wine.

I struggle with the foil covering over the cork and take a knife out of the drawer to loosen it. But the bottle is slightly wet with condensation and the knife slips as I try to slide it under the foil.

The next thing I know the bottle is on the floor and I'm gasping from the sting of the deep cut I've inflicted on my hand. I reach for a handful of kitchen towel even as my blood drips onto the tiles and mixes with the Sauvignon Blanc.

The smell of burning omelette reminds me to turn off the hob. When I've done that, I drop onto a chair, dizzy from the shock and pain.

The kitchen towel is stained red. The bleeding hasn't stopped yet. I'm not sure exactly where the cut is, and to be honest, I'm a little wary of looking. I'm not that good with blood.

I give myself a couple of minutes before I start to pick up the glass fragments from the floor. But leaning down makes me dizzy again, and I'm panicking a little. I take a tentative peek beneath the paper towel and it's like a scene from a Halloween movie, so I ring for a taxi to take me to the walk-in clinic in nearby Swords. It's a private clinic, but fortunately the health insurance that Cosecha paid for still covers me to the end of the year.

There's nobody ahead of me, so I get to see the doctor straight away. He says I'll need stitches for the cut that runs from the base of my palm to between my thumb and first finger, but assures me it won't hurt at all.

He lied. It's agony, and I have to fight to hold back the tears.

'Sorry we couldn't use skin glue, but the cut was too open,' he says as he covers it with a bandage. 'I don't think there'll be any nerve damage, but come back if your temperature spikes or you feel any increased pain. The stitches can come out in a couple of weeks. I'm also recommending a splint so's you don't move that thumb too much. You only need to keep it on for a few days.'

He applies the splint and I sniff a bit more before thanking him and ordering another taxi to take me home.

Once I'm back in my house again, I sit quietly for a while, hoping that the throbbing in my hand will ease and wondering if cutting my hand was a reminder from the universe not to get too complacent; that my personal black cloud is still directly overhead.

I dump the charred remains of the omelette into the bin, then check my phone. No messages, not even from Ed, although I wasn't really expecting anything from him because he's in Sligo for a couple of weeks on an engineering job. He was apologetic when he told me and hoped I didn't mind.

'Why on earth should I mind?' I asked. 'It's your job. You have to go.'

'Yes, but I'm staying up there for this weekend, maybe even next,' he said. 'The guys have arranged a target shooting day on Saturday and I can't not take part.'

'Of course you have to take part,' I agreed. 'Besides, you like target shooting. You've done it before.'

'I haven't done it since I went to Dubai,' he admitted. 'Carleen wasn't keen and I lost touch with the guys I used to shoot with.'

I've realised since I've been going out with him again that Ed doesn't have many male friends. He socialises with his colleagues and they go to sporting events together, but he doesn't have the kind of friendships that I do with Erin and Sheedy. It seems to me that lots of men have plenty of acquaintances but they don't form the same sort of bond that exists between women. The one where you let your defences down and admit that life can be overwhelming. Where you drop everything if your mate calls. Despite all the talk about changing attitudes, men still want to be alpha. At least all the men I know do. Perhaps there's a whole generation of younger men out there who'll form those close connections with each other and won't feel the need to appear on top of things all the time, but I have my doubts.

Anyhow, I insisted that he wasn't to worry about me and that we could FaceTime, and I waved him off with a certain amount of satisfaction for him and (if I'm a hundred per cent honest) a little relief too. He's my boyfriend, we're in a relationship, yet I'm afraid that I'm depending on him too much. Because he's always there for me. Always ready to help out or call over. And always ready to sleep with me, which is lovely and pleasurable and leaves me with a warm glow. I'm getting used to having him in my life. The question is, should I?

It takes nearly five attempts before I manage to take a photo of my bandaged hand, but when I eventually succeed, I send it to him with a message saying that I'm not safe to be let out alone. Normally he messages back straight away, but it's nearly two hours later before the phone rings and he's asking me what the hell happened.

'Do you need me to come back?' he says when I tell him.

'What?'

'Well, you can hardly manage alone in the house, can you?'

'I'm getting by.' Although I haven't actually tried to do anything other than take the photo yet.

'I can leave the shooting and be back for the weekend at least. Carleen has Joe because I'm supposed to be away, so I can stay with you if you like.'

I'm tempted to say yes, that I'd love him to come and look after me, but instead I tell him that it's important for him to do his bonding stuff with his colleagues and that I'll be fine.

'How long before it heals?'

I give him the doctor's prognosis.

'I'll call you tomorrow,' he says. 'But if there's anything you need, Delphie, let me know straight away.'

'I will. You're . . . well, thanks, Ed.'

'Anything for you,' he says. 'Take care.'

'You too.'

I end the call.

Anything for me.

Maybe Lindsey and Vivi and Mum are all right. Maybe living my best life should mean living it with someone by my side. Maybe that someone should be Ed.

Chapter 25

Despite my blithe assumption that I'll be fine, it turns out that managing by myself is a complete nightmare. Having a shower without getting my hand wet is a Herculean task that involves trying to sellotape a bin liner around my wrist using my teeth. It's almost impossible to hold the bag tightly enough and apply the sellotape at the same time, and leaves me with a mouthful of sticky tape as well as a raw spot on my lip where I accidentally sellotaped it to the bag.

When I eventually emerge from the shower, almost an hour after I first went into the bathroom (drying myself is another almost impossible task), I make an appointment with Mindy, because doing my own hair is out of the question. As is opening the carton of soya milk in my fridge. It has one of those plastic ring pulls, and I simply can't manage it with one hand. I eventually open it by sitting on the kitchen step, gripping the carton between my feet and yanking the ring pull with my left hand. The milk explodes from the carton and spills over my hands and trousers. I stare at the puddle on the patio and I want to cry with frustration. What the hell is happening to me? To my ordered life? Why is even the smallest thing going wrong for me? What did I do to deserve this?

It's not until the black cat that sometimes prowls the garden and has been watching me from the top of the back wall ambles up to the puddle of milk and begins to lap it up that I allow myself the tiniest of smiles.

I start to sneeze because the cat is so close, so I go inside, change out of my trousers and T-shirt, then remove the splint and carefully unwind the wet bandage. The wound is still painful, and it's difficult to put another bandage on. I keep dropping the pin that holds it in place. But eventually I succeed, and then spend another minute trying to secure the splint. From beginning to end, the entire episode has taken another hour.

It wouldn't have happened if I'd had someone living with me, I think, as I make a second attempt at my soya latte, using capsules instead of the metal eco version I bought last year, which are too fiddly to open in my current state. If Ed had been here, he would've looked after me. But I told him not to come, so it's just me, on my own, as I've always wanted. I think of all the men I've dated who didn't work out, and I think of Erin, who's made some compromises to be with Fintan. Then I think again about Ed, who I once thought might be a permanent part of my life. He didn't feel the same way then, but does he feel differently now?

I used to measure men against Ed: the fun we had together, the way he treated me as an equal and wanted the best for me. Until he left because he wanted the best for himself. Then I started to measure them against Conrad.

I miss that Ed's not here now. And Ed Mark II is a very different proposition to the Ed of eight years ago. People matter to him more than they did back then. Doing the right thing by his son matters. And me? I seem to matter a lot more too.

I take a cookie from the Orla Kiely container that Sheedy bought me for Christmas last year (less of a struggle as it's a screw-top), then sit at my gate-leg table and look around at my kitchen with everything perfectly in its place. I like it this way. Nevertheless, I can't help asking myself if Lindsey is right and I'm holding out for perfection in a man too. A perfection that can't possibly exist. Will I only ever know when it's too late?

I finish my coffee and cookie, then take a look at my jigsaw. It seems to have been on the table forever, and I haven't bothered with it since Granny Mertens' death. But in a flurry of activity, I manage to crack a whole portion of the left side of the picture. It's a section where brightly coloured surfboards are pulled up onto the golden sand of the beach. I think of everyone's desire for me to take time out and smell the roses, and I wonder if they're right. I wonder whether having nothing to do would sort out my head.

But I already have nothing to do right now, and I already know who I am. I also know who I'm not. I don't care if people think I'm crazy for wanting to work. I don't care if they think I'm crazy for being happy on my own. I'm living my life my way. All the same, if only to stop them talking about me in clichés, I'd better get a job soon.

At that exact moment my phone rings and Roberta Dillon, one of the recruitment professionals I sent my CV to, asks me if I can make an interview in Glenageary at 9.30 in the morning.

Glenageary is a southside suburb of Dublin, and the bonus is that it's on the Dart line, although I reckon it will take at least an hour and a half to get there. The interview is with a solicitor's office.

Three Weddings and a Proposal

'Denis Lawrence will be interviewing you,' says Roberta when I say yes. 'Good luck.'

I immediately look up the Lawrence and Associates website. I reckon Denis must have set it up when he first went into practice, because it's static and old-fashioned, with basic information, no photos and no drop-down menus.

I could help him with that.

I text Sheedy and ask if she knows anything about the firm, but although she's familiar with the name, she doesn't know anything more. Nor does Erin. However, as Glenageary is an upmarket suburb, I have to assume that Denis has a good client list and plenty of work.

I'm glad I made the hair appointment with Mindy; it's exactly the self-care I need, because there's nothing more soothing than having someone else do your hair. As I'm leaving, my phone rings again, and this time it's Dad, asking if we can meet up and have a chat about Granny Mertens' estate. Luckily the salon is close to the train station, so I tell him that I can be with him shortly.

'That'd be brilliant,' he says. 'Thanks, Delphie.'

Mum and Dad both make a big fuss over me when they see my strapped-up hand and hear my tale of woe. Mum wants to know how I'm managing, and I say it's tricky but I'm fine. They both ask about jobs, and I'm happy to be able to tell them about the interview I've already done with Tom Greene and tomorrow's with Denis Lawrence. Then Mum puts the kettle on and makes coffee for Dad and me.

'I'll leave you to it,' she says, putting two bright yellow mugs on the table along with a freshly baked lemon sponge.

Dad cuts the cake and deposits a slice that's way too large on my plate.

'Don't finish it if you don't want it,' he says when he sees the look on my face. 'But you need some feeding up, Delphie. You've gone too thin.'

There is no way in the wild world that I'd ever be considered thin, but it's true that over the last couple of weeks, what with the stress of Granny Mertens on top of my job situation, I've lost another few kilos. Although I've noticed it around the waistband, I don't really think I look any thinner. Nevertheless, Dad never usually comments about my appearance, so my weight loss must be apparent somewhere.

I accept the cake and take a sip of the coffee.

'I wanted to talk about Granny's house.' Dad isn't one for beating about the bush, which is good. I like people being direct.

'I've decided on a local agent who thinks she can sell it very quickly,' I tell him. 'She sold a couple of similar properties at the beginning of the summer and she says she can get a really good price.'

'I don't want to sell it,' says Dad.

'OK.' I swallow some cake and look at him in surprise. 'Do you want to rent it out?'

'Not as such,' he says.

'Oh? What's the plan, so?'

'I want Vivi and Jason to live there with Charley,' he says.

I digest this information. 'You mean gift it to them?' I ask.

'No. It'd be my house,' he says. 'But why shouldn't they live there? Despite all the efforts at making housing more affordable, it's still bloody difficult for them to get anywhere, and they need their own space. This way, they wouldn't be too far away from us, so that would keep your mum happy too.'

'I thought she liked having them here,' I remark.

'She does,' says Dad. 'But it's not right. They're a family. They should have a home of their own.'

'Fair enough,' I say slowly. 'D'you think that might cause some issues with André and Tory? After all, they're spending a fortune on rent, whereas this would be a real boost for Vivi and Jason.'

'Vivi and Jason have a lot of expenses with Charley,' says Dad. 'So they need a bit of a dig-out. And . . .' he gives me a guarded look, 'Vivi is pregnant again.'

Was two babies under the age of two part of her life plan? I wonder aloud.

'I don't know,' says Dad. 'Maybe it wasn't exactly a plan. But your sister is a great mum and I'm sure she'll be fine.'

I nod.

'Anyhow, you don't need to worry about André and Tory either,' he says. 'Councillor Palmer is helping them out.'

'How?'

'He's giving them a deposit for a house.'

I'm relieved. I would've felt bad for my brother and his wife if they didn't have the same opportunity as Vivi and Jason. Not that it's exactly the same, of course. But at least both couples will have places of their own.

'It would be a good idea to have a rental agreement done up between you and Vivi,' I tell him.

'She's my little girl. I don't need an agreement,' says Dad.

'Yes, but . . .' I hesitate, unsure of how to carry on.

'But what?'

'Well, everything is fine now, but what if she and Jason split up? Or what if she wants to buy the house?'

'If they split up, Jason can feck off out of there,' says Dad.

'I know that's what you'd want, but it's not always that easy in practice,' I tell him. 'It'd be better to get it all signed and sealed.'

'We're family,' says Dad.

'Especially because it's family. Sheedy could tell you stories that'd make your toes curl.'

He ponders this for a few minutes, then nods. 'Can you draw it up?'

'It might be better if Sheedy does it,' I say. 'She'll make sure it's perfect.'

'You're a good girl, Delphie, you know that,' says Dad. 'You give good advice too.'

'Thanks.' I grin and push the plate away. I've eaten about a third of the cake.

'I'm sorry you're going through a rough time.'

'Ah, my hand isn't too bad. A bit sore, but it'll get better.'

'I meant your job,' says Dad. 'I know you put your heart and soul into it. They treated you disgracefully.'

'I'm grand, Dad, don't worry. Besides, they had to pay me off.'

'It shouldn't have come to that,' he says. 'And I shouldn't be grateful that it did. But it's been lovely seeing so much of you in the last while. Work to live, not live to work, you know.'

It's always been his mantra. But I also know that when he was working, he gave a hundred per cent.

'I'm fine, really I am,' I tell him.

'You're strong,' he says. 'You've always been strong. So I have faith in you.'

'Thanks.'

'But even strong people need a hug now and again.'

I lean forward and he wraps his arms around me, holding me tight like he did when I was a little girl. It's unbelievably comforting.

'I can tell you're struggling with that hand, no matter what kind of brave face you're putting on it,' he continues as he releases me. 'Maybe you should move here for a few days yourself until you can cope a bit better. I'm sure your ma would love to have you. I would myself.'

'Oh, Dad, you're a pet, you really are. But I'll manage.'

'You always say that,' he says. 'But sometimes managing isn't enough.'

'Honestly.'

'You're alone in that house,' he says. 'What if something goes wrong?'

'What sort of something?'

'I don't know. What if you fall?'

'I'm not Granny,' I say gently. 'I won't fall.'

'You only have one hand to break it if you do.'

'Please don't worry about me,' I say.

'Well, if you change your mind . . .'

'I promise that if I'm struggling I'll let you know.'

'I'm not like your ma,' he says. 'I don't need to know everything. But . . . what about Ed? How's that going? Could he stay with you for a while?'

'Things with Ed are pretty good,' I reply. 'But he's away at the moment.'

'How is it that that always happens?' asks Dad. 'The one time you really need someone, they're not there.'

'He'll be back soon.'

'Will you ask him to stay?'

It would be very useful to have someone to open my soya

milk and help me fasten my bra (which took fifteen minutes this morning). I tell Dad that I'll consider asking Ed to stay when he's back from his work trip.

'I want you to be happy, Delphie.'

'I am.'

'If you're stuck for anything – for help, for money – you'd tell me.'

'I'm not stuck,' I assure him. 'Didn't I follow your advice and sign on?'

'All the same. You'd tell me, wouldn't you? If things were getting on top of you?'

'Of course I would.' I get up from the table and kiss him on the head. 'I love you, Dad.'

'I love you too,' he says, and then eats the cake I left on my plate.

I'm wrapped in a warm glow all the way home. Because even if my family as a unit doesn't always get me, my dad has done his best. He certainly understands that my work is as important as any other part of my life. He understands my desire to live alone too – even if he thinks that at times like this it's problematic. But unlike the others, he doesn't try to change me. And he doesn't judge me.

I call Sheedy from the train and tell her about his decision to allow Vivi and Jason to live in Granny Mertens' house, and she promises to draw up an agreement. She also suggests he update his will, something I say I'll mention to him.

'I'll have it for you next week,' she says. 'We could meet for coffee?'

'Perfect,' I say, and put my phone away.

*

The following morning, I catch the eight a.m. train, which should get me to my interview in time, even allowing for the fact that the weather has taken a sudden turn for the worse and heavy rain always seems to delay everything. The streets are slick with water, and when I get into the slightly too crowded carriage, I'm greeted by the damp smell of wet coats and rolled-up umbrellas. I do my best to avoid contact with the other damp commuters and heave a sigh of relief when we reach Connolly station, where many of them alight. Connolly used to be my stop, and it seems odd to stay on the train as it continues on a journey that takes it around the curve of Dublin Bay. This is always a stunningly beautiful part of the train ride, though today the sea is a forbidding grey, and seagulls screech as they wheel above the frothy waves. I think of the bay at Port d'Andratx and the calm aquamarine water. I see Conrad's body, broken on the rocks. I close my eyes to block the vision, but it's still there. I wonder if it will ever go.

The train pulls into the station on time. The rain is coming down more heavily now. I put up my blue and gold golf umbrella, emblazoned with the Cosecha logo, and hurry along the leafy Station Road towards the town.

Lawrence and Associates is part of a small commercial development containing a convenience store, a dentist, a newsagent, a craft butcher and an upmarket café. The solicitor's practice is in rooms above the shops, and shares a door with the dentist. When I ring the bell and go up the stairs, I hear the steady buzz of the dentist's drill.

I push open the green door with the gold nameplate and almost collide with someone coming out.

'Oh!' I look at him in surprise.

He returns the surprised stare.

'Delphie,' says Luke Granahan. 'How are you? What are you doing here?'

'Interviewing for a job.' I smile at my one-time employment solicitor.

He frowns. 'With Larry?'

'With Denis Lawrence,' I reply.

'Known to his friends as Larry.' Luke winks and then frowns again. 'I didn't think you wanted to be a legal secretary.'

'I don't,' I say. 'I'm interviewing for the executive assistant job. Although,' I add, as I look past him into the office, 'I'm not entirely sure that's what they want here.'

'Maybe they do.' There's an undercurrent of doubt in his voice. 'Larry's ambitious.'

'If he's doing business with you, he obviously has some good clients.'

'He's my brother-in-law,' says Luke.

'Oh.'

'Have you had other job offers?' he asks.

'You sound like you're warning me off,' I say.

'God, no, I don't mean to.' He shakes his head. 'Larry would be lucky to have you working for him. I'm sure you'd drag him into this century.'

'You've seen the website too?' I grin.

He laughs. 'I'm being unfair. He's a great guy. He doesn't need to focus on things like websites because he's well known in the community.'

'But I could help with it,' I say. 'I'd better let him know I'm here. Don't want to be late and create a bad impression.'

'Indeed.' He steps to one side and then looks at me with concern as I roll up my umbrella. 'What on earth happened to your hand?'

'Oh, it's just a cut. I needed stitches.'

'They didn't do a very good job of bandaging it,' he observes.

I tell him the story of the soya milk disaster and he asks me to let him have a closer look. I hold out my palm, and he puts down his slim briefcase then gently takes my injured hand in his. In less than a minute he's expertly unwrapped and rebandaged it.

'Wow,' I say as I look at his handiwork. 'That's amazing, thanks.'

'My mum is a nurse,' he says. 'I'm good with this sort of thing. It's healing well, but you should take it easy. You don't want to open it up again.'

'That's what they told me at the clinic,' I say. 'I've been doing nothing *but* taking it easy.'

'Why don't I entirely believe you?' he asks.

'Really, I have.'

'How did you cut it in the first place?'

I tell him, and he says that's why he likes screw-top wine bottles, no matter how sniffy people can be about them. 'I'm glad you're getting on OK, despite your injury,' he adds. 'Erin told me you all had a great time in Mallorca.'

Presumably she didn't say that the visit included an unexpected meeting with Bianca followed by a trespass order. Although maybe that particular situation would constitute a good time for most solicitors.

I say that I enjoyed the trip very much but I'm ready to get back to work.

'You're very focused, aren't you?' says Luke.

'Not as much as everyone seems to think,' I reply. 'But I like . . .' I hesitate for a moment, then, in a rush, it comes to me, and I can't believe I never realised it before now. 'I like an anchor,' I tell him. 'Having a job is something that tethers me. That makes me feel secure.'

'You don't always have to be tethered,' he says.

'So everyone keeps telling me. You'd swear losing my job was a lifetime opportunity.'

'I suppose big shocks in our lives give us time to press the reset button.' He then says that he hopes I find the job that's worthy of me. I'm getting the impression that he doesn't believe working for his brother-in-law's firm is it.

At that moment, the door to an inner office opens and a man steps out.

'You still here?' he asks Luke before looking at me and asking if he can help me.

'I'll go, Delphie,' says Luke. 'Great to see you. Take care of that hand.' He nods to his brother-in-law and tells him he'll give him a call. 'And you'd be lucky to get Delphie,' he adds before he goes down the stairs again. 'She's great.'

Denis Lawrence raises an eyebrow as he ushers me into his office and asks how I know Luke. The problem with this is that I then have to tell him about leaving Cosecha in more detail than I wanted to. He makes notes as I talk and then interrupts me to ask how much I was paid. When I tell him, he looks at me in surprise.

'I can't offer you that,' he says.

'I had a great salary,' I admit. 'But that reflected my responsibilities.'

'You wouldn't have anything like that level of responsibility here,' he tells me. 'We're a small practice. Efficient. Good. But small.'

'I don't mind. I'm ready for a bit of downsizing.'

'Really?' His tone is dry and I kick myself, because I've implied that his firm isn't worthy of my full attention.

'What I mean is that Cosecha was an international firm,' I say. 'I had to accompany Conrad on overseas trips and deal with clients from many different countries. I'm happy not to have to go abroad any more.'

'Why?'

I say that I have family commitments for the next few months that will keep me at home, and that leaves him looking at me with the kind of expression that suggests I'm someone who'll arrive on the dot and leave on the dot because she has better things to do with her life. This is, without doubt, the worst interview I've ever done in my life. The woman in the job centre could use it as an example of how not to do one. I hope Denis Lawrence doesn't say anything to Luke. He'd be disappointed in me.

'I'll be in touch,' he tells me after I've run out of things to say.

I stand up, and he asks when I think my hand will be healed.

'Hopefully within a couple of weeks.'

'I do rather need someone straight away,' he says.

And I know I've blown it completely.

Chapter 26

Although I'd like to get home as quickly as possible and put the trauma of the horrible interview behind me, my stomach is rumbling and so I go into the nearby coffee shop and order a cappuccino and a slice of chocolate biscuit cake.

I'm scrolling aimlessly through my social media feeds as I sip the coffee when my phone buzzes and I see that Martha is calling. Has Henry complained about her giving me Conrad's pen? Does she need it back? I can't think what else she could possibly want from me.

But after we've gone through the pleasantries, she asks if I can tell her anything about the Caldwell project.

'It's a buyout of some distressed mortgages,' I reply. 'Conrad had lined up a company that was taking them over but not selling the houses.'

'Oscar was talking to Henry about it,' she says. 'Apparently Cosecha had set up some kind of special-purpose vehicle to do the deal. And it seems I'm one of the signatories to that.'

Conrad must have used one of the companies Martha was a director of when finalising the deal. I did up the original paperwork but left blank spaces for whichever company and directors he decided to use.

'Is there a problem?' I ask.

'Only that Justin has been on to me and is saying that I have to sign the papers as soon as possible.'

'Justin is always last-minute about stuff,' I say. 'I'm sure he'll get the papers to you in plenty of time.'

'He sent them yesterday,' says Martha. 'But when I read them through, the deal isn't what I originally thought.' Martha never signed anything Conrad asked her to unless she'd read it through first. She's not stupid.

It's taken a long time to get the deal to this point, so it's not unreasonable for Justin to want to conclude it now even if he's made some changes. I say this to Martha.

'I remember talking to Conrad after it was set up,' she says. 'He'd done a lot of work and he asked if I'd be willing to remain a signatory despite our split to save him having to go through a whole heap of paperwork again. I agreed because I was happy at the idea of selling the mortgages and making sure people stayed in their homes. But that's not what seems to be happening, and I wanted to check with you whether Conrad himself had changed anything so that the houses could be sold.'

'Not that I'm aware of,' I say. 'It was one of the last projects I gave him papers on. In fact,' I say slowly, 'I think there was a written resolution not to sell to anyone who'd repossess the homes.'

'I don't trust Justin Delaney to do what Conrad wanted,' says Martha. 'Are you busy right now, Delphie? Could you call to the house and have a look at the documents with me?'

I'm free for the rest of the day, so I tell her I'll be with her as soon as I can.

I drain my coffee and cram the biscuit cake into my mouth.

Checking documents, being involved – this is what I like doing.

This is me.

'Come in, come in.' Martha opens the door wide and takes my umbrella, putting it in the stand so that it doesn't drip all over her beautiful tiled hallway. 'It's filthy out there.' And then she spots my bandaged hand and asks what happened. Once again I go through the story, and she tuts in sympathy before bringing me to the basement, where she has all the paperwork for the Caldwell deal.

On the train journey to Lansdowne Road I've been wondering how Hammersmith, the company ultimately buying the debt, has reacted to changing the terms. After all, their CEO seemed to be on the same page as Conrad about not selling the houses. But then I see that Justin has replaced Hammersmith with another company called Evergreen.

'So he's selling the debt to someone else,' I say. 'Wow. I bet Mike Ogilvy will be fuming at being dumped, especially as it took months to put the whole thing together.'

'How did Justin manage to change it in such a short time?' asks Martha.

'It's like he already had a replacement deal ready to go,' I say. 'I suppose he reckons it's a more profitable scenario to be able to sell the houses.'

'He's such a shit,' says Martha.

Yes, he is.

'I don't want this to happen,' she continues. 'Making people homeless is wrong.'

I agree.

'I'll tell Justin I'm not signing.'

'In the end he'll probably set up a completely new company for the project,' I say. 'It'll take a while, and Mike Ogilvy might be able to throw a spanner in the works, but it's not impossible.'

'I don't think he has the time to do that,' says Martha. 'He was peppering me to get this signed as soon as possible.'

'He could be under pressure from the new buyers,' I acknowledge.

'He said it was important for Cosecha.' Martha looks thoughtful. 'I hope it's not in trouble. Losing clients or anything like that.'

'It probably did lose some clients,' I say. 'That's the nature of things when someone influential isn't there any more. But it's a strong company, and even though I loathe Justin Delaney, he's a good business person. Cosecha will be fine, Martha, with or without this deal.'

'They're still working on the valuation of Conrad's shareholding,' she says. 'I planned to retain some shares for myself. But now I'm not so sure.'

'I would've got shares when I was made a director,' I say. 'I would've been proud to be a part of it.'

Martha suddenly tears up, and the next thing I know, she's sobbing helplessly. I feel a lump in my throat. I grab one of the tissues from the box on the desk and hand it to her.

'Why does it still feel like it only happened yesterday?' she asks when her tears dry up. 'When will I stop reliving it? When will I stop grieving? When does anyone?'

'I don't think you ever do,' I reply. 'I think you just grow a shell. Learn to live with it.'

'Conrad used to say that what didn't kill you made you stronger. I've always thought it was a ridiculous quotation.'

Martha blows her nose. 'Because it doesn't. I'm definitely not stronger after this. After Bianca either.'

'But you're strong enough to know that Justin was trying to dick you over.'

'I guess some of Conrad's business sense did rub off,' she says.

'You had your own business before Conrad,' I remind her. 'It was very successful. You have a good business head.'

'I'd kind of forgotten that.' She gives me a thoughtful look. 'It suited me not to keep going with things, but I had a lot of high-profile clients back in the day. And you, Delphie – he loved working with you because of your business brain.'

'Not that it's much in demand at the moment.'

'What d'you mean?'

I tell her about my fruitless job-searching and she looks at me with astonishment.

'Why on earth are you faffing around with recruitment agencies?' she asks. 'Why aren't you calling all the people you dealt with before? For heaven's sake, Delphie! You were a senior person in Cosecha. You're not someone who needs to be on a recruiter's mailing list.'

I say that I might have thought so, and Conrad might have treated me that way, but that most people seem to have regarded me as an overpaid secretary.

'Are you crazy?' she cries. 'Just because that idiot Justin Delaney didn't rate you – or, more likely, felt threatened by you – doesn't mean that everyone else thinks the same way. I remember Seb Mitchell telling Conrad that he'd love to have you on his team. And Richard Dorsey used to sing your praises.'

Richard and Seb were both clients of Cosecha.

336

'When did they say these things?' I ask.

'At our dinner parties,' says Martha. 'Why aren't you banging on their doors, Delphie? Why aren't you putting yourself in front of the people you need to put yourself in front of?'

'They know I've left Cosecha. If they wanted me, they'd call me.'

'But they don't know what you might be doing now!' she exclaims. 'They might think you're taking time out. Or working somewhere else. How will they know if you don't tell them?'

It's a good question. I assumed that people I knew from the business world would come looking for me if they needed someone. I didn't think I should be the one to show them that they needed me. But Martha is right. I've been an idiot.

'Do you seriously think that Justin wouldn't be putting himself about looking for a job if he'd been canned?' she demands. 'And not only that, he'd be putting himself about for jobs he's eminently unqualified to do. Because he's full of undeserving self-confidence. And yet you, Delphie, one of the most competent people I know, have apparently left your self-confidence at home.'

'I have plenty of self-confidence,' I assure her. 'I know I can do a good job if someone will give me the opportunity.'

'Listen to yourself! You shouldn't be waiting for an opportunity. You should be out there telling them how lucky they'd be to get you. You should be telling them that *you* are the opportunity!'

You'd be lucky to get her. Luke said that to Denis Lawrence. But Denis isn't going to give me a job. I know that. I'm not what he wants. Because for his practice, I am overqualified.

Wildly overqualified. So why exactly did I go to that interview in the first place?

Because, I acknowledge, my self-confidence was tied up in Conrad and Cosecha. And being booted out put a massive dent in it. I didn't realise it sooner, but now I do.

Martha's right. I've been selling myself short. I've always told other women never to do that. I can't believe I might be doing it myself.

Her grey eyes are studying me carefully.

'You could be right,' I concede. 'Maybe I need to do a radical rethink.'

'You definitely do,' she says. 'I can't believe I'm having to tell you this.'

'Thanks, Martha.'

'No,' she says. 'Thank you, Delphie. For all you did for Conrad. For what you did for me too. For coming here today. And for going to Palmyra for me. For dealing with the Bianca situation and getting the things that mattered to me. For doing it all so brilliantly.'

'Have you heard from her at all?' I need to deflect the conversation. It's uncomfortable to have to face up to how stupid I've been.

'Bianca?'

She still says the name as though it's a swear word.

'I know she's hard in some ways, but she was very upset,' I say carefully. 'She told me about seeing Conrad's body. It was traumatic for her.'

'I don't want to think about her,' says Martha. 'She threw herself at my husband and she didn't care what the consequences were.'

I keep silent.

'Oh, all right.' She sounds irritated. 'It takes two to tango. Conrad isn't exactly without blame.'

'Everyone makes mistakes,' I say. 'You, me, Conrad . . .'

'You really do think she should get something, don't you? For her time fooling around with him.'

I say nothing.

She shakes her head. 'I can see why you haven't been putting yourself about after all,' she says. 'You're a softie at heart.'

'No,' I protest. 'I'm practical.'

'I'll think about something to keep her happy, OK?' Martha gives me a look of pure exasperation, and I say that what happens between her and Bianca is nothing to do with me.

'Oh, Delphie. It's all to do with you somehow or another. You're part of our lives whether you like it or not.'

'I'm not part of anything,' I say.

'We'll see,' replies Martha.

I'm not exactly sure what she means by that.

Although I'm fired up after my conversation with Martha, I'm going to leave the cold calling until next week, when I can give it my full time and attention. I spend half an hour with my jigsaw, completing a section with multiple palm trees, then walk to the deli to get some food before sitting out in the back garden with the newspaper. I bought a takeaway coffee at the deli too, so there's been no trauma of opening cartons or messing around with capsules.

There's a sudden flurry of activity from next door, and squeals of excitement from Liam and Cathal, and I realise that their parents have bought them a trampoline and that Peter is erecting it in the garden. It isn't long before I see the top of Cathal's golden head as he bounces as high as he can, and the uncontrolled joy and laughter of the two boys makes me smile. I like hearing children having fun.

It still doesn't make me want to have any of my own.

Does that make me an unnatural woman? A bad person?

I don't think Ed is a bad person for not wanting to have a baby when he did. And yet in being the sort of woman who isn't frantically listening to the tick-tock of her body clock, I wonder if I'm missing an essential part of myself. Even Erin has succumbed, for heaven's sake! Her main motivation for moving in with Fintan, no matter what she might have told him, is the possibility of having a baby. Her elusive maternal instinct has finally kicked in. Will mine? And if it does, will I have left it too late?

The shrieks of the boys grow even louder as Cathal manages to jump high enough to see over the wall.

'Hiya, Delphie!' he shouts, his face red with excitement.

'Hi, Cathal.' I wait till he reappears at the top of the bounce.

'We have a trampoline,' he adds unnecessarily.

'I can see that.'

'Would you like to come in and jump with us?' His voice is breathless.

'That's very kind of you, Cathal. But I've hurt my hand. I can't jump.'

There's a silence, then a scrabbling sound, and Cathal appears at the top of the dividing wall.

'How did you hurt it?'

'I cut it with a knife.'

'Ooh.' His eyes widen. 'Mum says you have to be careful with knives.'

'Your mum is right.'

'Cathal Dunne! Get down off that wall and stop annoying Delphie.' Katie sounds harassed.

'He's fine,' I call back.

'He's not allowed on the wall.'

'I was being nice to her,' he tells his mum. 'She's hurt her hand. So it's OK for me to be on the wall.'

'If Delphie has a sore hand, you annoying her won't make it better.'

I give Cathal a conspiratorial wink as Katie's own head appears above the wall.

'What happened? Are you OK?' she asks.

It's Cathal who tells her that I cut it and that I have a huge bandage, and Katie gives me a sympathetic look. 'Can you manage?'

'It's on the mend.'

'We're having a barbecue this afternoon,' she says. 'Join us.'

'Oh, I don't think . . .'

'Please do,' she insists. 'Pete loves barbecuing and he always does way too much. It's only sausages and chicken skewers. You'll be able to manage. Save you trying to cook for yourself.'

I think about the food in my fridge from the deli run. It'll keep. So I say thanks to Katie, and a short while later I'm sitting in their garden while Pete chars the sausages and the boys divide their time between the grill and the trampoline.

'You should drop by more often,' says Katie as she fills my glass with a chilled rosé.

'You're very busy,' I say. 'You need your quality time.'

'There's no such thing as quality time when you have two

young boys,' she says. 'It's only time when there isn't a disaster either happening or about to happen.'

I laugh.

'Seriously.' She shakes her head. 'If I'd known what it would be like . . .'

'I'm sure you wouldn't change them for the world,' I say. 'They're great kids.'

'Nobody truly tells you how all-consuming it is, though,' she says. 'And how bloody difficult it is to juggle everything. Sorry.' She takes a sip of her wine. 'It sounds like I'm complaining, and I don't mean to. I love my family. But sometimes an hour by myself would be the greatest luxury in the world.'

I know what she means. To me, being alone is a privilege.

My phone beeps. It's a WhatsApp from Ed.

Are you OK? he's asking. *I'm at your door and you're not answering.*

What on earth is he doing here? He should've texted if he was going to come by. I tell Katie that I'll have to go because a friend has called around unexpectedly, but she tells me to invite him in too, so next thing I know, I've retrieved Ed and am introducing him to the neighbours.

'He's very handsome,' murmurs Katie when Ed insists on helping Pete with the barbecuing.

'Always a bonus.' I grin.

'Are you guys . . . Is it serious?'

Isn't it funny how quickly women get around to asking each other these questions? Ed and Pete's conversation, scraps of which float towards us on the air, is all about the relative merits of Volkswagen and Audi.

I tell Katie that I've no idea where Ed and I are going,

but that it's fun being with him. I add that he's divorced with a young son, which she appreciates can be tricky; then she asks about work, and I tell her about being let go from Cosecha, and she looks horrified and asks if I'm managing OK. I share my interview stories with her, and she counters with some car-crash stories of people she's interviewed herself – she works in the human resources department of a medical company. I tell her that I've also interviewed candidates for jobs but that most of them have been pretty professional.

'Lucky you,' says Katie. 'I had a twenty-five-year-old who turned up with her mother once. She was quite put out when her mum couldn't sit in on the interview.'

'You're kidding me.'

'Totally not. And then there was the guy whose dad rang to complain when his son didn't get the job. He wanted him to be interviewed by a man. Said I was biased.'

I try to imagine my dad doing that. I can't.

'Why didn't you give him the job?' I ask.

'Firstly, he wasn't qualified,' she replies. 'Secondly, he was rather too put out by our policy of random drug testing.'

We laugh a bit more and she tells me that I'm probably a dream interview candidate and wishes me luck in finding a job. Then Pete and Ed inform us that the sausages have been sufficiently burnt, so we help ourselves to the food, which is on the right side of incinerated.

Ed and I stay for a couple of hours before I say that we should be going and thank Pete and Katie for a really good time. She reminds me to call if there's anything I need, while Pete and Ed talk about meeting up for a pint together sometime.

'Lovely neighbours,' says Ed when we're back in my house.

'I don't see them that often,' I confess as I flop onto the sofa. 'But it was a great afternoon. Anyhow, Ed Miller, why are you here and not target shooting in Sligo?'

'The target shooting was yesterday. I had the day off today. And I suddenly thought it would be nice to surprise you. Though when I rang your bell and there was no answer, I thought you'd probably gone to your mum's and I was raging I hadn't messaged you first.'

'You should've,' I agree. 'I was at Mum's yesterday, so I couldn't do two days in a row. Although,' I add, 'ever since leaving Cosecha, I've been getting on so much better with all my family.'

'You have more time for them,' says Ed.

'True. But I think . . .' I have to consider this carefully, because the thought is only now formulating in my head, 'I think it's that I'm having a crisis. They relate better to disasters than successes.'

Ed gives me an amused look. 'I'm sure that's not true.'

'I really think it is,' I say. 'I've had more texts in the last few weeks from them than in the last year. Vivi sent a link to a receptionist's position the other day. She said it was better than nothing. And it is,' I add hastily. 'But my career was never about being a receptionist. I need to interview for the right job, not any job. Employers know that too.' I tell him about my disaster with Denis Lawrence. 'And that was even with Luke's endorsement.'

'Luke?'

'The solicitor who looked after me,' I remind him. 'Denis Lawrence is his brother-in-law.'

'Did this Luke guy get you the interview?'

I shake my head.

'Then how do you know he endorsed you?'

I have to explain then about bumping into him, and Ed asks if he would've known I was going to the interview.

'Of course not.'

'I thought you might have kept in touch.'

'Ed, are you jealous?' I look at him incredulously.

'Of course I'm not jealous, Delphie. He did a great job for you with the settlement and I thought perhaps you might have stayed in touch because he had good contacts or something.'

'Sadly, he didn't offer me his contact book.' I give Ed a rueful smile. 'Sorry, I was being silly.'

'You were a bit. Though I wouldn't like to think he was muscling in on my girl.'

And then he kisses me and one thing leads to another, and we go to the bedroom, which makes me very glad he called around today.

Chapter 27

Given that everyone's so keen on me having a good time and looking after myself, it's a bonus that I'll be heading on my spa trip soon, even if I'm not sure I'll be doing any swimming, because on my return visit to the walk-in clinic, and much to my frustration, they advised leaving the stitches in for another few days. I'll be going back again before I head to the Ardallen, but I can't count on them being removed in time for my trip. Nevertheless, although my hand is stiff and a little uncomfortable, it doesn't hurt any more and I'm managing much better. This is a good thing, as the first few days of the week end up being unexpectedly busy.

Monday starts early because Ed has to get back to Sligo for eight a.m. That means him leaving my house before five. At least it isn't dark – his departure more or less coincides with the sunrise, though he's up early to shower. I make him coffee and put it in my thermal mug, which I give him for the journey, along with a couple of the pastries I picked up in the deli yesterday. He kisses me before leaving and tells me he'll message me later in the day.

It's like being married, I think, as I go for an early-morning jog along the seafront. It's like being married with me at home sending my husband off for the day. Although that doesn't really happen in marriages any more, does it? Like Pete and Katie next door, it's more of a mad rush by both people to get out to work.

It's calm and glorious by the sea as the sun rises higher in the sky, its white light shimmering off the water. I'm not the only person out and about, and my fellow joggers acknowledge each other, enjoying both the beauty of the morning and the communal spirit of being up early enough to see it.

When I get home again, I have a long shower (I ordered a special cover online that goes over my arm and keeps my hand dry, thus speeding up the process enormously), then make myself some breakfast. As I haven't heard back from Tom Greene at Sycamore Investments yet, I decide to be proactive and call him to ask if he's made a decision. He's not available, but I leave a message. I haven't heard from Denis Lawrence either but I already know I've completely blown that and I'm not going to call.

I then send an email off to Sheedy asking her if the rental agreement for Granny Mertens' house is ready, and when she replies attaching a copy, I print it off to bring to Dad's later. She tells me that she's in the process of updating his will and that she'll send him an email directly with the amendments he asked for in place.

When I get to the house just after noon, Nichola and her girls are there. So is Vivi. I don't know if Vivi has made news of her pregnancy public yet, so I don't say anything. Then she gives me an exasperated look and asks if I'm not going to congratulate her and I realise that I was probably the last to know. I give the necessary congratulations while Mum puts on the kettle and makes tea. I bring a cup into the other room for Dad and hand him the agreement.

'Vivi and Jason both have to sign,' I tell him as I go through it with him.

'Thanks for this, Delphie,' he says. 'I appreciate it.'

'No problem. I'm delighted to have been able to help.'

I leave him with his newspaper and tea and go back to the kitchen, where Vivi is talking about her pregnancy, which apparently is going more smoothly than her first. Then she talks about having to find somewhere to live, which makes me smile, as obviously Dad is going to surprise her with Granny Mertens' house. I can't help thinking that even now, when we're all adults, our parents are looking after us.

'I'm glad to see you're looking more cheerful,' she says when she notices my smile. 'How's the job-hunting going?'

I tell her that I'm looking at a number of options and hope to have something really soon. I confess that I've put it on the long finger until my stitches are taken out. There's more sympathy about my injury, which disappears somewhat when I tell them I'm going to the Ardallen for a break.

'How fabulous!' The look Vivi gives me is envious. 'At least you're finally treating yourself.'

'Absolutely,' says Mum. 'You deserve it after the last couple of months.'

'I have a voucher.'

'Even better,' says Nichola. 'Who are you taking with you?'

'Nobody.'

'Delphie!' She looks horrified.

'What?'

'A lovely girlie break like that! You should bring your best friend.'

'My best friend wouldn't have time.'

'She'd make it for that.'

'The voucher is only for one person.' Martha knows me too well to have made it for two. Or maybe she didn't even think of it.

'I thought you were mellowing,' says Vivi. 'But you're not, are you?'

'Mellowing? How? Why?' I shrug. 'I'm going for a lovely overnight experience. I don't need anyone with me for that.'

Mum, Vivi and Nichola all look at me in despair.

I finish my tea and leave.

It's Tuesday before Tom Greene returns my calls and tells me I haven't got the Sycamore job.

'You're overqualified for us,' he says.

I want to say that I'm not, that I'd love to work for him, but I don't, because he's right. Instead I say that I was afraid that was the case but that I'd always liked his company and that was why I'd applied.

'Appreciate your words, Delphie,' he says. 'If anything comes up that matches your experience, I'll certainly give you a call. Though I guess you'll have something else by then anyhow.'

Later in the morning I turn up to a mandatory session organised by the unemployment office, which is pretty much a waste of time but ticks the boxes. I say this in a text to Ed. He FaceTimes me as I'm sipping a cappuccino in the nearby café afterwards. He looks very fit in his hi-vis jacket over a tight-fitting T-shirt and I say so.

'And you have a delightful frothy moustache,' he tells me, which makes me rub my upper lip. 'I miss you.'

'I miss you too,' I say. 'How's the job going?'

'With luck, we'll be finished by the end of the week. But more likely the middle of next. These things always take longer than you expect. I'll come back at the weekend anyway, though.'

'No target shooting on Saturday?'

'Not that I know of.'

'Whatever suits you,' I say. 'Let me know.'

'I'll call you later,' he promises. 'Have a good day.'

I forgot to mention that I'm going to Ardallen tomorrow, but I'll tell him tonight.

I'm finishing my coffee when I get a call from Martha telling me she has a meeting with Justin next Monday about the Caldwell deal.

'I managed to put him off earlier about the whole sign-right-away thing, and I'm in Cork this week with the children,' she says. 'As I told him, they're my priority. But Cosecha is important to me too. I want this deal to be the one that Conrad put together, not some nonsense of Justin's.'

'You're a fierce woman, Martha Morgan,' I tell her.

'If only,' she responds. 'He wants to talk about my share-holding as well. Apparently they've hired Haughton's to help, though I'm not sure how Henry feels about that.'

Erin messaged me the other day with that news. I sent her a hand-clap GIF in return.

'Henry also told me that the divorce file is closed,' Martha adds. 'It made me think about how things might have turned out, how messy it all might have become. I'm sure we would've worked it out in the end, but . . . well, things might have been said that I'm happy have been left unsaid.'

I'm glad I trashed the file on Conrad's computer. When we finish the conversation, I wipe the remote disk too.

Then I go to the clinic, where my stitches are finally removed and the nurse proclaims herself happy with how my hand has healed. The skin is pink and delicate, and I think I'm going to be left with a scar, but it's great to be bandage-free.

When I get home, I book a car on the app and pack for my trip.

As I zip my case closed, the conversation with Martha about Caldwell resurfaces in my mind. I recall the written resolution again and assume it's with Conrad's papers some-where, but I wonder if he also scanned it into his files. I open my laptop and click on the Cosecha portal, then type the password into the log-in screen. I'm half expecting it to be rejected. But it isn't. I'm in. Again.

I know I shouldn't be accessing the company's files, and there's a part of me that feels I only have a few minutes to find what I'm looking for before someone in IT notices that the system has been accessed using the anonymous password. But Conrad logged in like this all the time, so it shouldn't raise any flags. Besides, the Cosecha IT department is basically Tiernan and one other person, and their main focus is the financial database. Tiernan wouldn't know anything about random documents in Conrad's files.

I find the Caldwell folder straight away. The agreement and all the supporting documents are there, just as I originally filed them. I click on the one I'm looking for, the written resolution, signed by the board, not to sell the portfolio to any company that wants to take possession of the houses. Conrad signed it too.

I look at it for a while, wondering if it means anything any more. Hoping fervently that nobody is tracking me, I download the resolution and send it to Martha, saying that it might be useful to have in her conversation with Justin. She sends back an almost immediate response thanking me. She doesn't ask how I found it.

Then I access the client database and download a list of names to call when I come back from my break.

I close the laptop.

That's the last time I'll ever access the Cosecha files.

I've put Martha, Conrad and Cosecha completely out of my mind by the time I drive to Ardallen the following day. It's a glorious morning, and the sun is high in the sky when I collect my car. I pair my phone so that I can listen to an audiobook as I drive. I've chosen *My Cousin Rachel*, narrated by Jonathan Pryce, and his distinctive voice takes me from the dry grass and blue skies of Ireland to an altogether more dark and Gothic Cornwall, filled with drama and intrigue. I've always thought that much of the suspicion that falls on Rachel in the story is because the men of that time hadn't a clue about women. I'd like to think that today's men do a better job, but there are times when I doubt it very much.

As I pull into the magnificent grounds of the hotel, it strikes me that my mental image of the house that Rachel came to is not dissimilar to Ardallen itself, an eighteenth-century building with sash windows that currently reflect the cloudless sky. There's a portico to the front and a hidden parking area for cars off to one side. I leave my Prius in the nearest available space, then walk to the reception area.

The house is as magnificent as the gardens, and the tiled reception area is dominated by an enormous circular mahogany table standing on a richly coloured rug. A large vase of colourful flowers takes up the centre of the table, while an elegant chandelier hangs down over it, its crystals scattering rainbow shards of light beneath.

I'm not thinking of Rachel as I look around, but I do feel a little like Elizabeth Bennet when she first sees Pemberley and realises exactly how rich Mr Darcy is and what she's given up for the sake of pride. I've always liked Lizzie Bennet. I like how she stayed true to herself.

Although there's a lift to my top-floor room (given its location, it must originally have been a maid's room), I walk up the wide staircase, imagining the house as it probably was a couple of hundred years ago. The restoration is so authentic that it can hardly have been very different, although I suppose that modern heating and air conditioning have made it significantly more comfortable, certainly in the servants' quarters.

No servant would have had the luxury of the queen-sized bed I see when I open the door, or an en suite bathroom stocked with sumptuous Rathbornes toiletries. Standing here looking out of the window, I feel a sense of peace and ease settle on me, and I allow my breath to escape in a slow, deliberate exhale.

As I put away my clothes, I remind myself that you don't have to escape to one of the most expensive spas in the country to relax, but my goodness, being surrounded by luxury certainly helps. And I realise that no matter what has happened to me in the past, or what might happen in the future, I'm a lucky woman. I have choices. All I have to do is make the right ones.

I've made a conscious decision not to check my phone every few minutes while I'm here, so I leave it behind when I go for a walk around the sunken garden to the rear of the house. The fountains are shooting water high into the air, and the droplets, caught by the sunlight, cascade downwards in a rush of rainbow colours. I feel a sliver of regret that I didn't bring my phone after all, but remind myself that I can take photographs in the morning and that I should simply appreciate the beauty of where I am now.

Looking back towards the house, I see that there are two wings attached to the main building. Both are new. One, I know, is the spa, where I've already booked a salt scrub treatment. The other seems to be a ballroom, and it's clear that an event will be taking place there later today, because the hotel staff are bustling around moving furniture and arranging large tubs of flowers. Yet here even the bustling seems tranquil.

I return to my room and send a thank-you text to Martha, then head for the spa. My treatment takes place in a subtly lit room with a lingering scent of jasmine and lemon. It's superbly relaxing, although I feel slightly anxious when Samara, the therapist, leaves the room and I'm not sure if she's coming back. After what seems an age of lying there pretending to relax, I sit up, which is exactly the moment she returns with a glass of water for me.

'Take your time,' she says. 'There's no rush. You can sit in the meditation area afterwards.'

The meditation area has neatly spaced loungers where about half a dozen women are sipping water or green tea as they look out over the gardens and chat to each other in muted tones. I stay there for as long as it takes to finish my water.

Even if I haven't spent as long as I should clearing my mind and taking care of my body, I'm more relaxed than I've been in months, and my skin is smooth as silk after its sea salt exfoliation – although my hair is a disaster area thanks to the head massage that was included in the treatment. But it doesn't matter, because I'm not doing anything special tonight. I'm avoiding the elegant dining room and having a more casual meal in the bar. Samara told me to drink plenty of water, and even though I assumed I'd have wine with my dinner, my body feels like a temple right now, so I'll seriously consider following her instructions and skipping the alcohol.

There's a library in the hotel where guests can borrow books. I know I won't have time to read an entire novel today, but when I see a hardback edition of *Pride and Prejudice*, I select it and bring it outside.

Then I sit in the slanting rays of the sun and embrace my inner Lizzie.

Chapter 28

I stay in healthy mode at dinner and stick with water to accompany my seafood risotto. Afterwards, I go outside and sit on the terrace again. The temperature is still balmy, and even though I probably should've made a bit more of an effort given the beautiful surroundings, I'm perfectly happy in my loose red dress. I'm wearing flat ballet pumps with it, thus opting completely for comfort over style. But style doesn't matter, because it's an external thing, and today I'm looking after what's inside. Anyhow, I'm alone except for a couple at the other end of the terrace who are far more interested in each other than me.

Looking across towards the wing of the house that contains the ballroom, I can see that the event they were preparing for is in full swing. I discovered earlier that it's a wedding, and that the groom is a player on the Irish rugby team. He's marrying his childhood sweetheart. They were posing for photographs at the front of the building as I was coming back from the spa, him tall and muscular, her dainty and slight.

Maybe my relationships don't last because I'm not dainty and slight. Even as the thought crosses my mind, I know it's rubbish. But it occurs to me, as it has before, that there's a premium placed on looking feminine and helpless, even if you aren't. When it appears that you can perfectly well look after yourself, people assume you can. And you learn to live up to their expectations.

All through my schooldays, I was the one who was put in charge. Being taller than anyone else conveyed an authority I had to learn. I wasn't naturally good at being a leader and I used to complain that I always got the blame when things went wrong. I said this to Granny Mertens once, upset over a dressing-down from Mum because somebody had left the freezer door open and all her carefully stored meals had defrosted. She blamed me for not keeping an eye on things. She told me I was big enough to know better. I realise now that she wasn't really talking about my size, but back then I didn't think that way.

'Why can't I be like Vivi?' I asked Granny afterwards. 'Nobody ever gives out to her, because she's princess pretty and everyone likes her. But I get into trouble and people call me a big lump. It's not fair.'

Granny agreed that it wasn't fair, but she also insisted I should embrace both my leadership potential and my height. 'You only have one life, Delphie,' she said. 'Are you going to waste it wanting to be someone you're not? People will always say things that can hurt you. But the question is, do you want to let it eat away at you while they're simply getting on with it? Do you want to be the one giving orders or taking them? It's hard to be tough, but women especially have to be.'

Her words stayed with me. From then on I wrapped her strength around me like a protective shield. I've learned to ignore barbed comments and to keep it together, in public at least. I haven't been as good at that as usual in the past few weeks, but the only people who really saw me rattled were Erin and Sheedy, and if you can't let your guard down with your closest friends, then you're in greater trouble than I'll ever be in. Besides, after offering comfort, they also gave me practical advice. I'm always better with practical advice than sympathy. It's easier to cope with.

I get up from my seat, no longer wanting to sit around like a lady of leisure. I leave *Pride and Prejudice*, which kept me company during dinner, on the table, and stroll through the lush gardens towards the river that forms a border with the land on the opposite side. According to the hotel information, there's trout fishing in the river. Nobody's fishing here now, though, even if this is meant to be one of the best times of the day for it.

The sky is a palette of blue and pink, embroidered by the gold threads of the setting sun. The sound of the water as it spills over the riverbed is deeply calming. I slip out of my ballet pumps so that my bare feet are cooled by the dewy grass. I feel better than I have in weeks. Serene and hopeful. Like someone who can take control of her life again, someone who knows that everything is going to be OK.

I am in the moment.

I look back towards the house and step to one side so that I'm hidden by the trees and shrubs that run along the river-bank. Then I slide my dress over my head. Beneath it, my underwear is a tango-red Tommy Hilfiger support bra and shorts. I look at the river for a moment, but I'm certainly not going to swim when it might be teeming with trout. Instead, I stand facing the setting sun and stretch my hands high over my head before moving into the first position of my yoga routine. It's ages since I've done any of the poses, and I wobble wildly as I try to hold them, favouring my injured hand so that I don't put too much pressure on it, even though Gilda, my instructor, would want me to spread my weight equally. However, she'd be very pleased that I've emptied my mind and stilled the thoughts that have been buzzing around in my head for the past couple of months. This is the part I'm normally very bad at, but right now my mind and my body are one, and the only thoughts I have are of how cool the grass is and how beautiful the river sounds and how good it is to be alive. I finish up with my favourite warrior pose, then bring my hands to touch. I whisper *namaste* beneath my breath and think, with a flash of humour, that everyone wanted me to become all Zen and chilled, and to find myself and whatever, and that there can be nothing more mindful than doing yoga, however inexpertly, beside a river at sunset, with nobody else around.

'Hello,' says a voice behind me.

I spin around and see him silhouetted in the rapidly falling dusk.

'What the hell are you doing here?' I demand as I grab my dress and pull it over my head. 'Were you watching me?'

'I wasn't watching you, I swear.' Luke Granahan takes a small yellow tin from his jacket pocket and removes a narrow cigar, which he lights. The aroma from the spiral of blue smoke is surprisingly sweet. 'I've been here no more than a second or two, honestly. I'm at a wedding in the hotel and came for a walk while they're setting up the space for dancing. A walk and a quiet puff,' he adds. 'I only smoke about twice a year, but even having one of these tiny ones is such a terrible thing to do these days, I thought I'd better remove myself from the vicinity of the ballroom. I didn't realise you were here. And I didn't want to disturb you while you were balancing like that. It was very impressive.'

He sounds genuine. And my heart, which was racing with fear and then embarrassment, begins to slow down again.

'It might have looked impressive to you, but I'm sure my yoga teacher despairs,' I tell him. 'How come I keep bumping into you in the most unexpected of places?'

'Are you a wedding guest too?' asks Luke. 'I didn't see you earlier.'

'Do I look like a wedding guest?' I demand as I run my fingers through my tangled hair. I wish I'd brought a brush with me. But I wasn't expecting to meet anyone.

He hesitates, clearly unsure of the correct response.

'I'm here for an overnight stay,' I tell him. 'And it looked so lovely and was so peaceful by the river that I came over all Zen.'

He nods.

'In a place like this, it's easy to be grateful for what you have. At a price,' I add as I glance back towards the hotel. 'Obviously.'

He laughs. 'The best things in life and all that. Not always true.'

I smile in return. 'I've thought that over the last while. But I guess you can find a nice place to be grateful anywhere.'

'How's your hand?' he asks.

'Good as new,' I reply. 'Thanks again for your wonderful bandaging skills.'

He grins. 'My pleasure.' Then he asks if Larry called me back.

'You were right about that job.' I shrug. 'It was never for me. And although I don't have anything right now, I've got a strategy for when I go back to Dublin. Today . . .' I pause to gather my thoughts. 'Today is about putting a tough period behind me and taking control of my future.'

'I get the feeling that you're someone who'll always control her future,' says Luke.

'I think you controlled a major part of it for me,' I tell him. 'I was all over the place when I met you at your office.'

'I helped set you on the road, but you were a perfect client,' he says. 'Lots of people are on the phone to me every few minutes wanting to know what's going on. Asking for information I don't have. You were as cool as a cucumber. I knew you'd be OK.'

'As cool as a cucumber is pushing it,' I say. 'I wanted to phone you every few minutes but I knew it wouldn't help.'

He laughs. 'That's what makes you cool.'

I smile and tell him that panicking never solves anything, but that a little bit of panic in the privacy of your own home sometimes helps. As well as copious glasses of wine. 'But I'm over it now,' I say. 'It's all clean living and tranquillity from here on.'

'Excellent,' he says. Then he looks at me enquiringly as he takes a final puff of the cigar and puts the butt in the tin. 'I wondered . . . even though it won't be particularly tranquil . . . have you anything planned for the rest of your evening? Would you like to come back to the reception with me?'

'Are you crazy?' I ask. 'I haven't been invited, I'm certainly not dressed for it and I'm sure you're with someone, or a group or whatever, who won't want a gatecrasher.'

'I'm at a table with people I don't really know,' he says.

'It'd be nice to have someone else to talk to. I should've brought a plus-one but I kind of forgot about it and nobody was available at the last minute.'

I know that feeling.

'You don't really know me either,' I point out.

'I know you better than them.'

'Are you a guest of the bride or groom?' I'm not sure about rocking up to what is obviously a flash wedding in my very ordinary dress, messy hair and flat shoes.

'I'm Trevor's legal adviser,' he says, name-checking the rugby player. 'I've known his family for years.'

'It's nice of you to ask me, but I'm a total mess,' I point out.

'You look lovely,' says Luke.

I feel myself blush. The compliment is unexpected, and although it's highly unlikely I look anything other than hot and bothered after my yoga, it's nice that someone would say I look lovely. And that's what makes me think about seizing the moment and being nice to myself, and so I say OK, regardless of the fact that I'm pretty sure every other woman there will be looking more than lovely. She'll be looking perfect.

I'm right about the amount of glamour on show at the wedding reception, but the majority of the women have abandoned their five-inch heels for jewelled flip-flops, and the reception-only guests haven't made the same hair and make-up effort as those who've been here for the whole day. Nevertheless, as I'm not wearing any make-up at all, I'm taking casual to a different level.

But Luke either doesn't realise this or doesn't care, as he

introduces me to a couple of the rugby players. I fake a deeper interest than I really have in the sport and he leaves me chatting to a prop forward while he fetches a couple of drinks. Fortunately I don't have to say much, because the player is happy to talk about phases of the game and offloading the ball until Luke returns with the gin and tonic I requested. (The Zen clean living has gone out the window. If I don't have the armour of make-up, I'd like the comfort of an alcoholic drink.) We leave the prop forward chatting to some other guests and sit at an empty table.

'Everyone's dancing now.' Luke nods towards a group engaged in a complicated routine. 'I've two left feet.'

'I'm a bit too clunky for dancing myself,' I remark. 'I don't do coordinated. Or elegant.'

'You looked very elegant back at the river,' says Luke.

I splutter into the G&T. Elegance has never been my strong point.

'Seriously,' he says when I give him a disbelieving look. 'You looked fit and strong, and that thing you were doing when I saw you – standing on one leg with your body stretched out like that – was amazing. You were like a carving. And very definitely elegant.'

'I might just put you in a little box and bring you home.' I smile. 'Nobody has ever said so many nice things to me in one evening before.'

He smiles in return, and then I ask him about himself, reminding him that he knows all about me but I know nothing about him. He tells me that he's a widower and that his wife died three years earlier.

'I'm sorry for your loss.' I've had to say this too many times this year.

'Thank you,' he says.

I ask if he has children and he shakes his head. 'Lara became ill very shortly after we married. It wouldn't have been . . .'

I reach over and give his hand a sympathetic squeeze as his voice trails off.

'She was my best friend.' I can hear the grief in his voice. 'I thought we were forever.'

'You were her forever.'

He returns the focus of his gaze to me. 'That's . . . I never thought of that. Thank you.'

I squeeze his hand again, then release it.

'It's been hard,' he admits. 'For the entire first year afterwards I didn't even want to leave the house. People are kind, but they want you to get over it as quickly as possible. They say it's for you, but I think it's for them. Because nobody really knows how to behave with you. To be honest, for a long time I felt like getting over it was betraying her. It's only in the last six months that I've started connecting with the outside world again.'

'My grandmother passed away recently,' I say. 'And of course we lost Conrad before that. I know it's not at all the same thing as losing your wife, but getting on with your life when someone has gone is an adjustment that's not easy to make. It wasn't like I spoke to Granny every day, but I still miss her. I miss Conrad too. I can't imagine how you feel.'

'I should stop talking about her to everyone I meet,' says Luke.

I shake my head. 'It's fine.'

He exhales slowly. 'Well, thanks, but I didn't ask you to join me so that I could upset you with tales of my loss. I thought it would be fun for you.'

'I'm glad you asked.'

'I made an assumption,' he says abruptly. 'That you were on your own. Which is crazy, because you could've been here with anyone.'

'I like doing stuff by myself,' I tell him. 'Even yoga poses by a river in my bra and knickers.'

'I wasn't going to mention that.' He smiles, then both of us laugh. And suddenly the conversation is easier and we're talking about happier things, and the next thing I know I've finished my gin and tonic and he's asking if I'd like another one and I ask for a tonic on its own this time because I'm back embracing Zen.

He goes to the bar again. I scan the guests, not that I'm expecting to see anyone I know, just to take in the glamour and the style. But that's when I see them together, at the far side of the room. It's only because they stand up that I realise who they are. I saw them earlier but they both had their backs to me so it didn't register. But now it does.

Her blonde hair is up, showing off her blue silk dress with its deep V to both front and back. Around her neck is a diamond pendant. Long earrings drop from her ears. And around her wrist is the emerald bracelet I bought for her on behalf of my boss.

He's wearing a tux, although he's taken off the bow tie and jacket.

Bianca and Justin.

Together.

In the same room as me.

He gets up suddenly and walks in the direction of the bar. I wonder if I should go and speak to her, or leave the ball-room before she sees me. She hasn't noticed me yet and it might be better if she didn't. Honestly, I think with a touch of irritation, this was meant to be my self-care get-away-from-it-all night, and so far I've encountered Luke Granahan and Bianca Benton. Why is it so bloody difficult to go anywhere in Ireland without bumping into someone you know?

'Delphie Mertens! How are you doing?'

I turn around, and now I feel as though I'm actually in a parallel universe. Because I also know the woman who's standing beside me. Her name is Jackie Pearson and she's a client of Cosecha. She founded a communications company when she was in her early thirties and sold it ten years ago on her fiftieth birthday for an astronomical amount. She stayed on as the chair of the board for another few years but now heads up her own charitable foundation and divides her time between Dublin and the Bahamas. She's a formidable woman and she looks it too. Her royal blue dress (Donna Karan, I'm almost certain) is accessorised with chunky jewellery, and in the high heels she's wearing today, she can look me directly in the eye.

'I'm Trevor's godmother,' she says when we've exchanged greetings. 'His mum and I are great friends.'

I don't know Trevor's mum (one of the few people I don't seem to know at this wedding!), but apparently she and Jackie went to school together.

'It's great to be back in Dublin for something as fun as this,' she says. 'I was sorry I couldn't come to Conrad's funeral. I'm sure it's been hard on everyone.'

I nod.

'How are things in Cosecha now?' she asks.

When I tell her I've left the company, she looks at me in astonishment.

'But why? You were such a big part of it.'

'Not really.' I keep my tone light. 'I worked for Conrad, and they're going in a different direction now, so . . .'

'What d'you mean, a different direction?' she asks.

'You should talk to Justin. He's actually here too.'

'I spoke to him earlier and he didn't say a thing about you,' says Jackie. 'So what are you doing now? Where are you working?'

'I'm taking a bit of time out,' I say as lightly as I can.

Her eyes narrow, and I say that I needed personal time because of family issues.

'Oh,' she says.

'How are things at the foundation?' I ask, in order to get away from talking about me.

Jackie's foundation helps young people from difficult backgrounds to develop their skills and talents. From a slow start it has now disbursed millions towards various programmes in both Ireland and the Caribbean.

'Great,' she says. 'We've got a lot of new projects up and running and I'm really happy about how they're working out.'

'I'm delighted to hear that. I saw the newspaper interview with Ciara a few weeks ago. It was excellent.'

Ciara is her daughter and is on the foundation's board, along with Jackie's husband, Tim.

'Supporting disadvantaged women in getting into business is important to her.'

'I'm with her on that.' I nod. 'It's important to me too.'

Even though I'm not currently a woman in business.

Even though nobody has yet offered me a job.

367

Sadly the foundation is a very tight organisation that doesn't have any more staff than it needs, otherwise I'd ask Jackie about working for her. And then I remember my more proactive approach. She's a woman with a lot of contacts, and some of those contacts might be useful to me.

'Are you busy in the morning?' I ask. 'Would you consider having breakfast with me?'

She looks at me in surprise and then nods.

'Why not?'

'Eight thirty?' I suggest.

'Delphie! Are you mad? We're at a wedding reception. I'm not hauling my ass out of bed at the crack of dawn.'

I laugh. 'Nine thirty? Ten?'

'Nine thirty.'

'Look forward to it.'

I inhale deeply and then release the breath in a slow, steady stream.

I'm taking steps, proper steps, to get back in the game.

I'm looking after myself like I always do.

Luke returns with my tonic just as Jackie leaves.

'Sorry I took so long,' he says. 'Who were you talking to?'

He nods when I say Jackie's name.

'I think Haughton's sponsored her foundation,' he says. 'I'm not sure if we still do.'

'I added it to the Cosecha funding programme a couple of years ago,' I say. 'It's a really good foundation and Jackie's always been a bit of a hero of mine. I'm meeting her for breakfast.'

'Oh?'

I explain that she knows lots of important people, some

of whom might be in the market for an experienced executive assistant rather than an office dogsbody.

'Good idea,' he says.

'Hopefully it'll pay off.'

'Fingers crossed.'

I want to talk more about Jackie, but at that moment another of the rugby players and his very beautiful girlfriend join us at the table and the talk turns towards sport. I've almost finished my drink when I see Bianca walking back to her table with a glass of wine. Justin isn't with her. I murmur to Luke that there's someone I have to say hello to and make my way over to her.

'Delphie!' She's as surprised as I was that we're both at the same event. 'Were you at the wedding ceremony or were you just invited to the afters? I didn't see you earlier.' She frowns as she takes in my casual dress, ballet pumps and uncombed hair. 'Or are you casing the joint for jewellery you can rob?'

'Look, Bianca, I've already apologised about wearing the bracelet. You *know* I wasn't planning to swipe it. Either for me or for Martha.'

She touches it on her arm and then looks at me speculatively. 'I suppose I believe you.'

'And I'm sorry about how things went at Palmyra too.'

'Yeah, right.'

'Truly, Bianca. I . . . I hated being stuck in the middle.'

'You weren't,' says Bianca. 'You were firmly in Martha's camp. You still are. You sent me an email gloating that Conrad hadn't changed his will, and yet when you were in Mallorca to see him that last time, you had the nerve to ask me if I'd talk to him about giving her a decent settlement. And at

369

Palmyra when I was getting my stuff you took her side too. So don't talk to me about camps.'

'I certainly wasn't gloating in that email,' I say. 'I'm really sorry if it came across that way. And I don't want to be in any camp. At Palmyra, all I could do was follow the law.'

'The convenient excuse of people who are morally wrong.'

She has a point. Simply because something's legal doesn't make it right, not that it's a distinction anyone with a law degree generally allows themselves to be bothered by. But I tell her again that I was trying to do my best in a difficult situation.

'And all I can do is what's best for me,' says Bianca.

'Naturally,' I say.

She nods slowly and then asks again if I was invited to the wedding. I explain that I'm staying at the hotel and met a friend who asked me along to the reception.

'Just like that?' she says. 'Out of the blue?'

'Exactly.'

'You seem to know a lot of random people.'

'I do rather. And so do you. I didn't realise you knew Trevor. Or is it his wife who's a friend?'

'Neither,' says Bianca. 'I came with someone else.'

'I saw you earlier with Justin.'

'Trevor's dad has investments with Cosecha; that's why he's here.'

'Oh, of course.' I hadn't immediately connected the name, but I do now. 'So why did Justin invite you? Are you guys a thing?' I do my utmost to keep my voice as level as possible, but Bianca's no fool and she laughs.

'Oh, Delphie. You think I've turned my attention from

one CEO to the next. You have a really poor opinion of me, don't you?'

'I didn't think . . .' Well, actually I did. So she's right.

'Why are women so bloody judgemental about other women?' she demands.

'I'm not . . .' Oh, hell. She's right about that too.

'I've had a few meetings with Justin since Conrad died,' says Bianca. 'As you already know, I'm an authorised signatory to some companies he set up, and that means Justin needed me to sign things for him. Obviously we had to negotiate it. I can't sign my name for free.'

'Bianca!' I'm suddenly filled with a certain admiration for her. 'You're getting *paid* by Cosecha?'

'I have to look after myself,' she says. 'Besides, Conrad did want me to work with the company. It was always part of the plan.'

'In what way?' I ask.

'On the PR and branding side,' she replies. 'Meeting clients, entertaining, that sort of thing.'

The things Martha did because she was married to him. The unpaid support businessmen expect from their wives. The unpaid support she always gave him. But Bianca wasn't going to do it for nothing. She knew her worth. She still does. I could learn from her.

'Anyhow, he asked me to come along because he needs to present a good face to the clients and they prefer to think that a man has a woman at his side.'

I laugh. It's so 1950s. But then again, Justin often acts as though it still is.

'I haven't been out socially since . . . since Conrad,' she says. 'I thought this would be a good way to begin again.'

I nod.

'I did love him, you know,' she says.

I believe her. I really do.

'I'm sorry, Bianca. I hope you find someone . . .'

'Well, it won't be Justin Delaney.' She smiles suddenly. 'He's such a bollocks. But I need him at the moment so that I know what's going on. So that I can do what's best for me.'

I look at her with a new-found respect.

'Bianca?' I say after a moment or two.

'Yes?'

'In all the things Justin asked you to sign or be involved in, did he ever mention a deal named Caldwell? Or Hammersmith? Or Evergreen?'

She asks why I want to know. I explain quickly and she frowns.

'You think he's trying to pull a fast one?'

'I wouldn't put it exactly like that,' I say, although in all honesty, I would. 'Though he *is* reneging on a deal and a promise that the other directors made. Truth is, whatever came before will probably come to nothing now if he's managed to restructure it. There's always a way around this stuff. But Conrad was adamant that he didn't want people to lose their homes.'

'Yes, well, I can understand that,' she says. 'After all, I'm about to be thrown out on the street myself thanks to him not thinking about my future.'

'Don't you have somewhere else? A house of your own?'

She shakes her head. 'I was renting when I met him,' she says. 'I was hoping to build a place of my own eventually. So, no, I've nowhere. The Anglesea Road house has been my home ever since we got together.'

I understand how she feels. The thought of losing my own home always fills me with dread. It's the driving force making me want to get back to work as soon as possible. I can see why the prospect of having to move out of Anglesea Road is making Bianca both angry and upset.

'If there was something that could be done about Anglesea Road, would that help?' I ask.

She looks at me thoughtfully, then nods.

'Yes,' she says. 'It would.'

'And would it make you more inclined to maybe . . . well . . . not sign those forms for Justin?'

Her eyes widen and she gives me a slow smile. 'Perhaps.'

'Leave it with me,' I say.

I walk back to my table, where Luke is sitting alone.

'I think you know more people here than me,' he says as I rejoin him. 'Who was that you were talking to?'

'Conrad Morgan's girlfriend,' I reply.

He looks at me in surprise.

'She's here with the new CEO, Justin Delaney.'

His eyes open even wider. 'It's a convention of Cosecha staff! What's their relationship?'

'It's complicated,' I say.

'Complicated seems to follow you around.'

We sit in silence for a moment, then the music slows down. The people on the dance floor split into couples. I think of André and Tory's wedding, of dancing with Ed. And I think of how that day ended up.

'Would you like to dance?' asks Luke suddenly.

'I thought you weren't much of a dancer.'

'No. But I thought it would be a good thing to do. So that I don't look like the miserable git who won't bother.'

I smile at him and we move onto the floor together. He's right. He's not much of a dancer. But then nor am I, so it's fine.

We stay together until the music speeds up again, and then I tell him that even though it's only just gone midnight, I'm heading off to bed. I want to think about my meeting with Jackie in the morning. I want to think a little more about Martha and Bianca too.

'Thanks for being here,' he says. 'Thanks for dancing with me. It was . . .' He shrugs. 'It was nice.'

'Yes,' I agree. 'It was.'

'I'll head up myself. Do you . . .' He breaks off and shakes his head. 'I was going to suggest meeting for breakfast. I forgot you have a breakfast date already.'

'What can I say? I'm in demand.' I grin and he laughs.

As we stand in front of the lift, I suddenly lean in towards him and rest my head on his chest so that my face is hidden. I feel him tense up with the surprise of it, but I stay where I am for a few seconds.

'Sorry.' I straighten up again. 'Justin Delaney was coming down the stairs. I didn't want him to see me.'

'Why?'

'Um. No particular reason.'

'You can't move forward if you're afraid of being seen by your ex-boss,' he says.

'Actually I'm not at all afraid of being seen by him. I just don't want to . . . well . . . complicate something.'

'What are you up to, Delphie?'

'Just trying to sort out an issue that involves him. But it's nothing at all to do with me.'

He looks at me.

'Really it's not. It's about . . . loose strings,' I finish.

'Whatever.' He laughs. 'You're definitely one of the most interesting women I've ever met, Delphine Mertens.'

'It's no big deal,' I say, and then give a rueful smile. 'Well, it's a bit of a deal given that I didn't want him to see me. But it's not personal. And that's thanks to you and everything you did for me. It was nice to see you again tonight and spend some social time with you.'

'I enjoyed it too,' says Luke. 'You made it a lot more fun than I expected.'

Then the lift arrives and there's a moment where I feel we want to say more to each other, but we don't.

Instead he wishes me a very good night and I return to my room alone.

Chapter 29

When I close the door behind me I realise that I've missed three messages and a call from Ed. I debate whether to call him back, and then decide that messaging is best.

Sorry, I type. *I didn't realise my phone was on silent.*

It wasn't, but I didn't hear it over the buzz of conversation and music in the ballroom.

It rings almost immediately and I answer it.

'I was getting worried,' says Ed.

'Worried that I might've been massaged to death?'

'You never know.' He laughs. 'How was it?'

'Lovely,' I say. 'This place is amazing. Everything is so perfect.'

'What else did you do with yourself besides go to the spa?'

'Yoga,' I reply. 'Beside the river.'

'You've totally embraced the mindfulness vibe. Is it all health foods and mint water there?'

'Not entirely.' I'm not going to mention the gin and tonic. Or becoming Luke Granahan's temporary plus-one. Or running into Bianca Benton. 'How about you?' I ask.

'The project's going really well after a near disaster

yesterday.' He launches into a description of the crisis he managed to avert that would have meant a delay of at least a week.

'So will you be finished this weekend?' I ask.

'Middle of next,' he says. 'Which is just as well, given the wedding on Saturday.'

The wedding on Saturday! How could I have forgotten that my outing as yet another plus-one was so close?

'At least my skin is prepped and gorgeous,' I respond.

'You're always gorgeous.'

'Thank you.'

'I miss you. I won't be back this weekend after all, because we really want to finish next week. I'm sorry.'

'Don't worry. We'll see each other soon,' I say.

We chat for a little longer and then I tell him that I'm worn out from the yoga and need to hit my bed.

But when I do, I don't sleep.

I'm not quite mindful enough yet for that.

Jackie Pearson is already in the dining room when I arrive the following morning. She has a plate of fruit and a large silver pot of coffee in front of her.

I'd originally planned to have my 'holiday' full Irish breakfast, but instead I follow her lead and order the fruit selection. Jackie's not a woman I'd feel comfortable talking to with a mouthful of sausage and rasher.

'So how are you doing in your post-Cosecha life?' she asks as she pours herself a cup of coffee. 'I'm taken aback that you left. I know you said there were family reasons, but that doesn't sit entirely well with me.'

'I had family reasons for not looking for another job

immediately,' I correct her. 'As far as leaving Cosecha was concerned, it wouldn't have been my choice, but Justin and I have never seen eye to eye and he offered me a package to leave.'

'I see.'

'I know the company manages some of your investment funds,' I say. 'Please don't worry about them, Jackie. Emily Hunt is your investment manager and she's absolutely brilliant.'

Jackie smiles at me. 'I admire your loyalty.'

'It's not loyalty, it's honesty,' I say.

'And what about Cosecha's sponsorship?' she asks. 'Can I continue to depend on that?'

Given Justin's comments about the corporate responsibility programme, I'm not certain about the sponsorship and I say so. 'But,' I add, 'there's no reason why the directors won't respond positively to a firm proposal from you.'

'You think?'

'I do, if you make it yourself,' I say. 'Normally it's the CEO . . .' I search my memory and come up with the name, 'Daniel Horton who meets with them. But perhaps it would be better this year if you did it personally. After all, you're an important client.'

She nods. 'Daniel is planning to meet with someone,' she tells me. 'But I think you're right and I should set it up myself. Who do you recommend I see? Justin? One of the other directors?'

I consider for a moment. 'Justin,' I say, even though he's the least likely to respond well to requests for money. But he wouldn't take kindly to Jackie talking to Didier or Kieran instead. Besides, if she's smart (and I know she will be), she'll be appealing to both his ego and the fact that she could pull her investments from Cosecha. He wouldn't like to lose her as a client.

She helps herself to more coffee. 'It's probably a good thing for me to meet them anyhow,' she says. 'Daniel's leaving us shortly.'

I look at her in surprise.

'He's got a job with another foundation,' she explains. 'It's an excellent move for him, and given that he's been with us for five years and done so well for us, I can't be anything but supportive. However, it does leave a gap in our expertise. Our board is knowledgeable, but not in the way Daniel is, and we have other funders we need to talk to about renewing their support. And even more we want to talk to about initiating support.'

The board of Jackie's foundation is small. It consists of her, her husband and her daughter. Tim is a graphic designer and Ciara's background is in marketing.

I wonder if she's telling me all this for a reason. And I think of my own reason for asking to meet her.

'Are you going to appoint a new CEO?' I ask.

'Naturally,' says Jackie.

'Have you got anyone in mind?'

'I haven't started a formal process yet.'

I take a sip of coffee and replace the delicate cup on its saucer. My plan was to ask her about potential contacts for an executive assistant role. Yet there's about to be an interesting position available in her own foundation. Working for Jackie would be amazing, but I'm not qualified to be the CEO of a major charitable foundation. And yet . . . I think about Justin stepping into Conrad's role without a thought.

Of my colleagues jostling for position within the firm. Of how I always thought of myself as a senior person. Of how proud I was of my work. Of the experience I have. Of the fact that Conrad wanted to make me a director.

I think of the jobs I've applied for. The jobs I'm overqualified for. The jobs I'm not going to get, all in the same areas as before. Law and finance. I think of Bianca's remark that something being legal doesn't necessarily mean it's right, which is exactly why I'm so determined that the Caldwell deal will work out. And I think of Dad's belief that my work in Cosecha was simply about making rich people richer. Yet in the area I was in complete control of myself, I loved that our community grants project helped the people who needed it most.

'I said that I had family reasons for not looking for something new immediately,' I tell Jackie now. 'They were to do with the death of my grandmother and the administration of her estate.' I realise that this makes Granny Mertens sound like someone who's bequeathed a fortune to her descendants, but I don't care. 'However, I'll certainly be available in the very near future.'

She looks at me thoughtfully.

'I think I'd be an asset to the foundation,' I say. 'I think I could be an excellent CEO.'

'Do you indeed?' she asks.

'Yes,' I reply.

She taps her fingers against the table as she holds my gaze. 'So do I,' she says.

We look at each other in silence for a moment, and then she begins to tell me a little more about the foundation and the direction she sees it taking. The more she talks, the more confident I am that I want to be part of it. I know I can do it. I can bring new skills to the mix, and she seems to agree.

'I'm in Ireland until the end of next week,' she says. 'How about we meet in the office on Monday? I'll have a proposal for you then.'

'That would be wonderful,' I tell her.

'I'm so glad I bumped into you,' she says as she stands up. 'I think we can do amazing work together.'

'Thank you.'

We shake hands and I sit back down at the table. Jackie is going to make a proposal. She's going to offer me a job. The kind of job I actually want to do. Joy, excitement and sheer relief flood through me. A woman I admire values me enough to want me to work for her. And I want to work for her too. The right job was there for me, I simply had to reach for it.

I celebrate by ordering the cooked breakfast after all.

I'm happily tucking in when Bianca walks into the dining room. She spots me straight away.

'Delphie!' She looks in horror at my plate of sausages, rashers, tomatoes and fried eggs. 'What on earth are you eating?'

'A hot breakfast is good for you,' I say. 'Would you like to join me?'

She shudders and then tells me that if I plan to do anything about Caldwell, I need to organise myself quickly, because she's supposed to sign that document early next week.

'Right,' I say. 'Thanks for telling me.'

'Don't worry.' She gives me a tight smile as I look around. 'Justin had a room service breakfast. He's on the phone to the office now and I reckon he'll be gasbagging for at least an hour.'

'Are you having something yourself? Do you want to join me?'

She shakes her head. 'I couldn't possibly sit opposite you while you're eating that. Besides, I had a room service breakfast too. I hate mingling with people in the mornings.'

'So do I. Usually.'

'Look, Delphie . . .' Bianca sighs. 'I want to do the right thing. But I need to take care of myself.'

'I understand.'

'I hope other people do too,' she says, and leaves the room.

I'm packed and ready to leave when my phone buzzes with a message from Luke to ask if I'm still at the hotel. I respond that I'll be leaving shortly and he suggests meeting in reception in five minutes. I send a thumbs-up emoji in return. When the lift doors open, I see him standing beside one of the long sash windows.

'Hi,' I say. 'Everything OK?'

'Sure.' He smiles. 'Did you have a good breakfast meeting?'

'The best.' I beam at him. 'Jackie's going to put a job proposal to me next week.'

'How fantastic.' His eyes shine with pleasure. 'What kind of position?'

'CEO,' I say as casually as I can.

'Delphie! That's even more fantastic. It's so well deserved, and I bet you'll be brilliant.'

'You're basing that on very limited knowledge of me,' I tell him.

'I know enough.'

'So that's the second time you've been great to me,' I say. 'First with the whole Cosecha thing. And then by asking me to be your stand-in plus-one, because without that I wouldn't have met Jackie. You're my lucky charm.'

'You deserve that job,' says Luke. 'Let me know how it goes, won't you?'

'Of course.'

'It's certainly more your thing than being a PA to my brother-in-law,' he adds.

'Gosh, yes, that was a train-wreck interview,' I admit. 'It was so weird running into you there too. Do you live in Glenageary?'

He shakes his head. 'Sutton,' he says.

Sutton is another northside coastal suburb.

'I go to the supermarket in Sutton sometimes,' I tell him. 'When I'm trying to be properly organised and do a big shop instead of picking things up on the run.'

'You'll see me prowling the aisles there from time to time,' he says.

'I'll watch out for you skulking in the frozen foods.'

'Actually I'm a sucker for the fresh bread,' he says. 'I buy a couple of loaves and then realise that there's only me, so end up using most of it to feed the birds.'

I've done that myself and I nod in understanding.

'Um . . . Delphie . . .'

'Yes?' I look at him again.

'I wanted to . . . well, you were really good to join me at the reception last night and . . . it made it all a lot easier for me. I can be a bit antisocial sometimes, but having you to talk to was great.'

'I enjoyed myself tremendously,' I assure him. 'As for being antisocial . . .' I shrug. 'My family often complain that I'm too much of a loner. My sister-in-law was on my case about coming here alone. But it turned out fabulously well. Being alone can be good.'

He nods. 'My family get on my case too sometimes. Well, after Lara, I don't blame them.' He clears his throat. 'Actually, I was wondering if . . . if you don't think it's inappropriate . . . maybe we could meet up from time to time. For a coffee? Or perhaps dinner some evening?'

I'm dating Ed, so I suppose it is kind of inappropriate. But then I tell myself I'm being silly. This is a friendship thing, not a romantic thing, and Ed has already said he's not jealous of Luke.

'That would be lovely,' I say.

He beams at me. 'How about next Saturday morning?'

'Yes – oh, sorry, no.'

'Yes, no?'

'I'm busy next Saturday,' I explain. 'Believe it or not, I'm a plus-one at a wedding.'

'You'll be all weddinged out.'

'I did sort of gatecrash yesterday's,' I say. 'But Saturday has been in the diary for a while. How about the following week?'

'Sounds good to me. Will I call you?'

'Perfect.' I glance at my watch. 'I'd better go. I have to get the car back before two.'

'Oh, right. Of course. Sorry for delaying you.'

'Not at all,' I say. 'It really was nice to see you.'

'You too,' he says.

I head out of the hotel and drive home.

It wasn't quite the getaway I expected.

It was much better.

*

I'm back in Malahide in plenty of time to leave the car at the drop-off point and pick up a few bits and pieces from the deli. I think of Luke wandering the aisles of SuperValu and I send him a message suggesting that the Malahide deli is worth a visit from time to time. He responds almost immediately telling me he'll give it a try. Then I scroll to a different name on my contacts list and send a message to Martha asking if we could have a chat about Cosecha and a few other things.

She suggests lunch at her house the next day, and so by one o'clock on another fabulously sunny afternoon, I'm sitting in her kitchen, where I tell her about meeting Bianca at the wedding reception and our discussion about Caldwell.

'Let me get this straight,' says Martha. 'She's working as an image consultant for Justin – the exact same thing she did with Conrad? And she's worming her way into being part of the company? And she wants to blackmail me into . . . into gifting her a house? An actual house!'

'In a nutshell,' I agree.

'And you think this is a good idea why?'

'I don't know what's a good idea as far as Cosecha is concerned,' I say. 'Obviously the Caldwell deal meant a lot to Conrad, and it seemed to mean a lot to you too. Bianca is looking after her own interests, and while I might not entirely agree with how she's going about it, I understand it.'

'You'd never try to blackmail me to get anything!' cries Martha. 'That girl is amoral.'

'Maybe,' I concede. 'But when you think you might lose your home, the place that matters to you – like the people living in the Caldwell estate, like me – well, you'll fight like anything to keep it.'

385

'How were you going to lose your home?' demands Martha.

'When the whole thing blew up with Justin, I was out on my ear,' I tell her. 'I didn't have a job. I owed a lot of money. My mortgage had to be paid . . . I was in an absolute panic about what might happen.'

'Yes, but you got a good settlement in the end, didn't you?'

'I couldn't be sure of that,' I say. 'And while I accept that Bianca's situation is different, she's still stuck with worrying about where she's going to live in the future. Giving her the time you did was generous, but it goes by very quickly when you're trying to sort out your life and your finances. No matter what you think, Martha, she believed she and Conrad were forever.'

'As if.' Martha snorts.

'She had to identify his body,' I say.

'If he hadn't been there with her trying to act half his age, she wouldn't have been in that position.'

'I know.'

'You feel sorry for her, despite everything.'

'I guess I have a certain amount of empathy.'

'So basically you're saying that if I hand over a great house in a prime location to the gold-digger, the Caldwell deal will go ahead as Conrad wanted.'

'And all those other people will keep their homes too,' I add.

'For feck's sake.' She sighs.

'It's got nothing to do with me any more,' I say. 'I'm moving on from everything connected to Cosecha. I'm hoping to start a new job shortly, so it doesn't matter to me what you do. I'm only here to give you information.'

'You've got a new job? Where?'

I tell her.

'Jackie Pearson wants you?' She gives me an enthusiastic smile. 'That'd be a good move, Delphie. I like her foundation. I know Cosecha supported it, but Conrad and I contributed personally too.'

'Hopefully you'll also consider it for the future. If I become the CEO, I'll be the one who asks you.'

She laughs. 'You're a hoot, Delphie. I told you you were a complete softie, but there's a bed of hard nails under it all.'

'Not really. You said as much yourself before. That I didn't put myself out there enough. That I hung back. And I've done it again now, because I didn't say that I'm hoping for a massive six-figure sum from you the day I walk in the door.'

She laughs again. 'If I give the foundation money, is that enough to salve my conscience over Bianca instead of letting her have Anglesea Road? Not that I have a conscience where she's concerned.'

'They're two separate things,' I say. 'Bianca won't sign the contract if she gets the house, and that's a good result for the homeowners in this deal. Any contribution you want to make to the foundation has nothing to do with that.'

'Were you really afraid you'd lose your home?' asks Martha.

'Terrified,' I reply.

'I guess I've been lucky,' she says slowly. 'Even when I first met Conrad, he was doing well enough that we could buy a decent house. When he was setting up the company, he didn't need to use our home to raise the finance. I was always secure about having somewhere to live.'

I say nothing.

'And then we bought Bandon. And our Cork house. And the New York apartment. And Palmyra.'

'You deserved them all,' I say.

She gives me a sideways look. 'Deserved? I don't know. Maybe I was just lucky. I married the right man at the right time and I supported him in everything he did. I deserve something for that. But does anyone deserve multiple houses and more money than they know how to spend? I'm going to downsize, Delphie. I'll sell Bandon and I'm thinking of selling Palmyra too. I don't want to go back. I want to keep the good memories as they are.'

I nod.

'As for Anglesea Road . . .' She lets out a slow breath. 'Not my house. Never my house, despite everything. It was always his. And, you'd say, hers.'

'I wouldn't say anything.'

'You're thinking it, though.'

'Martha—'

She holds up her hand. 'Stop, Delphie. You're right. About all of it. I'll never forgive her for her relationship with Conrad and I'll never forgive him for dying before I could fix things. But I can't spend my time obsessing over that. I keep telling the kids that we have to grieve and move on. I have to heed my own words.'

I stay silent.

'I don't want to talk to her myself, but if you don't mind, you can call her and tell her that I'm prepared to sign the house over to her. Tell her she needs to talk to a financial adviser, because she'll end up with a tax bill and there's nothing I can do about that. But she'd better keep her end of the bargain. I don't want families with children being put out of their own homes. And then . . .' she pauses, 'then let me know what projects the foundation is looking at for next year, and I'll see what I can do to help.'

I smile at her. 'Thanks, Martha. You're a really good person. You always were.'

'Huh.' But she smiles back at me. 'Conrad would want this. And I always did what Conrad wanted.'

So she did.

And so did I.

And so did Bianca.

Chapter 30

On Monday morning, I arrive at the modern glass and steel building on Shelbourne Road where Jackie's foundation has its offices. I'm exactly on time.

'The developer gave us rent-free space here for five years,' she says when she greets me in the light-filled reception area. 'It's his way of supporting what we do.'

The main office itself is small but equally light-filled. Jackie introduces me to the current CEO, Daniel, and to the team of Keisha, Gabriel and Yui who liaise with the donors, come up with fundraising ideas and assess the projects looking for funding. Feargal, who's the financial guy and also looks after IT, is currently on holiday, although he'll be back shortly. They're all young and enthusiastic, and even if I wasn't here because I'm hoping to take over as CEO, I'd be inspired by their energy. But I *am* hoping to be their boss and so I sit down opposite Jackie while she talks through the ethos of the foundation and how they operate and what would be expected of me.

'Everyone here passionately believes in what we're doing,' she says. 'But we have to demonstrate to our donors that we're delivering results. We want to keep costs to a minimum while providing an excellent service. It's important that there are never any negative stories about the foundation. I don't mean that we want to hide any problems,' she adds. 'I don't want there to *be* any problems.'

'I'm good at troubleshooting,' I assure her. 'But even better at making sure there's no trouble to shoot.'

She grins and then pushes a single-page document towards me. It has printing on both sides, but I thought there would be more. I'm suddenly worried that she hasn't taken me seriously at all; that she's simply offering some kind of support role.

'What d'you think?' she asks.

I was wrong to be worried. The proposal is for me to be CEO. And although I've prepared myself for a significant cut in salary, because we're talking about a charitable foundation after all, I'm astonished to see that Jackie will be paying me slightly more than I earned at Cosecha.

'Something you should know,' she says when I glance up at her. 'The money that comes in from donors is spent exclusively on our projects. None of it ever goes into salaries or bills or anything like that. My contribution funds the running of the foundation, and that includes the wages bill. I pay people what they deserve. Every year I set a budget for this and I expect us to keep within it. That way nothing that's earmarked for the people we help is ever diverted away from our work.'

I nod slowly and turn over the page, looking at what would be expected of me. I note that I would have to visit various projects throughout the country and occasionally some of the overseas ones too. I would be the public face of the foundation. I would attend as many of the fundraising events as was practicable. I would have complete control of some elements of funding but would have to liaise with the board for any of the major disbursements.

'Do you have the most recent accounts?' I ask.

Jackie opens a drawer in her desk and takes out a folder, which she hands to me.

The numbers are impressive. The organisation is in a healthy state. I look up at her and smile.

'I'd be honoured to work here,' I say.

'And we'd be honoured to have you.'

I don't need advice from Erin or Sheedy on the contract. I take out my Montblanc pen and sign it straight away.

I'm the CEO of a major charitable foundation.

I couldn't be happier.

I'm almost bursting with excitement as I walk to Lansdowne Road station. A train is approaching so I hurry through the turnstile and manage to catch it with seconds to spare. All the other times I've caught the train from here it's been because I've had to call to Conrad and Martha's home. Now this station means something else to me.

I get off at Killester and pop in to Mum and Dad's. They're delighted – and relieved – that I've finally got another job. Dad is particularly pleased that it's in the charitable sector, and Mum is impressed that it's Jackie Pearson's foundation because she knew Jackie's brother back in the day.

'He used to come into the bakery,' she tells me. 'Brendan. Lovely man. Lovely family. Jackie was always a go-getter. Brains to burn, that girl.'

After coffee and cake, I head home. On the way, I text Erin and Sheedy, who both respond with delighted messages and suggestions of meeting up at the weekend to celebrate. I reply by saying that I'm going to Ed's niece's wedding so it'll have to be the weekend after that, and we agree to celebrate then.

I send Ed a text too, but I know he's completely caught up in his own work and I'm not upset when he doesn't immediately reply. As I'm still fizzing with excitement, I also message Luke Granahan. His response comes five minutes later, a GIF of a popping champagne cork. I'm just getting off the train at Malahide when he calls.

'That's brilliant news,' he says. 'I'm delighted for you.'

'Me too,' I confess. 'I love the idea of the foundation. The people seem great. The set-up is fantastic. The work is amazing.'

He laughs. 'Your dream job.'

'I always thought working with Conrad was my dream job,' I admit. 'But with this, I feel like I'm doing something worthwhile. I'm helping people who have money to do something good with it. That's empowering. And pleasing. And . . .' I run out of words.

'I'm very happy for you,' says Luke. 'Perhaps it really is true that when one door closes, another opens.'

'Thanks again for asking me to be your temporary plus-one and making it possible,' I say.

'I'll be finished here around six tonight,' he says. 'Would you like to have that dinner with me? Turn it into your celebration?'

I should really celebrate with Ed or my girlfriends first. But it's thanks to Luke that I met Jackie.

So I say yes.

*

We meet in a restaurant over a pub in Clontarf with a view across the bay. It was Luke's suggestion as he was coming straight from work and it meant he could get the train. I get the train too and arrive at exactly the same time as him. Which is a bit unfortunate as I wore my Skechers to walk from the station and had to change into my heels in front of him.

'I should wear trainers myself when I'm commuting,' he muses. 'It'd make the walk much more comfortable.'

'I've got used to trainers and flats over the last few weeks,' I admit. 'Shoving my feet into heels seems like abuse.'

He laughs and we walk up the stairs together.

Our table is beside the window and we look out over the seafront, where people are jogging or strolling or walking their dogs. A small group of young men are kicking a ball about on the grass, using the bushes as goalposts. Even though the heat of the previous few days has lessened, it's still a beautiful summer evening.

Luke orders a glass of Prosecco each and congratulates me again.

'You did such a good job with Cosecha, it gave me the time not to panic,' I tell him.

'My pleasure,' he says.

'To jobs well done.' I tip my glass towards his.

'And future success,' he says as we clink them.

He's an easy person to talk to. We chat about work, about employment law, about the importance of treating people well. But by the time we've finished our main course, we've moved on to more personal things, like our childhoods and our families. Luke's parents are older than mine and his father has Parkinson's, which, he admits, puts a strain on everyone.

'There's me, my older brother and my younger sister,' he

says. 'They're both married with families, and because I don't have a family, I seem to be the fallback for everything. Not that I mind doing my share,' he adds hastily. 'It's simply that sometimes I feel my life for the past few years has almost entirely been taken up with illness. Sometimes it gets a bit much.'

'Maybe they think that keeping you busy will help you,' I suggest.

'You might be right.' He gives me a rueful smile. 'You're good at putting a sympathetic gloss on it.'

'Fortunately both my parents are in great health so we don't have any issues like that to deal with, at least not yet,' I say. 'But my family think I'm work-obsessed and don't care enough about them.'

'And are you?'

'I guess I do obsess about work,' I admit. 'I thought recently that it's because I live alone and my work sort of validates my choice. I realise that sounds a bit . . . whatever. But I like being alone and I like bringing order to things. I suppose I'm not really your spiritual kind of girl.'

He laughs. 'You do yoga.'

'Not very mindfully,' I say. 'Not the way it's supposed to be done.'

'Why are you so hard on yourself?' asks Luke. 'You're living the life you want to live. What's so wrong about that?'

'I think that as a woman you're always judged,' I say. 'Judged for wanting it all. Judged for not wanting it all. Judged for whatever part of it you decide matters.'

'I've never felt judged,' he admits. 'But like I said before, I've felt the pressure to get over Lara's death.'

'Maybe we let ourselves feel pressure,' I observe. 'Maybe we have to not care so much about what other people think.'

'You might be right,' he says, then orders coffee from the waiter, who's hovering beside us. I ask for a decaf.

We linger over the coffees and then go downstairs to the pub. We choose a couple of seats in a corner, and because Luke insisted on paying for dinner, I order the drinks. I'm at the bar when my phone rings. It's Bianca. I spoke to her after leaving Martha's the other day and told her that Martha would sign the house over if Bianca didn't sign the Caldwell papers. She said she'd get back to me. I leave the drinks on the table and tell Luke I'll be back in a moment, then go outside to talk to her.

'Martha's solicitor was in touch with me today,' she says. 'He'll have papers for me to sign tomorrow for the house. Thank you.'

'And you won't sign the Caldwell documents?'

'Justin's already going mad because I haven't.'

'Have you said why?'

'No. But I will. He's not going to be happy.'

'He's never happy.'

'That's true.' She laughs. 'Thanks for talking to Martha.'

'You're welcome.'

'Maybe we'll meet up again sometime,' she says.

'You never know.'

And you don't. Bianca is a smart woman. She won't disappear from the scene.

I go back to my gin and tonic and Luke.

'Everything OK?' he asks.

'Right now, it couldn't be better.'

And in all honesty, it couldn't.

Chapter 31

I'm beginning to think that all Irish weddings now happen in flash country houses or renovated castles, because the one Ed and I are going to is also taking place in a castle, this time in County Tipperary. It's a three-hour drive and we have to be there for two p.m., so Ed stays over. He's already there when I get home, because I've been for a drink after work with the team at the foundation to celebrate my first week with them. It was a brilliant week. The term 'blessing in disguise' always irritates me, because I generally think that bad things are bad things and calling them anything else is nothing more than trying to make yourself feel better, but in getting rid of me, Justin has opened a whole new world of challenges and experiences that have totally energised me. Ending the week socially with my new colleagues was the right thing to do, although Ed remarks that he hopes it won't be like this every weekend, as it's after ten when I get in and I'm too flaked to do anything except lie on the sofa.

I have a 9.30 appointment with Mindy on the morning of the wedding, and she works her magic with my hair, so that when I get back, Ed gives a wolf whistle of appreciation. He slides his arms around me and kisses me hard on the lips, but

I pull away from him and tell him that we don't have time for faffing about, and he says it's not faffing about, and in the end we make love quickly and urgently before I do my make-up and get dressed in the Ted Baker frock I didn't wear to André and Tory's wedding.

We leave on schedule, but traffic on the M50 is terrible and I'm in a panic about being late and wishing that I'd stuck to my guns and not allowed Ed to push me onto the bed, even though he's as good at making love in a hurry as he is about doing it slowly and tenderly.

Things improve once we reach the M7, and I sit back in my seat feeling more relaxed.

'OK?' asks Ed.

'Absolutely,' I reply.

I'm more than OK really. All the things that have weighed on me over the past weeks have been resolved, including the Bianca/Martha situation. Both women have been as good as their word. The house is now Bianca's, while the Caldwell deal has reverted to what it was before. Martha went to see Justin and told him that if he didn't fulfil the promise Conrad made, she'd look elsewhere for a buyer for her stake in the company. Justin was so horrified at the thought that he backed down immediately.

'Perhaps we didn't need to ask Bianca not to sign that form,' Martha told me when she called me to confirm that everything was agreed. 'But it slowed him down and that allowed me to put the pressure on.'

She's going to sell her shares to the current directors. She'll be an even wealthier woman when she does. And the excellent part of that is that she's also agreed to a regular funding deal for one of the foundation's projects as soon as her cash settlement comes through. She wants to set it up in Conrad's memory.

'I'm delighted to be part of it,' she says. 'I hope we can work closely together, Delphie.'

I hope so too.

On the home front, things have also settled down. André and Tory have moved into their new house in Baldoyle, while Vivi and Jason are now living happily in Marino. Dad confided to me that he was relieved to have the family home to himself again, and even Mum admitted that it was nice not to be falling over other people's stuff all the time.

'Besides,' she grinned at me, 'they're here every day anyhow.'

As are Nichola and her girls. Dad will never quite get the absolute peace and quiet he craves, but he knows how much Mum loves having her family around, and he accepts it. I suppose that's what a really good relationship is all about. Recognising that there are some things you don't necessarily agree on but are able to compromise on regardless.

But not everything has gone as smoothly for everyone. This time it's nothing to do with the Mertens family. It's Erin and Fintan, who after only a few weeks together realised that it wasn't working out and have split up again, this time for good.

'Are you devastated?' I asked when we met for a very quick cup of coffee during the week and she told me about it.

'Not as much as I expected,' she confessed. 'Oh, Delphie, I thought it was what I wanted, but when it came down to it . . . Maybe there's someone I can change for, but it's not Fintan.'

'Did you really feel you had to change? After all, you've been going out with him for years.'

'There were too many things that didn't work when we were together all the time,' she said. 'And . . . well, it sounds awful, and I'm obviously a heartless bitch, but I didn't love him enough to want to leave meetings early or not to read papers at home if I needed to. Plus,' she added, 'he never once welcomed me with the dinner in the oven and a corkscrew in his hand.'

I laughed. 'What about your desire to have a baby?'

'It would be nice,' she said. 'But not at all costs. I'm probably not cut out for it. It was just that damn doctor telling me that I was getting old that made me feel . . . well, sort of unwomanly for not caring enough.'

We agreed that it's a myth that all women want to be mothers, but we also agreed that there's an inherent unfairness in the biological clock aspect of things that forces you to do something when you might not be ready.

'I suppose I could end up as a batty old childless spinster,' she said.

I laughed. 'I often think that about myself. But I prefer to think of myself as turning into a formidable woman.'

'Oh yes!' She grinned. 'Like Lady Bracknell in *The Importance of Being Earnest*.'

'Well, perhaps a bit more sympathetic. Lady B was a right old rip.'

'Maggie Smith in *Downton Abbey*.' Erin held up an invisible lorgnette. 'I know several couples who are perfectly happy. Haven't spoken in years.'

I laughed again. 'I know a few couples like that myself.'

'How about you and Ed?' she asked.

'We speak a lot.'

'Doomed, in that case.'

'Clearly.'

'I hear you've been seeing Luke Granahan.' Her words were so determinedly casual that I knew she wasn't being casual at all.

'Not seeing,' I corrected her. 'Certainly not in the sense you mean.'

'But you had dinner together.'

'We were celebrating my job.'

'Before you celebrated with your girlfriends?' She raised an eyebrow.

'You guys were busy.'

'What did Ed say?'

'For heaven's sake, Erin, Ed isn't my minder. I can have dinner with someone without him getting Neanderthal about it.'

'Did you tell him?'

'Well, no, I didn't. But only because I don't need to share every moment of my life with him. I don't need to share every moment of my life with anybody.'

Erin gave me a speculative look.

'You're tilting at windmills,' I told her, and headed back to the office.

Ed and I arrive at the castle with twenty minutes to spare, which in my world is almost unforgivably late. We barely have time to check in before heading to the room where the ceremony is taking place. I'm grateful that everything's happening under one roof, because it eases my overall stress levels. Both about cutting it fine time-wise, and also about seeing Ed's family again. Like me, he was living at home when we first went out together, and I met his mum and dad a number of times. But unlike my sprawling home-bird family, his brother and sister had long since married and moved out, and I think I only met them on one occasion. John, his brother, is twelve years older than him, and there's a gap of seven years between Ed and his sister Tanya. He used to say that he was the panicked afterthought.

'I'm sure you weren't,' I told him when he first said this, but even though he laughed, I could tell it bothered him.

The room for the wedding is beautiful, with high ceilings, long windows and off-white walls with gold-leaf paint that allow the vibrant colours of the flowers and ribbons to shine through. We slip into a seat near the back, and the ceremony starts almost immediately. Tasha, Ed's niece, looks as radiant as every bride does, and her wife-to-be, Lisbeth, is equally beautiful. Both women are wearing fitted white dresses. The bodice of Tasha's is covered with pearls, and it has a long train that flows out behind it. Lisbeth has gone for a plain white off-the-shoulder number, but the crystal necklace around her neck glitters and sparkles in the afternoon sun.

Despite never having met either woman before, I tear up when the celebrant presents them to us as the newly married Tasha and Lisbeth Miller-Brown. The applause is rapturous and the joy is infectious. I turn to Ed and hug him, and then he kisses me and it feels almost perfect.

There's a champagne reception after the ceremony, and that's when I meet Ed's parents again. His mum remembers me, but it's clear that his dad doesn't. Nevertheless, he's polite and charming and, I think, more laid-back than he was back then. I also meet Ed's brother and sister and their spouses. His family is less gregarious than mine, less interested in me than mine are in him. It's refreshing not to be quizzed by people and I'm feeling more at ease by the time we sit down to the meal. The speeches come before the food is served, and both Tasha and Lisbeth get up to speak. Their words are warm and witty, and their love for each other shines through. In a break with tradition, the two mums also make short speeches. Tanya says that she's never seen her daughter happier, and that she's never been happier herself either. Lisbeth's mum wishes them both a long and contented life together. And then the tables are moved, everyone mingles and the music starts.

'Having fun?' asks Ed as I lean against him for a slow dance.

'Yes. It's been lovely.'

He pulls me closer, his hand warm against my back.

When the music speeds up again, he goes to get more drinks. I tell him I'm going to nip outside for a breath of fresh air but that I'll be back before he is because it's probably too cold to be out for long. As I step into the dusky light, I have another flashback to the night when André and Tory got married and when, in the grounds of that castle, I heard the news about Conrad. My breath quickens at the memory, and despite the resolution of so many things since then, I feel a lump in my throat.

That was the night when everything changed in an instant. For me. For Martha and her family. For Bianca. For Cosecha. All because of a single moment in time. Life is unfair, I think as I walk along the stone path. It doesn't matter if you're a good person or a bad person. The unexpected happens, and it can shake you out of your chosen path when you least want it.

My phone vibrates. I'm reluctant to take it out of my bag,

even though I know it can't be bringing me the sort of terrible news that came only a few weeks ago. I tell myself not to be stupid, and open the message.

Hi, says Luke. *Are you around tomorrow evening? Would you like to meet up for a drink?*

Almost immediately, another text arrives.

Sorry. I forgot you were at a wedding. Have fun.

I'm looking thoughtfully at the messages and wondering if I should reply when I see Ed walking along the path to join me. I drop the phone back into my bag.

'Everything OK?' he asks as he hands me a glass of Prosecco.

'Oh, fine. No worries.'

'I saw you on your phone. I had a bit of a flashback,' he admits.

'Me too.'

He puts his arm around my shoulder.

'We've moved on a lot since that night.'

'I was thinking the exact same thing.'

'See.' He smiles in the gathering darkness. 'We're on the same page, you and I.'

'I guess we are.'

He pulls me closer and I tilt my face upwards. His kiss is deep and satisfying and I'm thinking that perhaps we should abandon the reception and head up to our gorgeous room with its enormous bed. We didn't have time to check it out earlier, what with being so late, but we could give it a really good test drive now. I murmur this to Ed, who looks startled and then, to my surprise, says that we should stay at the reception for a little bit longer.

'Really?' I slide my hand down the front of his trousers.

'You're a witch, Delphie Mertens,' he says. 'And tonight

I'm going to have you in at least five different ways. But honestly, I don't want to skip away too soon.'

'Five different ways?' I look at him in amusement. 'I look forward to finding out about them.'

We walk back into the reception together. There's been a pause in the dancing, and now there's singing. Ed's family are very musical – I remember him telling me that his sister was in a choir and his brother played the piano. It seems like that talent has passed on to the younger generation too, because as we find a space to sit down, Tasha takes her place behind the mic and launches into 'If I Can't Have You'. Then Lisbeth joins her and they duet on 'I Don't Want This Night to End', which has everyone up and dancing.

'They met at their college musical society,' Ed tells me when I remark on how good they both are. 'I guess that old chestnut of having interests in common makes sense.'

There's loud applause at the end of the song, then Ed's brother borrows a guitar from one of the band members and does a lively rendition of 'Whiskey in the Jar', which keeps everyone dancing. When he finishes, he beckons to Ed, who jumps up beside him, slips on the leather jacket that's on a chair beside the stage and launches into an energetic version of 'You're the One That I Want'. He's really very good, and as I clap along with the rest of the guests, he points at me and gives me the kind of sultry look that John Travolta would've been proud of. Sadly I can't do a convincing Olivia Newton-John, but I join in the chorus, and when he slides across the polished floor on his knees, I grab his hands and try to haul him to his feet.

But he resists my efforts and instead reaches inside the jacket.

'You're the one that I want.' He speaks the words as he removes his hand and holds out a small box.

There's an audible gasp from everyone around me. Ed stays on one knee, looking up at me. I stand and stare at him.

'I can't stay like this forever,' he says.

I take the box and open it. Inside is a ring. It's a simple hoop with a solitaire diamond.

'You can change it if you want,' he says. 'No problem. I wanted to have something to offer you, but if you don't like it . . .'

'Oh my God, Ed!'

He stands up, lifts the ring out of the box and takes my hand.

'You're the one that I want, Delphie Mertens,' he says. 'Will you marry me?'

The room has fallen silent. Everyone is looking at me, willing me to answer him. The man who left me and came back. The man who broke my heart and fixed it again. The man who's looking at me with love and hope in his eyes.

The band plays a suspenseful riff. I know I'm waiting too long.

I take a deep breath, then straighten my finger. He slides the ring onto it amid wild applause. 'The future Mrs Miller!' he cries. 'She said yes!'

And then he kisses me.

Chapter 32

I'm engaged to be married.

That's the first thought that goes through my head when I wake up. The second thought is that I dreamed it. So I roll over and look at my hand and I see the diamond ring on my finger. I catch my breath. I'm engaged to be married to Ed Miller, who's sleeping in the bed beside me.

Delphine Miller, I think. Delphine Mertens-Miller. The double-barrelled name works. That's a good thing. I don't want to lose the Mertens part of me.

I slide out of the bed and into the robe that I left on the floor the previous night. I walk slowly to the bathroom and stand under the shower, not caring that I forgot to put on a shower cap and so my hair is getting soaked.

Ed loves me.

I love him.

I'm ready to share my life with him.

He was there for me when I needed him most. Now we'll be there for each other.

I will no longer die alone mourned by my non-existent cat.

My mother will be happy.

Tasha and Lisbeth haven't arranged a barbecue as André and Tory did, but instead have organised an extensive brunch that lasts until two p.m. At that point they leave for their honeymoon in Mexico, while Ed and I drive back to Dublin.

'Will we call in to your mum and dad and share the good news?' he asks as we approach the end of the motorway.

I'd like a little more time to absorb the fact that I'm engaged myself before telling anyone else, but given that all of Ed's family know, it would be really awful not to tell my own parents, so I nod and he turns towards Killester.

As it's Sunday, Mum and Dad aren't alone. In fact they seem to be entertaining most of the family. Everyone except André and Tory is there: Mike and Nichola, Vivi and Jason, Martin and Lindsey and all the children. It's Noemi who, eagle-eyed, spots my ring before I have a chance to say a word, and she yells out to everyone that I'm engaged. Which causes a complete kerfuffle and immediately makes me the absolute centre of attention.

'Congratulations!' cries Vivi as she embraces me. 'I'm so happy for you.'

'Hallelujah,' says Lindsey, who immediately wants to try on the ring.

'Fabulous news.' Nichola kisses me on the cheek.

'Oh, darling.' Mum has tears in her eyes. 'I'm so thrilled for you.'

They really are happy for me. Happier than when I passed my law exams. Happier than when I got my first job. Than when I moved to Cosecha. Than when I was promoted. And happier than when I told them about becoming CEO of Jackie's foundation. This is the one piece of news that makes them uniformly joyful. My brothers are patting Ed on the back and telling him they hope he'll be able to keep me under control. Ed laughs and says it'll be hard to know who's controlling who, and I hear myself say that nobody is controlling anybody, that we're a partnership.

'There's a bottle of cava in the fridge,' says Mum. 'It's been there since André and Tory's wedding. Open it up, Julien.'

'One bottle won't go very far,' mutters Dad as he nevertheless does what he's told.

We don't have enough champagne flutes either, but he manages to eke a mouthful into a variety of glasses.

'Ed and Delphie!' He raises his own glass.

'Ed and Delphie!' echo my family.

And suddenly it feels real.

I'm engaged to Ed.

I'll never need to look for a plus-one again.

The next wedding I go to will be my own.

Erin and Sheedy are both delighted and astonished in equal measure.

'I know you and Ed have been a thing,' Erin says when we meet up. 'But I didn't think you were ready to escalate it into a life-long commitment.'

'Neither did I,' I admit as I turn the ring on my engagement finger. 'I can't quite believe he proposed to me the way he did. But . . . well . . . it seems like my life has taken a complete turnaround over the last couple of months. And Ed is . . . he's been wonderful. He's a rock of support. How could I not love him?'

'When will the wedding be?' asks Sheedy.

Ed and I had a long conversation when we arrived back at my house from Mum and Dad's. We agreed there was no point in a big delay, but I told him that we couldn't arrange anything until I'd met Joe.

'He might hate me,' I said. 'Then what will we do?'

'He won't hate you.'

'All the same, we need . . . well, we need his blessing.'

'He's four years old, Delphie. His approval isn't a deal breaker.'

'I'll be part of his life. It's a big thing for both of us.'

'He'll be fine and so will you,' Ed assured me.

'We still need to meet properly,' I insisted.

'I *had* hoped you'd meet him before I popped the question,' admitted Ed. 'But with your grandmother and your new job and everything else, you've been far too busy for anything else.'

'I'm sorry. The job stuff will die down soon,' I promised.

'I hope so. You're giving it your all at the moment.'

'It'll definitely ease off,' I said. 'Anyway, fingers crossed that Joe likes me. He's the most important person in your life.'

'And you're going to share that spot with him,' said Ed. 'So let's take his approval for granted right now and make some plans for the big day.'

'OK.' I was still nervous about Joe, but Ed was right. It would work out. I'd make sure it did.

Much to my surprise, given his complaints about the cost

of his first wedding, Ed was all for yet another big bash in a castle, which, I reminded him, would take ages to organise because castles were booked up months, if not years, in advance. Besides, I added, I was too old to prance up the aisle in a long dress and veil. I would be perfectly happy with the registry office and a meal afterwards, like I'd always expected.

'You're entitled to the very best,' Ed told me. 'And for everyone to make an enormous fuss over you.'

I told him I didn't need a fuss and he said I absolutely did, but, he added, he was glad that I didn't want to wait years for the right castle.

'If you go for the registry office and meal, you could have it done and dusted before Christmas,' Erin tells me now.

I spent last Christmas at Mum and Dad's, the only unattached woman among the group. I had to put up with the usual low-level nagging about finding someone to love, the normal stuff about a job not being enough and about me being too damn fussy. I thought then that perhaps they were right. But when I eventually left, I was relieved to sit in the silence of my own home without having to put up with the children's excitement and the way their laughter turned to tears and back again in less than a minute. I poured myself a large glass of wine and binge-watched *Money Heist* on Netflix. It was an excellent antidote to the sugar-rush frenzy that had been Killester.

'I'm glad you and Ed . . .' Sheedy gives me an awkward smile. 'He's a good man.'

'We both agree on that,' I say.

'I don't fancy him,' she assures me. 'You do know that, don't you? I've zero interest. It was a fling. We split up.'

'Ed and I split up too,' I remind her.

411

'Please, Delphie.' Her tone is anxious. 'There's nothing between us. Honestly. I'd hate you to think . . . I promise you, there's nothing.'

'Sheedy, I'm going to be honest with you,' I say. 'It's a bit weird to know that you and my fiancé were a thing. But I didn't even know he was in the country at the time, and like I said to you before, he was in the process of divorcing a woman who wasn't me, so I can hardly get upset about his sleeping partners.'

'All the same . . .'

'It's fine. We're fine,' I assure her.

She looks relieved and tells me I should embrace Ed's desire for it to be the best day of my life, and go full traditional.

'I suppose it might be exciting,' I muse. 'White dress, veil, high heels . . .'

They smile at me.

I smile back.

It is actually very exciting.

It's also weird.

Jackie left for the Bahamas after my first couple of days at the foundation, but Daniel will be around until the end of the month. I'm dividing my time between meetings and visiting some of the projects, something that's more uplifting than anything I've ever done in my life before. Seeing the difference that money makes to the lives of disadvantaged children is humbling, and there's a part of me that now feels ashamed for having flitted around the world and stayed in five-star hotels with my filthy-rich employer.

Martha comes with me on my second visit to my favourite project. Run by a couple of businesswomen, it's aimed at advising young women from diverse backgrounds on how to present themselves at interviews by organising a variety of workshops and support structures. It's modelled on other similar schemes where women are mentored in creating the right impression. Those running the workshops help with make-up and clothes too; if a woman has an interview, she can call in to the HQ, borrow an outfit and have her hair and make-up done.

'On the one hand, it's sad that we're so superficial about how people look,' says Hattie, one of the organisers. 'But if it's a game we have to play, we want to make sure that our girls can play it.'

'I love this place.' Martha is enthusiastic. 'I'd like to help as much as I can.'

'You could donate clothes,' says Hattie. 'I'm betting you have an entire wardrobe of stuff that you don't wear any more. Bags, too. Nothing says don't mess with me more than a great bag and killer heels.'

Martha nods in agreement and says she'll check out her wardrobe. But when we leave the building and walk towards the train station, she tells me that this is the project she wants to support financially. And she'll do a three-year deal.

'Are you sure?' I look at her in delight.

'Certain. You know,' she adds thoughtfully, 'Bianca might be someone to get involved too.'

'Bianca!' I stare at her in complete astonishment.

'No reason why they can't have an image consultant to help.'

'Oh, Martha. You're unbelievable. I'm shocked you're suggesting Bianca of all people!'

'I was thinking about her yesterday,' she says. 'About you too.'

413

'Oh?'

'I found Conrad's other three watches. They were in one of the desk drawers in Bandon. I'd like you to have one, Delphie.'

'I already have the pen,' I say.

'This is a gift from me, not from him.'

'That's very generous.'

'Not at all.' She smiles. 'I want to give one to Bianca too.'

'Oh, Martha!' I can't help laughing.

'She should have something personal to remember him by. The house doesn't count.'

I don't say that she has a gorgeous emerald bracelet to remember him by. The watch is very different. It's a nice gesture from Martha and I tell her that.

'Maybe I'm getting things into perspective,' she says. 'Not that I can really put her and Conrad into perspective but . . . I've been lucky, Delphie. And I never realised how damn lucky before. I've had great opportunities and a great life. Conrad's death . . . well, I don't think I'll ever properly get over the fact that it happened when he was with her. I don't think I'll get over the fact that it happened at all. But I know he'd like to think that in the end everything he built up was for something good. And,' she adds, 'given that Bianca did the right thing over the Caldwell deal, she's not the worst person in the world.'

'She only did that after you did a deal with her on the house,' I remind her.

'A deal that you thought was fair,' Martha points out.

'Because it was.'

'You always want the right thing,' she says.

'Don't we all?'

'And the right thing for you has come along too. I was gutted for you about your job. I could see you were devastated. And yet you managed to take something really awful and turn it into an amazing career move. Plus . . .' she smiles, 'you found yourself a fiancé along the way.'

She exclaimed over my engagement ring the moment we met, and I told her all about Ed and the fact that this was our second go at a relationship.

'I didn't have a second chance with Conrad,' she says. 'I wish I had. But at least you know that you love this man. You've met at the right time in your lives and you know you'll be really happy together. He sounds an absolute pet, by the way.'

'He is,' I tell her. 'I'm very lucky too.'

Ed has invited me to his apartment so that I can finally meet Joe. I'm more nervous about this than about any corporate presentation I've ever done. I'm terrified the little boy won't like me and will sense my lack of maternal instinct immediately. Not that I'm going to be a mother figure in his life. Not that Carleen would want me to be. My anxiety levels at getting this right are off the scale.

We're having fish fingers and beans for dinner, which has replaced omelette and chips as Joe's favourite meal. I tell Ed that it's my favourite meal too.

'You're joking,' he says.

'Total comfort food,' I say. 'You couldn't have chosen anything better.'

We sit at the round table and Joe eats everything in front of him, not in the least bit put out by my presence. He's kitted out in Chelsea football gear and I go up in his estimation by being able to name some of the current squad, thanks to the boys next door also being Chelsea fans. I finally start to relax.

'He's very self-possessed for his age,' I say to Ed after the meal, when Joe is allowed to sit in front of the TV and watch one of the Madagascar cartoons.

'Takes after his dad.' Ed beams at me.

I feel a surge of affection for my ready-made family.

Although when it's Joe's bedtime and he throws a complete and utter strop about it, rolling around the floor in absolute fury, I'm glad that he won't be with us every single day and immediately feel ashamed of myself.

The rest of the week is busy, and I'm grateful beyond measure when I get home on Friday evening and Ed has already made dinner. He's set the table properly and has even lit the Jo Malone tea lights I use when I'm chilling out at night. In fairness, though, it's not all tea lights and flowers. We're having burgers, and Ed has grilled them to within an inch of their lives.

'I was looking up wedding venues before you got in,' he says when we're seated at the table. 'There's a lovely place in Monaghan where they do the complete package. It's not a castle but it's a stately home. Looks fabulous.'

'Could be nice,' I concede.

'Alternatively there's a new hotel in Galway. Overlooking the Atlantic. Very rugged and beautiful.'

'Is there nothing closer to home?'

'It doesn't matter where it is if people are coming the night before and staying over,' he says.

'Isn't that making it into a big deal?' I ask. 'I realise that both weddings we've gone to have been like that, but honestly, Ed, I really do mean it when I say I'm happy with something simple.'

'I want to celebrate my love for you,' he says. 'Not rush up the aisle in your lunch hour.'

'I didn't mean that I don't want to make it lovely.' I give him a placating look. 'All I'm saying is that I don't want some over-the-top lunacy.'

'André and Tory's wedding was wonderful,' he says. 'And don't tell me you didn't enjoy Tasha and Lisbeth's.'

'They were both fabulous,' I agree. 'But I don't think we need to match them.' Times have definitely changed when the groom wants a bigger bash than the bride. 'Besides,' I add, 'you had the big do before.'

'But you haven't had one at all,' he points out. 'And it's your day.'

'It's not just my day,' I say. 'It's an important day, of course it is, but it's only a day and it's not like I've been waiting for it my entire life.'

'Well, thanks for that.' He puts down his knife and fork. 'Good to know that my future wife thinks her wedding is the same as any old day.'

'I don't think that,' I protest. 'All I'm saying is that us getting married is what's important. Not venues and people staying over and barbecues and all that palaver.'

'I never said anything about a barbecue.' He gets up and walks to the patio door, where he looks out to the garden. 'It'll be too late in the year for a barbecue.'

'We could leave it till next summer.' I walk over to him and put my arms around him. 'You could have a barbecue then.'

417

'Next summer!' He whirls around. 'What the hell, Delphie? I thought you wanted to do it quickly.'

'If we're having a winter wedding, we'll want somewhere warm and cosy,' I say.

'Mulligrew House is warm and cosy.'

That's the one in Monaghan, I presume. I suddenly think of Ardallen Lodge and wonder what it would be like in November or December. I suppose it would depend on when the Christmas decorations go up. I picture myself like the fairy on top of the Christmas tree in a big dress and with sparkles in my hair. There isn't a chance in hell Ardallen Lodge would be available. It's probably booked up at least a year in advance.

I'm back there again now, as I remember the beautiful ballroom, the elegant floral arrangements, the magnificent grounds and the peaceful river. I remember doing yoga by the river in my bra and pants, and my shock when Luke Granahan turned up beside me. I remember dancing with him, his arm around my waist as he did his best not to step on my toes. I remember the carefree feeling of being with someone who wasn't making demands on me. Who was kind and supportive and . . . Not that Ed isn't all of those things too, of course. And Ed loves me. He asked me to marry him, after all!

I haven't mentioned my plus-one evening with Luke or our subsequent dinner to him. I thought it was better just to consign it to the past. In any event, I haven't seen Luke since I got engaged. I'd say 'obviously', but that implies I can't be friends with a man because I'm engaged to be married to someone else, and that's not the case. But I need to commit to my new life, and a friendship with Luke, no matter how casual, would complicate things.

I texted him the news of my engagement the day after Tasha and Lisbeth's wedding. It took him a few hours to text back. When he did, it was a little GIF of a bride throwing her bouquet. He added, *Congratulations, you deserve to be very, very happy.*

'Does Mulligrew House have availability?' I ask.

'Midweek.' Ed stays looking out at the garden. 'At the end of November.'

I think about how I'd feel if I got an invitation to a wedding in a remote location on a weekday at the end of November. Probably pissed off, to be honest. I'd be all about the time off work, the drive in the dark, the staying overnight . . . I realise that I'm the worst person in the world to gauge things, because I'm so bloody non-weddingy. I'm sure Vivi and Nichola and Tory and Mum will all love it. As for Lindsey, she's already texted twice with suggestions on venues and caterers. She's also given me a pass on my new job. Despite being the boss of a foundation that manages millions, her reaction was 'Charity work! I'm so pleased for you, Delphie,' as though I was selling scratch cards or something. Not that there's anything wrong with selling scratch cards. Oh God, I'm falling down a rabbit hole of justifying my life to myself.

'If you think it's the best place, then perhaps we should book it,' I tell Ed.

He turns to me and smiles. 'Phew,' he says. 'Because they're keeping the date for us. I had until the weekend to persuade you.'

'It'll be lovely,' I say.

And I mean it.

Chapter 33

Ed has moved in with me, which finally makes it all seem real. He's not here a hundred per cent of the time, because he has to give notice on his apartment, and at the moment he prefers to be in his own place when he has Joe to stay. It's geared up for a young boy, whereas my house isn't, although I've talked to Ed about turning the study into Joe's bedroom and decorating it in bright primary colours. I prefer working in the light-filled living room anyhow, so hopefully having his own room will make Joe feel that he belongs here too.

Meanwhile, I'm adapting to having someone else in what I've always thought of as my space. So far I'm doing better than I expected, even if Ed's relationship with the dishwasher leaves a lot to be desired. But I'm OK with sharing the bathroom and the living room couch. And, of course, the bed.

At the moment, though, I'm staying at Ed's for one of the two nights of Joe's visits. We're getting along well, especially as I bought him the latest Chelsea away strip, which he now wears every time he stays over on the basis that he's 'away'. I laughed when he told me that and so did he. There hasn't been a repeat of his temper tantrum the first time we met, which I know was simply because he was over-tired; and I'm getting used to Saturdays being dominated by cartoons on TV. Carleen doesn't mind in the least that Ed and I are engaged and that I'll be a fixture in her son's life in the future, and I'm pleased that we're all being so adult about things, even though, despite how well things are going, I'm anxious about suddenly turning from a single woman into a stepmother. I wish there was another word. Every time I hear 'stepmother', I also hear 'wicked' in my head. The fairy tales told to us as children have a lot to answer for. However, I'm able to put the low-level anxiety I feel about all this behind me when I'm at work, because I'm so busy. Martha has made an initial donation that has thrilled everyone, and somewhat to my surprise, Bianca is also very involved. At first she was sceptical, but when I suggested she come and see the women's project, she became very enthusiastic. She's going to give workshops to them once a month about clothes and make-up. Despite Martha sending Bianca the watch (and Bianca accepting it), I'm keeping the two women apart from each other, but that might change in the future. In the meantime, there's something serendipitous about the fact that both of Conrad's partners have ended up helping out at the same place. And that I, the person who always organised him, have also organised this.

I hope he would be happy.

I always wanted him to be happy.

All of us did.

By the end of the month, I'm exhausted. I've been working late every evening because I wanted to be completely up to speed with everything before Daniel departed. He's been super-helpful, giving the lie to my experience that most male colleagues would be happy to stab you in the back. Although, to be fair, we won't be colleagues, so he doesn't need to show me who's really the boss.

Jackie is delighted with how things are going, and especially pleased that Martha is on board. She's also been impressed by some of my other contacts who are considering contributing or sponsoring various initiatives. I'm using the Cosecha client list I downloaded when I wanted to ask about jobs to ask about donations instead.

'I knew you were the right person, Delphie,' she says when I FaceTime her to give her an update at the end of the week. 'I won't be back in Ireland for a few months, but I look forward to reviewing everything in more detail with you then.'

'Sounds good.' I end the conversation, take my jacket from the back of my chair and leave the office. The initial job offer included a car so that I could get around the country as needed, but I've decided to stick with commuting on the Dart on the days I come into the office, and use the app to hire a car whenever necessary. It's far more economical for the foundation and ensures that money is spent on the work we do rather than my commute.

It's after seven when I get home and the house is silent because Ed is out at a get-together of the guys who worked on the Sligo project. I walk into the living room, soothed by the fact that I'm home before him for the first time this week. I drop my bag on the sofa and switch on the machine to make myself a cup of coffee. While it's heating up, I put the mug and spoon that Ed left in the sink this morning into the dishwasher.

I make the coffee, then wander over to my jigsaw. I've been too busy to look at it this last couple of weeks, but with Ed out and the house my own, I have time now. As I stand over it, I see that the incomplete right-hand corner is almost finished. All the pieces I neatly arranged have been locked together to form clusters of tropical flowers. Obviously Ed decided to do it one evening when I was out and I didn't notice until now.

I wish he hadn't. The jigsaw is my thing. He shouldn't mess with my things. What he should do is put dirty crockery in the dishwasher instead of leaving it piled in the sink. In my house, dirty dishes are never left in the sink!

I catch myself at my own words. I'm calling it 'my house' as though it's not Ed's too. We haven't made a decision on where our home will be in the future, but it would be crazy to sell the cottage and move anywhere else. Though if this is the way I'm thinking, maybe it would be better to live somewhere I wouldn't regard as mine. Somewhere that would be ours. Just as Fintan and Erin did.

Though Fintan and Erin split up.

I walk into the back garden, pulling my fleece around me because it's become autumnal over the last few days. I sit on the wooden bench and look back at the house. I try to imagine living somewhere else with Ed and I can't. I love it here. I love my home.

I have to make sure that Ed sees it at his home too.

It's Dad's birthday on Sunday, which means another Mertens family gathering. It's an even rowdier affair now with Ed added to the mix, but he's good at the banter and jokes that sometimes pass me by. And of course we're the centre of attention when he tells them that we've set a date and will be sending out invitations soon.

'Two weddings in one year!' Nichola exclaims. 'Who would've thought it when we were giving Delphie grief about her plus-one for yours, André.'

'I'm taking credit for the fact that she's getting married at all.' My brother grins at me. 'If we hadn't badgered her to find a decent plus-one . . .'

'I'm so glad I measured up.' Ed laughs.

'You're lucky to have met Delphie's exacting standards,' observes Lindsey. 'Most men get dumped after they profess undying love for her.'

'No they don't,' I object.

'Lindsey's right,' says Nichola. 'Every time we almost get to know someone, he's given the boot.'

'Oh, come on!' I make a face at her.

'It was because of her job,' says Lindsey. 'If she was still with Cosecha, you wouldn't have had a chance, Ed.'

'Lindsey!' I give her an exasperated look.

'It's true,' she says. 'You might have had other boyfriends, but the only man in your life was Conrad Morgan.'

'There's a big difference between a boss and a boyfriend,' I say as mildly as I can.

'You need to be the boss in your marriage, Ed.' Nichola laughs. 'Then she'll always have time for you.'

'Why are you all giving me grief?' I demand. 'For years you've gone on and on at me about needing someone in my life and how I'm failing as a woman for not being married, and now that I am getting married, you still won't give me a break!'

'Ah, lookit, we're only teasing you, Delphie,' says Vivi.

She turns to Ed. 'You'll find she gets a bit stressed sometimes. And that she wants a perfectly ordered life.'

'Who doesn't?' I demand.

'Anyone who's married,' says Nichola. 'As soon as you have a family, Delphie, order goes out the window.'

'But you have to lay down some ground rules,' Lindsey says. 'Otherwise he'll drive you mad.'

'Hey, men have to have ground rules too.' Martin gets involved. 'Everyone does something that gets up the other person's nose.'

Suddenly they all start sharing things that annoy them. It seems to go on forever. Martin doesn't put clothes in the laundry basket. Lindsey buys stuff on sale even if she doesn't need it. Mike wheels his muddy bicycle into the hallway. Nichola won't use cloths to wipe down surfaces, only paper towels. Vivi uses her pregnancy as an excuse for . . . well, everything according to Jason, although he smiles when he says this.

They're all laughing about each other's annoying habits, but I can't understand why nobody makes an effort to change. And then I realise that I'm not going to be able to change my apparently annoying habit of wanting to have everything in its place. I'll change something else for Ed. I don't know what it is yet, but I will.

'So what do I do?' Ed grins at me. 'What's my annoying habit?'

'You mess with my jigsaw,' I say.

'Huh?'

'You mess with my jigsaw. You did a big chunk of it.'

'The pieces were growing mould.' He laughs.

'My jigsaw is my thing,' I say. 'I'm the only one who should touch it.'

'Right,' he says. 'Is there anything else I should or shouldn't do? Best to find out sooner rather than later.'

'Putting the dishes in the dishwasher would be good. And hanging up your jacket when you come in instead of leaving it on the back of a chair.'

There's a sudden awkward silence and I realise I've misjudged the question. It was supposed to be an opportunity to say no, and allow him to point out one of my flaws, but I've answered it as though it was something he wanted to know.

He turns away from me with a murmured 'OK, so' and helps himself to a bread roll. Nichola starts talking to Lindsey about the autumn sales. Vivi says her back is hurting and stands up. I take a sip from my water glass and wish I'd kept my mouth shut.

Mum goes to the kitchen and comes back with a couple of perfectly made pavlovas, which has the effect of bringing Vivi back to the table amid a chorus of approval for Mum's baking skills. She passes around the dessert and everyone tucks in. Calm is restored.

I take the largest slice of pavlova on offer and eat every morsel.

Chapter 34

When we arrive home, Ed turns on the TV and watches a football match while I sit in the window seat to do some prep for the week ahead. We haven't actually exchanged any words since I enumerated my list of his flaws. I want to apologise, but I'm afraid of making matters worse.

I get the feeling that both of us want to be alone, but the problem about my house is that with such limited living space, you have to retreat to the study for a bit of solitude. But I'm already thinking of it as Joe's bedroom, and anyhow, I don't want to move. Which means I'm conscious of Ed and conscious of the edge between us even as I pore over my calendar for the week ahead.

When the football ends, he tells me he's going home.

'OK,' I say. 'Talk tomorrow.'

'Talk tomorrow.'

He walks out of the house and leaves me to my own devices.

It's probably not a bad thing right now.

He texts in the morning, though, as he always does, and tells me that he'll be in Wicklow for most of the day and so he'll spend the night at his own apartment. Until yesterday, I wouldn't have given it a thought, but now I wonder if him staying at his own place is some kind of statement. I send back a jokey text saying that it's fine, I'll just about manage on my own. He doesn't reply.

I debate whether I should send another message saying I'll miss him. I will, but if he's still pissed at me, it's better that we're apart until he gets over it. This is the problem with relationships, I think, as I head to the office. Men get into your head. You're always trying to second-guess how they feel, whether you've managed to annoy them, how to fix it. You're always trying to fix it. I should know by now that men don't think it needs fixing. They want to be left alone while you cool off. Because they've forgotten about it already. I bet Ed isn't even thinking about me, while I'm obsessing about him.

Fortunately it's a busy morning and I don't have time to overanalyse my relationship any further. By mid afternoon, when things have quietened down, I think that perhaps I should send him another text. But texting him when he's already told me he's going to be out of town and then spending the night at his apartment smacks of being needy. I don't want to be a needy girlfriend. I'm not. I'm not a girl either. I'm nearly forty.

Except there's something wrong and I can't rest until it's sorted.

I get home to an empty house and pop half of the lasagne I bought from the deli in the oven. I got a large one in case Ed changed his mind and called over anyway. He hasn't texted and I'm annoyed at myself for caring. He'll text when he can. Or when he wants to. It won't affect my evening either way.

Except it does, because I'm constantly checking my phone. I don't want to miss a text in case he thinks I'm deliberately not replying to him. In case he thinks I'm engaged in some kind of texting tit-for-tat. I know this is ridiculous. But I can't help it.

It's like déjà vu from my previous relationships. I go out with a guy, we get on fine, it's moving towards another level and then – wham – something happens and I always seem to be the one who's caused it. And the next thing I know, I'm questioning everything and obsessing over texts and trying to figure out exactly what it is he wants and what I want. And in the end, because it's too exhausting, it's easier to end it. But I can't end it with Ed because we're engaged and we've set the date and we have an appointment with the registrar next week. And because Joe has accepted me as a fixture in his life too. So we have to work out something that I don't even know if he realises needs to be worked out.

My head is melting.

I'm an idiot.

I'm an idiot because of a man.

It's nearly ten before he sends a message to say that he was late home and will be in Wicklow tomorrow too. I'm tempted to call him back rather than keep messaging, but I don't want him to think that I need to talk to him. So I say that's fine and ask if he'll be dropping over tomorrow evening, and he says he's not sure but he'll let me know. So I say goodnight and add a heart emoji. He sends a sleeping emoji in return.

At least we've moved to emojis.

That's progress.

I'm in meetings with project managers all of the next day, but every so often I check my phone to see if Ed has messaged me. By the time I leave for the evening, he still hasn't been in touch. I remind myself that we're both grown adults and this text-or-not business is utterly childish. And so, on the train home, I send him a text and ask him if everything's OK and whether he knows his schedule.

He replies within a couple of minutes saying that he'll be leaving the site shortly and should be home in about an hour and a half.

I release a sigh of relief and reply with a couple of thumbs-up emojis.

When I get off the train, I go to the deli. I'm about to buy two of their fabulous pad thai dinners when I think that perhaps it would be a nice thing to cook something from scratch myself. So instead I choose some chicken breasts and seasoning, along with fresh vegetables and potatoes. I cheat by adding a tub of mushroom sauce, which I plan to use with the chicken. I also buy a couple of bottles of Ed's favourite white wine, a crisp Pazo Cilleiro Albariño, as well as a pretty bouquet of freshly cut flowers from the florist next door.

At home, I put the wine in the fridge, season the chicken, prepare the veg and potatoes and then set the table with my decorative table mats and matching napkins and place the vase of flowers in the middle.

I'm feeling proud of my efforts and I reckon that the women in my family would be astonished at how I've finally embraced the whole domestic goddess vibe. I have to admit that I've quite enjoyed it. There's something very satisfying about knowing that the well-laid table and the aroma of food coming from the oven is all down to me. I've got my timings almost exactly right, planning to have the food ready about fifteen minutes after Ed gets home. I nip upstairs and change into a fresh top and a multicoloured skirt, then, hoping that he'll appreciate my transformation, I open one of the bottles of wine, pour myself a glass and wait.

He said an hour and a half, but I know traffic can be heavy, so I based my timings on two hours. But when there's no sign of him twenty minutes after that, I send yet another text to ask where he is.

Just got in now, he replies. *Traffic was terrible*.

He means he's just got in to Ballinteer. But he said he was coming home. So is Ballinteer home, or is here? A few days ago I would've said here. But now I'm not sure.

'Are you coming over?' I ask.

'Leaving now,' he replies.

It takes him forty minutes to get to me.

When he arrives, I don't say anything about having cooked dinner, but I do ask if he planned to be here this evening. 'Because you said you'd be home in an hour and a half and I thought you meant here, but obviously you meant Ballinteer,' I add.

'Force of habit to call that home,' he says. 'I had to leave some stuff there.'

It's only now that he notices the set table and the vase of flowers. And that the oven is on.

'You cooked?' He's utterly astonished.

'I thought it would be nice. But it might be a bit dry now.'

'Give me a minute to wash my hands and I'll be ready to eat,' he says.

He dumps his bag in the hallway and goes upstairs.

I take the chicken breasts out of the oven. They're definitely looking a bit wizened, but with the sauce poured over them, they'll be edible. The mashed potato looks OK, and I'm doing the veg in the microwave now, so at least the carrots and broccoli will taste fresh.

When Ed comes downstairs again, I put the food in front of him and pour wine for us both.

'I'm sorry,' he says.

'No worries. It's fine.'

But it's not. It's nothing to do with him, and everything about me trying to do something good and it all going wrong. Despite the mushroom sauce, it's obvious the chicken is rubbery. The mash is drier than it should be, and although Ed eats the carrots I remember, too late, that he's not keen on broccoli.

'Lovely,' he says when he's finished everything but the broccoli. 'Dessert?'

'No dessert,' I say.

'Not needed.' He nods. 'Thanks, Delphie.'

My mobile rings. It's Jackie, FaceTiming me from Barbados. She's generally been very hands-off, but there were a couple of things I put in an email to her earlier and I suggested that calling me might be quicker than having emails going back and forward.

'I have to take this,' I say.

He gets up from the table and stretches out on the sofa while I talk to Jackie. When we finish our conversation, I begin to stack the dishes in the dishwasher.

'I was going to do that,' he says. 'But I know I never do it right, so it's easier to leave it to you.'

He turns on the TV.

I sit at the table and work on my jigsaw. But it's hard to concentrate when all I keep thinking of is that Ed is still punishing me for the moment in my parents' house. I was insensitive and he's not letting it go.

I know I have to change, and I'm doing my best. Despite him being Ed Mark II, he's reverted to the silent treatment he used to dish out whenever he was pissed at me in the past. Which, to be fair, wasn't that often.

How do we deal with this?

How do I fix it?

I jump as I feel the touch of his fingers on the back of my neck.

'I've been an absolute dick, Delphie,' he says. 'You were great to cook dinner and it's my fault if it wasn't as perfect as you'd planned. Come on, let's go to bed.'

I sigh with relief, and we head upstairs together.

Chapter 35

I meet the girls on Friday evening. We've all had a busy week, and Sheedy has spent most of it with a divorce client and her barrister. The couple has been married for twenty-five years, but the husband doesn't want the divorce and is making things difficult.

'She's not happy any more,' says Sheedy. 'Their only child has finished college and got a job. She doesn't see the need to keep the family together.'

'If there hadn't been a child, would she have left sooner?' I ask.

Sheedy nods. 'She knew it was a mistake after the first year. But she was pregnant by then.'

Ed and I have discussed having children. He's not against having another one, but it's not high on his agenda. We've filed it away as something that might happen at a future date, but not something to worry about now.

'There's no need for him to be difficult about it, but it's his form of revenge,' continues Sheedy. 'The perceived wisdom is that women are the emotional ones, but when it comes to divorce, it's men who let emotion get in the way more often.'

'Which emotion?' I ask.

'The desire to hit back,' she says. 'They don't like being beaten and that's how they take being divorced, unless they've got someone else. And of course they do tend to get someone else as quickly as possible. But even so, far too many seem to think that their wife instigating divorce proceedings is some kind of insult that has to be dealt with. It's such a waste of energy.'

Sheedy has a point. Each time I broke up with someone, the man concerned was angry. They nearly all told me that I'd be lucky to find someone as understanding as them. Someone who treated me as well as they had. Someone who would put up with me. The one time the man broke up with me – the time Ed broke up with me – I went home and cried because I thought I wasn't good enough myself. So either way – dumped or being dumped – I always felt that it was my fault.

'How are you coping without Fintan?' I turn to Erin.

'Better than I thought,' she replies. 'But every so often I put my head down and have a little weep.'

'Oh, Erin.'

'At least I didn't have to work on your divorce,' says Sheedy.

'Sorry that you lost out on the business.' Erin grins at her.

'Will you ever get married, Sheedy?' I ask. 'Or are you too cynical?'

'I'm not cynical at all,' says Sheedy. 'I'd love to find the right man and spend the rest of my life with him. It's just that I won't settle for the wrong one. Mind you,' she adds, 'my mum never shuts up about wanting me to be happy. Although in her case it's really about wanting me to produce a grandchild. She's the only one of her gang who can't participate in the cuteness one-upmanship when they take out their videos and photos. And being an only child myself, I feel a certain responsibility.'

'That's exactly it,' says Erin. 'Everyone says they want you to be happy, but it's their version of happy that they want.'

'There's nothing wrong with being married if it works,' I say.

'We weren't trying to get at you.' Sheedy gives me a horrified look. 'Ed is a great guy and you're going to knock it out of the park together.'

She slept with him. I usually don't think about it, but whenever she says his name, I do. I wonder if I'll ever totally get over it. If I'll ever be able to see them in the same room and not think of it.

'The wedding's going to be great,' says Erin. 'I'm looking forward to it already.'

'Hopefully it won't make you think of Fintan.'

'Fintan and I were only ever going to live with each other,' she says. 'Besides, I've plenty more things to occupy me till then.'

'Like what?'

'Cosecha,' she says. 'There's a massive row among the board about a particular deal that went pear-shaped. I'm looking at the legal ramifications.'

The Caldwell deal, I think. I presume the legal ramifications are from Hammersmith being dumped out of the picture.

'Your name came up,' she adds. 'It was on a Post-it note stuck to a bundle of papers.'

'What did it say?'

'It was only your name, with a series of question marks. As though they felt you could've been involved.'

'I'm not involved any more,' I say. 'Though I know the deal you're talking about.'

Erin gives me a quizzical look, and I shrug.

'Anyhow,' she says, 'splitting from Fintan has worked out for me time-wise, because I've a lot on my plate and I don't have to keep worrying that he'll think I'm ignoring his messages.'

I tell her I know all about the ignoring messages thing, and even Sheedy chimes in with her reminiscences of being tethered to her phone looking to see if a message had been read, wondering why it hadn't been answered. I thought I was the only one.

'What was the decider in you and Fintan splitting up?' Sheedy asks Erin.

'I couldn't be the person he wanted,' she says. 'I don't know if that makes me selfish or not. But I didn't want to be the one who defaulted into household chores or looking after all the domestic things. And yet because he's the sort of man who's quite happy to let things pile up and up and up, and I like to keep it all under control, I was suddenly doing the laundry and the ironing and the dishwasher unloading and I was resenting it. Massively.'

'Out of such apparently trivial things my divorce business thrives.' Sheedy grins.

'Ed and I had a row about my jigsaw,' I tell them. 'I know it's ridiculous, but I got stroppy about him doing it when I wasn't there.'

'If it's only a jigsaw that comes between you, you shouldn't end up in my office,' she says.

'We're actually having a bit of a tough time at the moment.' As I say this out loud, I feel a monumental surge of relief. I'm tired of pretending everything is perfect.

437

'Why?' They ask the question in unison.

'It's been different since we got engaged,' I say slowly. 'He's treating the wedding like a military operation. I think he wants to outdo the ones we've been to this year. He's insisting that I deserve the best for the happiest day of my life, but the best for me is something a lot more casual than he's planning.'

'Tell him you want to scale it down a bit,' says Sheedy.

'He wouldn't understand.' I shake my head. 'He seems to think he owes it to me. He's got his heart set on this place in Monaghan. It's absolutely gorgeous, but it's not me.'

'If he loves you, he'll want what you want,' says Sheedy.

'Though that's not what happens the other way around, is it?' I ask. 'When women insist on big fancy weddings, the guys just have to go along with it.'

'It's a bit of a role reversal all right,' Erin acknowledges. 'Despite his Prince Charming heroics over being a plus-one in your hour of need, you're not exactly the helpless princess who needs the happy-ever-after wedding.'

She's right. Ed was great when I needed him most. And I love him. So I should do this for him.

I need to get over myself.

I need to get with the programme.

I need to get married.

On Saturday morning, I leave him in bed and go for a run along the seafront. He stayed up late to watch a horror movie, and now he's sleeping like a baby. I was happy to leave him to the movie, because I can't watch horror. Instead I headed up to the mezzanine, where I put on my headphones and watched a saved episode of *Bake Off* on my iPad. When I checked my emails afterwards, I saw one from Jackie asking about the possibility of me visiting Barbados in a few weeks' time to check out a women's project that's very similar to the one in Dublin. She added that I might like to continue on to Atlanta afterwards for a philanthropy conference she's chairing. I was thrilled at the idea and immediately mailed back saying yes. I was going to shout down to Ed about it but decided against interrupting his horror viewing.

I'll tell him when I get home with fruit and pastries from the deli for breakfast.

I'm sitting on a rock overlooking the estuary, catching my breath, when I look up and see Luke Granahan walking towards me. Despite the fact that he lives on this side of town, I've never seen him here before, and as he approaches, I'm not sure he recognises me in my running gear. He's dressed casually in jeans and cotton shirt, his face unshaven. My contact with him fizzled out after my engagement to Ed, and I feel slightly awkward seeing him now. I'm not sure if I should say something, but he strides past me without even acknowledging me.

I'm surprised at how hurt I feel.

And then he turns back.

'Delphie!' he says. 'I didn't recognise you there for a moment.'

'I'm not looking my best,' I say as I stand up.

'You look great.'

That makes me laugh, because I know my face is red, and my hair scraped back into a short ponytail is not in the least bit flattering.

'How have things been?' Almost without thinking, I free my hair from the bobbin and let it fall around my face. It's damp and a bit ratty from my exertions, so I'm not sure it was one of my better ideas.

'Good, and you? How's the new job? Erin tells me you're going great guns there.'

How often do he and Erin talk about me?

'I'm loving it,' I admit. I tell him about my possible trip to Barbados and Atlanta, and he smiles broadly.

'You're clearly playing a blinder. I'm really happy for you, Delphie.'

'It's all thanks to you,' I say. 'Like I said before, Cosecha and then meeting Jackie were both big wins for me on your watch. You can't deny being my lucky charm.'

He laughs.

'Seriously,' I say.

'Well, it's nice to be someone's lucky charm.' He looks at me. 'I was going to buy an ice-cream cone. Would you like one?'

I look at my watch. It's only ten in the morning.

'It's never too early for ice cream,' says Luke.

'Oh, go on then.'

As we walk to the shop together, I ask him what he's doing in Malahide, and he says he often walks around the estuary because it's so beautiful.

'You should run,' I say.

'I'm not mad about running,' he confesses. 'I've taken up badminton again. I used to play with Lara and I really enjoyed it, but I haven't wanted to go back until this year.'

'I play too, although I'm not very good,' I tell him.

'You're probably better than you're letting on,' says Luke. 'You're tall and strong and—'

'Wildly inaccurate,' I say.

440

He grins at me as we stop at the shop, where he asks what kind of cone I'd like.

'A 99,' I say.

'As if there's any other kind.'

We take our whipped ice cream with chocolate flakes back across the road and sit on the small wall facing the sea.

Although there are quite a few people out and about – mostly runners and dog-walkers – there's something very tranquil about sitting here beside him with my ice-cream cone. It brings me back to the days of my childhood, when Dad would pile us into the car and drive us here or to nearby Portmarnock and we'd play on the beach or run through the sand dunes. Afterwards, always, there were ice creams.

I ask Luke how things are going for him, and he says that he's busy. I mention that Erin says she's busy too, so Haughton's is obviously doing well. And then I ask how things are going personally, and he says not bad, and I wonder if he's been to any more flashy weddings, and he says no, but that he's been invited to one in January. A second-time-around couple, he tells me, so it'll be a less frothy occasion than Ardallen Lodge. Probably better fun as well, he remarks, although he enjoyed Ardallen House because I stepped in as a plus-one. He adds that he hasn't managed to add to his list of plus-ones so he doesn't know where he'll get one this time.

'Sorry, sorry.' He looks at me with an appalled expression after he says this. 'That sounded . . . I didn't mean to imply . . .'

'No, I understand. It's fine.'

'And your own wedding?' he asks. 'When is that?'

'November,' I say. And then I nearly choke on my ice cream. 'Shit,' I say.

'What?'

'I'm supposed to be going to Atlanta in November. To that conference I mentioned earlier!'

'You've let a conference clash with your wedding?' Luke is looking at me in disbelief.

'I didn't mean to . . . I was so excited about it and I didn't think . . . Well, no need to think, actually.' I exhale in relief as I work it out in my head. 'It's the week before the wedding, so it's not like I'm going to miss it or anything. It's all good, I didn't really forget, it's just that the timing is a bit tight.'

He's still looking at me in disbelief.

He's judging me.

I'm judging myself.

'What's wrong with me?' I ask abruptly. 'Really, Luke, what? I mean, I know I'm not the girliest girl in the world, but it's my wedding, for heaven's sake. I need to be back the week before to do all sorts of weddingy things.'

'Have you got the dress?' he asks.

'Not yet. But I'm going out next week with my mum and my sister. That's what women do, isn't it? They go with their friends or their family and they make a big day of it. So I'm doing that right at least.'

I don't say that Vivi was the one who told me I was leaving it far too late to get the perfect dress. I told her that I wouldn't be going full bridal, there wasn't going to be a long dress and veil, so there wasn't the same degree of urgency.

'You'll still need time to find the exact right one,' she said. 'You want to give yourself a few weeks, Delphie.'

'Shit,' I say again.

'What?'

'The dinner the week beforehand. Female relatives. It's a

thing, apparently. My sister is organising it, but I won't have time for a dinner if I go to Atlanta. I won't have time for a hen night either, though for feck's sake, I don't care about that.'

Luke says nothing.

'The dinner is more important than Atlanta, isn't it?' I look at him in despair. 'How can I possibly change if I don't realise straight off that the dinner is more important?'

'Are you expecting to change?'

I explain about wanting to be a formidable woman, a woman who doesn't spend hours second-guessing herself, contemplating her failures, thinking she doesn't measure up. But I point out that I can't entirely be that woman if I want to get married. I have to knock the edges off her. I have to be nicer. More thoughtful. Less driven.

'No you don't,' says Luke. 'You're smart and professional and you've pretty much got it together in life. What the hell is wrong with that?'

'Men are threatened by strong women,' I say. 'We have to at least pretend to prefer going to a spa to going to a meeting, to not know one end of a screwdriver from the other. To be needy.'

'Is Ed threatened by you?' he asks. 'Does he want you to be needy?'

'Well, no, I guess not, although he likes looking after me.' I sigh. 'But I don't put him first. That's wrong.'

'Does he put you first?' asks Luke.

'Yes. Mostly.' I lick the remains of my melting ice cream from my fingers and put the cone in the nearby waste bin. 'At least, he puts what he thinks I want first,' I say as I sit down again, 'even if he gets that wrong sometimes. Oh God, I'm a terrible person.'

'You're not,' says Luke. 'You're the woman you want to be. There's nothing wrong with that. And yes, you might have got carried away with the job thing and forgotten that you needed some pre-wedding time, but in the end, you remembered. So all's well.'

'Not really,' I say. 'Because I'd much rather go to Atlanta than have a pre-wedding dinner.'

He laughs, and I can't help smiling.

'But Ed deserves me to do it properly,' I say. 'He's been so brilliant and so wonderful to me. He was my plus-one when I was stuck. He stayed around after Conrad's death. He was there when my grandmother passed away. He's been with me for everything. I couldn't have managed without him.'

'Forgive me if I'm getting this completely wrong,' says Luke. 'I don't want you to think that I . . .' He hesitates.

'Oh, for heaven's sake. What?' I demand.

'Are you sure you're not marrying Ed as a thank you?'

'A thank you?'

'For being there.'

'Of course not!' I exclaim. 'I'm marrying him because . . .'

Why am I marrying Ed?

Because I love him.

Because he loves me.

Because my family loves him.

Because they want me to marry him.

Because he came back to me.

Because he asked me.

He's the only man who ever asked me.

And I said yes because he's Ed Mark II.

I love Ed Mark II.

But do I love him enough to marry him?

To be a stepmother to his son?

I must.

I knew what I was taking on.

I absolutely did.

'Delphie?' Luke is looking at me.

'I'm sorry,' I say.

And then I burst into tears.

I don't believe it. Through everything that's happened this year, I've managed to keep the tears away. Even though I might have wobbled from time to time, I've been strong. I've been – with the odd exceptional moment – the formidable woman I've wanted to be. Except for some happy tears at the three weddings I've been to this year, I haven't cried. Not once. And now here I am, sobbing in front of Luke Granahan.

He takes a neatly folded hanky from the back pocket of his jeans and hands it to me, telling me it's clean and unused. I don't want to cry into his hanky, but I've nothing else. I hold it to my eyes while my shoulders shake. I can feel him beside me, close but not touching me. I remember leaning my head against his shoulder at the Ardallen Lodge. I did it so Justin Delaney wouldn't see me, but I recall the comfort of Luke's arms around me. They're not around me now, but he's sitting beside me, saying nothing.

I take a deep breath, stop crying, and mop my eyes.

'Sorry,' I say. 'You must think I'm a complete fool.'

'No,' says Luke.

'I don't know what brought that on.' I keep my voice as steady as I can. 'Sorry again.'

'It's fine,' says Luke. 'Are you OK now?'

I nod.

'Is there anything I can do?'

'I don't think so.' I give him my best smile. 'You've done enough already.'

'But not in a good way.'

I shake my head, then look at the hanky balled up in my hand. 'D'you want this back in this awful state, or will I wash it and return it?'

'Keep it,' says Luke.

He stays sitting beside me while I twist his hanky around in my hand. And all the time, I'm thinking. It's as though the tears have cleared my mind. Because it's obvious to me now. I love Ed. I really do. He's a good person who wants what's best for me. And I want what's best for him. He deserves that much.

'Seems to me that this is the second time you've helped me out of a crisis,' I say to Luke.

'Oh?'

'I've sorted things in my head. I know where I'm at now.'

'Good,' he says.

'Though it's not very strong-woman of me, is it, crying on your shoulder.'

'You can be a strong woman and still let the guard down sometimes. It's not the end of the world.'

'I never let my guard down.'

He grins suddenly. 'Yes, you do. I saw you in your bra and pants, remember?'

I laugh. It feels good to laugh.

'You know that saying about nobody on their deathbed ever wishing they'd spent more time in the office?' says Luke.

'My sister-in-law quotes it to me on a regular basis.'

'It's very true,' he says. 'But nobody ever regrets spending time on the things they love either. And if you love what you do, you shouldn't feel the need to do something else just to make other people happy. Or to fulfil someone else's idea of what you should be. You can't live your life based on what other people expect. Only on what you know will work.'

'You're the least legal lawyer I've ever met in my life,' I tell him. 'Being with you is like being with my own personal counsellor.'

'I probably picked it up over the last few years.' He gives me a wry look. 'After Lara, I needed it. You do when you lose someone you love. When you become unmoored.'

Martha used that exact word about herself. I remember thinking how well it described how I was feeling too. How anyone must feel when the fabric of their life has unravelled. But Ed has been there for me. Keeping things on an even keel. Helping to anchor me when things have been tough.

'I love Ed,' I say.

'In which case, he's very lucky. I'm glad you've come to that conclusion.'

I gather my thoughts before I speak again.

'But I'm not going to marry him,' I say. 'I love him, but I don't love him enough for that. It would be a monumental mistake, and he doesn't deserve me to make a monumental mistake with him.'

Luke's face is impassive. 'Well then, it's good you've decided that before it's too late.'

That's exactly what Erin would say.

447

And Sheedy.

But somehow I don't think they're the words Ed will use.

There's no way of telling someone that you're not going to marry them without hurting them. Ed looks at me in disbelief and then asks if I'm having an anxiety attack. A case of cold feet. Nerves about being a stepmother.

'It's normal to get the jitters,' he says.

'It's not jitters.'

'And I understand if you're anxious about Joe.'

'I'm not anxious about Joe.'

'It's normal to feel a bit overwhelmed too,' he says. 'I did, before I married Carleen.'

'And you and Carleen got divorced.'

'You and I know each other better than Carleen and I did,' he says. 'We've history together.'

'We went out for a while and then you left me to go to Dubai,' I remind him.

'So what is this? Some kind of revenge?' he demands. 'I broke up with you, so you're breaking up with me? We weren't engaged back then, Delphie!'

'I know they say it's a dish best served cold, but honestly, Ed, d'you really think that when I saw you on the plane, my first thought was to lure you into proposing to me so that I could dump you?'

'How do I know how your mind works?'

'Not like that,' I say.

He gives me a look that's equal parts hurt and disdain.

'Joe will be upset,' he says. 'He really likes you.'

'I'm truly sorry,' I say. 'I thought it was right for me, but it's not. And you don't want a second broken marriage, Ed. It wouldn't be fair to you. Or to Joe.'

'I would've made sure it worked for everyone.'

'It takes two,' I remind him. 'And I'm the variable in the equation. I'm the one who would've messed it up.'

'You already have,' says Ed, and walks out of my life for the second time.

Vivi calls me when she hears.

'What the hell?' she says. 'This takes the biscuit, Delphie. You only dumped them before. Now you've called off a wedding.'

'It was the right thing to do.'

'You have guts, that's for sure.'

'It doesn't take guts to do the right thing.'

'I'll never understand you.'

'Sometimes I don't even understand myself.'

'Are you OK?' Her voice softens.

'Never better,' I assure her.

I'm telling the truth.

Lindsey sends me a text.

Are you out of your freaking mind? Ed is adorable. You'll never meet anyone like him again.

I know, I reply. *And it's because he's adorable that I don't want to ruin his life.*

Do you really think working is better than loving?

No. But it's better than marrying the wrong man.

You've let the right one slip through your fingers. You're an idiot, Delphie.

449

An idiot who's made the right decision.

She carries on with a few more texts, but I don't reply.

Nichola's text is more understanding

I'm sad for you, but I'd be sadder if you married him and it didn't work out. Besides, this way you remain my kick-ass role model.

I reply that I'm not a great role model of any description, even as I process my surprise that I'm apparently one for my sister-in-law.

You do what you want and what's best for you, says Nichola. *I admire that. Don't ever feel you have to be different.*

I'm cheered by her words.

But when I drop around to see Mum, she's almost as upset as my now ex-fiancé.

'Why?' she asks as I prop myself against the kitchen table. 'You were good together. You had a rapport. Everyone could see it. He understood you, Delphie.'

'Not entirely,' I say.

'You'll be alone again,' she says. 'I don't want you to be alone for the rest of your life.'

'If I am, I am,' I say. 'Better that than to mess it up with the wrong person.'

'I didn't think he was the wrong person. You loved him before.'

'Maybe we simply got the timing wrong.'

'Will there ever be a right time for you?' she asks.

'I hope so. But I don't want to make a bad mistake just because I'm afraid it won't come around.'

She's silent.

So am I.

'You know I'm proud of you, don't you?' she says eventually.

'I—'

'Your life is your life,' she's speaking quickly, 'and you're right to take the decisions that work for you. Yes, I'm sad it didn't work out with Ed. Having the right person in your life is . . . well, it's great, Delphie. It really is. But more than anything, I want you to be happy. And I know you are. I know you're strong. You were strong about the whole job thing. You were strong about Granny Mertens. And you're strong about this. So I'm sorry if I've been . . .' she hesitates, and then beams, 'projecting – isn't that the word? I'm sorry if I've been projecting what makes me happy on you. Because it's obvious you're happy doing what you're doing now. I'm delighted that you're running a great organisation. And whatever you want that's best for you, I want that too.'

'Oh, Mum.' I move closer to her and she hugs me. Then she opens the kitchen cupboard.

'Have some cake,' she says, putting a large slice of lemon drizzle in front of me.

And I do.

I meet the girls the following weekend.

'Our strike rate is pretty good.' Erin gives me a knowing look. 'You and Ed. Me and Fintan. Sheedy – well, you haven't got into the living-with-someone, getting-engaged-to-someone, nearly-marrying-someone thing yet, but you've had your fair share of expendable relationships. Generally speaking, ladies, we're hopeless.'

'Only when it comes to men,' I say. 'At everything else, we're great. Even my mum admits that.'

'And we're not hopeless at men either,' says Sheedy. 'Because we haven't made disastrous mistakes over them. Trust me, I've seen how that turns out.' She's finished with her big divorce case and has negotiated an excellent settlement for her client. Or, as she puts it, the appropriate settlement given the circumstances of their marriage.

'Will any of us ever get married?' I wonder.

'*I've* been married,' Erin reminds me.

'OK, will any of us find someone we love enough to want to get married in the future?' I amend. 'Don't we all want somebody to love?'

'Yes,' says Sheedy. 'But maybe we're deluded about what love is. Maybe that's why so many people get married when they shouldn't.'

'It'd be nice to think we might. And that it would work out,' I say.

'My mum married my dad because she was afraid of being single,' Sheedy remarks. 'It worked out; they're still together. But sometimes I think they're more like a business partnership than anything else. I don't want to end up in a business partnership.'

'If I do, it'll be one where I set the terms,' says Erin.

'I don't think it's about setting the terms,' I say slowly. 'I think it's about knowing them already. Like you said before, knowing when to compromise and when not to. But not resenting it. That was the problem for me. I started resenting Ed, and I didn't want to resent someone I cared about.'

'Perhaps when you meet the right person, the compromises simply fall into place,' says Erin. 'No matter how much we told ourselves otherwise, you and I didn't meet the right person, so that's why it didn't work out.'

'Or maybe it was because we really are trying to have it all. You know, the career, the husband, the family . . .'

'No,' says Sheedy. 'We're trying to make sure that whatever we choose is the right thing for us.'

I nod. She's right. You can't live your life with the fear of missing out. You have to make choices. You have to believe in your choices. And you have to have confidence in the future. I have all those things, even if I'm going home alone tonight.

My house is quiet when I walk in the door. Everything is exactly as it was before I left earlier. The worktop is clean. The dishes are in the dishwasher. The cushions are arranged the way I like them on the sofa.

I switch on the garden lights and walk outside.

It's cool in the night air, but I sit on the wooden bench anyway.

I'm alone.

I'm not lonely.

I'm more relaxed than I've been in months.

The decisions I've made might not have been the ones that other women would've made, but they're the right ones for me. I hope I'm not going to be single for the rest of my life, but if I am, I know I can cope. Because I'm actually OK with myself. With my own company. With whatever it is I want to do. I'm not a recluse. I have lots of things going on in my life. And even if I don't have a man in it right now, I have a large and loving family, all of whom might criticise my choices but who love me anyway. I'm closer to them than I was before. And that's a good thing.

I'll be OK.

My phone buzzes with a message.

Hope all's well with you, says Luke Granahan.

I look at it for a long time.

I'm fine. I'm not engaged any more.

There's a delay before his response arrives.

I hope you feel you made the right decision.

Yes. Definitely. At least I'll have more time for yoga.

Badminton too! You can improve your accuracy.

Ha ha. Perhaps I'll take you on some day.

He responds with a smiley face.

I don't send another text, and neither does he. But I'm smiling to myself when I get up and go inside again.

I stop at my jigsaw.

There's only a small corner left. It's the difficult corner because it's mostly blue sky and a tiny wisp of cloud. That's why it's the last bit to be done.

I stand in front of it, shifting the pieces around until suddenly I find one that fits into the top edge. And then another. And another. Until the jigsaw is complete.

I look at the picture for a while. The almost cloudless sky, the tranquil beach, the tropical flowers, the green palm trees, and the hint of adventure in the surfboards.

I'm glad I've finally finished it.

Tomorrow I'll break it up and scatter all the pieces again.

But for tonight, right now, everything is exactly where it should be.

Acknowledgements

Writing a novel during lockdown was a very different experience for me.

I realised that although I'm a solitary person during the writing process, it's the interaction with people and life that sparks off the many different thoughts that take my original idea into places I never expected. During the writing of *Three Weddings and a Proposal*, my interactions, like yours, were at a two-metre distance, or by Zoom or social media. But every single one made a difference to my writing, so if we communicated in any way during 2020 – thank you! To writers, artists, musicians and all the creative people who've touched our hearts and minds, and who sparked my own creativity in a difficult year, thank you too.

A very special thanks to readers who joined me for virtual events. In a year when I'd scheduled more live events than ever before and then had to cancel them, it was wonderful to be able to reach out and chat with book lovers virtually. It was especially nice to talk to people who don't normally have the opportunity to come to library or bookshop events, and to people in countries I wouldn't have had the chance to visit. So, a warm thank you to readers in the US, Australia,

South Africa and Europe who joined me on Facebook, Zoom and other channels. Every single one of you contributed to keeping my own creativity alive, and my desire to write the best book I possibly could. I hope we meet again soon.

To the booksellers who did such an incredible job during immensely difficult times – thank you for staying open whenever you could, for setting up online sales systems from scratch, for going above and beyond in supporting authors, making recommendations to readers and getting books into their hands.

Libraries and librarians were a great source of comfort to readers too as they rolled out click and collect options, and organised virtual events to keep books and writing as accessible as possible. Thank you for everything you do.

In thanking people, I also have to mention those I didn't necessarily interact with directly, but who were an integral part of life while I was writing this book: the frontline workers who kept, and are still keeping, the entire show on the road. The health workers, the retailers, the postal workers, the delivery people – you have been amazing. I've needed every one of you at some point, and you've always been there.

For those of you who read the acknowledgements before the book – the action in *Three Weddings and a Proposal* takes place in a post-pandemic environment. I couldn't ignore some of the changes that 2020 wrought on our lives, but, at the same time, references to the virus are fleeting and not relevant to the story. I'm sure there will be plenty of pandemic novels in the future, but I won't be writing any of them!

Although many things were different during the writing of this novel, others remained comfortingly the same, even if our methods of communication changed. And so the usual suspects were there to offer advice and encouragement, particularly my lovely editor Marion Donaldson and her exceptional team. Thank you, Eli, Rosanna, Jo, Alara, Ellie, Yeti and everyone at Headline Publishing in the UK, and the Irish crew of Breda, Jim, Joanna, Bernard, Elaine, Siobhan and the Ciaras. A very special thanks to Ruth – we will eventually do the M50 tour again! Thanks also to my wonderful agent Isobel Dixon and her team of brilliant people – Sian, Tia, Hana, James, Lizzie, Daisy and all at Blake Friedmann.

As always, thank you to my copyeditor Jane who spots the fatal flaws and not-so-deliberate mistakes, and to Colm who checked that I corrected them (as well as reminding me that the coffee machine was on and that I could take a break . . .)

With each book, I thank my family for their unstinting support. Like everyone else, I haven't seen as much of them this year as I would have liked. But I'm saving up my hugs for that day when we can all be together again.

I hope you enjoy *Three Weddings and A Proposal*.

SIGN UP TO SHEILA'S NEWSLETTER

Keep in touch with the world of

SHEILA O'FLANAGAN

For up-to-date news from Sheila, exclusive content and competitions, sign up to her newsletter!

You can sign up on her website, www.sheilaoflanagan.co.uk

We will never share your email address and you can unsubscribe at any time.

REVIEW